HUDSON GANGA MERGER

2

Union of America's Hudson River with India's Ganga

Policy of Democratic U.S. and India, Discovering World's Love, Hate, Tolerance and Intolerance, with Prejudice, Pretense, Persecution, and Passivity

By

SACHI G. DASTIDAR

(Assisted by Mr. Shuvo Ghosh Dastidar)

Published in the United States of America

ISBN 979-8-9920800-3-2 (Paperback)

ISBN 9 979-8-9920800-6-3 (Hardback

ISBN 979-8-9920800-7-0 (eBook)

Book Haven Literary
1524 Lakeside Dr. Jackson,
Mississippi 39216
www.bookhavenofficial.com

For Book Rights Adaption and other Rights Permission.

Call us at toll-free **601-914-6178.**

Table of Contents

Chapter 1
Southern Hospitality

Welcome to Southern Hospitality and Progressivism of the North

The 1965 Used Mustang Manual Convertible, Bought in 1972
with Some Damage on Driver's Door. It gave Rides to Many Foreign Students
in Tallahassee, Florida, Without Car for their Chores

1976 4th of July Independence Celebration at Athens, in North Alabama,
with Gov. George Wallace of Alabama

Being an insignificant and new ethnic Indian minority in 1970s, whether in the South or in the North of U.S., it had a distinct advantage, whether welcomed, ignored, mistreated, appreciated, or treated like everyone else. Being a foreigner when first arrived, even any uneven treatment is always overlooked as one does while being a tourist in a new country. There are always differences in cultures, and their values.

On Sachi's very first trip overseas in 1971 on his way to Florida as he took a ride in the elevator of Eiffel Tower in Paris, there were boys and girls, men and women tightly embracing and kissing each other in that cramped area which was unthinkable in Indian culture, but not in Parisian culture. Living with parents, grandparents, uncles and aunts under one roof is unthinkable in Parisian culture, but not in India and Africa. Thus, in India, indigenous families of North and South America, and in Africa one lives knowingly in family-based cultures creating a sharing and caring tradition. Showing Parisian affection in public in many cultures is considered "uncivilized," but not showing affection and respect in public. But Paris is gradually influencing the East, and vice versa. Going to places of worship in churches with shoes is acceptable in the West, but not in the East. Footwear is not acceptable in *mandirs* (temples), churches, mosques, *gurudwaras*, and *viharas* in the East. Western traditions have developed for cold climate, whereas Eastern traditions developed in tropical climate. One is not better than the other, but is a product of values and nature. Once we change to other faith, we adopt other traditions. There are good and bad everywhere. We were fortunate to meet mostly the open-minded ones, here in North America, and in India, Europe, Africa, Asia, Australia, South America, and elsewhere. Unquestionably there are many intolerant people everywhere but they were generally absent from our journey. Exceptions are exceptions. However, in gun-based violent culture of the West, especially the U.S. for over two centuries, somewhat paralleling the armed, violent Islamic culture of the East, with mass killing of non-believers and non-armed persons for over a millennium.

Mass killing in the United States is protested daily around the nation. Yet, in the name of gun rights, we have indirect support of gun killing in America. Discussion and condemnation are common. In the future, will these two militant ideologies come to conflict? God only knows. However, how many protests of mass killing and genocide of unbelievers have taken place in true-believer-culture-majority nations in the last 1400 years? In 1971 there was an anti-Hindu genocide and anti-secularist-Muslim extermination killing by the Army of Islamic Republic of Pakistan and their Bengali Islamist allies. How many Muslim-majority nations protested and barred the killers from their lands in the past 50 years? One sees daily mass murder of kids and adults in America through our guns, and of kefir kids and adults and disobedient believers in many nations. In 2021 and 2022 we've witnessed demonstration to protect women of Afghanistan and Iran. How many demonstrations took place Muslim-majority nations? We are happy to see worldwide demonstration against killing and taking hostage of Israelis by Palestinian Hamas, as well as happy to see demonstrations in the U.S. and Europe against killing of persecuted Palestinians. Persecution of disobedient followers in Christian-majority nations is gone for some time, especially after Enlightenment and Reformation. We wonder how many Christians are persecuted for not following the scripture even in countries like Italy, Spain, Poland, Mexico, Brazil, Kenya, or Greece, as compared to non-followers in faith-majority nations like Afghanistan, Pakistan, Iran, Saudi Arabia, Qatar, Algeria, Bangladesh, Somalia, and more? We found very warm welcome of "Hindustanis" – pre-Christian and pre-Islam words in old cultures of Indians in old Egypt, Morocco, Jordan and Uzbekistan, to name a few. Challenging true believers often means death in many nations, but not in Christian-, Buddhist-, or indigenous-(Hindu)-majority nations. By the way, both the words Hindu and India are foreign words that entered Indian society after British colonization. Christian, Buddhist, Hindu, and Jain philosophies are full of pacifism, tolerance and non-violence that in the past millenniums have not changed that much. For indigenous faiths – Hindus and Jains, their preaching has created a self-destructive, fatalistic, coward, resistance-free, and suicidal mentality. Sorry about that. They have lost the basic instincts of living beings, like birds and animals, in protecting themselves and their family.

Way back in America in January of 1976 when Sachi returned back to work after their wedding, his colleagues extended their warm welcome, and said that they missed his wedding as well as his absence during the Christmas celebration in the office. Hearing that Sachi's newly married wife Shefali, a doctoral student with student visa, wasn't allowed to return back with Sachi, and the role of U.S. Consul in Kolkata, all were angry with the U.S. Consulate. This is America! They presented Sachi Christmas gifts, and Sachi gave gifts that he brought from India. As he was going through his mails in that first hour at his office at 8 am in the morning, there came a call from one Mr. Cr of Alabama. Sachi couldn't talk as his boss walked into his office. Sachi apologized. Cr called back and invited Sachi for an interview for a teaching job at the Alabama A&M University in Huntsville. Mr. Cr didn't say how he learned about him. Sachi said he couldn't do that as he cannot take any time off from his work for interview as he has exhausted his leave. Mr. Cr called again a week or two later and asked Sachi for a visit. By that time Shefali had arrived in their new Florida State University's (FSU) married student housing called Alumni Heights, a five-minute drive from the campus.

Their regular routine was for Sachi to drop Shefali off at the campus at 7:30 am in the morning, report to work at 8 am, then leave work at 5 pm, pick her up at 5:30, then go home and have dinner, then drop her off at campus after dinner and bring her back at 10 or 11 at night or later based on her work. The evening was for Sachi to do his academic and social work. These were the days before cell phone, so schedule had to be worked out beforehand, and followed closely.

Florida State University Pre-Graduation Ceremony Workshop for Graduate Students with Shefali on Left Center wearing Sari, 1978

After a few days, Mr. Cr, a professor in the City Planning and Urban Studies Department, an Afro-American, came up with a new offer that was difficult to ignore. A team of top A&M officials and academics will interview Sachi on a Saturday, an off-work day, and Mr. Cr would host Sachi at his home. Sachi and Shefali was excited to think that a stranger will host another stranger in their home! After discussion with Shefali, Sachi accepted to travel to Huntsville, Alabama. Mr. Cr gave him many tips for travel, research interests, possible courses to teach, as well as Huntsville in general. He suggested a six hour 400-mile journey route via Dothan, Montgomery, Birmingham and Decatur, that Mr. Cr traveled many times. Alabama A&M is a historical Afro-American university with a great heritage, academic achievement, and is a product of the era of institutional racism in America when African-Americans were not allowed to attend state-funded White-majority institutions. In 1970s America, all the colleges opened to all, including for Whites and Blacks, and through Black's struggle they were open to other non-whites, i.e., Asians, Africans, and Hispanics. Hearing Sachi was heading to Huntsville, Sachi's colleague Ellen, a Black American, got excited as she lived in Huntsville, and went to Alabama A&M for her studies. At that point Ellen didn't know Sachi was going for a job interview. Ellen and Sachi traveled together for their state work to visit many job training centers in Miami, Orlando, St. Petersburgh, Jacksonville, Ft. Lauderdale and more. Ellen told stories about her good life in Alabama.

Journey from a White-Majority Campus to a Black-Majority Campus:

Sachi and his wife Shefali reached Mr. Cr's home, just across the campus entrance, before noon. True Southern hospitality was waiting for Dastidars. It felt more like coming to Shefali's uncle's home than a stranger's place. It was a well decorated spacious home, in an African-American neighborhood. Right across his front yard, across the street, began an open space that belonged to the university. From his living room one can see most of the buildings of Alabama A&M University. Mrs. Cr immediately took Shefali to their guest room and for a girl-to-girl talk, much like her newly acquired aunts would do in India. Seeing Shefali's sari outfit, she was very happy. After some time, she returned to the living room where Cr and Sachi were chatting with an announcement, "My God, she is a new bride! We must treat her likewise," and started treating us like her newlywed niece and her husband.

Soon, Sachi headed out with Mr. Cr to the campus while Shefali stayed with Mrs. Cr. Sachi met with top administrators, department faculty as well as a few department chairs. He toured the campus, and walked to a greenhouse of the agriculture department. But then, this was Saturday. One doesn't expect faculty and students on weekends. In the evening, they were invited to a dinner with a few campus faculties that included one or two Indian faculty members as well. Sachi had no idea that Alabama A&M had attracted such a diverse faculty, with mostly Southern Black students at that historically African-American institution. Next morning on Sunday there were further discussions. After breakfast and tea Dastidars left for Tallahassee. The Vice President called and asked about Sachi's plans for the immediate future. Sachi had many queries for the campus as well. One of the things he was brought to light was that the Department will be applying for certification of their graduate planning degree to the American Institute of Planners. Sachi said he will be happy to be the lead person for that application process. A&M was happy too. Eventually, A&M will be the first or second Black-majority graduate program to receive AIP's recognition.

Soon after Sachi's return back to Tallahassee from his interview he was offered a faculty position of associate professorship at Alabama A&M asking him to join immediately. Dastidars were happy yet stressed as it would mean hardship for Shefali to complete her doctorate, and living by herself without a car in Tallahassee. We negotiated a joining date of 1976 May, not March, after the end of spring semester. Alabama A&M assigned Sachi immediately to teach from the summer session. Our original plan for a quick honeymoon in India was disrupted by the U.S. Consul. Now we had to postpone that for our August summer break. Hearing our plan to move to Alabama, both sets of highly educated refugee parents in India were worried about Shefali's doctoral work and would remind us regularly through letters. In March while at Tallahassee we arranged for our wedding reception where Mrs. McClure, wife of the department chairman Dr. McClure, wore an orange, red-bordered sari that she asked Shefali to bring back as we headed to India for our wedding. At the reception Shefali wore her new purple *Benarasi* wedding sari with golden thread, a must for Indian weddings, that she wore again at our 35th anniversary in Queens, New York City. Sachi put on his favorite cotton dhoti (*dhuti*) or outerwear and long Bengali *punjabi* shirt.

Mrs. Anne McClure with Shefali

Chairman Dr. Ed McClure at the Wedding Reception

Dr. Andrew Dzurik, Shefali's Advisor at FSU with his Wife and Student Shefali

In August of 1976 during our summer break, we left with our Subaru station wagon for a camping trip that took them from Alabama to the West Coast via the mountain states reaching up to Northern California, then to Vancouver, British Columbia via Oregon and Washington states, returning via Alberta, Montana, Dakotas, Minnesota, and Illinois. This was their delayed honeymoon. Camping was introduced to them at our campus in Tallahassee, Florida. It was exciting. Let's discuss that later.

Students at Tallahassee, Florida and Huntsville, Alabama campuses were similar in many ways, like typical American college students, first time free from parental guidance, yet there were differences as well. Students at Alabama A&M were mostly Black-Americans, with a few White, Indian, and African, mostly Nigerian, students. Florida State was mostly White, with some Black, Asian, Hispanic and African students. Alabama students rarely missed classes, and some families encouraged their kids to wear formal outfit, whereas Florida students had informal outfit, as in New York. Absenteeism was higher in New York, where most of the students had to work to support themselves. Among students, Alabama attracted mostly local students, whereas Florida attracted many out-of-state students, especially in their graduate programs. In New York, it was mostly local students, meaning from New York City and Long Island. After returning from their cross-country tour, Shefali went back to Tallahassee to work on her dissertation. Soon, Sachi would be an expert on travel between

Huntsville and Tallahassee. One could drive 400 miles in 6 hours, or take a bus that took 10 to 12 hours or more, or one can fly, either directly from Birmingham 90 miles south, about an hour-and-a-half away, or drive to Montgomery, a two-and-a-half-hour drive for a non-stop flight to Tallahassee. From Huntsville, one had to change airplane at another airport adding time to one's journey. Shefali did all those routes, except bus as it took too long and had to change bus in another city. In Tallahassee her friends gladly provided airport shuttle service. Soon, RatnaDi, Older Sister Ratna, a famous statistics professor's wife, took it on herself to be the elder sister of Shefali. RatnaDi was married to Dr. Basu, a world-famous statistician, a Hindu refugee from East Pakistan, now Bangladesh, who was one of the pioneering professors of Dhaka University, East Bengal, now Bangladesh, started their statistics program before 1947 Indian partition. Basu's story of forced migration is recorded in a book. When Basu, a Bengali Indian, arrived at Florida State Univ in the fall of 1975, one of his former students Dr. Raman, a Tamil-Indian-American statistics professor, called Sachi to extend help to Basu family, as Basu was Bengali-Indian. Dr. Basu was not allowed to drive because of high-powered glasses; thus, his wife did all the chores, including taking kids to school and back, as well as her husband. Soon RatnaDi and Shefali developed close friendship. Shefali's major professor, Dr. Dzurik, provided lots of logistical support as well.

On the very first day at Alabama A&M in Huntsville, as Sachi was walking up the stairs, an Indian lady was walking down. Seeing her, Sachi said, "Hello, do you teach here?" She replied, "No, I work at a lab here. My name is Sw Mukherji." Sachi replied in Bengali, "Namaskar (Greetings), my name is Sabyasachi Ghosh Dastidar." Mukherji is a typical Bengali last name. Hearing Sachi's Bengali, Sw almost fell on the steps as she was so shocked, being the only Bengali in the city. She said holding the railing tight, "I couldn't believe that I am hearing someone speak Bengali in Huntsville. We are the only Bengali family in town, although we have a few Indians here in Huntsville." With that Sachi became a part of Subcontinental subculture in Huntsville, as Mr. Cr made Sachi part of the native culture in Huntsville.

Shefali at Doctoral Graduation with Daughter Joyeeta at Tallahassee, Florida, 1978

Students, Faculty, Neighbors and Friends:

People like Cr and Sw kept suggesting to put our roots down by buying a home. We came across a ranch style house in the southeast of Huntsville, close to Tennessee River, yet a long distance from the campus which was on the northeast. This was close to Sw's home who at times biked to our home with their little daughter Sangeeta. On our block, Tom and Elsie, a mixed Jewish-Catholic couple, lived with a little daughter Mary, Sangeeta's classmate in elementary school. From our backyard we had a view of a hill. Our southern neighbor was researcher at the National Space Research Center originally from the Northeast, and the northern neighbor was a former resident of Levittown, Long Island. Dastidar family would end up living in a Levitt home in Hicksville, two blocks north of Levittown boundary, after moving to Long Island, New York.

Huntsville, Alabama was a very cosmopolitan city. Locals called it a Yankee City. It had a huge Redstone Arsenal with two major Army divisions, a Space Center, three college campuses, and presence of many multinational corporations, attracting a diverse population.

Soon after arrival in Huntsville Sachi got a call from Dilip of Birmingham, "SachiDa, Older Brother Sachi, welcome to Alabama." It was the result of the proverb: Words spread through the air. Dilip was a graduate of Bengal Engineering College of Calcutta University, India, one-year junior to Sachi, thus

Sachi was his older brother, Dada, and invited them for a dinner to introduce to some of his Alabamian friends. We did that ritual for three years, until we moved to New York, and then in 2022 he got a call from Dilip informing Sachi and Shefali that they have finally moved to Virginia, close to their daughter. From our Huntsville home to get to Birmingham we took a shortcut going south crossing Tennessee River, then west via local road 36 which connected to Interstate 65. At the crossing of Route 67 and Route 36, it used to be 4-way stop. Frequently there were groups of white-hooded, white-robed KKK peoples collecting money from stopped vehicles. Seeing a strange looking colored couple, one wearing sari, the folks were a bit bewildered. Shefali or Sachi didn't lower their windows to pitch into their bucket, as they moved on. When we shared this with our African-American colleagues at Alabama A&M – a historic African-American university, they asked again and again, "Are you sure Shefali didn't drop something in the KKK bucket?" One said, "That's why I avoid those back roads." In that crossing we came into white supremacist Ku Klux Klan rallies several times, and each time we refused to pay. This was not the first time we would come across KKK folks in Alabama. But if we met some big shots of KKK, it was unknown to us. In Sachi's second year at Alabama A&M, the university was expanding its reach in different towns. Our campus started offering courses at Northeast Alabama Community College located at Rainsville, about 60 miles northeast from the campus. They asked Sachi to teach an introductory Urban Issue course. It was a wonderful ride through a great hilly countryside, and the campus looked new and sparkling. One downside of that experience was that classes were offered in the evening, and returning back in winter through pitch dark with many curved roads without any streetlight was scary. In that sophomore-level Urban Studies course, students were to write short papers on societal issues. One student wrote an excellent paper, with inside intrigues, on the growth of KKK in northeast Alabama, colloquially referred as the headquarters of the racist movement in the state. Sachi was surprised to see that one of his students knew so much of the inside story. At the end of a class, one student pulled Sachi to the side, and said, "Sir, do you know who that is?" Sachi said "Yes, John with his nine-year old boy." The student replied, "He is the head of the KKK cell in our area." Earlier, in the semester, student John in his thirties, close to Sachi's age, asked politely, if he can invite his son to meet an "Indian" as his son hasn't seen any Indian before. When his son came, he sat in the back of the classroom till the end of the class. Sachi treated father and son with ice-cream. As a teacher there was normal relation with John, as with other students. It was an all-white class. There was no personal discussion.

We bought our Huntsville house from a veteran Mr. Rhow. During our last meeting they pointed to a house saying, "Another Rao lives there, but he is Indian." In single family home areas, one rarely meets neighbors down the road as driving starts from one's garage and returns back to the garage, rarely getting opportunity to meet neighbors in person. That was true in Huntsville, Long Island, or in our single-family neighborhood in Queens, New York City. In Queens our kids or Shefali knew many people in the neighborhood as they walked to the bus stop bumping into neighbors, or while standing and waiting for the bus, but not Sachi. He drove to work. In Huntsville Sachi later met Dr. Rao as he too was teaching at Alabama A&M. And it was after returning late from a weekend dinner party at Rao's home Sachi had to rush Shefali to Huntsville Hospital for the birth of their first child, a daughter named Joyeeta.

Alabama provided for close friendship with students, faculty and neighbors. One Nigerian student Nwarisi of the eastern Ibo region, going for a graduate planning degree, missed his wife and kids. One day he appeared in our home. Since then, Nwarisi and some foreign friends became regular visitors, often having lunch and dinner with us, while playing with our kids. He became a part of the family keeping in touch after we left Alabama. After graduation he moved back to Rivers State, Nigeria. It was really heartening to see him crying when he learned that we were planning to head to New York. We stopped his grief when we said that we'll keep in touch with him. Nwarisi helped us pack our stuff for our move to New York. He brought back our memory of Shefali's Nigerian roommate Vicky at Florida State University. Three foreign students supported each other, while Vicky encouraged Shefali to wear sari on campus.

At our wedding reception Vicky put on a Bengali sari and gorgeous makeup to feel joyous. In early 1980s in our Long Island, New York campus started a host program for foreign students. On one Thanksgiving we hosted several students, among them were two Nigerians, Kadjaliou and Barry. Those young men frequently visited our home to play with our little kids. Kadjaliou became a successful American man and TV producer, and philanthropist. Barry married a Jamaican-American classmate rising to a top position in an international cosmetic corporation.

Thanksgiving created many opportunities for us to give thanks to our Mother, the Creator, who gave us life. While at Huntsville, Alabama we received a request to host foreign visitors who came for training at an Army base. In 1977 when we moved into our new home, we decided to welcome Army guests to our home. Army decided who and how many to send. We had army officers from Europe, Africa, and Asia. Once there was an Indonesian officer named Wardoy. At first, we couldn't get the correct spelling, and we could not say properly in Indonesian accent. He was a bit annoyed and asked us, "What kind of Indian are you? Don't you know my name means heart in Sanskrit?" We said, "Of course." In Bengali accent it is said as Hridoy. As Sanskrit is millennium old language from which many European and Asian languages had risen, but with accents it is said and written differently. This was a big surprise for Sachi and Shefali when they took Russian language course while teaching at Kazakhstan as almost all the Russian numbers from one to ten were Sanskritic. Once, seeing our little baby in Huntsville, Alabama, a Saudi high ranking military man came to revisit us a few days later with a bouquet of flower and some candy. As he was having lunch together, Shefali asked about his family. He said with a smile, "It is going to get bigger." She asked, "It is a boy or a girl?" He replied with a laugh, "No it is a woman. I am going to take another wife."

"What happened, why are you going to divorce your wife?"

The brigadier laughingly replied, "I am going to have another wife. I am not divorcing anyone."

Shefali asked innocently, "Do your current wife knows that?"

"No, I don't have to tell her." He responded, ending the conversation. He came to visit us again before he left U.S. He was a wonderful man, and knew a lot about Indian culture than us.

Another army officer came was Lt. Col. R. Ull of Bangladesh. He felt at home with us speaking in Bengali, and discussing about our ancestral homes, as did another top officer from Bangladesh Lt. Col. Rash. Both were Muslim, and both of them invited us to visit "Your Homeland." It immediately moved to the top of our list of places to visit and opened connection to our ancestral home. There was another Bangladeshi officer, seeing Shefali waring sari at a departmental store, rushed to ask if she was Bengali, and later became friends of the family. We would give ride to them from their apartment in the base, at times to stores as they didn't have car. Once two young German officers, our neighbors in our apartment complex before our single-family home, invited us to an army store in the military barrack. They didn't know that it was only for army families, not for their friends. The store guard asked us to leave the store. We told our hosts not to worry and waited outside, as they picked up their supplies to bring them back to their apartment off the base.

In 1982 we visited Bangladesh for the first time, and Mr. Ull, a Muslim, picked four of us up at Dhaka Airport, and took us to their home, saying, "Welcome to your homeland!" His wife Rani waited at the door to welcome us. Then Ull gave us the bad news, "Look, your Lakshman village is in deltaic Barisal District. It must be too small, or too unimportant to be in army map!" Two days later, we left on our path to discovery of our ancestral land of 1500s from where our parents were driven out from their "new" 500-year-old village in Barisal district of Bangladesh.

It opened the universe to us. Later we visited our old pre-1500 ancestral village Gava from where they migrated in 1500s to establish a new village Lakshsmankathi, after receiving honorific Persian title "Dastidar" when eastern India was ruled by a Persian-Islamic king. As a result, our New York's

Persian/Iranian colleague Alireza calls us Indo-Iranian. Living in Gava goes back to almost 40 generations, or to First Millenia.

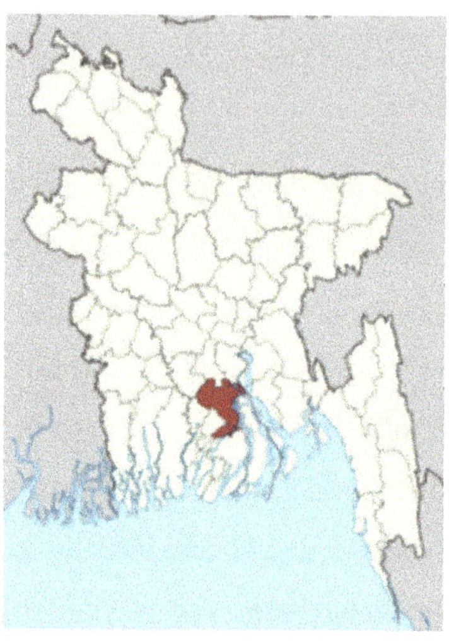

Barisal District of Bangladesh

Once during Thanksgiving in Huntsville, Alabama, one Dr. Chattopadhyay of Indian Institute of Technology (IIT) at Kharagpur, India was visiting us in late 1970s after receiving Fulbright Award from the U.S. He delighted our army guests by making fresh *rasogollas* or cheeseballs, dipped in sugary liquid, a typical Bengali and Indian delicacy. In another Thanksgiving Dr. Arjun T joined us, who was a former classmate of Shefali at Presidency College of Calcutta University, the top and oldest educational institution of India. Arjun was a Singapore-Chinese-Buddhist-Bengali-Indian-American who joined as a physics professor at our university in Alabama. Shefali and Arjun were meeting after more than a decade!

In Alabama A&M's graduate program had many army personnel who were posted at the army base in Huntsville. Ned, a Black-American, with a high rank, really stood out, yet was afraid of statistics. After his initial debacle instead of being frustrated, Ned said he understood his mental blockage that he worked out with Sachi's help. He then gave us the good news of his wife's imminent child birth. As the day approached, we asked him about the good news. As soon as the baby was born the couple invited us to meet the baby at Huntsville Hospital. It was great to meet the happy parents and their little princess. After a few minutes of chat, Ned said, "Can you suggest a name for our girl?" We felt honored. This is possibly the best tribute that a student can give to a teacher. Shefali started with normal popular names like Barbara, Linda, Joey, Cathleen, Laura, etc. when they stopped and said, "No, we want an Indian name" and held our hands tight, and said, "What about Shefali?" Shefali said, "What about a different one?" as it is very uncommon in Indian culture among your relations and close circle to keep the same name. It is also because one doesn't call older persons by first name, so by mistake if one calls the same name in presence of an older person, it is often considered improper. They wanted the name immediately as they have to give it for birth registration. Shefali and Sachi sat down to come up with a name matching the princess and her parents. After some discussion, we suggested the name Shamolee, the Green of the Mother Earth, but made simpler as per Bengali accent, as opposed to Shyamoli, a more common spelling in India. Shamolee matched with the mother's name, Shelly, a professor. They were excited! For African-American Ned, it meant the rolling green of Kansas where he was from. Poet Rabindranath Tagore popularized the name with a poem by the same name. Three decades later we got a call from a medical doctor at our home in New York introducing her as Shamolee Elizabeth asking for the meaning of her name. Her parents forgot to tell her the meaning. Shamolee was glad to know the meaning and we were overjoyed with little one's progress in life.

As we were putting our roots down in Alabama, we were introduced to the Indian cultural groups, which also included few Pakistanis speaking the same language. Apart from festivals of Diwali or the Festival of Light, and Holi or the Festival of Color, presence of two Bengali families were honored by rest of our friends in Huntsville through a Baisakh New Year music party in mid-April. It was one more excuse to have one more party. Our get-togethers were generally held at Dr. Lal's apartment complex with a party hall. Shefali didn't go back to Tallahassee in the following fall semester in 1977 as she was expecting our first child. Baby was born in October, and one of my students, Patricia, arranged for a card from Sachi's graduate students and a cute stuffed turtle for the baby. Patricia, a Caucasian, became a successful real estate broker, with a huge Alabama farm with horses, who kept in touch forty years after graduation.

Initially, in our three-bedroom house one bedroom was occupied. This was a time when new immigrants were arriving, mostly with higher education as that was the only way Asians and Africans could get visa. One Dr. Mathur, an economist from Hindi-speaking northern India, arrived in Huntsville and was living with a friend in a small apartment. The host asked us if Mathur can live in one of our unused bedrooms. We thought this was a good idea. Soon, our house would be even emptier as Shefali had to head back to Tallahassee in February leaving our three-month old daughter in care of Sachi and our babysitter. The baby talked to Shefali everyday via Mrs. Basu in Tallahassee. These were days before cell phone. Before trip to Tallahassee, Mrs. Basu, wife of Professor Basu, whom we called Boudi or Sister-in-Law, insisted that Shefali stay with them till her doctoral defense in May, not in an apartment. On Commencement, her major professor Dr. Dzurik, a person of Ukrainian heritage, insisted that she bring along baby Joyeeta with her to the graduation. There were a few other Shefali's special guests, besides Boudi, present at the Commencement.

Shefali with Major Professor Dr. Dzurik at Graduation

Mother Shefali's New Journey:

Soon after a celebration in Huntsville, Shefali was invited for an interview to teach at the Economics Department of the Alabama A&M University. Digging deep into full-time work, we planned to celebrate summer break with baby Joyeeta. This time in 1978 summer we headed for a camping trip to Northeast America and Atlantic Canada. We were unable to reach Newfoundland as the ferry from Sydney and other ports of Nova Scotia was fully pre-booked in August. We headed for a camp site in Cape Breton Highland National Park on the tip of Cape Breton Island. It was August 15, the day of India's independence and British-created partition. At the gas station near the park entrance the helper said "Today is the end of summer for us," reminding how far north we have traveled. On that trip we met Jayanta, at Saint John, New Brunswick, an architect from Indian Institute of Technology whom we met in India. Jayanta introduced us to Chanda family, a Bengali-Indian physician couple, who then invited us to their home for a chat and talking about their plans for permanently returning back to Kolkata, India. One of them followed Hindu tradition, while the other followed monotheistic Brahmo tradition. Both of them were post-partition refugees from East Pakistan, now called Bangladesh. In 1990s Chandas were able to fulfill their dream and buy an apartment near Gariahat More junction, a 10-minute walk for our home in southern Kolkata. As they were furnishing their new apartment, they expressed desire of getting some house plants, as they had in Canada. Sachi told his Ma about the Chanda family's wish. Ma said, "Would they like to have our plant collections, except our *tulsi* plant?" *Tulsi* is a mint-like plant where all Hindus offer water, in lieu of giving food to all plants, once after sunrise and the other time before sunset. This tradition my mother followed all of her 94+ years of life. Sachi's parents' collection included several one-of-a-kind plants, including an 8' feet tall decades-old cactus plant that could have been sold for lots of money. It became difficult for Ma, a widow, to take care of those plants, some of which were on third floor rooftop while Ma lived on second floor. Dr. Chanda rented a pushcart to take those plants away, and with that part of our parents' memory stayed with our friends. At least three decades later Rana, our parent's grandson and my nephew, a medical doctor, seemed to fulfill his grandparents' wishes by creating beautiful greeneries in rooftops of second and third floors. Seeing this, in 2022 it mesmerized all of us.

The building takes one of the small lots in the city of Kolkata, possibly smaller than many front yards of single-family homes in U.S. suburbs.

Roof Garden in Kolkata, India; 2022

Roof Garden in Kolkata, India; 2022

2nd Floor 18" Wide Balcony Garden Visible behind Aunt Satya Debi, center in White Sari and former Caretaker of our Mother

1977 was the first time that Shefali and Sachi would have a Christmas break together. Our parents constantly reminded us to have a second Annaprasan – a traditional Bengali first Rice-Eating or Going into Solids ceremony for Joyeeta – again in Kolkata. We had Annaprasan celebration in Huntsville, and the first rice was fed by Swati's husband, Dr. Trip. Traditionally, the honor of first feeding is given to a maternal uncle, followed by blessings with flower petals, husked rice and grass tips placing on top of head of the blessed baby by all attendees. Sachi had the honor of offering first rice in August of 1971, right before leaving India, to his nephew Dhruba, and again in 1975, two days after his wedding, to Dhruba's younger brother Amit, both sons of middle-older sister Mejdi. She made sure that Sachi had that honor.

Son Shuvo is on lap, right, at his First Rice Eating Annaprasan Ceremony in Huntsville, Alabama. Daughter Joyeeta is in front.

Before Shuvo's birth every letter from our parents would remind us to bring their granddaughter Joyeeta "Home." So, we planned for a trip during Christmas holidays. This was also the best time to travel, as temperature in India is like American spring, with lots of flower and freshly-picked vegetables available. Sachi's parents arranged for a party for their granddaughter. To visit Shefali's father we had to visit the hilly Nagaland State bordering Burma (Myanmar) on India's eastern border. Getting there is a bit complicated because one has to get a visa to visit an Indian state by Indians, called "Inner Line Permit" which colonial Britain started to introduce a foreign culture and divide the population. And someone coming from America, it could take ages to get the visa. That visa is issued by state governments. This is a remnant for colonial Britain's "Divide-and-Rule" policy when they decided that in border regions, mostly tribal, even from their own Assam state residents won't be allowed to enter, but colonialists and Christian missionaries from Europe will be allowed. Some such areas included Nagaland, Mizoram and Arunachal Pradesh districts of Assam, now states of northeast India. It would be like if there was a law here in America that needed Americans to get a visa to enter New York, West Virginia or Arizona, or to indigenous tribal areas, to name a few. Unbelievable? True. All of those states were parts of Assam State during British rule, yet Britain created a law that didn't allow entry of Assamese into parts of their own state, but allowed colonial oppressors, and Christian missionaries to change identities of native peoples. Britain didn't allow cooperation within its own state, but allowed cooperation with foreigners. Unbelievable? But true. There were similar restrictions in border tribal regions of both Pakistan and Bangladesh, formerly parts of India, which their governments completely wiped out those restrictions and began settler colonization. But India, and Hinduism being the face of extreme "fatalistic democracy and tolerance," she wasn't allowed any change, often by supporters of colonialism in disguise of supporter of "democracy." No one is allowed to invest or buy land there. It has become a recipe of perpetual backwardness. But India being India where law is one thing, and enforcement by local administration is another matter, sometimes enforced, other times not enforced, and sometimes bribery changes everything.

Then there are state governments' partisan sectarians whose police may completely ignore Federal rules. So, during our trip to Nagaland Shefali's older brother Dada or Hironmoy, who was a medical doctor there, just asked a local transport to pick us up from the airport, which was in the plains of neighboring Assam state, while most of the state was mountainous. Border Security didn't check people in state cars. Since 1950s a group of Nagas wanted secession from India. Many Nagas took to Christianity and used Roman script for the same language spoken across the border in Assam State, to which it was a part. There was low level warfare, yet Dr. Hironmoy and his family was never affected. Nagas were very friendly to him as well as to us, especially to the baby. They presented fruits and sweets, like your own neighbors. Migrant Bengali Doctors' families spoke fluent Nagamese, Assamese, Hindi, Bengali and English languages. Nagamese is a dialect of Assamese written in English script. British Christianization has divided a people speaking the same language through their religious conversion, much like the work of Islamic converters in Punjab, Sindh and Baluchistan of Pakistan, and rest of India. In Nagaland's capital Kohima, hearing our arrival through grapevine, appeared Anju to chat with us, as he received Architecture degree from Jadavpur University of Kolkata. He became our guide to Naga culture, known earlier for beheading and hanging the enemy's head in front of homes. Decades later Sachi would enter another restricted state for plains Indians: Mizoram. In 2008 when he was at the Jawaharlal Nehru University in Delhi, he got an invitation to visit a remote corner called Tuichawng of the remote Mizoram state of India to help build a school by Probini Foundation for extremely poor villagers. But going there posed a problem as it required to have an "Inner Line Permit" which some call visa. And to do that for an American it needed six-month notice, and a clearance from the federal Foreign Office, etc. He didn't have even 6 days. Luckily for Sachi, the Mizoram House, the state government office-cum-lodge was around the corner from Delhi's Jawaharlal Nehru University campus. He headed there with his American passport and passport photo. The lady at the counter took the completed forms, 400 rupees – a huge fee for Indians traveling within its own country – and asked Sachi to comeback after a cup of coffee. At the state capital

Aizwal's airport there was a counter for visa check, but no visa checker, as some Christian missionaries walked ahead of him. Mr. Daneswar from the village was waiting for Sachi. Journey from Aizwal to Tuichawng must have been one of the most wretched trips we have ever taken anywhere in over a hundred countries and territories that we visited. Recently Indian government has improved infrastructure a lot, told by locals.

Welcome to the Minority Buddhist Chakma Village in Christian Mizoram

Chakma Homes

Tuichwng Market Area

Students Helped by Probini Foundation of U.S.

Welcome to Sachi G. Dastidar with a Banner to Tuichwng Village

On his return trip back to the capital on January 10, 2009, Sachi planned for other visits, yet he found that it was a State Holiday as "Missionary Day" to celebrate the arrival of two British crusaders, and starting preaching, converting from indigenous faith, changing script, and identity. Everything was closed on that state holiday. This was shocking in Hindu-majority, secular, partition-divided, refugee rehabilitated India. How can this happen in a democracy? Would U.S. allow celebration of slavery or holiday for arrival of Spanish?

*Bangladeshi Minority Buddhist Chakma Refugees in Assam,
India Cleansed from their Homeland*

A Group of Bangladeshi Buddhist Refugee Students in Assam, India

Buddhist Kids waiting for Dinner, Assam, India

In 1890s Colonial Britain enacted a law forbidding teaching by the natives of Assam Province to which the district belonged, prohibiting them from entering parts of their state, and allowed only British Christian missionaries to conduct teaching, preaching and converting from their indigenous belief. If any other Indian state had enacted similar Hindu-Jain missionary control, entire world and neo-colonialist Indians would have written tons of editorials. Entrapped in hotel Sachi wrote a letter to the Chief Minister that he mailed on February 9, 2009 from the U.S. The letter reads:

Dear Chief Minister Lalthanhawla:

Re: Road to Southwest

Please accept warm greetings from me, my family and friends in the U.S. Recently I was in Mizoram and enjoyed the hospitality of the people and loved the spectacular beauty of the land. Having traveled all seven continents and every state in India I wondered why your state is not on the world map of tourism through which many parts of the world have pulled themselves up economically. ... Ironically I was in Aizawl on January 11 when the state celebrated Missionary Day holiday as two English Christian missionaries J. H. Lorrain and F. W. Savidge arrived in Mizoram on January 11, 1894 to guide Mizos away from their nature-worshipping Hindu-like belief. I wonder if there is a contradiction as coming of foreigners is being celebrated yet we are restricting countrymen from traveling to the state!

My trip took me towards the Bangladesh border via Lungsen, Matri Chhara (Tlabang) and towards Chakma Autonomous Area. I was moved by the warmth of the people yet I was appalled by the condition of the state road from Lunglei onwards. I witnessed a large number of trucks rumbling towards the Bangladesh border for creating a fence. People told me of the rationale for the fence. However, if the connection with Lunglei is not quickly improved, and Bangladeshi Chakma areas are cut off economically I am afraid that the region may become a virtual prison without any prospect for economic improvement. I wonder if you can secure funds to rebuild the road and bring prosperity to the area and the state....

Best wishes and belated Happy New Year.

With that trip we were able to help build a school and a dormitory in Mizoram, making an emotional connection to the state. For several years a Mizo

National Front, supported by many anti-India and anti-Hindu groups, tried for secession from India. There was a peaceful resolution of the conflict through creation of a separate state giving a small Christian-Indian tribe a self-rule. Yet the Mizo-Christians followed an extremist path by expelling all indigenous non-converted Mizos – called Brus and Reangs, almost a fifth of the population – for refugee camps in the neighboring Tripura state where many of them have been living for two decades or more, ignored by Western and Indian press, Indian elites, pro-Hindu and anti-Hindu activists, ruling Congress Party of the federal government, and by the ruling Communist Party-Marxist of the neighboring Tripura sheltering Hindu Bru and Reang refugees. http://www. thestatesman.com/news/northeast/wehavetakenmeasurestorepatriatebr urefu-gees-rijiju/77261.html, Statesman July 22, 2015. How many articles were written in New York, London, Washington, and on Lahore dailies? Only after 2010s the federal government of India tried to impress on Mizo government to allow return of Brus and Reangs to their ancestral village, yet demonstrations against return to their homeland by natives was routine in Mizoram's Christian movement. U.K.'s Scotland never had laws stopping English folks not to enter Scotland. Unlike rest of India, in a Mizoram restaurant, or a Bengali tea shop, or in Assamese clothing store, or Mizo-Chakma gift shop, or a local food shop of Hindi-speakers, they had no bilingual or trilingual signs, as is common in India, instead only English signs. A Bengali shop owner, a Muslim, most likely from Bangladesh as his accent suggested, said he was from Cachar District, a Bengali-Hindu majority district of Assam. Mizoram's only land connection with rest of India is via Cachar district, yet Cacharis are legally forbidden to enter Mizoram, but Mizos are allowed to enter Cachar without any paperwork. At the time of Indian partition in 1947, the Assamese politicians wanted to push the entire Bengali-majority Sylhet District of Assam to Islamic Republic of Pakistan for their hostility to the Bengalis, however, a quick and only referendum of 1947 partition saved Sylhet district's Hindu-majority area to be part of India, and rest of Sylhet went to Pakistan. Muslim-minority Bengalis of Sylhet district stayed in Hindu-majority Cachar area of Sylhet district in Assam,

India, but the Hindu-minority of Sylhet District of East Pakistan, now Bangladesh, was mostly cleansed for India, increasing Assamese hostility to the Bengalis for fear of Assamese becoming minority is Assam.

This is the sad and discriminatory part of world politics that when the indigenous Hindu minority is cleansed from any area no one complaints, but if reverse happens all medias and politicians complain against India or "Hindus". Tragically, Assam's Assamese-Hindu politicians embarked on anti-Hindu-Bengali racism, as Bengalis in Assam asked for retention of teaching in Bengali, like British time, resulted in mass killing of Hindu-Bengalis by Hindu-Assamese assisted by East Pakistani, now Bangladeshi, Bengali-Muslims in Assam in 1962's *Bongal Kheda* or "Cleanse the Bengalis" movement. This is India! And how many remembrances were made in Western or Eastern media? In 1961 Assam police murdered 11 young Bengalis as they demanded retention of Bengali-medium schools in Bengali-speaking Cachar, formerly Sylhet, district and other areas of Assam, as before.

11 Young Hindu Bengalis were Murdered by Assam Administration for seeking Instruction in their Bengali Mother Tongue, as Before. Killed were: Ms. Kamala Bhattacharjee, and Male Members were Kanailal Niyogi, Sunil Sarkar, Shukomol Purakayastha, Hitesh Biswas, Tarani Debnath, Sachindra Pal, ChandiCharan Shutradhar, KumudRanjan Das, Satyendra Deb and Birendra Shutradhar.

\- *Courtesy: Paschim Banger Jonyo, or For West Bengal*

In India, this type of identity nationalism, promoted by Colonial Britain and strengthened by democratic Hindu fatalistic-pluralism with pacifism lacking of unified identity, then partition of India, has created new sub-nationalisms with new identities. Thus, in Assam, with the rise of Assamese exclusivist nationalism created other separatist nationalism – from small population of Mizos, Nagas, Garos, Khasis, Bodos, Karbis, Kukis, Dimasas and more, and from Bengali Muslim activists, most with Bangladeshi root. The world, including present-day India, never recognize that all countries around present-day India indigenous populations from Afghanistan, Pakistan, Sri Lanka, Myanmar (Burma), Bhutan, Tibet (China-controlled), even in Hindu-majority Nepal's Hindi speakers, called their indigenous population as "Hindu" and cleansed from their homeland for India. And, India accepted all without any question! How many progressives or conservatives protested? Afghanistan is 0% minority now, Pakistan from a quarter to 1% now, Bangladesh – fifth most populous nation then – almost a third to 7% now and similar situation in other places. In Sri Lanka many believe that Tamil speakers are "new" as they came only in 2nd Century B.C., not 4th Century B.C. like the majorities, thus should be cleansed. Nepal expelled Hindi-speaking Nepalis during monarchy, while Bhutan expelled Nepali-speaking Hindu citizens. Who protested? Even Bangladesh which was born in 1971 with millions of Hindu lives and lives of Secular Muslims, with 10 million+ sheltered in India, has declared an Islamic Republic, no more a secular one, moving away from its founder Sheikh Mujibur Rahman's principle. In May of 2024 secularists – Muslim and Hindu – protested in New York City against this change, then started another pogrom after August 5, when Prime Minister Mrs. Hasina Wazed was driven out of the country. No one knows how long the pogrom and destruction of temples, deities, minority homes and businesses will continue. There was a Tamil genocide in Sri Lanka. Did East or West Protest? If such narrative happens in India, will East and West protest? Or, do we operate double standard? If U.S. followed Indian mentality, by now we would have several Native-American-majority states, African-American, Jewish, Catholic, Hispanic, French-speaking, German-speaking states, and more, and all its illegal residents would have been legal.

In India, as in old cultures like that of Italians, Ethiopians, Spanish, Peruvians, English, Chinese or Greeks, the definition of "new" and "old" is very different from America, Canada, or Brazil. In 1960s during a college trip to the eastern Orissa state some of the students got lost, but they knew that their class was working on architecture of a Krishna Temple. So, they asked a stranger with a vegetable carrier on top of his head about the direction of that temple. The stranger asked the lost students, "Which temple, the new one or the old one?" The "new" one was only 700 years old, and the "old" one was only "900" years old! This is Subcontinent! In 1979 we were visiting Sachi's sister's family in Jaipur, Rajasthan State in western India, possibly 1,200 miles from Bengal, crossing six cultures. Sachi was supposed to meet his Alabama friend Govind's father, but Sachi lost the address. Only thing he remembered was that Govind's father was a priest at a Hindu temple. Our brother-in-law suggested that we talk to the local temple priests, who often know other temple priests. We went to the neighborhood temple, seeing Sachi's Bengali brother-in-law, the Rajasthani-speaking priest said, "Go to that Kali Mandir temple, there is a Bengali priest." When we said, we are looking for a different one, the priest informed us, "Then go to Durga Mandir temple, where there is a Bengali priest." We met both of those priests. Ancestors of one family was brought from Bengal 700 years ago by a ruling king, the other was brought by another king "only" 500 years back, yet both of them spoke fluent Bengali with Rajasthani accent; and wore Bengali-style dhoti and *fotua* shirt. In India this extreme tolerant is expected by one's neighbors. Foreign Islamic and Christian rule for 1,000 years changed some of those mindsets.

Trip to another "restricted area" of Arunachal Pradesh in the Northeast, bordering Tibet and Burma (Myanmar) it was much simpler. Sachi came to Dibrugarh in Assam to take part for a Buddhist Chibar Dan Offering Ceremony, and to look into the possibility of helping an orphanage run by a Buddhist Vihar headed by monk Ven. Karuna Shashtri. After an early morning service, Sachi left for a sightseeing trip. The area is spectacularly beautiful with rivers, streams, mountains, wild animals, birds, and villages. By marketing the nature, the region could have become one of the most desired tourist destinations of the world, as we were reminded during a tour of Iceland, how the nation became one of the highest income countries of the world through tourism. The rental car was driven by a young local. He said, "Uncle Kaku, have you been to Arunachal? We border Arunachal. Let me take you to Tezu, a three-hour ride." On May 6, 2001 we journeyed through wide open thinly-populated picturesque hilly countryside, stopping for water falls, fast-flowing streams, looking at colorful birds, deer, and raccoon, rhododendron and other flowers, crossing a stream by foot while he drove his old car over the stream, and stopping at lonely vendors. Our car had to take a ferryboat crossing on a branch of Brahmaputra River. There were no signs on this remote road. We most likely crossed Changling District of Arunachal, before entering Lohit District. Finally, we arrived at Diwon village, before the town of Tezu. There were few residential buildings, a sprinkling of shops, a regional government office building, and a bunch of school boys and girls in blue-and-white uniform returning home from school, each holding a big paper. These tiny places are good for watching nature. Our young driver-cum-guide, asked "Uncle Kaku, go and say hello to the head of the office." As Sachi walked to the front door, four steps above the ground level, a man came out, and said "Namaskar! (Greetings!) Welcome to our village," with folded hands. The man, Mr. Das, became our instant tour-and-history-guide. He was a Bengali-Hindu from adjacent Assam State, where Sachi was staying. In Assam, as in some parts of diverse India, everyone spoke three, four or more languages. Thus, the linguistic-cultural identity is often self-identified. As he took visitors for a walking tour of the village, officer Das said, "Uncle, it is a very important day in the region. Do you see that all the students are carrying a Citizenship Certificate?" Then he took certificates from two of them to show us. "All the kids were born here. They are Buddhist Chakma refugees from Bangladesh. Their families were driven out of Bangladesh, and Government of India sheltered them in these desolate, uninhabited areas, yet some tribal groups in distant parts of Arunachal, who never set foot on these land in thousands of years are objecting to Chakma refugee rehabilitation, and asking India for deportation to Bangladesh, which Bangladesh refuses to accept. But, where would these refugees go? Their land and homes have been confiscated by Islamic Republic of Pakistan, and later Bangladesh. Thus, Indian Supreme Court ordered giving these kids citizenship paper based on their birth.

Their parents have not been issued those certificates yet." And this is how democratic pluralism looks in India. One small group of Buddhists and Hindus are objecting to another Buddhist group getting shelter on a land not of their forefathers. As we drove, we saw posters in English and Thai demanding education in Thai medium. This is a small group of people – 20,000 or less spread over a large mountainous area – who migrated to northeast India 200 to 300 years ago. We wonder how many school districts in Iowa, Alabama, England, France or Poland, to name a few democratic areas, would provide full-fledged K-12 education in Swahili, Ibo, Tamil, Inca or Thai, 300 years from their arrival in those areas? Or, in German, Russian, Finish, or Norwegian medium of instruction in publicly-funded schools for folks who came to America 200 years ago? A suicidally tolerant indigenous (Hindu) tradition allows the presence of such a demand, at times such tolerance has proven to be miserable.

Host Mr. Das in Arunachal with Kids Holding Indian
Citizenship Certificates walking to Their Home

Is it good, or is it bad? In India, under Hinduism's pluralism one allows such diversity, and ultra-tolerance, even at the cost of self-sacrifice. In other parts of

India which became Islamic Republic of Pakistan, a non-native Urdu language of north India basically wiped-out local languages like Punjabi, Sindhi, Baloch, Kashmiri, Pashto and more, using Arabic, not Indian, script. In trying to Arabize Bengali, it created Bangladesh movement opposing that. In Indian Kashmir, Kashmiris demanded their language to be taught, but in all-Muslim Pakistani Kashmiri area there were no such demand. Why? Even in Bangladesh, born after a language movement, the Founding Father Sheikh Mujibur Rahman asked the tribes to forgo their identity and "Become Bengali" further diminishing their culture. No one in refugee camps of those Chakma tribes in India asked them to give up their identity. Secular and non-partisan media need to promote tolerance, but not sectarian intolerance.

In the U.S., after returning from India in 1979, we decided to strengthen our connection by buying a land near our Alabama campus, on top of a slope with a nice view. Sachi had a dream of designing his home using his architecture degree. In March of 1979 we were blessed to be a parent of a son, Shuvo. It was on a Monday morning that Sachi had to take his wife to the hospital. And in a hurry, he stopped at a bank to withdraw cash, and an elderly man hit him from behind as he exited the bank. Within minutes' police, and in true to Alabama hospitality, said, "Sir, please don't wait here. Head to the hospital. I will bring my report to you," which he did.

Huntsville is a fascinating place. One would hardly realize that Tennessee River flows past the city. We lived in southern part of the city and frequently took the highway to south for a pleasure ride for ice-cream for the kids, and coffee for us. Soon we found a shack selling fish. This was a eureka moment for a fish-eating Bengali. But we were apprehensive too as we learned from a project Sachi was doing at the university for a small poor Black-American town of New Hope and Triana on Tennessee River, with deadly dump of DDT and pesticide that was affecting health of the residents. The poison was possibly sipping into the river. So, there was fear that it may be polluting Tennessee River's fish. Still, not being able to suppress temptation, on one weekend we went to the shack to buy fish. We found the owner and a hip of shad fish, a bony fish, very similar to *ilish* or hilsa, the most prized fish in Bengal. This is the first time we were seeing hilsa fish in America. We offered to buy one, but the owner said, "Take all of them for free." There were probably 100 of those bright silver colored fish. Owner said, "This is Alabama." We didn't understand his humor, but he was serious. Soon he started loading shads into our trunk. Finally, Sachi had to close the trunk to stop owner loading more fish into the trunk. Shop owner was very, very reluctant to take money, but we forced him to take money. After return home, Shefali had to beg our fish-eating friends to take hilsa for free. We had to home deliver to some. Afterwards, whenever we passed that shack, we waived at the shop owner.

Undecorated a Pair of Hilsa or Ilish Fish

- *Courtesy: Social media*

Before the end of spring semester, a friend told Sachi to apply to a campus on Long Island which was looking for someone with Urban Studies background. On one hand, we were happy to be teaching in one institution where we were getting same breaks together, on the other hand for our academic, cultural, social, and inquisitive minds attracted metropolitan area that could be more productive we thought. That is also what our friends thought. It put us between a rock and a hard place.

Welcome to Progressive, Cosmopolitan New York:

Coming to New York was full of challenges, excitement and hardship. Hardship, because coming from a low-cost area to an area of high cost of living makes you poor. Tax was high too. All of a sudden for a relatively hassle-free living in Alabama, it became hassle-only living in close to poverty. Now, we were not students, but a family with two kids. As it was already summer, Shefali's department chair requested her not to quit with a short notice, and urged her to stay for the fall semester, which she did. Our one-and-a-half-year-old daughter Joyeeta decided to join dad, while the 5-month-old son Shuvo stayed with mom. Our search for apartment was going nowhere, when a sociology professor gave a lead to a one room apartment in Westbury that cost more than our home mortgage in Alabama, but it was close to our campus. Shefali found a wonderful Dominican family who would babysit in the evening in Westbury for our daughter Joyeeta when she won't be at the campus daycare center. To find an apartment, for several days we traveled from our classmate Vasant's home in New Jersey.

He cautioned, "Be careful, some areas do not welcome colored people, including Indians. Take a look at the home of my friend Ravi from our hometown in Maharashtra State (India) down the block which was torched recently." In one place, next to an underpass in New Jersey, there was a sign reading, "Indians Go Home." Coming from South, hearing about North's progressivism, this was new to us. This was in 1979. Nevertheless, when our Alabama secretary Mary, a Black-American, learned of our imminent departure, she asked, "Why go there? You'll be shot dead in a week." Then again in New York, secretary Eleanor, a White-American, who was trying hard to find us a place to live asked, "Were you ever attacked by KKK? I won't live there. Welcome to New York."

Our struggle was just beginning. Shefali found a great babysitter several miles south of our home in Huntsville, Alabama, as she was going to keep the 5-month-old baby, then drive to campus over twenty-one miles. Our Alabama friends provided logistical support to Shefali. Shefali's department chair asked her to teach for the fall semester as Sachi received the contract very late.

The difference in cost of living was so significant that a newspaper on Long Island asked Sachi to write an article for them. Salary difference was not there. Property tax was more than 10 times higher in New York, income tax was significantly higher, utility was many times higher, as was car insurance. Our Dominican babysitter Muriel took care of 2-yeat old Joyeeta with great care, especially when Sachi had evening class. A big help for childcare was a daycare center on campus called Child Care Educational Center or CCEC, directed by Dr. Sylvia, a Black lady. One year later, our baby, Shuvo joined CCEC. Educating two kids, Dr. Sylvia became a family friend, visiting our home with her daughter. And in 1982 we rented her center for our Sunday morning Bengali language Nassau Pathshala school bringing her some financial help, and providing our language school a space. We became friends with quite a few families through CCEC.

Before Joyeeta moved to kindergarten in our Long Island public school, we came to know of Mrs. Florence, a Black banker, whose grandson was attending the childcare center. We became close family friends for the past 45+ years. We became a Board Member of her non-profit, Pomoja International. When her son in his 30s was harassed by New York police in 2000s for petty reason, we wrote a petition to New York Governor for abuse of police and state power. In 2016 our family of three generations joined a summer Pomoja festivity and kids' outdoor competition at Braser Falls, a tiny village in Upstate New York, near Massena, across from Canada on the south side of St. Lawrence River.

On our way to Brasar Falls we passed a village named Bombay where an Irish immigrant from India with wife from Bombay, now called Mumbai, settled in 1805. From hustle and bustle of Brooklyn, Florence moved 400 miles north, as far away as one can go from densely-populated Brooklyn, to a very rural, open atmosphere.

CCEC Kids Center with Shuvo, 5th from left, and Joyeeta, Left, 1982

Mrs. Florence with Dastidar Family, 2016

Two Former Classmates of 1981 of the Child Care Center at Old Westbury, 2016

Families Joining Festivities at Brasar Falls, New York, 2016

In 1980, one housing activist group on Long Island asked Sachi to join a lawsuit demanding zoning change on Long Island townships covering Nassau and Suffolk counties – where the areas are called "Villages" with zoning power – to accommodate apartments in addition to single-family homes. But, once we bought a house in Hicksville in 1980, we couldn't be a part of the legal challenge.

Putting roots down in New York was full of pleasure and pain. Our first pleasure came when we found a house on P. Lane in Hicksville, Nassau County, Long Island, a place for working-class folks, and a suburb of New York City. As we went to sign the contract with a cashier's check, insults started flying when we said, "Listen, even if you give us your property free now, we are not going to take it, and walked out of the deal." Our real estate broker, a cheerful Irish-American, possibly in his late sixties, said "There are lots of other properties for you to choose from," and he found us a Levitt home on Picture Lane, six blocks from P. Lane. At Picture Lane, when we arrived, some neighbors told us that there were at first some consternation hearing as a colored family was moving in, although they were happy to learn from the real estate agent that both of us were professors, one on Long Island, and the other in New York CIty. We believe it was a fear of the unknown than racism or prejudice. In reality, we're welcomed with handshake by saying "Welcome to our neighborhood," by all of our neighbors, that was uniquely New York-type. This was a wonderful experience. We became quite close to our neighbor to the north, Pallellas, with whom we'd frequently have tea. After four years when they retired to Florida, they called us to tell us that they have an "Indian" neighbor, and their doctor is "Indian." Our southern neighbor, Mrs. Wallace's father, a first-generation Italian-American would often visit them. Grandpa was so happy to see our kids play across the 3-ft high fence, that he would stand across the fence and chat with our kids like a true grandpa. He used to talk about his childhood in Italy. We couldn't figure out why our German-American neighbor across the back fence, Grandma Angela, cheered my mother, as she saw Ma offering water to the plants, grains to the birds (animals) after Ma's morning prayer to the Sun God welcoming a productive day. They didn't understand each other's language, yet developed friendship. Mrs. Angela wanted to see Ma every day, and in summer offered vegetables to Ma from her garden. Ma visited New York in 1986-1987. Who could predict that by mid-2010s Hicksville will be a place full of Indians and South Asians, Indian culture, Indian businesses and restaurants.

With Shefali joining a New York City job, we moved to Queens with access to public transportation for her, and easy auto ride for Sachi. Ironically, Sachi was twice further away compared to Hicksville, yet it took half the time as he traveled via expressway whereas before he had to travel through city streets with traffic light on each block. Our plan to move to Queens, New York City in the summer of 1987 was dashed because of nationwide financial crisis until it completely collapsed on October 19, 1987, a special day for the family. Our calls to banks were never replied, neither our request for refund of mortgage deposit money was not responded. So, in December, after Sachi's classes ended and before exams began, he went to the bank headquarter in a county, north of NY City. At first the guard didn't allow Sachi to see or talk to any officers. Then realizing he was planning for a sit-in protest, one of their junior officers took him to upper floor and tried to sweet-talk him. Realizing, it wasn't working, he arranged for a meeting with top officers. After our discussion, they asked Sachi to come back after lunch when they delivered Sachi the paperwork for a mortgage, and with a stipulation that we had to move in three weeks during our winter break. We had to arrange for admission to Public School in New York City for our kids, and inform Lee School in Hicksville of our departure. Hicksville principle tried to persuade us to stay as both Shuvo and Joyeeta were admitted into the newly created Magnet Program for 4th and 5th grades in his school. We were sorry too, but had to give him an unfortunate news that since they were admitted to the special program, one of the 5th grade boys in the bus started teasing our kids with "nigger" slang. We tried to convince our kids to ignore by saying "nigger means smart," but the kids were not convinced. Principal was shocked. In early January our kids joined their New York City school on the first day of the school after Christmas break. Our new neighbor with three kids in the same school offered to bring back the kids, if Sachi gave them ride to school in the morning. Each year the number of kids went down as they graduated from elementary to join junior high school within walking distance from our home. Routine was disrupted one day as Joyeeta returned home crying with a letter from the principal saying that he is going to give her a special prize as she stood second in Spelling Bee competition. Our congratulation to our daughter was rejected by her. She said, "I stood first, not second." In the midst of our confusion came two telephone calls from two unknown ladies, one with a Southern-Indian accent, and the other with East-European accent, both urging us to protest, as "I was there. Your daughter stood first, and they won't give that to an immigrant." These competitions are held in public at the school auditorium where Joyeeta stood first, but not the girl the principal groomed. Then he took Joyeeta into his office, and in presence of four 5th grade colored boys he declared Joyeeta runner up. Next day, after class Sachi met the principal. His reaction was baffling: "You are not like other Indians!" Seeing Sachi, Joyeeta's class teacher, a Jewish-American said, "Thank you my friend for objecting. We all are with you. This is bad." Principal then rolled the dice to District Superintendent, the administrator of all 25 schools of the district. Few days later, Sachi was invited for a meeting with him, but the clock was ticking as the next phase of regional competition was two weeks later, and the school had to send the name in a day or two. He called for a second meeting with the parents of the other girl suggesting that both the girls be sent to the next phase. Sachi said, "Why not send all the six semifinalists to the next phase, but declare Joyeeta as the winner, as parents and teachers had observed that." This was 1988.

Bellerose Neighborhood

As Indians started to move into the neighborhood, two years down the road there appeared painted signs on lampposts on Union Turnpike between 249th Street and Little Neck Parkway (252rd Street) saying "Hindu Go Home," and on the door of our neighbor John, a Christian-Indian. Some of the neighbors suggested to ignore it. Seeing no action, Sachi called our police. A young police officer came to our house. Sachi took him to those lampposts. Soon neighbor John repainted covering the slogans in his door, but the lamppost slogans were still there. The officer felt disturbed, and said necessary actions will be taken in a few days. After several weeks, slurs were still there. Then it was painted by locals, not the police.

Bellerose Home

Although police action wasn't prompt, but at least police responded. In India, especially in extremist-, regional- and partisan-run states, there wouldn't have been any response at all. In "leftist" Kolkata (Calcutta), a large number of Hindu monks and nuns were hacked, then burned alive in broad daylight in a Hindu-majority land. West Bengal state and City of Kolkata were run by Hindu-refugees fleeing from Muslim-majority homeland to Hindu-majority West Bengal State. Communist rulers chose not to live with their Muslim-majority neighbors in their homeland, yet murdered pacifist Hindu monks, and not arrest a single killer although pictures are available on social media. They joined hands with anti-India religious extremists who cleansed them from their homeland.

It is within 150 yards from our home in Ballygunj. Yet not a single murderer has been arrested or prosecuted in that democratic nation in the past three decades, whether by the ruling communists, or now (2025) by the ruling anti-communist party. This is sectarian India that West ignores.

Memorial march by Monks and Nuns at Ballygunj Kasba
Bridge for Arrest of Murderers

- *Source: Social Media*

Running for Public Office:

1996 was New York School Board election year. Sachi decided to throw his hat for the nine-member board, of which seven of the Board Members were incumbents. For him this was a first-hand learning experience for an academician. He was learning firsthand what he was teaching: How theory can be different from practice, especially when politics is often controlled by elites. There politicians' preaching and practice were often deceitful, and joining the ballot box was determined by an elite few, at times with no connection to the people. So, in New York collecting signature for ballot petition was a humble, grass-roots experience. Reaching out to diverse groups was another learning experience. In America this is lowest-level of elected office. But New York City being what it is, the district had over 225,000 people with 110,000 electorates of which only 500 voters were of Subcontinent-origin. Ours was the best school district in the entire state, barring one or two districts with extremely small enrollments. About dozen-and-a half candidates qualified to run for election. There were Whites and Non-Whites, Protestant, Catholic, Jewish, Korean, Chinese, Hispanic, and more. There were four candidates of Asian origin. This election was non-partisan so political parties couldn't directly play any role, or financially help the candidates. It was an unpaid job. There were candidates who belonged to both Democratic and Republican parties, but couldn't identify as such, but party volunteers could help as individuals. There were 16 open debates in various places, generally in school auditoriums. There were activists of countless interest. Some activist groups interviewed candidates and endorsed some of them. There is no such thing in India. Even village-level elections are manipulated by parties, thugs and partisan press, but openly. In Bengal in India, we witnessed the rise of Communism in the 1960s with oppression of free thinking, and the rise of majority-Hindu oppression by Hindu-atheist leaders who ironically fled from their Muslim neighbors and Islamic power in Pakistan-Bangladesh for the safety of India, while claiming to have no religion. As young person we supported them. This thought process is still active in many parties in India, especially after the demise of nationalist Congress Party with family rule. Still, the 2020 American election revealed limitations of democracy in an open system. U.S. is a settler-colonial model, where the indigenous peoples have had no voice at all. But that is a separate issue for discussion. In the School Board election we all stood for the best schools, highest student achievements, lowest tax, finest administration, and best teachers. All of us looked for those. By default, our ethnicity, religion, place of birth became important. Thus, if all the Protestants voted for Protestants, it won't be any surprise. So, if Poles voted for Poles; Koreans for Koreans, Jews for Jews, Biharis for Biharis, Dominicans for Dominicans, and so on it won't be any surprise. We won't be surprised in the primaries of city, state or federal election, if such identities play important role, diverting the principles of democracy, and heading towards sectarianism. In debate, in evenings on working days, there were at times more debaters than listeners, but always there were people asking questions. With newly arriving "Indians" there were always questions for Sachi about why "Indians" do not volunteer for individual school committees.

We believe this was true. However, it had more to do with being new immigrant, trying to survive, working more than eight-hours a day, balancing two cultures, than being "Indian." This was true for other immigrants as well. Indians were a new ethnic group in America, distinct from Caucasians, Africans, Hispanics, and East Asians, as there were such nationalities present before new immigration policy enacted in mid-1960s, in post-Civil Rights era. "Indians" were also easily identified by their non-European names, food, and outfit, something new in American history. Thus, non-participation from other immigrant nationalities were not so obvious.

Sachi was lucky that several individuals and groups liked him. That included Sachi's son's Boy's Scout parents, parents of Sunday Bengali Nassau Pathshala free language school that we started while in Hicksville, Long Island, volunteers of Probini Foundation that we started to create a bridge with native-born and immigrants and help educate the poor and the orphaned in Bangladesh and India, our friend Rani's *veena* string musical instrument student families, and more. Still, it was an uphill task. In late afternoon on the election day, some families called Shefali, Sachi's wife, to tell her that they were denied from voting by a police officer in Public School voting site, where Dastidar family voted. The police would tell Indian voters, "Here comes Indian! You can't vote." Around 7 pm in the evening we were able to bring back three Indian families to vote. A few more families couldn't come back as their kids had returned from school. We suspect there were other families too, but they didn't call us. The policeman was furious at Sachi, who made a formal complaint to the police precinct. Several months later, one top officer called Sachi to inform that they investigated Sachi's complaint and "found that indeed many Indians were denied from voting," and said "a copy of the confidential report will be filed in the officer's folder, but their finding can't be shared with the person complaining." On the other side of trust, when Sachi gave his campaign literature to a person heading to a voting site, the man gave the paper back and said, "I know who you are. I am going to the booth to vote for you, as it is the first time I am voting for an Indian candidate." We understand Sachi was the first person of Indian origin to run for office in New

York State. There were write ups in Queens Chronical, the New York Times, and Channel-4, elsewhere about the candidacy. Sachi worked with another novice, Mr. Alam of Bangladesh, a Bengali Muslim, who ran in another school district. New York City School district election had a rank-order voting that made candidates work with other candidates for suggesting second choice for their supporters. Sachi worked closely with several candidates, among them was a first-time candidate, Mrs. Kim, a Korean-American. Even counting of votes was a learning lesson. It went for days. Questions many candidates asked, "How do full time workers like ourselves spend day after day, leaving our work, and attend those ballot count?" This also reminded us of questions raised by some attendees of the possibility of corruption in unpaid jobs where one has to spend thousands of dollars to get elected. Just to send one postcard to all the 100,000-plus voters could cost over $50,000 dollars in any district. How many people can afford to spend that amount of money without getting it back? Many politicians in the U.S. have argued for state funding of election, which is opposed by others. This is also a serious contradiction in democracy where wealthy individuals have advantage over the vast majority of commoners. As vote count continued, Sachi was at the bottom of top nine candidates, and was about to displace an incumbent, a lawyer. The losing 10th ranked candidate went to the court asking the court to declare him elected, as he argued during one stage of the count, he was ahead by a vote or two. Hearing the case, Asian American lawyers offered Sachi free legal help, which otherwise would have cost thousands of dollars. Sachi planned not to challenge as he realized it would be better to spend money for his kids' education, or given to our Probini Foundation which was educating the poor and the orphaned children. Learning from newspapers, he got calls from Ms. Chen and Ms. Young, both lawyers of Asian American Legal Defense Fund, to help Sachi, free of charge. They were like angels! At the end of the hearing, one of lawyers asked Sachi, "How come Asian American Defense is defending you? You are not Asian but Indian!" We asked, "Is that true?"

In the world's largest democracy of India, this speedy investigation, and coming up with a conclusion is beyond imagination, but it has changed. This is another face of corruption. Of course, in India it depends on state administrations as police is run by states, like the U.S., not the federal Delhi government.

On the School Board and the Campus:

The School Board met once a week in the evening, but Board Members were invited to meetings and events in schools throughout the week. In the first year Sachi was elected Secretary of the Board. By secret ballot, our Board elected a president, a secretary and a treasurer. In rest of the country School Boards decide property tax to balance their budget on educating children, but not in New York City. This is a huge responsibility rarely understood by many nations. Once Sachi lectured in India to a top university's graduate economics students. It more than baffled the students hearing that districts have to balance their budget, as in India and most of the world, it is assumed that "government" will pay for education irrespective of budget consideration. Sachi made it a point to visit all schools in the district. This was a great experience. Each school developed its own identity based on the neighborhood, but all had to follow the same curriculum. Class size was similar. Our new Board had six whites, all incumbents, and 3 Asians, all first timers.

The first meeting of the Board with all the 25 school's Parent-Teacher Association heads went on smoothly, except for one last item on the agenda, to "Asian Board Members must know that they do not represent Asians only." Sachi was the last speaker in the meeting, and pointed out how this innocent mistake could be construed as unfair because they didn't talk about the behavior of our other nationalities, to which all the hands of the school PTA Presidents went up in protest. There was one strong defender of Sachi's position was Ms. Berni, who later became a Judge of New York Supreme Court. Sachi was honored to be invited years after he left the School Board to her inauguration in a new court building in Jamaica, Queens.

NYC School Board 26 Oath Taking, 1996

Dastidar decides not to run again

Decision Not to Run in 1999

Our district had magnet programs for better performing students. The district was attracting many talented colored students, but the magnet program was almost exclusively white. The District Superintendent, a Jewish American, wanted to broaden it, and not controlled by few families. He discussed his proposal with the Board, where there were differing opinions. He needed five votes from the nine-member board to change district's policy. It needed a public hearing. Parents of the magnet program mobilized, sending Board Members dozens of letters, phone calls and more. The hearing lasted till 3 or 4 am in the morning. Within hours of returning home, Sachi had to head to his class for 8 am in the morning. The motion passed 5-to-4. This is very different from schools in India where there is hardly any parental involvement, parental influence, parental volunteerism, or curricular debates. Some schools have tried, but not with success. In India all are determined by the state political parties, violence, threats of violence, traditional and regional political machinations, as educations is a matter of state. During Congress Party rule in India, political leaders were more approachable than the Communist-Marxist rule of Bangladeshi-Indian-Hindu-Refugee-run regimes in eastern India, under whose rule Hindu-run private schools were discriminated in West Bengal state, as opposed to Christian, Islamic or other non-Hindu schools. As a result, the scholastically-famous monks of Ramakrishna Mission-run schools had to go to the Indian Supreme Court to declare themselves as a "non-Hindu" order. This is certainly one of many racist and anti-majority decisions made in India, especially by Bengal's and India's Left-Communist politics, and neocolonial intellectuals, although almost all the leaders in Hindu-majority partitioned West Bengal in India were Pakistani-Bangladeshi-Hindu-Refugee-Indians who chose not to live in their Muslim-majority homeland for safety of Hindu-majority India while criticizing Gandhi, India's independence fighter Congress Party, Hindus and India, but not Pakistan, Bangladesh/Pakistan Muslim League Party who cleansed them for their identity, Islamist/racist partition leader Jinnah, or Suhrawardy, the Islamist ruler of British-era Bengal. There is no word for this politics. Will U.K. react if huge numbers of citizens in neighboring Ireland, France, Belgium, Netherland and Norway drove from their homeland or killed them by calling them English? Or, would France react if her neighbors acted similarly?

After our School Board term ended in 1999, New York City's new mayor, billionaire Mr. Michael Bloomberg, and New York City Council, got rid of New York City's elected school boards. They exist everywhere else in America. However, the New York City School Boards didn't tax residents and balance their budgets, unlike elsewhere in America. Sachi didn't run for office again as he headed to Kazakhstan with a Fulbright Award.

Chapter 2

Wonders Of Wild-Open America and Wide-Open World

Traveling is a bug, as is popularly known. Even Ma used to tease Sachi when he was in college with a Bengali proverb, "Were you born with wheels under your feet?" although we did not have money for travel in our financially-stretched refugee family. Most likely Sachi got that bug in undergraduate residential engineering college when students had to take field trips across a diverse, colorful, and relaxed India with other boys and girls of the department to study architecture of various regions of India. This was a really wonderful experience giving us exposure to architecture and engineering of buildings, mostly old or unused *mandirs* (temples), going back to hundreds or thousands of years, or on occasion abandoned *masjids* (mosques) and *viharas* (Buddhist temples), as well as old palaces, that exposed students to diverse India. Architecture department used to rent one or two train's sleeping coaches for two weeks or more in summer. The coaches, called bogies in India, used to be attached to regular long-distance trains going in our tour direction, starting and ending in Howrah Station in Howrah City, across the Hooghly River from Kolkata (Calcutta). Hooghly is a branch of Ganga (Ganges) River. Our Bengal Engineering College campus was located in Howrah district on the bank of Hooghly River across from Kolkata.

Tour was an academic requirement. Those who couldn't afford long distance tour, used to go to nearby sites in West Bengal State. Campus was never worried about hotels, as those coaches had three tier sleeping berths with toilet. When our train moved, our campus tour manager bought lunch, dinner, breakfast, tea or coffee from the railway catering service, as well as arranged for discussion, chat, and music forums on the compartment. When we stopped for our projects, local restaurants supplied our food. Those rented coaches were disconnected from the train, when we needed break, the coaches were kept on the side parking tracks until our next move. And when we stayed for days in one place, we moved to hotels while the rented locked coaches waited in storage area. Hotels provided all that was needed for survival. Our projects involved measuring the structure, drawing of new plans, elevations and perspectives, then suggesting for preservation and landscape design of historic *mandirs* (Hindu-Jain temples), at times *masjids* (Muslim mosques), *viharas* (Buddhist temples), *girjas* (Christian churches), millennia and centuries old and historic buildings, often abandoned or unkempt. As we traveled food changed from state to state, architecture changed from region to region, signs on railway platforms changed with different languages, people's outfit changed, flora and fauna changed, even words of greetings changed, as India is often referred as "Nation of Nations," lot more diverse than European Union. Still, it is one country. It opened our eyes how diverse and tolerant is the nation in its language, culture, food, dress, tradition and architecture. Even the look of the deities changed with time and culture. This is also a political and cultural problem to bring the nation together.

The campus had to take permission from local authorities for our architectural work, when bunch of college students will be hovering around. Scale of structures, mostly brick- or stone-built, varied. Then again this was India in 1960s. In a rational situation, local archeological preservers could have used professionally supervised work for their own benefit. I don't know how many used them. However, we doubt if locals ever used our final report with measurement, sketches, and architectural drawings. Even Sachi's master's thesis of downtown revitalization of Howrah City, the second largest city in West Bengal state, was highly rated and appreciated by the Calcutta Metropolitan Planning Organization, but we don't know if they used the data with acknowledgement. Sachi learned about the use when he joined the office after graduation with master's degree from Indian Institute of Technology (IIT) at Kharagpur. There were places we visited where we didn't understand a single word locals spoke, and they didn't understand us, but socialized very cordially.

We were able to visit all far-flung regions in five years. Getting travel funds, though modest amount, was not very easy in that difficult economic time for a refugee family like ours. Sachi's parents and his older brother Mejda, Middle Older Brother Amitabha, supported his travel, and from second year economic pressure eased a bit as Sachi had a part-time off-campus job, almost at the entrance to the campus. Few dollars Sachi earned went to Ma, who then saved it in her *Lokkhir Jhapi* or Ma Lakshmi's Saving Bowl. Ma then gave Sachi from the bowl when he needed funds. This protocol was very normal in Indian families for generations, if not for millenniums. It is worth mentioning that unlike in America, that studying and working to support oneself was/is extremely unusual in India, and in poor countries. Exception was for the very poor and the refugees from Pakistan, Bangladesh, Burma, Nepal, Sri Lanka, Afghanistan, Tibet (China) and more whose families were driven out from their home for India. Sachi may have been the only student in our residential engineering college working while studying, certainly in his class. One of Sachi's teachers, Prof. Salil, introduced Sachi to a building contractor who needed some part-time drafting help.

Looking back, the first travel by himself was in his mid-teen before his college life, in the summer of 1961 after the School Final Exam. He headed to visit his oldest brother, Dada, Dr. Sankar, a medical doctor in a remote forest area called Dandakaranya Forest in central India where poor, oppressed Hindu peasants of East Pakistan driven out from their ancestral homes in Pakistan through genocide and successive pogroms, were being settled by the federal Indian Government under Dandakaranya Refugee Rehabilitation Project. Big socio-political problem was no one, including refugees, ever protested killing of their families or confiscation of their ancestral land by calling them "Enemy of the State" by using Enemy Property Act of Pakistan that allowed calling indigenous non-Muslim minorities as "Enemy of the State," and confiscate their property without paying a penny. Dada, Older Brother Sankar, was a very sincere man and decided to serve the refugees like himself for a meagre pay, giving up high paying jobs in cities and the U.S. A long-distance train from Howrah station headed for Madras, now called Chennai, in southern India, a 1-

night train ride took one to northern Andhra Pradesh state. The train heading south passed the entire state of Orissa, now called Odisha, then stopped at Vishakhapatnam Station, in Telugu-speaking Andhra state. Travelers got off around 10 PM at night, then they had to catch a bus that would take them to Koraput, deep in the jungle, which was the headquarters of the Dandakaranya Refugee Rehabilitation Project, where hospital and medical facilities were established for the refugees and for the local tribal and non-tribal communities. At Vishakhapatnam people spoke Telugu which Sachi didn't understand at all, besides many spoke Oriya, which he didn't know, but was close to Bengali, the language he spoke. This is where Sachi soon learned his first second-language. He noticed many passengers as soon as they got off the train rushed to a bus parked nearby, and after getting a seat, rushed to restaurants for dinner. Sachi noticed most of the ticket buyers were saying, "*Motay gutey ticket dio*," meaning "Give me one ticket" in Oriya. The words were very close to Bengali except the word for "one." Sachi learned "*gutey*" means "one," and ordered his bus ticket accordingly.

Dandakaranya Forest Area

These buses left before midnight, driving at night through thick dark forest in mountainous road bringing passengers to Koraput bus stop in early morning.

Sachi had no idea where his brother was living, except the town name, as the communication address was his office address. But this was India! As soon as he got off the bus, he asked a shopkeeper if he knew Dr. Ghosh Dastidar. Soon, a crowd gathered, speaking many languages, men and women, tribe and non-tribe, refugee and forest dwellers, and everyone wanted to take him to his brother; and one of them did. Dada was already at his office, before 8 AM, although the official opening was hours later. As the stranger took Sachi to the office Dada was looking through a microscope and almost fell from his chair seeing his brother. He became mad at Baba, our dad, for not informing him of Sachi's travel plan. Dada was extremely happy to see his youngest brother, no doubt. Dad sent him a letter weeks ago, but the mail hadn't arrived yet. After Sachi's return to Kolkata, Sachi bought a trilingual book to learn Oria language and alphabet, the second language that he learned. That language is still with Sachi, although many languages he learned later – French, Spanish, Russian, Hindi – he forgot a lot for lack of practice, except Oria and Hindi languages.

Traveling in India was mostly by train, while in America it was always by car. Later in life, in both India and America air travel helped. In Bangladesh, our travel was helped by boats, overnight boat journeys, including our most enchanting world travel: a river journey on a Hindu monk's boat, with hot food cooked by the monk, and hearing cheers from locals on riverbank when they could notice the monk. In rest of the world road, air, and water travel helped depending on the journey. He had a wonderful experience in another boat ride in 2023 at Arial Kha River in Madaripur City with monk Maharaj where his mother's family lived before cleansing.

India and Bangladesh, Partitioned East Bengal, now Bangladesh and West Bengal State, India:

As just mentioned, in India we got introduced to travel in that vast, tolerant, fatalistic, and extremely diverse nation through our Bengal Engineering College's architecture summer program when students traveled to different regions of India to an old structure – *mandirs* (Hindu-Jain temples), *viharas*

(Buddhist temples), (Islamic) mosques, *pathshalas* (schools), and shrines, generally abandoned or in disrepair, but with interesting architecture. Some of those structures are hundreds, at times thousands of years old. Each year the project took students to one of the regions of India, except Bengal where the college was located. In Bengal as in eastern and northern India, Pakistan and Bangladesh most of the old temples were victims of non-native Islamic destruction, including our family's 1700s and 1500s old *mandirs* (temples). Thus, in India ancient temples only exist in southern India, Odisha in the east, and Assam in the northeast where Islamic rule didn't penetrate, and in Rajasthan in the west where Hindu kings resisted destruction.

We learned not only architecture and history but also learned to live in places where they didn't understand one word of Bengali, or living in fully vegetarian culture for a fish-eating Bengali, or seeing signs on railway platforms, offices and shops that appeared in different languages and scripts that we didn't understand. One good impression in young mind was of acceptance of diversity and tolerance, even in a nation still suffering from partition-affected Hindu cleansing from Pakistan and Bangladesh.

Fortunately, cleansing of Indian Muslims who voted under British rule for partition of India on the basis of religion didn't take place. Even the first groups who went to Pakistan called themselves *muhajir* or volunteers of Lord of Islam's associate who went with Him to conquer and Islamize non-Islamic Medina. As Bengalis developed a tradition of travel to faraway places for pilgrimage, we were surprised to see so many traders dealing strangers in Bengali language – from Varanasi and Agra in Hindi-speaking area, to Ladakh in Tibetan-speaking area of Kashmir in the north, to the southern-most point of India at Tamil speaking Kanyakumari. Here is an art of painting seashell. The Bengali inscription of Sabyasachi's name was done by a Tamil-speaking artist:

Title says: Sabyasachi Ghosh Dastidar in Bengali Script Written
by a Tamil Artist; 1960s

Traveling in India, a culture bearing millenniums-old ancient tradition, makes you realize the term "new" has different meaning than a nation like the United States, Canada, or Brazil. With respect to ancient culture and architecture India may be compared with Italy, Spain, Egypt, or China, with a significant difference. In those old cultures, the ancient tradition of nature worship, deities representing different forces of nature are not part of modern life with the introduction of monotheistic Christianity, Islam, or Atheism, but not in India. Thus, reverence of ancient beliefs is part of modern Indian and Hindu/Jain/Buddhist culture. During one trip we were in Odisha (Orissa) in eastern India known for ancient architecture. That's why during a class discussion when Sachi told his students that when you walk the streets of Varanasi in India, Rome in Italy, or Xian in China you must realize that people walked the same path 2,000, 3,000, or 4,000 years ago! Sachi's own family called their ancestral home in Lakshmankathi village in Bangladesh as their "new" home as they established the village in the 1500s, as opposed to the "old" home before that at Gava village in Bangladesh going back to almost First Millennium, as per written record.

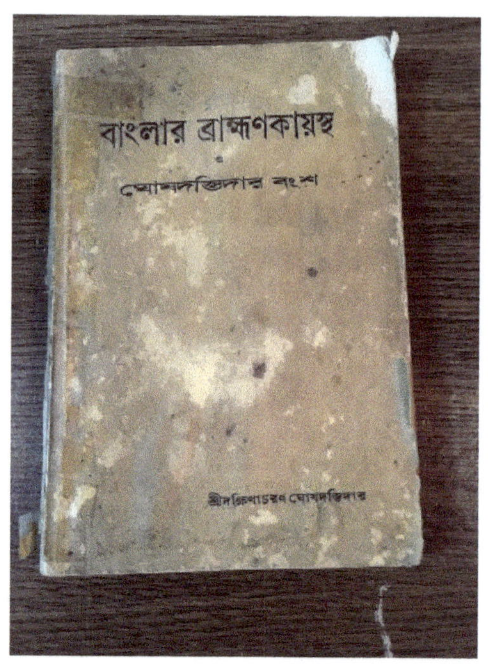

Banglar Brahmankayastha (Bengal's Braman-Kayastha & Ghosh Dastidar Family) by Sri Dakshina Charan Ghosh Dastidar; Published in 1942.

-   Courtesy: NY Partition Museum

From NYC Partition Museum: A Century or Two Old Lakshmir Jhapi (Saving Monetary Bowl of Ma Lakshmi, the Goddess of Prosperity) brought to India when a Hindu Refugee Family was Forced to Flee their Ancestral East Pakistan/Bangladesh Homeland

2021 Rededication of Lakshmankathi Sri Bishnu (Vishnu)
Mandir of 1500s Barisal District, Bangladesh

1982: Remains of the 1500s Sri Bishnu (God of Creation) Mandir (Temple) after Post-Partition Attack During Pogroms in early 1950s.

Sri Bishnu Deity, 2023 August, at Rededication of Mother Kali's Destroyed Shrine

This idea of new and old was exposed again in India when Sachi's older sister Didi and him visited Gaya, in Bihar State in eastern India. Gaya is a very old place with historic and religious importance. It is where Siddhartha Gautam or Lord Buddha, came to meditate under a Bodhi tree 600 years before Christian Era. Bodhi trees are similar to banyan trees, which are also considered sacred. Cutting down banyan tree is considered inauspicious as it gives huge shade in that hot tropical country, as well as it is home to almost 30 species of birds and animals. As Buddha rose after days of meditation without food and water, a wondering oppressed Hindu woman named Sujata offered Him his first drink from a nearby pond. Where Buddha meditated Mahabodhi Mandir was built. In another part of Gaya people offer food and water to their departed souls on the banks of Falgu River. People must have been making trips to that place for millenniums, most likely well before 600 B.C. Older sister Didi or Pratima and Sachi went there in early 2000s to offer food and water to our departed mother and ancestors on the banks of Falgu River. There exist many old, shrines, and viharas at Gaya. A Muslim invader destroyed scores of Hindu mandirs and

Buddhist viharas. To desecrate Hindus and Buddhists, and to make Buddhism nonexistent, the Islamic invader cut down the Bodhi tree and filled up the pond from where Sujata brought the first drink to Sri Buddha. In late 1800s during colonial British rule the temple site was discovered and the temple was rebuilt, and a new sapling of Bodhi tree was brought from Sri Lanka to grow a new one, as our Buddhist guide told us. We were fortunate to get several fallen dry leaves of the Bodhi tree that Sachi framed for our home, and presented to many of our friends. As you go through the area, tour guides often point out at old temples and say, "That is a temple of Mother Sita, but only a thousand-year-old. And that is a Ganesh Mandir, only 500-year-old," and so on. As one goes towards Falgu River Ghats, or river landings, where many small shrines are located for offering of food and water to the ancestors, huge numbers of brokers carrying thick hundreds-of-years-old books surrounded us asking for our home village, district, region and state. As one mentions one's home state, the crowd thins. It becomes smaller when one mentions district, then police station, and finally the village. Someone was carrying our family history going back to hundreds of years. When we mentioned our Lakhsmankathi village in Barisal district of Bengal, now Bangladesh, only two agents carrying our family history were left. They asked us to choose one of them. We chose one where our oldest brother Dada (or Sankar) came in 1980s to offer symbolic food and water called *pindu daan* to our departed father and to other ancestors. The biggest surprise was that the 3" to 4" thick book contained my ancestors' names going back to 400 to 500 years or more. It takes a long time to go through the book as one lineage goes in one section, and another in a separate section. Documentation started long before road and rail travel. For us it took just four hours by express train from Kolkata to Gaya costing a few dollars. Our ancestors must have come by boat from Barisal district, and we assume it must have taken them weeks to travel to offer their prayer at Falgu River, and weeks to go back home by boat. It was quite revealing just to think of their dedication, and courage to travel. Of course, Lord Buddha also traveled hundreds of miles in 600 B.C. from north Bihar and Nepal border to come to Gaya in southern Bihar in eastern India. He must have walked hundreds of miles to come to Gaya.

Sachi (not in picture) and Older Sister, Didi, Left, with a Hindu Priest, right, offering Water and Symbolic Food to our Departed Mother and Ancestors on the Bank of Falgu River, Bihar State, visible through trees, where Lord Buddha Came to Meditate in 600 B.C.

As we travel to our Bangladesh homeland via our refugee homeland of Kolkata, West Bengal State of India from the new homeland of the United States, what was very reveling to us of the reaction of the Hindu refugees in India. They were all very excited, and blessed our family for safe return, but were terrified to visit their homeland by themselves, even by so-called "revolutionaries." What was even more shocking that many of these individuals in their fifties, sixties or seventies fought with the British before 1947 independence, sometimes risking their own lives and spending years in British oppressor's prison, at times in remote Andaman Islands in the Bay of Bengal, but were afraid of oppression and butchery of Muslim League Party of India-Pakistan-Bangladesh. This is incomprehensible! Why were they afraid and silent in defending their own families? This is inhuman! We always wondered if that was because they witnessed anti-Hindu genocide of Pakistan in 1946, 1947, 1950s, 1962, 1964, and more, and in 1971 during Bangladesh's independence war. Did that fear continue after independence of Bangladesh in 1971? Why? These were high energy, self-sacrificing individuals. They didn't mind to sacrifice their lives for Mother India and Mother Bengal. Yet after fleeing to India, they never protested pogroms, genocides, killings including family members, or torching of their own family homes in their homeland or confiscation of their home and properties by the state and Muslim League Party. Witnessing the 2022 invasion of Ukraine, and fleeing of innocent citizens to neighboring countries, a comparable situation will be if those who found shelter in Poland, Moldova, Slovakia, Germany, the U.S., England, or Hungary didn't say a single word of their oppression. We always wonder why this is so for "liberal Bengalis, liberal Hindus and tolerant Indians?"

What is also remarkable is that soon all those refugees including India's freedom fighters found solace and peace in our journey. They would invite us and our kids to as many events as possible. As soon as we would return home from their Bangladesh homeland these luminaries would come to listen to our experience. Before our departure for Bangladesh, some of them would give us some a few rupees to give to their schools, orphanages, shrines, etc. Soon, we became so important in their mind that we were made members of Barisal Society, a 1905 organization in Kolkata (Calcutta) to help the remote Barisal District of Bangladesh, our ancestral home. We were made members of Gava Society of Kolkata. Gava is the ancestral home of our family before they moved to Lakshmankathi village in the 1500s. In our late 30s and early 40s we were invited to sit on the dais with governing Communist ministers – a very big honor in traditional India. Still, it was confusing of their fear for not to return back to their homeland. These letters are from pre-Partition (1947) organizations.

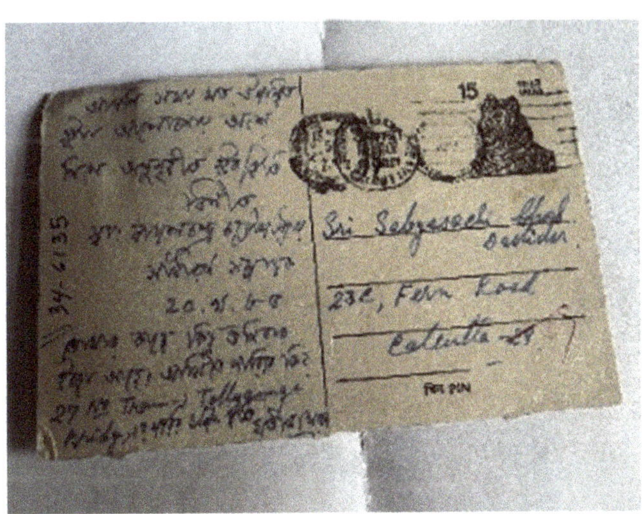

Post Card Letters from Older Hindu Refugees and East Bengal/Bangladesh-Based

Organizations in India after Learning our Visits to their Homeland in 1980s Onwards

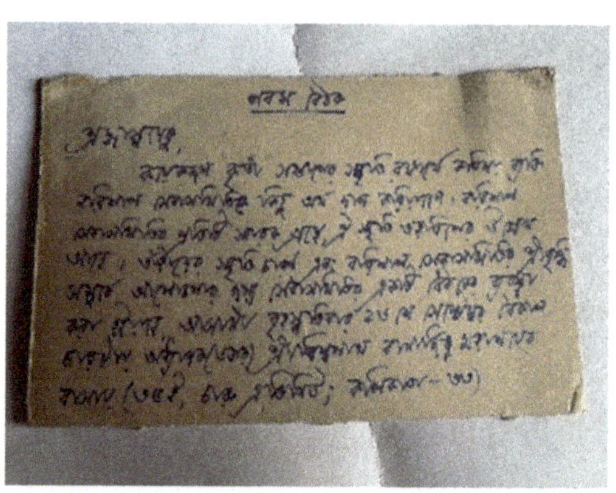

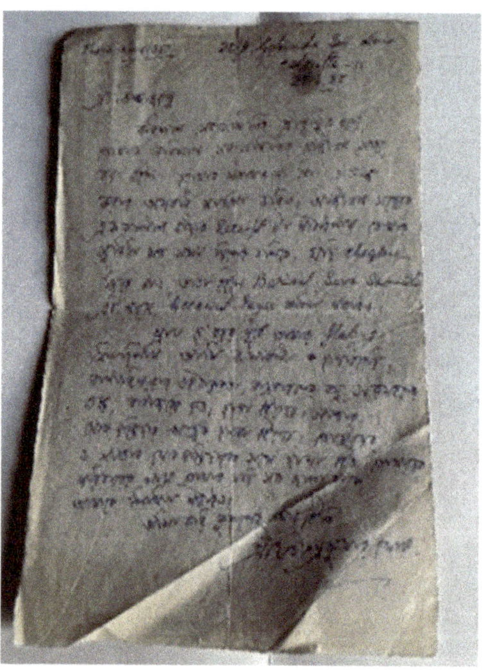

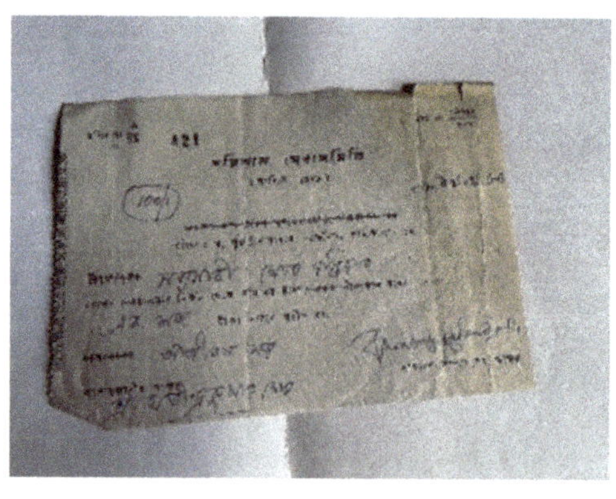

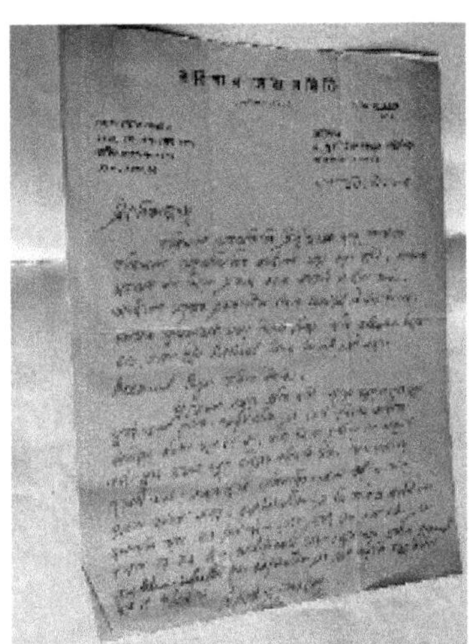

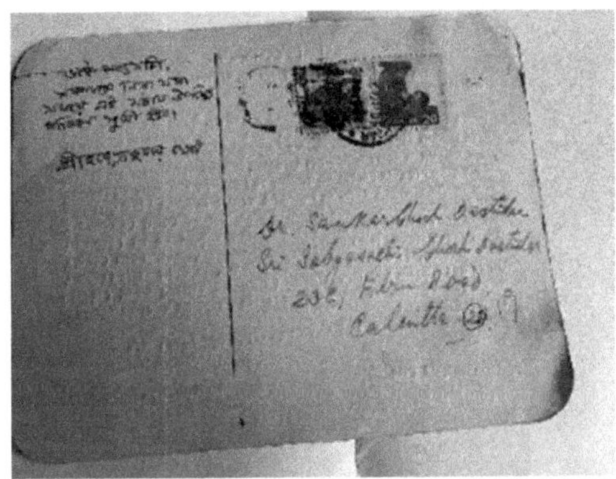

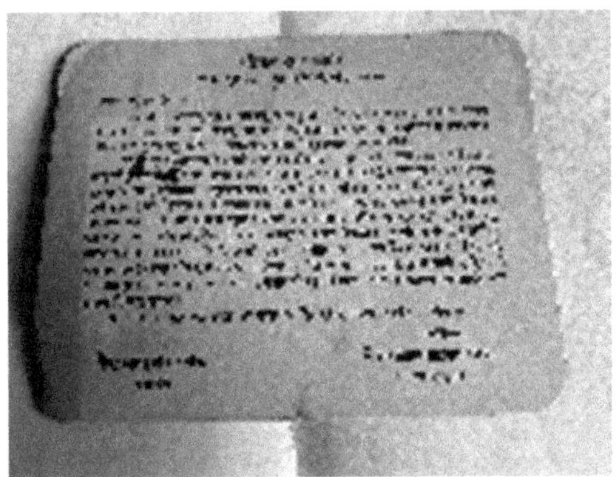

Soon we got invitation to be a part of Gava Sammelani (Society) of Kolkata, India. This was a pre-1947 organization. We accepted that. Gava is in Barisal District of Bangladesh is the ancestral homeland of Ghosh-Dastidar family for tens of generations before our family moved to Lakshmankathi in 1500s, also in

Barisal District, possibly 30 miles from Gava, and established the village. In the days before roads and bridges in the coastal area full of rivers and tributaries, it easily took half-a-day or more to get from Gava to Lakshmankathi by boat. One family moved to Lakshmankathi and established the village, after they received the honorific title "Dastidar" given by a Persian Islamic ruler. The word "Dastidar" is derived from Persian language.

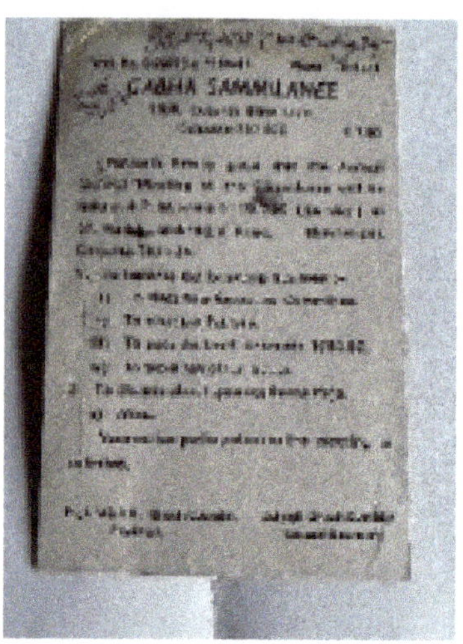

A Formal Invitation from Gava Society of India

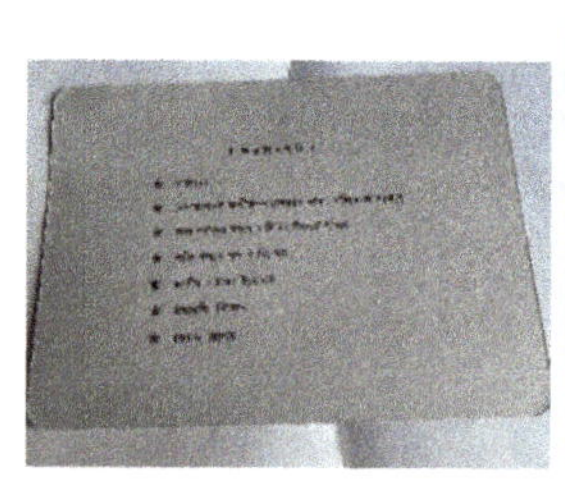

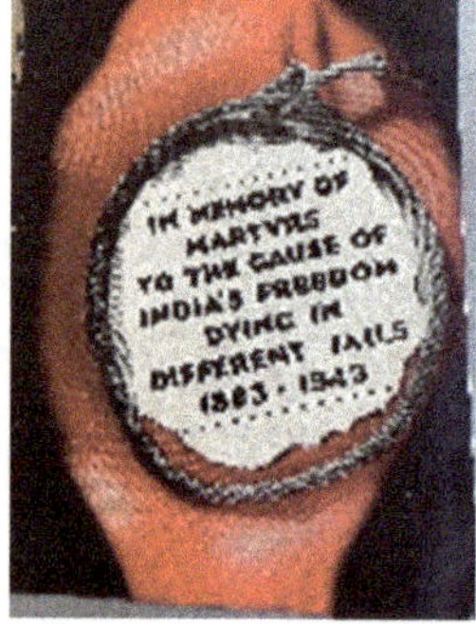

Then there were invitations from others intellectuals and many
Indian freedom fighters who fought against the British colonial rule,
but not against Islamic racism.

We also didn't realize that our visit to our homeland of 50 million Hindu refugees (till 2001) in India, just across the border, could inspire self-examination for so many people. One journal Kahon questioned Bengali's collective motivation. Kahon even introduced a word "Sachi like" or "Sabyasachi like" to question our identity, hypocrisy, bias, and prejudice.

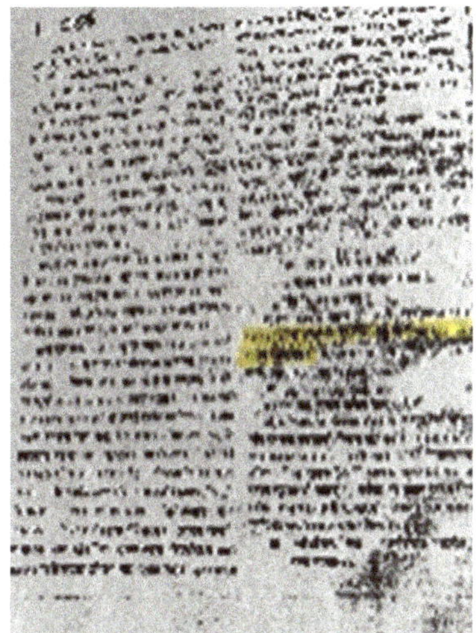

Kahon

Simultaneously, it brought warmth to a visitor to picturesque and warm rural areas of the Subcontinent. To a 100% urbanite it opened the vast green and watery landscape of rural Bengal. As refugees we had hardly any opportunity to visit rural areas as we had no connection to rural areas any more. Warmth of rural and poor made our family's visit really exciting. People even wrote us letters; at times the postage cost was a day's earning for some folks. We always wondered why did they spent that money. We felt helpless when we started getting letters seeking protection from local oppression. This was too much for someone living 12,000 miles away. At times, strangers called us spending huge amounts of money, often from public phone. During 2021 Durga Puja Autumn (October) Festival pogrom we received a call from a stranger, "Uncle Kaku, please help us. Jihadists are marching in our neighborhood saying 'We must eliminate all kefirs (Hindu) minorities in Bangladesh,' Uncle Kaku, please do something." Below are from the era before iPhone and WhatsApp, when we received postal mails.

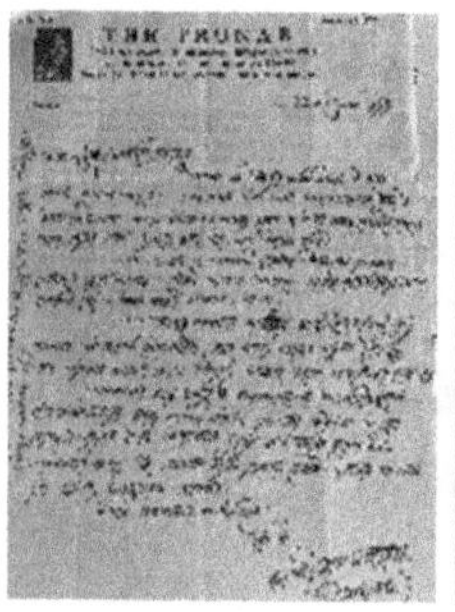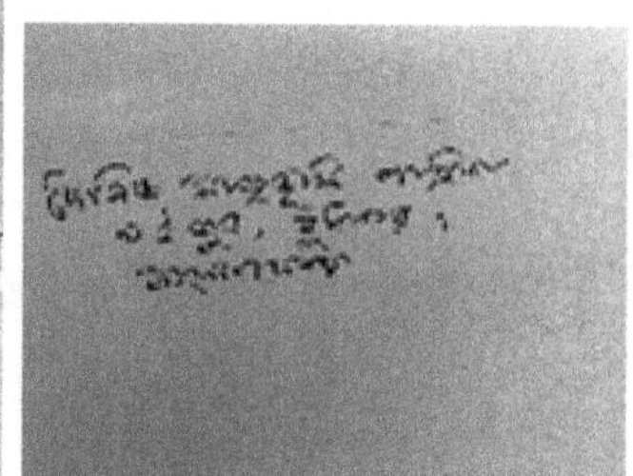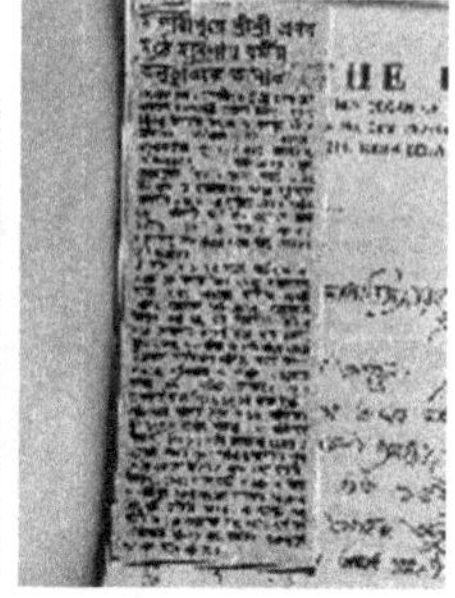

Letters from Pronab Ashram (Hindu Monk-based Relief Organization), Dainik (Daily) Matribhumi Patrika (paper), Bangladesh, and from Sri Sri Pranab Mott of Bangladesh when They Were Attacked.

From Tallahassee, Florida to Wide Open America:

Sachi's $200-dollar 1965 Mustang convertible bought from a Libyan undergraduate student introduced us to open, bustling America. The car door was damaged on the driver side, but rest of the car was excellent so much so that frequently workers at gas stations wanted to buy the car. Then Tom of Nashville, Tennessee reintroduced Sachi to camping again, after first introduction by Florida State University friends. It was an era of fast ride in sleek roads with 75-mile speed limit or more, before the Arab-Israeli War and Arab Oil embargo on the U.S. which permanently raised gasoline price. Gas was relatively cheap, quadrupling the price during the embargo. Camping allowed us to see the natural beauty, Mother Nature's marvel, and meeting open-minded adventurous people. We also witnessed firsthand the result of settler colonialism on indigenous peoples. U.S. is the first country in the world to experiment with elective government away from monarchs, kings, priests, generals, imams and pundits. Thus, rest of the world looks at U.S. and our constitution as their guide. Yet our experiment completely wiped-out indigenous peoples, that we rarely think. As we have pushed that model, including our media, in the old settled continents of Africa, Asia and Europe, it has caused many ethnic conflicts with internal colonization and ethnic cleansing.

We have traveled from one end of America to the other end in all 50 states. We also crossed into Canada from our westernmost border crossing at the

Peace Arch between Blaine, Washington and Surrey, British Columbia on Interstate 5, to the easternmost Ferry Point Crossing at Calais, Maine on Route 9 connecting with St. Stephen, New Brunswick. We also passed through the northernmost Top of the World crossing in Alaska on Route 5 connecting Chicken, Alaska with Dawson City in Yukon Territory of Canada. Chicken, although shown on travel maps, one of its permanent residents – who was the owner of the grocery store-cum-gas station-cum-post-office – said "the number of permanent residents in winter is less than double digit, while it becomes a 'big' place of about 50 residents in the summer." The family told us that all the books and supplies for their little kids are delivered before the pass closes for the winter. This border crossing remains open from 8 am to 8 pm during summer months. Route 5 takes one to Dawson City, Canada via Yukon River ferry before one enters Dawson City. The town had about 1,500 permanent residents, and for the first time in our lives we noticed that all the sidewalks are made of wooden planks because of permafrost. For us it still looked like a pioneer town of early settlers we saw on movies and on History Channel. Seeing us, assuming we were Indians, the owner of a gift shops showed us a 4"x1.5"x1" soap bar named "Bengali Tiger" made in Yukon. We couldn't believe our eyes: a Bengali finding a Bengali Tiger near Arctic Circle, a world away! We bought a few of those bars.

Bengali Tiger Soap

After walking up and down the entire business strip, we decided to drive north towards Inuvik, past Arctic Circle. We drove through the completely traffic-free unpaved highway, then took a snack break at a rest stop.

Welcome to Yukon

Top of the World Highway

Ferry from Alaska on Yukon River to
Dawson City, Yukon

At the border check point, the same lady officer was in duty when we returned. While heading towards Dawson City, seeing our driver's license, she jokingly said, "Are you sure you are driving back to New York?" On our return back to Alaska, she said, "Welcome back. Did you have a good time?" Our drive back to Anchorage along Alaska Route One followed hills and valleys, and at one stage it followed a stream that was full of migrating salmon that we could catch with bare hands especially those that got caught between stones. We let them head for spawning. This was National Geographic coming true! We witnessed not only the beauty of Alaska, but also her hospitality. Hearing through the grapevine, we received a call from Dr. Biswas, a Bangladeshi-Refugee-Indian-American professor of University of Alaska at Fairbanks who asked us to visit him. We received another invitation from our friend's sister-in-law Ms. Lauren for visiting her at Kenai Peninsula, south of Anchorage. We were gratified to receive the invitation as she was a good oral historian of Alaska. She worked for the federal government. Her house was a real fancy one, yet she had an outhouse as sewer lines had not been established in that region. All evening, she told us stories about Alaskan life, and asked us about life in New York City. We visited some of the nice spots she mentioned in costal Alaska. Later, our drive to Fairbanks in the middle of the state revealed how daylight extends past 10:30 pm, but becomes pitch dark almost instantly. Dr. Biswas didn't want us to spend a minute at home, instead as soon as we reached his home, he took us for a city tour, followed by a candlelight dinner at a resort-style restaurant on a lakeside. Driving through empty highway, it felt very pleasing. Apparently, restaurant owner knew the professor and brought a special wine. Next day, it was time for visiting the campus and a drive to Arctic Circle, but heavy fog made the ride unpleasant as we couldn't see anything beyond 15 feet. It was dangerous to drive in that condition.

Many of our friends always tell us that they want to travel with us in our wanderlust travel but at the final moment they all backed out, except for Prasanta visiting his ancestral home in East Pakistan/Bangladesh from where as a boy he fled with his family to India after an anti-Hindu pogrom. He is one of the very few Indian-Bengali-Hindu-refugees – Congress, Communist, Socialist, nationalist party supporters – who overcame the fear of marauding Muslim League Party to visit his homeland, with Sachi as a guide. On another journey, we as her guide, our Tamil-speaking friend Mali joined our road trips to

Michigan. During that trip we visited many places including Ann Arbor, Detroit, Lansing and the auto-free Mackinac Island. Mackinac was a special place near the world capital of auto manufacturing, Detroit. During another trip our Hindi-speaking friend Raman and Mira joined us when they heard we are heading to Las Vegas. The Capital of Gambling had a special vibe as the airport was so close to the strip. We walked around the strip up and down many times, day and night, and some time at the slot machine which we tried in Atlantic City in New Jersey. We rented a car to drive around the desert state. One day we decided to drive around the region of Las Vegas, and Grand Canyon. Ram and Mira wanted to join with us in our day-long outing. We stopped at the Mother Nature's wonder called Grand Canyon. Instead of returning back to Las Vegas, we headed east to Navajo Nation Native American area in Arizona for dinner. Then we headed north to cross Colorado River, and had to head west for Las Vegas making a full circle. As it turned dark, there began thunder and lightning. There were more lightning than rain, and strong wind. We didn't realize the seriousness of the situation. Soon we found fires all around us. As we headed in that darkness some fires at the street level were already doused by fire trucks, and most of the lower-level fires were gone as we drove further. Soon, we saw an unreal spectacle of fire in pitch-dark night on top of a long mountain range. Sachi drove as fast as he could for our lives while witnessing something we see on TV, but this time witnessing through our own eyes. Son Shuvo gave us a running commentary as Sachi focused on the dark road in front of us.

In 2022 April during our visit to Hawaii it revealed how a distant land in the middle of the ocean is able to develop such a high standard of living, that most developing nations with similar beauty and climate could not exploit for their development. In many of the tropical areas of Asia. Africa, South America and the Caribbean there exist similar opportunities of development based on climate and Mother Nature's beauty. We hope one day some of those areas will be able to develop further uplifting their economy, as Singapore has done, or Goa in India, Dubai in United Emirates, Iceland, and Aruba in the Caribbean, have become a tourist attraction increasing their standard of living. Visiting

Pearl Harbor reminded us that Hawaii is the place through which United States officially entered WWII after Japanese bombing of Pearl Harbor, destroying naval ship Arizona taking hundreds of lives. That bombing demanded immediate action by the U.S. to save the world from destruction by Japan and Germany. Thousands of books and articles on WWII are available in libraries, but visiting in person was different. Arizona Memorial is located on the opposite side of Pearl Harbor visitor center in the city of Honolulu. A short ferry trip from the Visitor Center takes visitors to Arizona Memorial.

The visitor center has many museums, a nice tropical garden, memorials, shops and book store. In the Indian Subcontinent there are thousands of such examples of atrocities by the British and Islamic-Persian-Arabic rulers for over a thousand year. Yet in the Subcontinent's fatalistic, self-destroying, history-avoiding culture such examples – from Kuttab Minar to Mathura to Varanasi to Noakhali Killing of 1946 to Kashmir cleansing to Churchill-created 1943-44 Bengal Famine to 1964 Hazrat Bal Genocide in East Pakistan to 1971 Bangladesh Hindu Genocide and extermination of secular Muslims, to Kolkata Hindu Monk & Nun Killing by Hindus, to many more, such oppression is neither memorialized nor taught in history books. (For Churchill's action, see Madhusree Chatterjee's *Churchill's Secret War: The British Empire and the Ravaging of India During WW II*, Basic Books, NY, 2010, and for Hindu genocide, see *Bengal's Hindu Holocaust: The Partition of India and its Aftermath*, Garuda Prakashan Publisher, Delhi, India, 2021). One doesn't have to be anti-something to learn from history. We are told that "if people who do not learn from history, history may repeat itself" on them. This is very true in India and the Subcontinent. As we didn't learn from Islamic colonization and British oppression we had India-Pakistan religious-sectarian partition. As we didn't learn from Indian Partition we had Pakistan-Bangladesh minority-majority partition and Hindu genocide and Secular-Muslim extermination. America and the West have tried to teach their citizens of their history through places like Pearl Harbor, Berlin memorial, Black Lives tribute, Irish Memorials, and hundreds more places. Hawaii also taught us that how a Americans can teach and promote indigenous Indian and pacifist tradition through a monastery established in 1979 that locals in India aren't able to do.

Here are few pictures from Aruba, 2023:

Honolulu, Hawaii, 2022:

Shriya-Lakshmi at a Honolulu Beach

At Kualoa Point

At a Boat on Moanalua Bay

Honolulu from the Bay

A Kauai Park with Wild Chickens

Kauai Island Hindu Monastery:

Founder of Hindu Monastery at Kauai

Inside Monastery

Forest of Trees for Dry Nuts

Friendship in Distant Corners:

Travel in the U.S. and around-the-globe showed that friendship can develop instantly, and over a short period of time, whereas some friendships develop over a long period. In poor nations friendship developed at very intimate surroundings, mostly around people's homes and huts, whereas in rich countries it is at restaurants, conferences, parties, campuses, and for us, during travel. Most of our experiences were joyous. Then there were pain seeing homes, shrines, *mandirs* (temples), schools and deities destroyed during pogroms, or when our luggage was stolen in Guatemala City, Guatemala, and in Gondar, Ethiopia, or wallet stolen by thugs in places like Prague, Delhi, Durban, and Washington D.C., and iPhone and money stolen in Bali, Indonesia! But these were personal loss which we survived. Seeing pogrom mayhems were painful, but even more painful was when we couldn't help except sharing a little money that we were carrying in our wallet, or giving a hug to pogrom victims, or offer *pronam* (obeisance) with folded hands. One of our first encounters with warmth of strangers came during our cross-country camping trip in the summer of 1976. It was our long-delayed honeymoon. We were camping with our orange station wagon, carrying our tent and supplies in the trunk, and on a roof carrier. In late afternoon as we set up our tent at a South Dakota campsite while Shefali was fixing hot tea, a white couple in their early forties walked into our site saying, "We are from Alabama too. We miss our families. Seeing your license plate, we thought we'll chat with our Alabamians." Then added, "We are here for prospecting." We didn't know what was prospecting's pull, and that people travel such a long distance for that. Thus began a long conversation. They told stories about their kids, and family. They were missing their children whom they left with their parents. We offered them hot tea, and conversation continued. We supplied more hot tea in Indian style. In faraway place two new colored immigrants, one wearing sari, became their close friends. Our color, our heritage, our outfit didn't make any difference to them. We became close to them. We were all Alabamians, all Americans. They gave us lessons of Midwest culture and economy. Next morning, before heading out, they came back to our campsite to say goodbye and give us a big hug. Here are a few of the places we visited.

Mount Rushmore, South Dakota, 1994,
with Shuvo and Joyeeta standing in front

Best Lake Wild Life Refuge

Park Introductions

Earlier on that trip we camped in northeast Nebraska. We stopped to buy some supplies at a store in a Native Indian reservation, most likely of Omaha or of Winnebago peoples. Seeing us a Native American mother said something to her seven-year-old daughter. We came almost face to face. Then she asked, "Indian?" We replied, "Yes." She said, "We too, but we are Indian from here," and then she started convincing her daughter about "Indian" similarities pointing to Shefali's long hair and sari, "All Indian women have long hair like us. They wear long dress like ours...." This was her way of making us feel at home and finding similarities. This is a good side of human nature, when one finds similarities. Decades later on our way to return home with our kids, we camped at a Navajo Nation campsite in Arizona. We came down through a mountainous road in Utah with steep fall that kept us breathless till we came down to the street level. Sachi was terrified that he may lose control in turns every few hundred feet, but couldn't say a word to his wife and kids to scare them. Luckily there was hardly any traffic so that we could drive in the middle of the two-lane highway keeping a safe distance from the edge. He was driving his stick shift car on our way on Route 89 in Utah going towards Arizona via Kanab village. This is a dry and barren region of America. "Welcome to Navajo" sign felt great, but one resident reminded the visitors, "It is tough living here," and pointed to a few people walking on the side of the road carrying water and grocery on hand as those rural roads had no sidewalk. "Look, they are walking miles back home with their grocery. They have no grocery near home. They have no car. Some people do not have running water." This was in 1990s near the Four Corners Region of Navajo Nation where Colorado, Utah, Arizona and New Mexico meet. This was not that different from seeing women and children, at times men, carrying water in big bowls on their head in India, South America, or Africa.

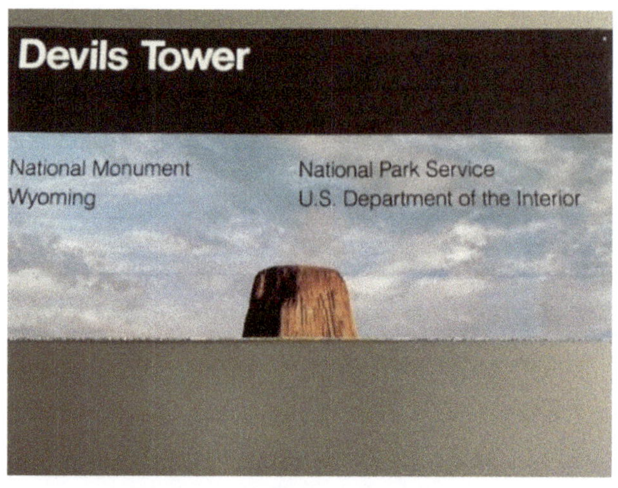
Devils Tower
National Monument
Wyoming
National Park Service
U.S. Department of the Interior

Dinosaur

Fossil Butte

glacier

GRAND TETON

Hot Springs

Jewel Cave
National Monument
South Dakota
National Park Service
U.S. Department of the Interior
Official Map and Guide

Joshua Tree

Introduction of National Parks

In 1990s trip to the mountains from Montana down to Arizona and New Mexico, we spent all day enjoying the beauty of Yellowstone National Park with kids. We exited the park from the north heading east on I-90 to look for a camp site. Our plan included visiting Big Horn National Forest, Black Hills National Forest, then Badlands National Park, and more. Soon we realized that it may not be that easy to find a campsite as we noticed hundreds of motorbikes on the highway. The first camp site was already full of hundreds of bike travelers, and we soon learned that there was no space in the site. A couple in their full bike outfit overheard our family conversation, then came forward and said, "Listen it would be hard to find any empty camping spot here, but let me contact my friend at two exits east, and ask for a place for you." We were so lucky to get that spot and live with bikers who come to Sturgis City Annual Convention.

Fourth of July:

On 4th of July 1976, the year of America's Bicentennial, all cities and towns celebrated with fanfare. Huntsville, our new home, was no exception. It was the largest city in north Alabama. Our Governor George Wallace was coming to a nearby town of Athens, about 25 miles west of Huntsville. Shefali and Sachi headed for the mid-day celebration. It was a typical 4th of July fair with hotdogs and roasted corn, with speech by politicians. The speeches were brief as Governor Wallace had to hop around all the regions of the state. We two non-whites were attending Governor's presentation who was known as a segregationist in American politics, but we weren't segregated. Everybody was in a joyous mood.

200th 4th of July 1976 Celebration in Athens,
Alabama with Governor Wallace

Governor Wallace in the Center

Travel Hardships:

Travel always brings pleasure; however, all travelers have to be aware of possible adversities. We had to face pick pockets from Prague of Czech Republic to Washington D.C. to Delhi in India, and handbags were stolen by a taxi in Guatemala City, and in Gondar, Ethiopia. In Bali, Indonesia Sachi's iPhone and some money were stolen by a couple in the next room of the hotel in 2023. Shefali's small camera was pickpocketed in a secured and gated museum with entry fee in Durban, South Africa. It exposed varied treatment in diverse countries. Luckily our passport and necessary documents were not lost. In Washington D.C. Sachi lost money and credit cards. He called police and within minutes arrived half-a-dozen police riding bicycle. But, as Sachi was speaking with police at the subway entrance, the thief was at a nearby Home Depot two blocks away trying to use Sachi's credit card as Sachi received texts from the credit card company. No one went to Home Depot to check video camera, barely a few steps away. We were more than convinced that it was a bus worker riding from New York City who pushed Sachi to get Sachi's carryon luggage from the bus storage, but neither the police nor the bus company were interested to hear that. Delhi police, on the other hand, was very energetic in trying to catch a group of pick pocketers working together in the nearby bus stop.

Within minutes a group of police brought a man and tried to scare him by thumping tables and shouting in loud voice. We are sure expert pickpockets are aware of those techniques. A group of 3 or 4 gang members pushed Sachi hard on the bus to take the wallet out of his front pocket. He was pleasantly surprised as one of the officers offered him money to buy bus ticket for his return journey from Gandhi Memorial on the banks of Yamuna River to his campus. Luckily, he had some cash left in his pocket. This time loss was some money, plus ID. In Ethiopia it was hard to find police for reporting. It was even harder to make an international call in 2014 to our credit card companies as access to overseas telephone was almost nonexistent. Finally, we paid for a toll-free call from a local shop. In Prague, Czech Republic in 1999 there was nowhere to report his loss. He had to call his family in New York to report to his banks for credit cards, and his campus for his new ID. In Guatemala City locals were very helpful, but language was a big problem. In the police station one English-speaking officer was very helpful in taking details of the taxi which took our carryon suitcase. One of police officer's assistants commented pointing a nearby market, "Why not go there tomorrow? You may find many of your objects on sale there. Lots of stolen properties are sold there." Whereas in Indonesia when we went to Police Headquarter who could easily trace Wi-Fi connected iPhone but showed no interest at all. On his return back home, he wrote a letter to the Governor of Bali Island giving all details, including the thief's cell phone number.

A tribal man in Arizona welcomed by saying, "Welcome to your Indian land!" and started making our life a bit relaxed. On the same trip as we drove earlier on a dirt road when the car slipped but survived from flipping. Camping made us aware of the beauty of the landscape, but its hazards as well. On the same trip we got up in the morning at a camp site in Wyoming with noise outside our camp. It was a herd of wild bison who were grazing there. Camp guards asked campers to keep calm and enjoy the behavior of wild animals. This was scary for the kids, but enjoyable. But not enjoyable was camping two days earlier in a park in Iowa. We were the only one camping in mid-week. We didn't get any indication that a storm was approaching. A few minutes before a huge downpour the sky became real dark in late afternoon as we were setting up our tent. Shefali was getting ready to make hot tea, and the kids were touring the camp; our normal routine. As it got dark in the midst of storm, we decided to board the car and head to the bathroom, the only lighted area in the camp. As soon as we reached the site downpour started with strong wind that continued for hours. Storm ended around midnight, but we spend the night in the car. In the morning, we found that our tent was completely flat and wet. The tent survived because it was under a tree that gave it protection. Later a park ranger told us that we were very lucky to be safe. Tent was flat, stuck on the ground.

Here are some descriptions of camp sites:

oregon
caves
national
monument

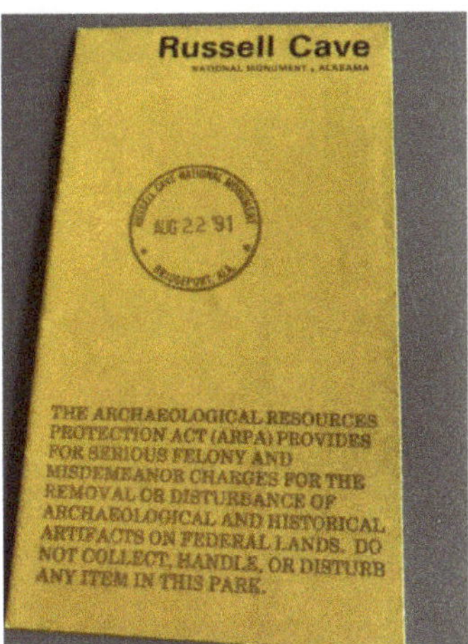

Russell Cave
NATIONAL MONUMENT, ALABAMA
AUG 22 '91
THE ARCHAEOLOGICAL RESOURCES
PROTECTION ACT (ARPA) PROVIDES
FOR SERIOUS FELONY AND
MISDEMEANOR CHARGES FOR THE
REMOVAL OR DISTURBANCE OF
ARCHAEOLOGICAL AND HISTORICAL
ARTIFACTS ON FEDERAL LANDS. DO
NOT COLLECT, HANDLE, OR DISTURB
ANY ITEM IN THIS PARK.

Oregon Trail

Shenandoah

Sleeping Bear
Dunes

Valley Forge
Official Map and Guide

Great Smoky
Mountains

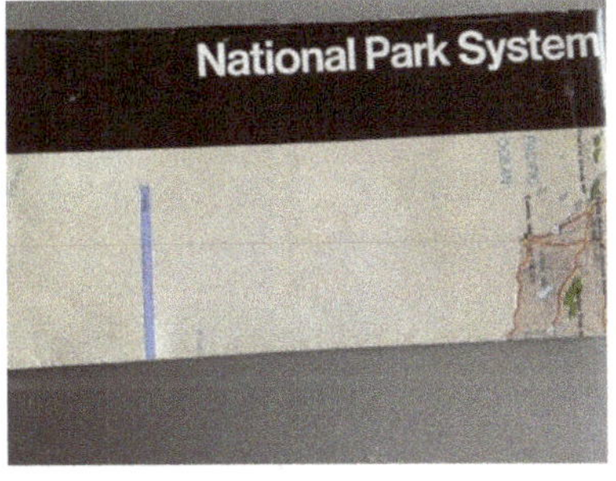

National Park System

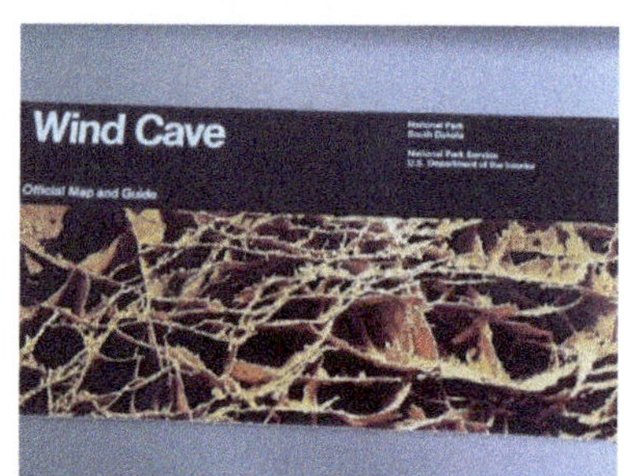

Introduction of National Parks

Travel Overseas:

Language can be a problem while traveling in non-English-speaking countries. In Lima, Peru there is a big daily celebration at Palacio de Gobierno or Government Palace with military-style parade. It is a big tourist attraction before lunchtime. After that we went to a restaurant managed by a lady. As we struggled to find items, the owner came to us and asked, "Hindu, not Peruvian?" We learned from our trip to Central America that in many Hispanic countries Indians are known as Hindu, or at least what it sounded like. So many times, the first question was, "Hindu?" She brought her lunch and joined with us saying that she has a friend who is Indian; she is learning yoga; that she watches Indian movies, likes Indian dress, and more. We spoke in sign language, and in monosyllabic Spanish. She gave us tips what to see and what to avoid. We felt at home in that distant land.

In 2019 September we had a similar experience in Manaus, the huge metropolis in the middle of Amazon Rain Forest. After a walk at the nearby riverfront, we came to rest at our hotel and cool down in that tropical heat and humidity. Soon arrived a young street vendor with a box hanging from his shoulder, and asked the receptionists if he could sit to cool down. The young man was around 20 years of age, and could easily pass for someone from India. He sat down with a big smile, and said something in Portuguese. We smiled in return. He continued speaking, but we couldn't respond. Soon he realized our predicament, and asked us, "No Portuguese?" We nodded. He asked, "Indian?" and we responded, "Si." With a laugh he said, "Namaste!" surprising us. We folded our hands and returned his greeting. Then he kept asking us, "Do you read Veda? Do you do yoga? Are you vegetarian? Do you worship trees and animals? And more." We were dumbfounded. And this was coming from a street vendor in Amazon Rain Forest! Then he asked, "Do you have a guru? What mantra do you chant?" We realized he is more intelligent, more "Sanatani or Hindu" than we are. We tried our best to respond with our Spanish monosyllables. The vendor boy used some English words. In our disbelief, he was overjoyed to talk to us, and presented us his Brazilian fruit juice filled in a foot-long plastic tube.

We were more than honored by his gesture, but couldn't accept such sacrifice from a struggling boy, instead we bought three of those tubes, offering one to him. Those are Amazonian delicacies. On our trip to the city's most important landmark, Teatro Amazonas or Amazon Theater, we were surprised again to see kids practicing a Hindu/Indian epic drama in colorful Indian outfit. In overseas, understandably, everybody saw us as "Indian," not "American."

As we were walking back from an Indigenous Museum on Avenida Sete de Setembro a man rushed inviting us to a home saying, "Come to my boss's home. He is Mr. Ahmed. He is Indian." Mr. Ahmed's assistant wanted us to feel like local Amazonians. If landing in the big urban metropolis of Manaus was a surprise, the experience of Amazon was revealing. This is the place that Shefali and Sachi would dance with bare-breasted women and speedo wearing men, of indigenous Amazonian tribes in the middle of Amazon Rain Forest. Because of the surroundings it felt very normal, not with any sexual connotation. This would also be the place where we would try roasted caiman meat and small insects. There were live insects for eating, but we tried only the roasted ones. At the forest lodge, at night one of the workers brought a baby caiman for us to hold, a first and last of such experience.

Teatro Amazonas or Amazon Theater

Kids at Teatro Manaus Practicing an Indian/Hindu/Traditional Epic

Inside Amazon Rain Forest a Tour Attraction

Dancing with Bare-Chested Women and Men with
Skimp Outfit with Amazonian Tribes Felt Very Normal

Roasted Caiman and Other Animals

England has always been a place with mixed emotion for Indians and the followers of indigenous religion. India was Anglicized during its wealth transfer from India for two centuries. Yet England turned Farsi-based Islamic rule of India into transitional majority yet colonial rule. Then again, Britain brought 'divide and conquer policy' and a new form of racism into India. All the Indian political leaders had to travel to England to plead for freedom from colonial oppression. Later many of our friends migrated to Britain for job. They gave shelter for many of her colonial subjects, as well as to many criminals. Thus, we learned English. Sachi's father and older brother Mejda both studied engineering at Glasgow University in U.K. And England is halfway between the U.S. and India, and a stop on our flights introduced England, until non-stop flights developed in 1990s. We stopped in England many times. Knowing the language made it easy to communicate. During a trip to Bristol on western coast in search of Raja Ram Mohon's *samadhi* (memorial) we were pleased to find there were many people at that grave site museum and the shop knew more about Ram Mohon than people in India. Ram Mohan is known in Indian history as the person in early 1800s who lighted the first lamp of Indian Renaissance, Bengal Renaissance, Hindu Reformation Movement, and the founder of Brahmo Samaj, the monotheistic, casteless, gender-empowering movement in Hinduism based on dialectical Upanishad. Stretch of Hinduism is such that it has God in many forms and deities, but it also recognized a Supreme Power energized by all deities, of all genders. It also allows for discourse of *Nastikbad* or Non-Believing. Theology and tolerance have allowed this formulation, as in the U.S. Upanishad has many theological discourses, originating long before the arrival of Lord Buddha or Lord Jain in 6th Century B.C. It is possibly the oldest secular thinking of the humankind with written words. In the dark days of Hinduism in the second millennia, Ram Mohan was the first Hindu to travel to England in early 1800s. To avoid ostracization by the powerful narrow-minded Hindu "elites", when he traveled by ship, he carried live cows for milk to avoid banishment by the oppressive Hindu unenlightened elites.

Raja Ram Mohon's Grave Site in the City of Bristol:

Ram Mohon's Grave

Ram Mohon's Grave

The Cemetery

For more information, please see:

https://empireslastcasualty.blogspot.com/2013/04/raja-rammohon-roy-and-arnos-vale.html. Ireland, across the Celtic Sea, is proud of her struggle with Britain, and for her Catholic faith. It was inspiring to see how villages, towns and individual families have been saving the history of their struggle against the British Monarchy, in public and at home museums. There is so much for Indians to learn from the Irish. Ireland has transformed herself into a more relaxed European identity, electing a Protestant as President, and a mixed Irish-Indian gay person as its Prime Minister. During visits to her pre-Christian sites – which many tour companies offer – it was revealing to see how so many Irish Catholics are anxious to learn about their heritage. Life would be lot relaxed and rewarding if all the monotheism-majority nations allowed their citizens the same opportunity, including Muslim-majority nations, to look into their old roots, instead of destroying it. Even in relatively tolerant mixed Egypt, there have been attacks and kidnappings of Copts, and desecration and defacing of many antiquity paintings, sculptures, deities, and pharaoh statues. Drawing of face, humans or animals are prohibited in some faith. Tolerant Muslim-majority Bangladesh's story is not as good as Egypt's although hardly known elsewhere. Internal and external hostility, rise and influence of ISIS, Jamaat, Tablighi, Taliban, Al Qaeda, Ansar and denigrating of indigenous pre-Islam-believer kefirs could be neutralized should monotheistic nations allow arts, music, literature and tolerance to flourish as Christians have done, as well as Hindus, Jains and Buddhists who follow that tolerant tradition from its inception. First Islamic theologians have to come forward. Islamic kings, monarchs, imams, ayatollahs, presidents and prime ministers should join them. What can we expect if Muslim schools in tolerant Bangladesh teach math to First Graders like this? "Example No. 23: 'A mujahid (Islamist fighter) on the *maidan* (arena) of Jihad kills 24 enemies on the first day, 18 on the second and 12 on the third. How many enemies did he kill in all?" (Source: Bengali Madrassa Islamic School math book; April 2020.) During our trip to a madrassa in Bangladesh, we found that books there are devoid of any traditional Bengali names, but with only Arabic or Persian names. Bengali language section of 8th grade madrassa book didn't have a single Hindu, Brahmo, Christian or Buddhist writers, although overwhelming majority of Bengali literature is by pre-Islam indigenous Hindus with non-Arabic names. This is in 2020 in a country where three million Hindus, secular Muslims and Awami League supporters were killed by Islamic Republic of Pakistan's army and their Bengali Islamic supporters. The nation was born with secularism as one of four pillars of the nation! Bangladeshi non-secularists, and Atheist-Bangladeshi-Indian-Hindus haven't challenged the killing, cleansing, and dehumanizing of minorities in their homeland, although many secular Muslims have been challenging intolerance since its founding. Even on May 5, 2024 Bangladeshis demonstrated for secular constitution in New York City.

Demonstration for Secular Bangladesh at Diversity Plaza of New York City

In 2005 Sachi was traveling from Kolkata, India to Dhaka, Bangladesh in a Bangladesh airline. It is a 30-munite flight. He took an evening 5 PM flight, after his day's work in Kolkata. He made evening appointments in Dhaka. After checking in, travelers were told that the flight will be five hours late, putting our arrival close to midnight. Everyone was worried as traveling in Dhaka Road at that hour is considered unsafe. But travelers had no choice. After receiving their luggage at Dhaka, and seeing absence of our friend at outside the terminal, Sachi started to wonder about his next step. Most of the passengers were gone except a few like him. The departure lounge was almost empty. Soon came an elegantly dressed lady in orange sari. Her first words were, "You must be Hindu." Sachi was stunned. He never knew he looked "Hindu." Before he could answer, she begged, "Please, please Dada, Older Brother, do not leave me alone. I am Madhabi. As a single woman I trust a strange Hindu in my land. I know you won't harm me. I am the granddaughter of eminent scholar Roy Chowdhury, who was murdered by Islamists in 1971.

Everyone in this country knows our Hindu family. I am looking for someone from home to give me a ride, otherwise I will have to stay in the lounge till morning." As our cell phones and lounge phones were not working, Sachi went out to the armed police station to make an emergency call with a fee. Madhabi also added, "I would like you to come and stay with us." Sachi's call worked, and within an hour Madhabi's family friend, Hasan, a young bright Muslim engineer with Hindu last name came to pick us up. Young Hasan too warned Sachi not to travel by himself at that hour, "especially for a Hindu." Sachi's tight schedule and Probini's annual meeting didn't leave time for him to visit homes of Madhabi or Hasan. We are sure it would have been a pleasant experience as Bangladeshis are very warm to guests.

Travel between partitioned India and Bangladesh, and India and Pakistan always highlight contradiction and identity issues that is for another discussion. Yet complexities, corruption and conflict are always in the background. Once Sachi was traveling from western Bangladesh's Kushtia district to Kolkata, barely 150 kilometers, and would have taken only two to three hours before 1947 partition, but now it may easily take half-a-day, if one is lucky. Our friend Prabir dropped Sachi off on the Bangladesh's Darshana side of the crossing. It seemed so few people cross the border legally that it looked as if the departure office was located in the middle of a bush with a few parking spaces. Then Sachi was asked to walk along the train track to the next station Gede on the Indian side. Scores of vagabonds, illegal money exchanger, possibly drug and human traffickers sat on the unused track and asked for your business. The railroad track crossed over a small stream separating the two nations, and one could watch how illegal border crossing is taking place as dinghies were taking Bangladeshi daily commuters across the border. Once one got on to the Gede railroad platform, visa, security and customs began on the platform. Corruption on the Indian West Bengal side was wide open. A man walking with stick going to Kolkata for medical treatment was openly robbed as cash was picked up from side pockets of his loose *punjabi* shirt. Protest didn't mean much, though American passport holders were not touched. Gede is the end of one suburban commuter line that takes to the heart of Kolkata in two hours. Corruption is so rampant that many Bangladeshis carry many passports. Those travelers normally bribe workers at customs and immigration.

Once Sachi objected for taking too long for Bangladeshi passport holders. The officer laughed at him and said, "It takes time to figure out which is real and which is not." Two days later one Kolkata paper reported that over 80% of Bangladeshi passport holders in Sachi's flight had fake passports. And in June 20, 2020 one Kolkata daily reported that on that flight one Bangladeshi passport holder carried 12 passports.

To be fair, one Bangladeshi, now an American citizen, came to see us in Kolkata, India in early 1990s, crossing the border without any paper. Huge number of illegal traffickers work on both sides of the border. Corruption is serious yet normal, as operated under regional sectarian rule. It was brought to light when Bangladesh's Founding Father, Sheikh Mujibur Rahman's one of the killers, Abdul Majed, was found in Kolkata in 2020, 40 years after mass murder of the Founder's family. It is during the rule of Bangladeshi-Indian-run Communist Party-Marxist rule that Majed not only got Indian passport, but local Ration Card and State ID, all of these need local West Bengal police and administrative endorsement. (See Bangladesh daily *Bhorer Kagoj*, April 13, 2020; and again, during anti-communist sectarian rule of Trinamool Party, an elected parliamentarian was murdered and cut into pieces by a Muslim-Bangladeshi group of half a dozen criminals all with Indian ID, and one also with American ID. See daily Prothom Alo, May 25, 2024 https://www.prothomalo.com/ opinion /column/brluyz8adw by writer and Deputy Editor Sohrab Hassan).

Surprising many moments in life are always enjoyable and energy producing, when it carries positive force. After visiting Vancouver, British Columbia we went east to Alberta during our cross-country camping trip in 1976. Crossing the Rocky Mountain Range was exciting. After camping in Waterton Lake National Park in Alberta, Canada, we decided to enter Glacier

National Park in Montana, south of Waterton, that we heard so much about. Glacier Park continues north to Waterton, Alberta.

We headed south via Canadian Route 6, which became Route 16 in the U.S. [1]There was a border crossing through two national parks, opened only for few hours a day. The post had very few employees. There was no traffic ahead of us. The guard was sitting inside the small office. As we drove to the check point, we held our IDs out through the driver's side window. A young man came in his uniform, and took our IDs. Soon he hollered, "Is that you Shefali?" to our surprise we found it was Jonathan, a Florida State University student from Montana, possibly the only student from that state at the campus, who surprisingly hung around with Indian student group which Shefali attended many times.

Jonathan also attended many India Association events, though he had no "Indian" background, but loved Indian food. We got out of the car, hugged each other, before the next car arrived. Jonathan was doing a summer job at his home state in that remote locale. During our stay at the Glacier National camp, we tried to figure out the probability of meeting someone from Tallahassee, Florida at a remote Montana-Canada border check point! Or, is that called God's Wish? In this book I bring such godsend miracles and coincidences to our attention.

In September of 2022 we traveled to Kolkata, in eastern India. Then, headed to the oldest National Museum of India, established in 1800 during

––––––––––––––––––––

[1] *Editor Hassan correctly points out "The murder of Anwarul Azim shows many weaknesses of our state machinery. We have seen that any person can get a passport in any name by dodging the eyes of the administration. You can get a visa. Killers can cross the border at any time for the purpose of killing, and can return home safely after completing the task. So much security, so tightness, is it only for the common man? The same applies to visas to India. People also have to pay for medical visas. But the killers got visas easily. Some of the killers went without visas and passports. How was that possible?"*

British colonialism. However, as during British oppression, their atrocities and persecution was shielded in that museum in post 1947 independent era. So, when Sachi found an exhibition on Indian Independence Movement, and genocide during British and partition era, his eyes opened. There was brief mention of Hindu holocaust. There were large numbers of high school students volunteering on that display so that they also learn of their history. This is new! Soon, girls started asking grandpa Sachi or Dadu, many questions, and said that they are learning about Indian Partition and aftermath. When grandpa mentioned he is involved in researching that, and mentioned that he has written on that issue, some of those youngsters immediately searched on the Internet and found his two recent publications, *Bengal's Hindu Holocaust: Partition of India and Its Aftermath*, and *Mukti: Free to be Born Again: Partitions of India, Islamism, Hinduism, Leftism, and Liberation of the Faithful*, and asked "Dadu, are those your books?" One of them said "I am going to ask Baba, Dad, to buy the books." The other girl, with the same double last name as Sachi's, Ghosh Dastidar, said "You are my grandpa too. I want to read those too."

Very next day Sachi went to Alipore Civil Court to attend a hearing. At the end of the hearing, a lawyer invited the attendees of the group for tea, and hearing Sachi is visiting from the U.S., asked Sachi, "Uncle Kaku, have you heard of two books on Partition with the author from the U.S.? My daughter found that out last night at the National Museum and wants to read the books." Hearing Uncle was the author, the lawyer immediately asked how he can get those two books. Was this a coincidence?

People with Multiple Identities:

All of us have multiple identities, although some think so, while others don't. Travelers like us face that all the time as we do not fit into the majoritarian identity. While living in Kazakhstan we faced that question all the time, not with any malice. This we felt more problematic while crossing international borders between Kazakhstan, Uzbekistan and Kyrgyzstan. This was true while visiting Pakistan, South and Central America as well. There were times it took immense amount of time to check our passports compared with locals. This posed a big problem while traveling with others as we were held back behind others, or vehicles behind us while traveling by car. We were also told by regular travelers, it could have been a function of corruption as well, i.e., looking for bribe, though we didn't pay anyone any bribe. Sachi was in Kazakhstan as a Senior Fulbright Award recipient, and because of that he came in contact with U.S. Embassy officials. Twice U.S. Ambassador came to events at Kazakhstan Institute of Management organized by Sachi.

The building earlier was the headquarters for training of communist bureaucrats. And with transformation came instruction in English, not in Russian, although everyone spoke Russian. What a revolutionary change from communism to capitalism! At the same time because of our look, we were invited by the Vaishnav (Baishnab) followers of ISKCON, or Hare Krishna pacifist Vaishnav movement, for their events at Almaty, the largest Kazakh city, the old capital, and through them we met a few Indian officials, including the head of embassy Education Section who was a Tibetan-speaking Indian. We met many more locals at the opening of Novie Vrindavan or New Vrindavan, a new ashram of local devotees, who invited "Indians." In most countries the words India and Hindu means the same. There we met Mr. Wanoo, a Hindu Kashmiri-Indian, and local head of a German organization building "villages" for orphans worldwide. For one of his graduates from such a home in India, Anjali, we became the uncle and aunt in the U.S. she never had before. After graduating from India, Anjali studied in Ohio, then became a journalist in New York City, marrying a conservative Jew. Surprisingly a few months before, Sachi met another Tibetan-Indian diplomat at our Long Island campus' graduation ceremony. He was the Education Counselor who visited the campus as Sachi received the "Distinguished Service Professor" award at the graduation ceremony.

Multiple identity confused a bunch of kids traveling on a tour bus in Iguassu Falls of Argentina and Brazil. Our tour bus was full of tourists from Italy, except for two of us. We realized the kids were debating among themselves as to where are we from. After couple of stops, a gentleman finally asked us in broken English about our home. Hearing New York it confused the entire group. After some time, he came back to ask, "But you are Indian, right?" Just days back, our Afro-Brazilian guide, told us to keep a distance as "our Indians, many in traditional outfit, are demonstrating at the Parliament Building in Brasilia," the planned capital of Brazil. This was in 2019 when the new Brazilian government encouraged Amazon settlement. Several forest fires were visible as we flew over the forest's edge.

On our way to a forest lodge east of Manaus we got to a ferry stop to get on to Route 319. On that road, following settled areas within the vast Amazon Forest, we witnessed small-scale fire by land owners possibly to extend their property into the forest. Boat ride through Amazon Forest is comparable to ride through Sundarbans Forest in Ganga delta on Bay of Bengal. But tourism is lot more developed in Amazon as opposed to Sundarbans Forest of India and Bangladesh. Recently, in 2022, Sachi and Shefali visited Indian Sundarbans to establish a school for the poor, where the forest was cleared by locals a century or two ago.

Vith Puja or Foundation Laying Ceremony for a School at Sundarbans

Ferry Boat Connecting Villages

Dancing Welcome by Students

During a trip to eastern Quebec, we camped at a private campground, next to a private museum, in Rivere-du-Loup on the south shore of St. Lawrence River. This region of Quebec was monolingual. After dinner in a nearby French eatery, we sat down to have tea near our tent. A lady walked to our site and asked, "Can we invite all of you to come and live in our house for the night?" We were stunned. Before we could respond, she said, "We are the owners of the camp site, and we noticed that you are playing with your kids. Why not come and join us for an evening chat? There is a possibility of rain tonight." We were hesitant. She then took charge of our kids, and led us to her home where we would have endless discussion of life in Quebec with French desserts and drinks. The owner refused to accept additional rental from us. It was hard to say goodbye to them. We still have a Native-Quebec sculpture that we bought at that museum.

A Quebec Museum Collection

Next day in a river ferry we headed north crossing St. Lawrence River, driving further east to Baie-Comeau via Route 138, which then takes one to Labrador which is a day's drive on the unpaved Route 389. We decided to camp at Forestville, a small quite town on the bank of the river. We were the only guest at the camp, making us feel a bit lonely. The camp site was practically in the middle of the town. Before dark, a lady came to say hello, and chat with us. It was nice to get a taste of local historian. She said, she is the only one in town who knows English, and said she will bring her son Jason next morning. Jason was a charming 15-year-old skinny boy, who too knew English. Mother and son invited us to a pond for fishing. As they had no car, we took them in our car, and followed their direction. First, we headed west. After a short distance they asked to take a right turn into a dirt road which was blocked by rows of cars of road repair crews. As we couldn't find a hole among the cars and getting frustrated, the boy said "Don't worry, I am going to remove one of the cars making a passage for the dirt road. Here everybody leaves their key in the ignition," and pulled a car up making space for our car. This beauty of Canadian life was completely unknown to us.

In mid-2010s we were visiting Poland. Journey from Vilnius, Lithuania through the rolling meadows reminded us of our Midwest. After a break in the

Polish hotel, we headed out for the city, when a stranger said, "Wrong direction." As we were utterly confused, he held Sachi's hand and led us to a huge open air summer festival which was about to begin. Food and festivity continued late. Then at Treblinka Death Camp, about two-hour journey from Warsaw, we were impressed about scores of Jewish groups coming to pay respect to their ancestors who were murdered there. We wish we did that to our ancestors who were killed and driven out of Pakistan and Bangladesh. Both Shefali and Sachi had shirts with Indian or Bengali flair. As we were going from area to area in that death camp, a couple in their sixties, asked us, "Are you Jewish?" We nodded our head. Then the man asked, "Why here?" We replied, "Why not?" They laughed, and said "We appreciate our answer." They showed us the ritual of putting stones on memorials, and said that they are from Israel, and visiting their ancestral villages in Poland, and finding lots of information. We said to them, "If my Indian friends and families had a tiny bit of your spirit for their family, then Bengal, Bangladesh, Pakistan, India and Indian Subcontinent would have moved further ahead in life."

At Treblinka Memorial

At the entrance to Treblinka, there is a small museum which contains a model of the Death Camp. This is one of the camps Nazis destroyed before the Soviet troops liberated it. There were rows of books, journals and pamphlets, mostly in Polish. As we were going through the museum, a skinny lady with blonde hair, possibly in her sixties, who was the cashier-cum-guide, came and gave us some journals, *Romano Atmo*, or Polish Gypsies. We returned those back as we couldn't read Polish. In gestures and words, she said that those were gifts for us, and that she is a Roma, as such she is Indian too. We were so proud to give her a hug to our long-lost cousin. We brought back several copies of the journal. Through her introduction, we got connected with *Romano Atmo* journal, and with Mr. R. Chojnacki, President of Polish Roma Association, who sent us an important article on identity for our 2016 Partition Center Journal.

Romano Atmo Journal of Polish Gypsies

Poland was forerunner to our visit to Belgrade, Serbia that we heard a lot in 1960s from Congress and Communist Party leaders in India: Congress Party because of Tito's leadership in Nonaligned Movement, and Communists because of Tito's communism. In 2018 we were visiting a new land of former Yugoslavia, that Tito couldn't imagine how communism failed to bring people together after 70 years of rule. People were massacring each like animals. People's identity changed overnight, paralleling identity issues of British partition of India. Genocides were committed, but this time being in Europe some trials were held. United Europe is trying its best to stop the rise of extreme Christianity, Islamism, Communism, or identity politics. What did we learn from socialist egalitarian ideology? Outcome is not clear yet in 2020s. Nevertheless, travel through these areas seemed to be relatively peaceful. For us language was an issue. People were friendly to help. We were surprised to see almost all the signs are in English script, not in Serbian. It reminded us of Thailand and Bali, Indonesia. During a welcome reception at a university in Bangkok, Thai capital, all the signs were in English, but not a single student spoke the language or understood it. We survived. It was very close to that in Bali. About Belgrade, my friend Edi suggested that we visit the famous Skordalia Street and visit one top restaurant. It has old elegance. The neighborhood reminded us of Lower East Side of Manhattan, and Park Slope of Brooklyn, but for pedestrian traffic. Language was not a problem there. The historic site of the confluence of rivers of Danube and Sava is a "Must See" for all tourists as it contributed so much of European history. It was nice to see how Serbia is trying to preserve her socialist, Serbian, Ottoman, Christian, and pre-Christian identities in her museum located at the Belgrade Fortress at the junction of the rivers.

Before our arrival in Poland, we traveled through newly independent Baltic nations. As in Balkans, one oppression has brought another headache. Anti-Soviet identity has brought exclusivist identities in the Baltics, creating new contradictions. As we arrived in Tallinn, Estonia by a ferry from Helsinki, Finland, there were no taxis available, but a number of local buses were standing at the stop. There was a language problem, as no one spoke English. All the signs were in Estonian, but everyone spoke Russian, that Sachi understood little bit. Our hotel was not far, but the bus driver refused to tell us if it takes us to our hotel, and was about to leave the stop. Sachi's Russian didn't help much. A Russian-speaking lady in her sixties started cursing the bus driver and stopped him from leaving without us. She then invited us to the bus, and told us to sit. Three or four stops down the road, she showed us our hotel, where we got off. With monosyllabic Russian, we thanked her. Estonia, Latvia and Lithuania provided us with a glimpse of struggle of nations to retain and project their pre-WW I, and post-WW II identities, and post-Soviet open society. In the Subcontinent there are similar struggles in Pakistan, Bangladesh and India in highlighting their pre-Islam, non-native Islam, British Colonial era, Portuguese-English Christian era, independence struggle, post-independence era, and the Islamic Pakistan era for Bangladesh.

Pre-Soviet Era Building in Estonia

Soviet-Era Memorial in Estonia

In southeast Asia one aspect of its daily life was impressive. After office hours, many of its parking lots are transformed into food courts. In some places, each vendor just caters to one item of cooked food. There were various types of soups, noodles, rice, and seafood. Thus, a step from hotel, one is in the midst of an open-air restaurant. In Bangkok, Thailand we were asked to visit the "biggest restaurant of the world," as per its ad. Waiters and waitresses brought food on roller skate. There are many stories about open prostitution in Thailand. We believed it was fake news not until our visit to Pattaya. Pattaya City on the Gulf of Thailand changed our knowledge. As soon as men got off the bus or taxi, hordes of agents would appear asking for guests' choice. On the famous Walking Street on the beach, agents wait with their offers. It seemed like some out-of-towners walked holding more than one Thai woman. This was quite revealing. During one van ride, an English-speaking father revealed that he brought his young teenagers for sexual tourism. One of our old classmates from Tallahassee, a Thai native, and a senior planner in Bangkok, said that the Thai nation is trying hard to change such social practices. Bangkok temples were very impressive, as were markets on the banks of rivers and lakes, which resembles somewhat like Dhaka's Sadar Ghat, the main ferry terminal of Dhaka City in Bangladesh. But Bangkok's floating markets looked attractive. Its speeding commuter boats through canals added one more mode of transportation, that Kolkata in India or Dhaka in Bangladesh could have copied to reduce their traffic congestion, and add to tourist attraction. Unfortunately, in Kolkata a subway line was built through the middle of Tolly Nalla canal, reducing its future in water transport, and natural beauty. During a trip Sachi took a night train from Singapore to Kuala Lumpur, Malaysia. In a small coupe there was a young, friendly Malaysian family in their thirties, with a little boy. As the train left Singapore territory, the man opened up, and offered Sachi a beer. Mr. Ahmed revealed that he is a Malaysia-born Tamil Hindu, but "had to change my religion and take an Islamic name," as he married his Malay Muslim girlfriend. He said he "needed that to survive in Muslim Malaysia." There are large numbers of Hindus and Christians in Malaysia. Chinese Malaysian, almost half of the population, are Christian and Buddhist. In Sumatran Malay Muslims are a tiny minority. Mr. Ahmed didn't reveal what forced him to do so: country's law or social fear? Kuala Lumpur prides itself as having famous Hindu temples in the city, including the Batu Cave Temple. Recently, in 2020, its aged Malay-Indian Prime Minister rebuked India and Indian Prime Minister Modi for deciding to count who is an Indian citizen and who is not, while Malaysia is deporting Bangladeshis and others on a regular basis. This is institutionalized anti-Indianism. In April of 2020 Malaysia expelled

Rohingya Muslims from its territory. Again, during Covid crisis Malaysia arrested hundreds of migrants based on its 1959 and 1965 Citizenship Law (see *Daily Observer*, Dhaka, May 11, 2020), but faults India for asking of citizenship identification for illegal migrants. Hypocrisy or new racism? It is true that Indian politicians didn't care that much for the nation or states as for power. Thus tens of million – possibly 50 million till 2001 census who vanished from Bangladesh and got Indian citizenship through corruption of neighboring West Bengal, Tripura, Assam, and Meghalaya states, but mostly in West Bengal. In trying to copy Malaysia, both Islamic Saudi Arabia and Kuwait criticized India for coming up with citizenship registrar, while those nations deported working Muslims to Pakistan, Bangladesh, Afghanistan, India or Nepal, during 2020 Covid crisis. Many were working there for decades. They did not give citizenship for babies born there with foreign identity. Why not give citizenship as India has given to tens of millions of refugees and regional colonizers? What this double standard is called? At the same time, many Muslim migrants to Europe, U.S. and India, criticize those nations if they do not get migration documents to these nations, but not Saudi Arabia, Kuwait, Qatar, Bahrain, and other wealthy Muslim nations, where many of them spend their entire working lives.

Welcome from the Poor and the Very Poor of the Fourth World Countries:

Growing up in urban areas in refugee family cut us off entirely from the enchanting village life that we all heard from our parents, grandparents, uncles and aunts. During our adult life in India, only twice Sachi spent time in a village. First time for Sachi was in his mid-teen as he was working part-time outside campus when a colleague, Sasanka, working for the same construction company, invited him to their village for the autumn Durga Puja festival of Mother Goddess, killer of demons, when men couldn't kill those demons. This was in mid 1960s. It was in Hooghly district, adjacent to Kolkata, yet it took bus, then train, then bus, then a river ferry, and finally a short walk to their home, possibly taking three hours to cover 60 miles. It was wide open, full of trees and shrubs, and the entire extended family welcomed Sachi. Puja, offering to deities, rituals start in early morning, yet preparation starts before sunrise, and most men and women start their puja work after a bath. Puja work include cutting fruits and vegetables, arranging wet rice in a plate based on family tradition, decorating the deities, again in a family tradition handed down from generation to generation, arranging *pradips* (*diyas* or oil lamps) in tiny boat-like containers, arranging *baran-dalas* or plates to welcome the Mother and Her Family symbolically containing all the necessities of life, i.e. grains, seeds, sweets, coins, fire, water, plants, and more. This was the first time Sachi stayed away from home during Durga Puja holidays of the Mother Goddess who killed demons, to bring peace on Earth. At our Kolkata friend Tapan's home they are celebrating this puja for about 300+ years. It is a huge expense for the family. To keep the tradition going, we have been sending Tapan our contribution for the past 50 years.

The other rural experience was in mid-1980s when Shefali and Sachi stayed with Shefali's older sister Chhordi, meaning Younger of the Older Sisters, Anjali, and her family in Raina village of Bardhhaman District of West Bengal. This was about 100 kilometers northwest of Kolkata taking 3 ½ to 4 hours by train and bus. Both of them were high school teachers, and popular in the area. Generally, teachers in India are held in high esteem, as in America, but their pay was not high. Chhordi's family lived in a rented mud-hut with typical Bengali-style thatched roof. The hut had electricity but no gas. So cooking was done in coal-burning portable *chula*, like our bar-b-que grill. Close to their retirement, they built a regular brick-and-concrete building in the same village. Going from America it was one of our dreams come true to stay in their village home with modern amenities. As we walked with a teacher, the brother-in-law, ShymalDa, or Older Brother Shyamal, at every corner people offered their *namaskar* or greetings with folded hands. Every shopkeeper offered special welcome. With him, we felt like a hero. At the fish market all sellers invited their "Uncle Mesho (maternal uncle)" giving tips and family news. Hearing of our visits to Bangladesh, many local Indian activists asked Sachi to visit the elected village council head belonging to the ruling Communist Party-Marxist, a Hindu who fled from his Barisal District of Bangladesh, as did our parents. First thing next morning Sachi headed to his house. Not knowing where his home was, he asked a Santhal tribal woman grazing her goats for "the Village Council Chair's home." She gave a surprise look saying, "How come you don't know that he lives in the biggest, newly painted white building in the village?" Sachi was taken aback as a communist head is represented by the "biggest building" of the village. In India you don't need an appointment to see such persons. One just walks in. So, he knocked at his home. The man was wonderful, soft spoken, and talked about serving the oppressed. He said he was atheist, not Hindu, but migrated from Muslim-majority East Pakistan to Hindu-majority India. When asked as he has no religion, why did he leave his Muslim-majority homeland, and how does he not live with the oppressed Hindu minority in his homeland, and why he never spoke out against daily oppressive acts against his family members back in his homeland? After some silence, he spoke like a non-political person, "I never thought about that." This is not the first time we came into communist politicians in West Bengal identified with wealth. In 1986 as we returned from a long-distance trip to Ballygunj Railway Station in south Kolkata, near our home, we needed to rent a taxi or rickshaw to carry our suitcases, but the entire stretch of Ballygunj Station Road was blocked by Party Cadres and mourners. To every person when asked came the same answer, "Our Communist Marxist parliamentarian has died. He was the richest person in this area owning several buildings on Station Road." Finally, after dragging our suitcases out of the huge crowd, we were able to get a kind Hindi-speaking hand-drawn rickshaw puller who put our kids on the seat, and our luggage of the floor of the rickshaw, while we walked with him to our home.

The rickshaw puller gave us a philosophical observation of the hypocritical nature of his society.

At Raina village of Shefali's older sister, it was wonderful to see the talented nephew Sanjoy and niece Ruma from that mud hut to grow up to be a professor and a successful teacher.

Brother-in-law ShyamalDa (Older-brother Shyamal),
next to his Thatched-Roof Rental Home.

Bangladesh and Barisal:

In search of our ancestral home, Col. Ullah, a Bengali-Muslim military veteran, took us to the office of "Rocket", the most-desired overnight ferry ship to Barisal City of the coastal Barisal District of Bangladesh. We heard of this boat journey zillions of times from our parents. Most of the lower Bangladesh and lower West Bengal, are parts of the world's largest delta of Ganga and Brahmaputra rivers, is accessible only by boat, similar to Amazon River of South America, although many bridges have been built, including in 2022 on the huge Padma River in Bangladesh. As we came out of the ticket office of Bangladesh River Ferry Office, and looking at our tickets, Sachi asked some questions to the ticket counter. A stranger heard Sachi asking questions to the ticket seller about Barisal City, places to stay and places to visit, etc. The stranger was a big guy, a vice president of one of the largest corporations, like the important jute crop big business of the country in 1980s. Mr. Hasan Rahman Talukdar, not his exact name, a Muslim, thought Dastidars are Hindu minority traveling "alone" with wife and kids, and he guessed that the family is a first-time visitor to the country.

He interrogated strangers with many queries, "Who else is going with you?" "Where are you staying?" "Who lives there?" and many more. Then the stranger said, "I won't allow you to go. I think you are Hindu minority, and you don't know how risky is their lives are in my country." After some conversation Mr. Abdul told Sachi, "I must come to protect you. You are Hindu. You are not safe here. You don't know my country. It is dangerous for you." We thought he was kidding. So, we said, "Dada, Older Brother, please don't worry about us. With your blessing we'll be fine." But before the ship's departure in late afternoon, Mr. Abdul met us on board, and said that he is coming with his eight-year-old daughter Putul to protect us. And that he will be in the lower crowded deck as he couldn't get a room in the upper deck. It was unbelievable as to how far one could go to help others! There is terrible fear among Hindu refugees across the border in India for visiting their homeland. Yet our experience in 1982 as tourist, and later during dozens of visits, proved otherwise. Almost every stranger, every well-wisher, every indigenous or Sanatani minority, and majority Muslims, were always cautioning us, as Mr. Hasan, a deputy of a large industry of Bangladesh.

On the boat, a free-rider shoe polisher approached us for our business. He recognized us as "Sanatani or Hindu," and asked for our shoes to be polished. Seeing Shefali, he advised us, "Mashi and Mesho, Aunty and Uncle, be careful. This is a Muslim country. People can harass you," then started telling how a few days back a boat full of "Sanatanis" were attacked by pirates in the middle of Meghna River, and no one was arrested. This was alarming that a shoe-polisher knows something as a matter of daily occurrence which papers in Kolkata, Delhi, Mumbai, New York, Washington, and London censor! At a micro level, relation between Muslim and non-Muslim is amicable. But what happens beyond the village or the neighborhood? Seeing our kids Joyeeta and Shuvo were talking to each other in English, one Army Officer riding the overnight ferry started chatting with us, and realized that we live overseas. For security reason we try to avoid disclosing where we are from when they assume we are from India, Bangladesh, or Subcontinent. The ferry stopped at the big Chandpur Ghat, after about 3 hours down the river on southeast. Right across the dock were many sweet shops that were clearly visible from the deck. Sachi went down to buy some Bengali snacks while Shefali stayed on the upper deck with kids. They waived at Sachi from the upper deck. He chatted with few shopkeepers and bought delicious snacks. He said goodbye, *namaskar*, with folded hands, in typical Bengali manner. Small shop owners were mostly poor Hindus. Hindu and Muslim shop owners were very warm to Sachi. Returning back to the ship, with pride Sachi offered those treats to his family, and offered to the traveling army officer, a Muslim, his family and a few other travelers. Apparently, army man watched Sachi's movements from upper deck. After some time, he asked, "How come you went to the shops of those *malus?*" *Malu* is a slur meaning lowly Hindus derived from *malaun*, an Arabic word for non-believers who are to be despised for their non-Islamic beliefs. We are told by victims that minority Hindus hear that slur in schools, colleges, buses, shops, work, ferries, sidewalks, paddy fields, and more on a daily basis. This is worse than our "N" or "J" or "I" word in the U.S. for our minorities. Sachi was stunned, and said, "I am *malu* too." The officer was speechless and vanished instantly. His face turned pink. He didn't believe that a family coming from overseas would identify with the very oppressed. We never met him again.

Heading to our ancestral village, Talukdar father-daughter stayed with us all morning for the discovery of our ancestral home. The overnight journey by ship reaches Barisal Sadar Ghat Ferry Terminal very early in the morning. A terminal worker, Amit Michael, a Christian, realizing we were non-local, came and warned us "Do not to leave the terminal before sunrise as you are Hindu minority. And if you have problem of getting your reserved cabin on return journey, tell them that you are related to Amit Michael, although I am Christian." A complete stranger was giving us protection against corruptive practice of selling reserved seat to another person. And, one minority warned another minority. This was in 1982 when Christians were not targeted for killing or forced conversion. That would start after the First Gulf War, which was portrayed in Muslim-majority nations as war of Christian America. As a matter of fact, on our journey from Barisal city towards our ancestral village in the north, a Catholic minister became our friend, guide and advisor, as the bus had to stop at all river ferries and it had to be loaded to a ferry boat to take it to the other side of the river. Sometimes one has to wait for hours for the ferry to be fully loaded. Realizing that this was our first visit, he told Sachi what to do and not to do, and what should we look for. During one conversion he urged Sachi, "Dada, Older Brother, please save your Hindus, otherwise they will be gone in a few years. Being a Christian, I cannot protect Hindus. Please tell people on the other side of the border to help us. West Bengal is run by East Bengali Hindu refugees." This was very revealing to us that victims finding shelter across the border are completely ignoring their broken family and neighbor's oppression while trying to protect families in America, Palestine, South Africa, Vietnam, and more.

Playground of a Church in Barisal District

Truly speaking, a few years down the road, a Muslim statistician in Muslim-majority Bangladesh would say the same thing to Sachi in Bangladesh capital Dhaka, about which we too were completely oblivious and ignorant through brainwashing during our college days. (Please see Abul Barkat, Shafique uz Zaman, Md. Shahnewaz Khan, Azizur Rahman, Avijit Poddar, Shafiul Hoque and M Taher Uddin, forwarded by Justice Mohammad Gholam Rabbani, *Deprivation of Hindu Minority in Bangladesh: Living with Vested Property*, Pathak Samabesh

Book, Dhaka; 2008, and Abul Barakat, Shafique uz Zaman, Azizur Rahman, Avijit Poddar and Subhas SenGupta, *An Inquiry into Causes and Consequences of Deprivation of Hindu Minorities in Bangladesh through the Vested Property Act*, PRIP Trust, Dhaka, 2000). Our promise to the Catholic priest and to the statistician produced many essays and books. The first published article "Ai Bangla Oi Bangla" (This Bengal, That Bengal) was in the most popular Indian weekly *Desh* appeared surprisingly on August 15, the day of partition of India, of 1989, as we were heading to Pakistan with entire family, including two minor kids. It was our brother-in-law "JamaiBabu" or NareshDa, Older Brother Naresh, in Delhi asked Sachi showing a copy of weekly *Desh*, "Is that your writing?" In Bangladesh while waiting at ferry crossings, at times half an hour or more, the Bengali Catholic priest told us many stories, and updated historical facts, while our Muslim protector Talukdar entertained little Joyeeta, Shuvo and his daughter Putul. At Sandhya Nodi River crossing, they pointed out to an ancient Hindu temple, hundreds of years old, and one of the 51 *Pitha* or *Pithasthans* or Holy Black Mother Kali's Place, where a Body Part of Mother Kali fell, during Lord Shiva's mourning Tandava Nritya dance with the corpse of His wife Kali on His shoulder.

This *pithasthan* is known as Sugandha Pitt on Sandhya River. The universe was on its way to be destroyed through His dance, according to the Indian mythology. Fifty-one *pithas* stretches from Baluchistan in Pakistan, near Iranian border to Tripura in the east close to Myanmar, and from Kashmir in the north to Sri Lanka in the south where 51 parts of Her dead body fell. There are five *pithasthans* or Sacred Places in Bangladesh, each faced wrath of terrorists, although pre-conversion ancestors of those thugs offered prayers there to their beloved Mother Kali before their conversion. We paid a quick visit on our return journey when the bus had a long wait to catch the ferry at north shore of Sandhya River. During a visit in late 1990s, a small crowd of devotees welcomed us. This was a warm welcome to a long-lost relation. Very warm indeed. We visited again in 2019 with Sachi's older sister Didi and a Hindu monk Swamiji, when the old building was being repaired and renovated by a Hindu family.

Entrance of Sandhya River Sacred Site

Newly Repaired Interior, all with Local Private Help,
not From the Wealthy who Fled to India

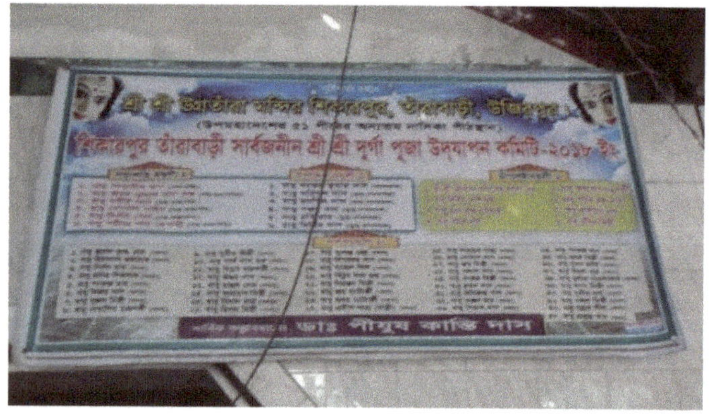

Schedule for Durga Puja of the Mother Goddess's Autuman Festival

Inside of the Shrine

Interiors of the Newly Repaired Shrine

In our onward journey to Barisal City in southern Bangladesh, another lady came to socialize with us. Hearing us calling our kids Joyeeta and Shuvo, she asked us, "You must be Sanatani, right?" We nodded. She was relieved, and responded "I am Muslim. I like Bengali names. They are so pretty. I even like more of the names of our deities like Lakshmi, Saraswati, Parbati, Durga, Kali, all of those names. But I can't give such names to my children. Sometimes I use those names as nicknames at home." With that we became a part of her family.

After crossing river ferries, we reached the bus stop of my ancestral "home" of 1500s. Several poor strangers, especially a Hindu monk Rakhal Sadhu, were chatting at nearby shops. Monk was wearing a gunnysack, possibly earning no more than $10 dollars a month. We enquired at shops about the village at the bus stop. Hearing our destination, a shopkeeper hollered asking Sadhu to take us to "Bishnu Bari" or Home of Lord Vishnu, the Creator of Universe. Sadhu with warmth became our guide without even saying a word, welcoming us with folded hands. When we reached our "home village" where only the extremely poor indigenous families survived, one family offered us a resting place who had only a torn sari as a bed, stretched on a bare floor, with a roll of hay as pillow. They offered that bedroom for the night as well, "Uncle and Aunty, please stay here overnight." This was a big honor for the family to consider us as part of their family. They graciously invited us to join with their rice and boiled green lunch. The family of eight earned no more than $30 a month, still we felt fully secured to leave our cameras and valuables worth more than a year's income for them, without worrying for a second.

Losing those never crossed our mind. To welcome us, poor families offered us cucumbers from their vine, and guavas from the bush. They sent boys to climb big *chalta* (elephant apple), and coconut trees for green cocoanut water. What was so rewarding is that we never felt insecure even for a moment because of their warmth. On our return to the bus stop, monk Sadhu, walking with Shefali, kids and some villagers, in passing said to Shefali, "Didi, Older Sister, you should have also visited my Mahilara village with a very famous 350-year-old Radha-Krishna Mandir (temple)." Sachi was walking behind with another mostly male crowd. Shefali couldn't believe what she was hearing. After a brief interrogation of the monk Sadhu, she realized that it was indeed her maternal village where most of her brothers and sisters were born at "Headmaster's Home." Her maternal home was called "Headmaster's Home" as generations of her ancestors became headmaster and teachers of the local school. For centuries it was a tradition among Hindu families to open schools, often called *pathashalas* and *bidyalois (Vidyalaya)*, to educate residents irrespective of family background, religion, gender, or wealth, at times free of charge. After British colonization many of these families opened colleges or *Mahavidyalaya*. We decided to head to that village, saying goodbye to Talukdar and Putul who then headed further south to Jhalokathi, Shefali's paternal village.

Welcome Party, 1982: Monk Rakhal Sadhu on Left, Who Became Our New Family Member, Mr. Hosain Talukdar, a Muslim, Center Back, Our Protector from Dhaka

Redication of the Shrine in 2020, with the New Priestess, Mrs. Karmakar, Sitting in Front, and a Hindu Monk offering Service to the Deity

Remains of Our 500+Year-Old Sri Bishnu (Vishnu) Mandir Temple, 1982. The Granite Statue of the Deity Survived Pogrom.

Redication of the Shrine in 2020 With Hindu Monk offering Prayer

Statue of Vishnu Deity after 2020 Repair and Re-Dedication or Puno-Prathistha

See https://empireslastcasualty.blogspot.com/2021/03/re-dedication-celebration-of-ghosh.html.

Shrine of 1700s of Black Mother Kali Destroyed during 1950s Pogrom Represented by Ghot or Pitcher

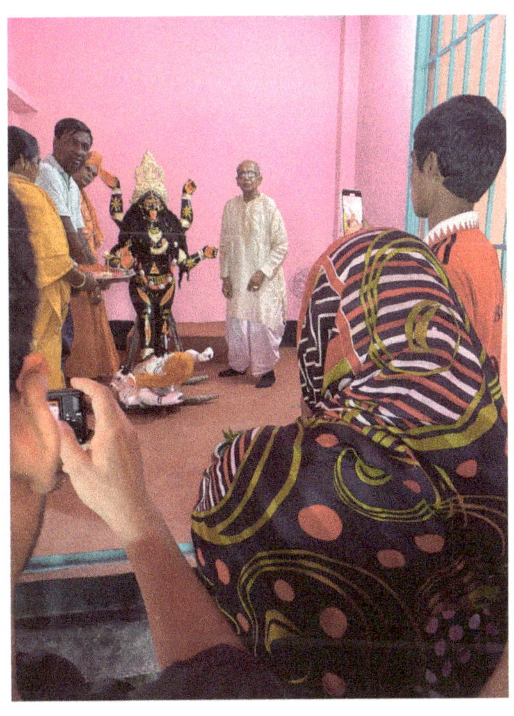

Rededication of the Shrine on August 18, 2023

Monks who Rededicated

A Village Celebratory Crowd

When the first offering was made at the newly built temple in 1987, a devotee and priest, a dirt-poor man, Mr. Nani Gopal Mukherjee, wrote a letter that is beyond belief for anyone. Here is the letter with translation by Prof. Dr. Judith Walsh, a Bengali language scholar. Our family was honored just to realize that the cost of mailing that letter could have been several days income for Mr. Nani Gopal.

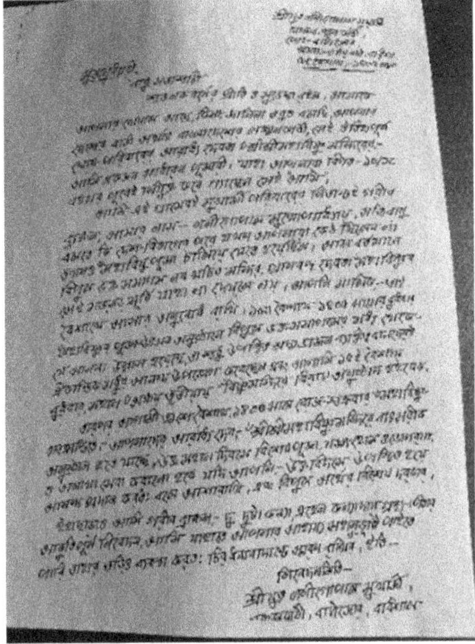

Translation:

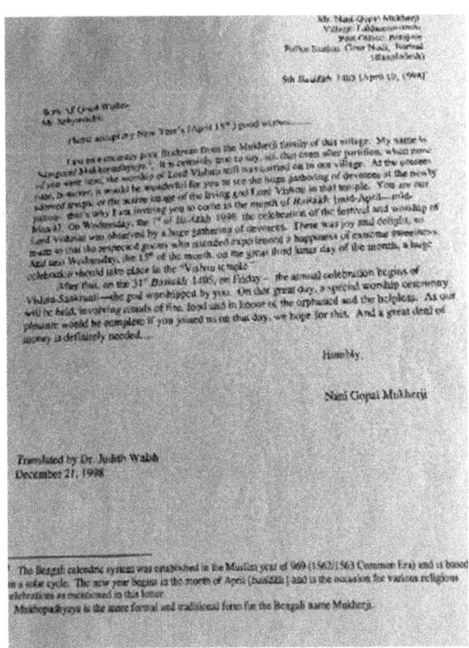

Mr. Nani Gopal Mukherji
Village: Lakhnaur-sundri
Post Office: Ratujore
Police Station: Gour Nadi, Borisal
(Bangladesh)

5th Baisakh 1405 (April 19, 1998)

To All Good Wishes
Mr. Sabyasachi:

Please accept my New Year's (April 15th) good wishes——

I am an extremely poor Brahman from the Mukherji family of this village. My name is Nanigopal Mukhopadhyay[2]. It is certainly true to say, sir, that even after purification, what now ... if you were here, the worship of Lord Vishnu still was carried on in our village. At the present time, however, it would be wonderful for you to see the huge gathering of devotees at the newly ... temple, or the active image of the living god Lord Vishnu in that temple. You are our ... patron, that's why I am inviting you to come in the month of Baisakh [mid-April—mid-May]. On Wednesday, the 1st of Baisakh 1998, the celebration of the festival and worship of Lord Vishnu was observed by a large gathering of devotees. There was joy and delight, so much so that the respected guests who attended experienced a happiness of extreme sweetness. And next Wednesday, the 13th of the month, on the great third lunar day of the month, a huge celebration should take place in the "Vishnu temple."

After that, on the 31st Baisakh 1405, on Friday – the annual celebration begins of Vishnu-Sankranti—the god worshipped by you. On that great day, a special worship ceremony will be held, involving rituals of fire, food and in honor of the orphaned and the helpless. As our pleasure would be complete if you joined us on that day, we hope for this. And a great deal of money is definitely needed. ...

Humbly,

Nani Gopal Mukherji

Translated by Dr. Judith Walsh
December 21, 1998

[1] The Bengali calendric system was established in the Muslim year of 969 (1562/1563 Common Era) and is based on a solar cycle. The new year begins in the month of April (Baisakh) and is the occasion for various religious celebrations as mentioned in this letter.
[2] Mukhopadhyaya is the more formal and traditional form for the Bengali name Mukherji.

On our second trip to our homeland in 1986, a minority monk in Dhaka, Bangladesh, told us to meet a minority Hindu monk at the famous Ramakrishna Mission in Barisal City before going to our hotel. Soon, we headed to Barisal in the south. Seeing Barisal City was a dream come true as so many of our ancestors lived there, went to school and college there, and worked there. As usual, the head monk called Swamiji, immediately canceled our hotel in Barisal City, and arranged for us to stay with a minority businessman Mr. Natta. We visited many famous places like the home of poet (minority Hindu) Jibanananda Das which was confiscated by a Muslim family, Sankar Mott or Sankar hermitage and meeting place for Indian nationalists during fight for independence against Britain but attacked by Pakistani and Bangladeshi

Islamists, the old Muslim mosque, the Christian Baptist Mission, Braja Mohon School and College, A. K. (Aswini Kumar) Hall of the City, the Old Kali Mandir temple of our Mother, Indian nationalist and folk singer Mukunda Das Kalibari (Kali Temple) which also came under attack by Islamists, the old Zamindar Bari or Home of the Landed Gentry, the *Ghats* or Boat Landing areas, and lot more. Everywhere we went we found warmth as well as inquisitiveness as refugees have come back to their homeland, as this was something unheard of. In early morning as well as in the evening, we joined prayer and meditation with our kids at the Ramakrishna Mission. Mission building was built by a Zoroastrian, also known as Persian in India. We will visit Barisal again and again, latest being in 2023.

Poet Jibananda Das' Confiscated Home in Barisal City

Remains of Poet Jibananda Home, Barisal City

Prayer (1986) at Ramakrishna Mission built by a
Zoroastrian in Pre-Independence India

In a 2019 visit, a son of the man who evicted our family from our home of 1500s welcomed us by saying, "Welcome to Ghosh Dastidar Home of tens of generations." I'm not sure if the son, now in his fifties, knows how his parents caused so much misery, pain, eviction, forcibly taking our home and land of hundreds of years making us homeless.

2019 Visit to the Shrine with Older Sister Didi, 3ʳᵈ From Right,
Friend 1ˢᵗ from Right, and a Monk.

The rebuilt 1500s Sri Vishnu Mandir (Temple)
and Welcome to Visitors, 2019

Didi almost Drowned in early 1940s in the Pond when She was a Toddler, saved by a Small Girl of the Local Villager Dhopa or Laundryman's Daughter. Didi met Members of that Family During the 2019 Trip. The wonderful Laundryman's family didn't know that.

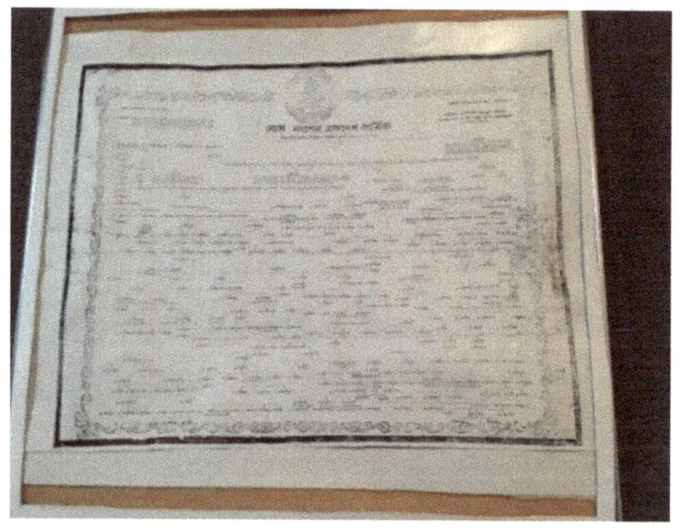

Ghosh Dastidar Family Tree of about 40+ Generations.
From Partition Museum in New York

See https://empireslastcasualty.blogspot.com/2019/11/lakshmankathi-2019.html

On the neighboring village from where Shefali's family was evicted, a host of dirt-poor surviving high-quality Hindus led us to that house, still called "Headmaster's Home." On a bend of that dirt path waited an elderly Hindu widow, Aunt Shil Mashi, of the village barber's family, to give Shefali a "New

Bride's Welcome" as Mashi, aunt, did to Shefali's mother 50 years ago. They started crying in joy. Then there were three poor day laborers, working with mud at *paaner boroj* – wooden frame where the *paan leaf* vine grows – or *paan leaf* farm, next to Shefali's ancestral home. Their first words from their worksite were, "Uncle, are you Hindu?" Sachi nodded. Immediately, they jumped over a small drain to run rain water, and asked, "Can we touch you?" Sachi was shocked, but said, "Sure, but why?" They said jointly, "*Aamra boll paai*, we get strength." They were Mr. Subhas Kulu, Mr. Manindra Gharami, and Mr. Haran Kulu, very poor oppressed Hindus, but very high-quality indigenous people. They started crying in joy. They wanted to touch Sachi's feet, a traditional ethos, but Sachi embraced. The embrace lasted a long time! Sachi held them saying, "We are like brothers, equal."

Subhas Kulu, 4th from Left, Manindra Gharami,
5th from Left, and Haran Kulu, 7th from Left

On our next visits we looked for them, but the day labor jobs take them far and near, returning home in the evening. Thus, we were unable to embrace them again. Hearing Shefali's and Sachi's families were refugees and lived as neighbors in Bangladesh, our Florida professor and chairman Dr. McClure asked us to find the probability of two people finding each other in distant Tallahassee but were neighbors for centuries, and refugees for decades! Soon we will reestablish our roots there with repair, renovation, and reconstruction of the 350-year-old Mahilara Mott (Shrine), now almost 400-year-old.

The 350+ Year Old Mahilara Mott at Shefali's
Maternal Ancestral Home; 2000

Transferring New York's Probini Foundation Documents in 2001 after Construction of a
New Building, on right, Mahilara Village, Bangladesh

Mahilara Mott Shrine After Restoration. There were attacks on the Shrine in 1991 and 1992 Pogroms. After Sachi's Request the Temple was Repaired by the Bangladesh Government.

During a 1980s visit, the family met one of our uncles who still lived in Barisal City. Ma wrote him a letter introducing us, and telling uncle of our itinerary. He came to receive us early in the morning, wearing a traditional dhoti, now regarded as "Hindu" outfit, as Bangladesh has Islamized herself replacing their ancestral outfit. There are recent changes among women's dress as well. Uncle told us sadly, how even kids would humiliate minorities pulling dhoti down to make one naked in public. This was unthinkable only a few years back. Even his wife told us as to how she has to hide her "*Hinduness*" in public, in her Hindu-majority neighborhood because of the presence of a small number of Muslims who have moved into Hindu homes and businesses by evicting them. During a dinner chat, they told us that they plan to migrate to India, without telling any of their neighbors. "If we tell them, no one will buy our furniture, utensils, ceiling fan, and other salable items, as Muslims believe, they can force Hindus to give those away free of charge." We didn't want to believe that. However, we have heard this from almost every corner of the nation, including from majority

Muslims. Many years later, we would meet his very talented son Sabyasachi, a topper of Dhaka University doing his doctorate at University of Illinois. Sabyasachi received three gold medals including Nara Narayan Padak (Prize), and possibly Neelkantha Sarkar Padak of Dhaka University. We were very proud of that as our father was a graduate of Dhaka University, most likely in its very first graduating class.

Once our host Sadullah, a Bengali Muslim, gave us a tour of Dhaka City, and Savar, 30 miles west of Dhaka, where the Bangladesh Independence Memorial stands. Savar is also an old Hindu-majority city with a very famous Rath (Chariot) festival of Saints Jagannath, Balaram, and Shuvadra was held. Keeping Islamic tradition, Pakistan Army and Bengali Islamists destroyed the big colorful Chariot during Bangladesh independence and Hindu genocide of 1971. Parts of old Savar town was also destroyed, then connected by canals in that riverine nation. The town contains beautiful Bengal-style homes of 1800s. There lived many famous learned minorities.

Original Statue of the Deity at Dhakeswari Temple of
Dhaka Destroyed during 1991 anti-Hindu Pogrom

A Typical River View in Bangladesh

Bangladesh Martyr's Memorial at Savar

Bangladesh Martyr's Memorial with Mr. Ullah

At Ekushey (21ˢᵗ February) Language Martyr's Memorial, Dhaka City, Where Pakistani Police Killed Citizens asking for Bengali, the Majority Language of Pakistan, to be a National Language, Beginning the language and Independence Movement of Bangladesh

Bangladesh Martyr's Memorial, Savar

Sadar (Main) Ghat Ferry Terminal, Dhaka City

Sadar Ghat Ferry Terminal, Dhaka City

Puja Prayer at Dhakeswari Mandir, Temple of Dhaka. (Possibly the Last Picture of the Centuries-Old Statue of the Deity before it was Destroyed by Islamists During 1991 Anti-Hindu Pogrom)

Since our first visit to our Bangladesh homeland, we visited many, many times, at times twice in a year. We fell in love with our homeland. However, our lives changed forever after witnessing two successive anti-Hindu pogroms of 1991 and 1992, as well as pogroms of 2001, 2021, 2024 and lot more. We traveled from village to village with our backpack, that many Muslim majority and Hindu minority friends thought was risky, although they were our host and guide. After 9/11 terror there was rise of Islamic pride, and a pro-Islamist party of Mrs. Khaleda Zia came to power. Earlier with 1992 anti-Hindu pogrom Islamist Mrs. Zia came to power. Surprisingly, after both 1991 and 1992 anti-indigenous minority pogroms an eminent New York paper sent one female Christian reporter, and after 2001 pogrom sent a Bengali Hindu reporter, none of whom wrote a word of mass destruction of indigenous homes, shops, temples, ashrams and abduction of girls, but praised a Muslim dictator's wife coming to power. Shocking! They maintained the same fake and partisan reporting after a month-long anti-Hindu minority pogrom during the millennia-old Fall Festival of Mother Durga, Durga Puja, beginning in mid-October of 2021, when thousands of deities were destroyed, hundreds of temples gutted, thousands of homes and businesses torched, and many minorities were hacked to death which are still available online due to cell phone technology. There were even demonstrations at their headquarter in New York City for censoring atrocities against the indigenous minority. To some of our elites' Black lives do not matter, and indigenous lives do not matter. There were demonstrations again in New York City's partisan media after overthrow of Prime Minister in 2024 August and beginning of another anti-minority pogrom.

Hindu Lives Matter Movement Demonstration in the U.S.; 2021

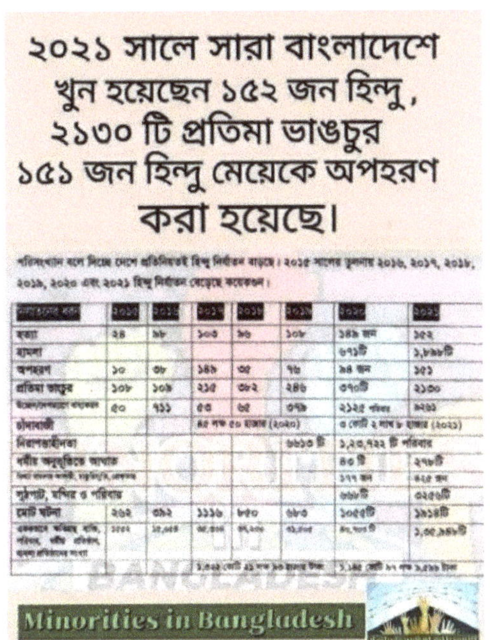

পরিসংখ্যানে বলে দিচ্ছে দেশে প্রতিনিয়তই হিন্দু নির্যাতন বাড়ছে। ২০১৫ সালের তুলনায় ২০১৬, ২০১৭, ২০১৮, ২০১৯, ২০২০ এবং ২০২১ হিন্দু নির্যাতন বেড়েছে কয়েকগুণ।

পরিসংখ্যানে ঘটন	২০১৫	২০১৬	২০১৭	২০১৮	২০১৯	২০২০	২০২১
খুন	২৪	৮৮	১০৩	৯৬	১০৮	১৪৯ জন	১৫২
মামলা						৬৭১টি	১,৮৯৮টি
অপহরণ	১০	০৮	১৪৯	৩৫	৭৬	২৪ জন	১৫১
প্রতিমা ভাঙচুর	১০৮	১০৮	২১৫	৩৮২	২৮৬	৩৭০টি	২১৩০
উচ্ছেদ/সম্পত্তি বেদখল	৫০	৭১১	৫৫	৮২	৩৭৯	২১২৫ পরিবার	৮৭৩৩
চাঁদাবাজী			৪৫ লক্ষ ৫৫ হাজার (২০২০)			৫ কোটি ২ লাখ ৮ হাজার (২০২১)	
নিরাপত্তাহীনতা					৬৬১৩ টি	১,২০,৭২২ টি পরিবার	
ধর্মীয় অনুভূতিতে আঘাত						৪০টি	২৭৮টি
						১৭৭ জন	৪৫৫ জন
পূজামণ্ডপ, মন্দির ও পরিবার						৬৮৮টি	৩২৫৩টি
মোট ঘটনা	২৬২	৫৯২	১১১৬	৮৭০	৮৮৩	১০৫৫টি	১৯১৪টি
[illegible]	১১১১	১২,৪৪৪	৬২,৪০০	৪৫,২০০	৪১,৭০৮	৮০,৭০৩ ৳	১,৫৫,১৪৮টি

2021 Statistics of Bangladesh Minority Plight: Murdered 152 Hindus, 2,130 Deities Destroyed, 151 Hindu Girls Abducted.

- *Source: Minorities in Bangladesh.*

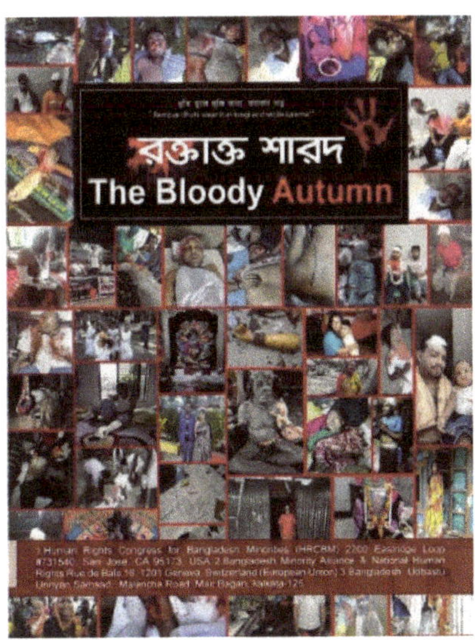

A book, The Bloody Autumn, on 2021 Durga Puja (Autumn) Festival Pogrom

"The Bloodied Autumn," Documentation of Atrocities Censored by U.S. and Western Media.

- *Source: Bangladesh Hindu Buddhist Christian Association of New York, USA; 2022*

Calcutta-Kolkata Reaction:

Every time we went to Bangladesh our parents, brothers and sisters had mixed emotion. They were joyous, appreciative and apprehensive. Appreciative because we are reconnecting them with their painful yet glorious past, but apprehensive because of fear of killing and abuse of minorities. All East Bengal Refugees as they are known in India, also called *Bangals,* our older brother Dada's anti-British Indian independence activist friends – all refugees – came rushing to hear every detail of our homeland journey. We had to tell them in Dada's *aadda* chat party with hot tea and fried vegetable *singara,* a popular Indian snack food after his medical office closed. This would happen almost every single day we were present in post-return Kolkata. Incidentally, almost a third of Kolkata's population, and that of the state of West Bengal with 90 million people, are Bangladeshi origin or more, specifically Pakistani-Bangladeshi-Hindu-Refugee-origin, including 2nd and 3rd generations. Hearing our firsthand experience, they would often remark that there are reasons for fear and good reasons to seek shelter in India, being Left and Ultra-Left in politics. A few non-politicians would comment as to "Why have we been silent towards our own oppression while bringing 'Million-Man March' for distant lands, and peoples whom they have never heard of." Some of them would also say in frustration, "It is time for India to expel atheists like us back to our homeland to live with our Muslim-majority neighbors, but that couldn't happen in self-hating politics of secular India." Some of them invited us to write in old anti-British nationalist papers like *Anushilan, Jugantar*, etc. – many started after Bengal Partition of 1905, and after India's Swadeshi or Self-Reliant Movement, but by 2000 they were almost at the stage of evaporation. These were the elderly people who would take Sachi and Shuvo to Indian nationalist programs, then mostly sponsored by the ruling Communist Party-Marxist of West Bengal, although Communist Party was not active in India's independence movement. One of them suggested that we write either at the weekly *Desh*, the largest circulation weekly of India, or at the daily *Anandabazar Patrika*, the largest circulated Indian daily, both in Bengali language. One of them gave Sachi the contact number of the editor, also a refugee from Pakistan-Bangladesh, who immediately invited Sachi to meet with him. The article in *Desh*, "Ai Bangla Oi Bangla" or "This Bengal That Bengal" was published on August 15, 1989. In August of 1989 we all headed for Pakistan via Delhi. At Delhi Railway Station our brother-in-law NareshDa, Older Brother Naresh, came to receive us and the first thing he asked, showing the article, "Sachi, is that you?" We were surprised to see that as we didn't know when it will appear. Soon, there was turmoil in Bangladesh and West Bengal about that article, and for six months' debates continued in *Desh* about the plight of minorities in Muslim-majority Bengal, with total silence of refugees. A book by the same name would appear in 1991 in India, that too brought debate in both Bangladesh and West Bengal about the killing and cleansing of pre-Islam indigenous Hindus in Bangladesh. Contradictions of writings of treatment of Hindu minority varies. There are many extremely powerful, conscientious Muslim writers in Bangladesh, but their power and influence over ruling elites is limited, in both sides of the border, and censored in "liberal" West Bengal, and the West. There are courageous journalists too, who write at times at their own risk. But the acceptance of oppression of minority has entered the DNA of majority Muslims, especially if they are from another village, and supported by West, possibly because India is the only surviving indigenous nation, with Nepal. This oppression, including killing and forced conversion has been justified by Arab preachers, Holy Book, Sharia and Hadis. Even our own Muslim university student whom we helped to graduate with free coaching as he was from our ancestral district, when loaned money, he refused to pay back the loan. A common friend said, "No Muslim pays back money of Hindus." We hope this is not true.

Visiting Bangladesh for our family has been more than tourism. Gradually, it became a part of us. This is natural. In 1980s, we bumped into a young, energetic American at a Kolkata tea shop. He said India has become a part of him, and now he wants to be Indian giving up his American citizenship. He was desperate. He said "I am living here for over ten years, required for Indian citizenship, and now I am applying for citizenship. So did Mother Teresa, Congress Party President and Freedom Fighter Nellie Sengupta, Sister Nivediata, Congress Party head Sonia Gandhi, Anthony Firingee, and more, but it is taking time for me." In post-Independence era most Indians go the other way for American citizenship, although they maintain strong bond with their nation they grew up in. But in Bangladesh, as we speak the same language, eat the same food, celebrate the same festivals, it is certainly different from other places, especially when people themselves see you to be part of them, Hindu or Muslim, Christian or Buddhist. However, witnessing anti-Hindu pogroms through our own eyes in 1990, 1991 and 2001 changed our lives altogether. Seeing temples and ashrams destroyed and desecrated, and people like Ma wearing the same sari for days standing on top of bare plinth of her home of generations is difficult. Seeing everything one built through decades of hard work destroyed though torching is beyond pain, and beyond description. Seeing destroyed deities is sin, but even bigger sin is to know that some people sincerely believe that destruction of religious objects is pious acts, promoted by religion. Seeing through one's own eyes the destruction of cremation areas of last rights is a sin, but it is even bigger sin is to know that religion teaches that giving last rites to non-believers is an anti-spiritual act, cursed by God. Meeting a grieving father who lost his only daughter to God-believing rapists and killers is hard. It is harder when you meet believers who believe it is one more way to go to heaven is to rape, kill, or convert a non-believer. But then again, it is a blessing to be able to sit next to the victims in their dark days, and with other faith believers who are equally shaken. That is also when one realizes one's limitation.

Without any question our firsthand witness to victims of 1991, 1992 and 2001 anti-indigenous pogroms have changed our lives forever, in addition seeing at other times too.

Grandma Standing on the Remains of her
Torched Property of Hundreds of Years: 1991 Pogrom.

During the pogrom of 1991 Sachi witnessed the old Ramakrishna Mission in Sylhet City in Bangladesh torched by true believers. The temple existed well before the birth of Pakistan in 1947. After initial resistance, the police guards allowed Sachi with hosts to offer a traditional prayer with grass-and-flower to the destroyed Mother and preacher monks' statues. In the capital city of Dhaka, we were able to brief the head monk Swami Aksharananda. Years earlier Swamiji gave us a lead of a boy at an orphanage whom we wanted to adopt, but couldn't because of local issues. We met Swamiji last time at a Ramakrishna

Mission hospital in southern Kolkata, before his death, offering him flowers and Sachi's book. Soon, the orphanage will become part of us as a dictator tried to close it down.

Remains of Destroyed Jumala Prasaad Smasan
Crematoria of Sylhet, 1992 Pogrom

Thus, our journey began to help the poor and the orphaned through P. Foundation. From early 1990s through early 2001 the orphanage with 75 boys, would come under attack, twice destroying the cremation area, the temples of Lord Shiva, and Mother Kali, and scores of memorials going back to hundreds of years adjacent to the orphanage. Was any one punished? Of course, not. Did West and East media cover? No, local lives didn't matter.

Newly Repaired Centuries-Old Hindu Memorial next to a Boys Hostel. Crematoria and Mother Kali Temple were Destroyed in 1992 Pogrom; 1991 Pogrom Destroyed Father Shiva Temple and Memorials.

As Foundation was getting connected with Bangladesh, and India's West Bengal, Assam and Mizoram states, we were very happy and honored to meet the three founding co-Presidents of the Bangladesh Hindu Buddhist Christian Unity Council, BHBCUC, representing the three minorities of the Muslim-majority nation. Minorities were being oppressed but censored in the Western and Indian media, not in Bangladesh. Since early 1990s we got connected with Gen. Chitta Ranjan Dutta, a Hindu minority and member of Independence Army, Ven. Bodhipal Mohathero, a Buddhist monk, and Mr. T. D. Rosario, a business professional, joint head of Bangladesh Hindu Buddhist Christian Unity Council from its inception. Our Foundation was completely non-political, and they were able to give us good advice.

Three Heads of the Bangladeshi Human Rights Organization,
BHBCUC, at Our New York Home

BHBCUC at Our New York Home

Buddhist Monk Ven. Bodhipal Mohathero with
Dastidar Family in New York, 1990s

In a pristine area of north-central Mymansingh region we were able to bring back to life a girls' orphanage run by a minority Hindu monk, Nayan Sadhu. At a time with no political tension, some thugs wanted to kidnap the girls. This time the monks urgent telephone call, and our calls to the police chief stopped the carnage. Yet, no thug was arrested. The same orphanage, was able to take in several minor Hindu girls who were abused during the post-9/11 election as a pro-Islam party came to power in Bangladesh. Some of the girls were as young as 6-years old. These crises also taught us providing help is complicated, and idealism may not help. In many orphanages, because of lack of space, sometimes two boys or two girls share a cot. So, where do you find space? How do you connect abused with their parents, who are grieving too? It was almost a day's journey from their island. How do you provide medical and psychological care? How do you separate the victims from regular hostel residents? How do you explain sexual violence to little kids, when such experts do not exist? In another orphanage, some victimized girls were sheltered in dining room. So, how are the resident students going to eat? How are the abused going to eat? Do we always ignore these pogroms? History books of Bangladesh, Pakistan or India ignores these. Even in 2013 an Indian history professor in England, graduate of Nehru University of India, and a Bengali, completely denied our eyewitness account, although he never cared to visit his Bangladesh homeland. We were further reminded when we visited the Gandhi Ashram in Noakhali, Bangladesh, and writing the booklet for the Gandhi Ashram Museum. Hardly anyone there knows, especially the Muslim majority, why the ashram is there, except for the word of mouth of a few surviving Hindus. Gandhiji went there in 1946 to stop an anti-Hindu genocide and abduction of mothers and daughters for forced conversion that began on the auspicious Lakshmi Puja day of Mother of Prosperity in October of 1946 during colonial British rule when Bengal Province was being run by the pro-partition Muslim League Party. Hundreds, perhaps thousands, of Hindus were killed, and tens of thousands of Hindu girls and mothers were kidnapped, forcefully converted then married off to believers (see *Empire's Last Casualty: Indian Subcontinent's Vanishing Hindu and Other minorities*, Kolkata, 2008, and Ashoka Gupta, *Noakhalir Durjoger Diney* [An Account of the Aftermath of Disaster in Noakhali in 1946], Naya Udyog, Calcutta; 1999, and *Bengal's Hindu Holocaust: Partition of India and Its Aftermath*, Garuda Publication, Delhi; 2021), and thousands of homes and shops destroyed, crops lifted and ponds owned by Hindus cleared of fish, and at times bodies dumped there. Britian didn't punish any killers or rapists. Very few Indians, Pakistanis, Bangladeshis, Hindus and Muslims know of this. We are not taught in school.

"Noakhalir Dujyoger Diney (Terrible days of Noakhali)"
by Ashoka Gupta, Kolkata, India

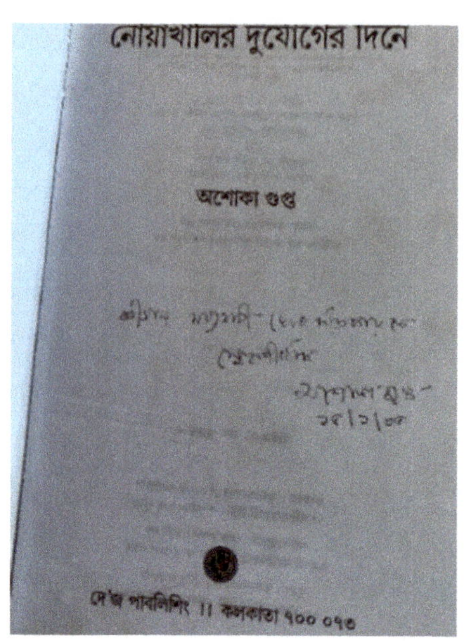

"Noakhalir Dujyoger Diney (Terrible days of Noakhali)"
Presented to Sabyasachi, 15/1/2005

In 1971 the Army of Islamic Republic of Pakistan murdered remaining few of the elderly Hindu residents of that Gandhi Ashram, followers of pacifist, unarmed movement of Gandhi. Their memorial at the entrance mysteriously gets destroyed regularly. There is no memorial for the 1946 mass killing, and West Bengal and Tripura in India where most of the victims fled haven't built any memorial to 1946 genocide either. Barrister Ghosh, an indigenous Hindu minority of Noakhali during British colonial era, donated all his ancestral land, ponds and buildings to Gandhiji, after Gandhi stayed at his home for a night during his 46-day walking rescue and bridge building mission in 1946. During Pakistani rule, all the donated land and ponds were confiscated by terrorists in the name of religion. A bamboo mosque was built on top of Jayag Lake, by confiscating it. The lake produced fish to support poor and orphaned children. Sachi wrote several letters to Bangladesh ministers and district administrators to liberate the place from illegal occupation, who also took over agricultural land. In post-2008 pro-secular rule, the ashram was liberated and the lake was returned back to the ashram, but not the 2,500 acres of agricultural land to support the ashram, orphanage, school, residents and a shelter for the destitute. The center now runs home for the poor and abandoned mothers, schools, dorms, a job training center, self-help projects and more. Yet, the 1946 massacre is hardly known to Bengalis and Indians or taught in history books in India, Pakistan or Bangladesh. Censorship is a serious and self-destructive problem of modern India that a young American medical doctor of Western Indian ancestry said on November 13, 2023 that he never knew that Bangladesh (and Pakistan) was part of India, and that so many people were killed and cleansed. Noakhali genocide was the turning point to convince British masters that Muslims and non-Muslims cannot live together – to make this narrative Britain paid a non-native Urdu-speaking Muslim in 1905 to start a Muslim League Party in Bengal, and seek Muslim-Non-Muslim separation. British imported him from north India, gave an honorific title of Prince/Nabab/Nawab, paid him hundreds of thousands of rupees to start a separatist Muslim League Party to oppose India's independence and support partition of India based of Islam.

Ironically, we were able to interview three individuals, Mrs. Ahoka Gupta, Mr. Rabindranath Datta, and monk Swami Purnatmananda who went to Noakhali to rescue kidnapped girls, mothers and families, and provide food for the homeless. Sri (Rev.) Purnatmananda and Mr. Datta's interview are available at Partition Center's ispad1947 channel at YouTube. In 2010s Datta still carried pictures of hundreds of Hindus killed in 1946 in Dhaka City, that he witnessed through his own eyes. As a young man he gave last rites to hundreds of Hindus with dismembered bodies dumped in front of him in Dhaka City, as told in the interview. Mrs. Gupta wrote several books on Noakhali experience, among them, *Noakhalir Durjoger Diney* (An Account of the Aftermath of Riot in Noakhali in 1946, Naya Udyog, Calcutta, 1999). She presented a copy of the book to us on January 1, 2015. There are many books available on Noakhali Hindu genocide and forced conversion, nevertheless those publications are treated almost like illegal or underground literature by elites, for example V. S. Godbole's *Horrors of Noakhali Massacre of October, 1946* (www.india-forum.com/forums/ index). Many prominent, learned Bengali Hindu luminaries were killed by Muslim mobs inspired by British disrespect, encouraged by Bengal's Muslim League Premiere Suhrawardy, and led by legislator Maulana Golam Sarwar Hossaini, a *pir* or Muslim saint. Parents, siblings, and extended family of an Indian (Hindu) Mayor were asked to dig their own grave before being slaughtered, but some of the recent publications in democratic India are censoring this. For more details, please see "*Empire's Last Casualty*" book. Britain didn't punish any killer. At Jayag, Noakhali, we became a part of the larger family, and came to know Ms. J. D. Chowdhury, a bachelorette, who was like a Hindu *Swamini* or nun, took us to meet many luminaries, including the District Commissioner. We met a few surviving Hindu families' of 1946 genocide. Some of them survived on floating boats stationed in the middle of rivers at night to avoid killer activists who were kidnapping girls and mothers for conversion and forced marriage, and killing and dismembering men.

There were similar attacks in 1971 when all Hindu minorities were targets of killing of the Army of Islamic Republic of Pakistan, but not Buddhist and Christian minorities. Pogrom after pogrom have revealed a very peculiar Bengali character, especially of Bengali Muslim killers of Pakistan and Bangladesh, and of surviving Hindu minority and refugees in India. Many mass murderers of Hindus have killed thousands, and then confiscated their homes and livelihood. Strangely a few of those mass murderers protected their minority Hindu neighbors in their own villages while killing outside the village. This is a strange loyalty to one's own village, but oppressing next door. One of the best examples of that is Brooklynite (New York City) Mr. Subhas of Noakhali, where the 1946 Hindu genocide took place. Subhas revealed in the interview for Partition Center how his Hindu family was saved in 1971 by a notorious Islamist Hindu killer, while the killer was engaged in Hindu genocide outside his village. (See ispad1947 channel at YouTube for Subhas' interview, https://www.youtube.com/watch?v=3EqMs5R_7zCA.) In 1971 almost all minority Hindus had to flee to India for shelter, otherwise murdered, except Subhas, and Mr. & Mrs. Sakkhi Gopal Saha and Chhaya Rani of Tangail, north-central Bangladesh. Sahas fled from village to village, at times walking miles through back roads, bushes and riverbanks. They said that "only 23 Hindus of their extended family members were killed." (See YouTube's ispad1947 channel https://www.youtube.com/watch?v=Qm3kC-GXrc.) One of his protectors, a famous Hindu industrialist and builders of schools and colleges, Mr. Ranada Prasad Saha, and his son, were murdered in cold blood by the Army of Islamic Republic of Pakistan. World hasn't asked for prosecution of these murderers. Why? During anti-Hindu pogroms in Bangladesh, Sachi was taken to various sites by Hindus as well as by Muslims. It was surprising that there was an indescribable relief on the part of the victims, just seeing and touching us, under that dire condition, although we didn't come to help them! According to the victims, this was the first time that an "Indian East Bengali Hindu refugee" has come to be with them. Sachi asked, "How could that be as India was partitioned in 1947, and in four decades none of those refugees in high position came to be with them?" Looking back, what is even more shocking is that our refugee brothers and sisters took to atheism and extreme leftism to grab power in two Bengali-majority states of India – West Bengal and Tripura, who were known to demonstrate for the oppressed around-the-world, but not for their own families. Shocking! Inhuman? A new form of racism? In Chittagong, the second largest metropolis and the main port of Bangladesh, during the 1992 pogrom huge numbers of historic building and temples were destroyed, homes torched, furniture stolen, and pet cows at homes slaughtered. American priest Sankar's 300-year-old temple in the heart of the city of Chittagong was destroyed, as was the Chatteswari – the Goddess of Chittagong – temple. An oppressed poor Hindu neighborhood across a Police Station was destroyed, as was Koiblya Dham Mandir and Ashram.

Student Dilip's home was burned, as was Priyo's, both in Chittagong. We visited so many destroyed homes that it is still etched in our memory like we saw those yesterday. No one was arrested. Who helped the victims to survive with food and shelter? At a public protest meeting at the historic J.M. Sen Hall in Chittagong City there were national luminaries – Hindu, Muslim and Buddhist – who were protesting against these atrocities. For no reason, Sachi was invited to sit on the podium with luminaries which he declined. Then the organizers made room in the front row. He refused that too, as he said, he is with them 100%, but no one should have any idea that he had any role in protecting them. Sachi stood on the back looking at pictures of destroyed villages, neighborhoods, crops illegally harvested, ponds cleaned of fish, cows slaughtered and deities destroyed. At Rangamati, Chittagong Hills District, a Buddhist-tribal area, a monk narrated how they are not allowed to pray at mid-day during Muslim call for prayers in recently-built mosques, which started as the area was forcibly colonized in Tibet-style by bringing Muslims from plains area to make the tribes minority in their own land. One of the Chakma tribesmen showed us the top of their king's former palace submerged by the newly constructed Kaptai Lake. Most of the arable land in that hilly area was inundated and the landless Buddhist peasants driven out of Bangladesh for India. This was done during the rule of military ruler General Zia. All the tribes kept reminding this over and over again. The dam was built to produce electricity for the plains area, but not for the indigenous inhabitants.

The Noakhali Gandhi Ashram was attacked in 1971, farmland and the Jayag Lake were confiscated by an Islamic group, and an illegal Mosque was built on the property, as mentioned earlier. After repeated pleading, the illegal mosque was removed outside the ashram and the lake was returned back to the ashram for raising fish to support the ashram. After helping Gandhi Ashram come back to life, a new Bangla Government raised the ashram's status as a National Museum, with schools and shelter for abandoned women. Sachi wrote a booklet containing the history of the place with maps and pictures, to be sold at the museum bringing little income and sharing its history. Ashram residents produce food, garments, and souvenir as sources of income for students and teachers. We are fortunate to taste some of those delicious snacks produced by Gandhi Ashram. The ashram produced the booklet, however, for unknown reason Sachi's name as the editor didn't appear. Ms. Chowdhury aka JharnaDi, Older Sister Jharna, wrote him a letter of apology for that. For her dedicated work among terrorists, Sachi nominated JharnaDi for an honor from an international organization.

Here are booklet covers, JharnaDi's letter of apology, her nomination for award, pictures of school and women at training school.

Booklet Cover: Editor Ms. Jharna Dhara Chowdhury

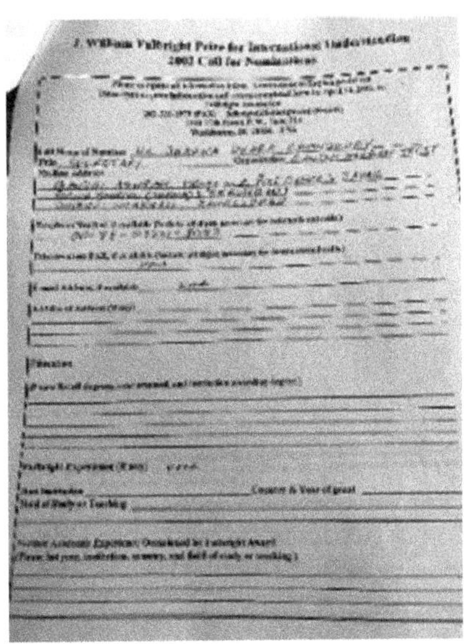

Nomination for Award, 2002

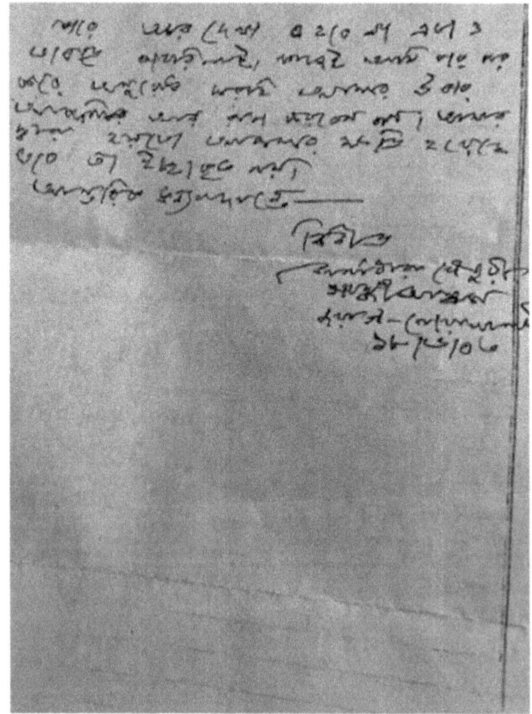

Two-Page Letter of Apology for not Including Sachi's Name as the Editor

Gandhi Ashram School, 1990s

Gandhi Ashram Women's Shelter, 1990s

Gandhi Ashram Secular School, 2022

Post-Covid Students, 2022

Ashram Honoring Sachi in Front of Gandhi's New Statue, 2022

Ms. JharnaDi, Center in White Sari, at
Probini Foundation Meeting at Dhaka, 2005

People like JharnaDi is always under pressure from killers and partisan bureaucrats. During our visit after reconstruction of the lake, she immediately rushed Sachi to the District Administrator to tell him, "Sir, this is the guy who was writing those letters to remove illegal occupiers. He saw those through his own eyes, and wrote those letters." Sachi told the boss, "Sir, I am the culprit, not the sister. She didn't tell me anything." In Subcontinent style, we just pushed through the door without an appointment. In typical Bengali hospitality the Administrator offered us hot tea, and thanked Sachi for asking the removal of illegal occupiers. Some locals think the liberation of the lake and handing over to its rightful owner, Gandhi Ashram, was a top breakthrough since Partition of Bengal and India in 1947. It is always good to see broadminded individuals.

The Liberated Jayag Lake, 2022, Illegally Confiscated after 1971 Hindu Genocide

One of the wonderful benefits of travel has been for poor villagers in Bangladesh and India to welcome our family among their families. It is truly a blessing when someone who barely has two meals a day, with no furniture at home invite strangers. It was good thing that distance with wealth and ability was gone in our mind. They see Shefali as their own aunt, and Joyeeta and Shuvo coequal with their kids. Our Foundation projects of schools and dorms at various distant corners of Bangladesh, Assam, West Bengal and Mizoram have brought us closer to peoples of diverse, economic, and distant places. It is good to know that poor and oppressed have found strength in themselves. Our foundation has built a girl's hostel in a north-central village in Bangladesh, bordering Indian Meghalaya state. It is really great to see kids who could have perished at their home instead going to school are moving ahead. Kids have found a shelter and finishing school which initially supported 45 girls. A few years after construction, we got an urgent call from the head monk that a group of thugs is planning to attack the hostel and kidnap the girls. In the middle of the night Sachi called police chief, and soon our friends started calling the police from different corners of the world. This was during anti-Hindu and pro-Islam rule in Bangladesh in 2000s. Many Bangladeshis protested, but no so-called secular newspapers in America or India printed a word. Why? Our lives don't matter? In late 2010s during another anti-Hindu pogrom, large number of Hindu girls and mothers were abused by Islamists, especially in the coastal Bhola island. This monk sheltered several victims. Youngest was only 6 or 8 years old. Did our papers write about that? No.

Residents at the Ashram School with Monk Nayan Sadhu

Eight Victims of anti-Hindu Atrocities in Bhola Island in 2001 are with Other Resident Girls at an Orphanage, a Day's Journey from Bhola Island Home

In 2017 a homeless teenager minority Hindu girl Monira was to be sold to smugglers. The monk traveled to Rajshahi district, a day's journey, then rescued the girl and sheltered in his ashram. The girl became homeless at five when her mother married a Muslim and converted, and in despair the father left home, never to be found. For many years Monira was sheltered by her grandma, who later became incapable of doing that. Below is Monira with the monk in white outfit.

Monira with the Monk in White Outfit

Here is the monk's letter translated in English by Prof. Dr. Judith Walsh.

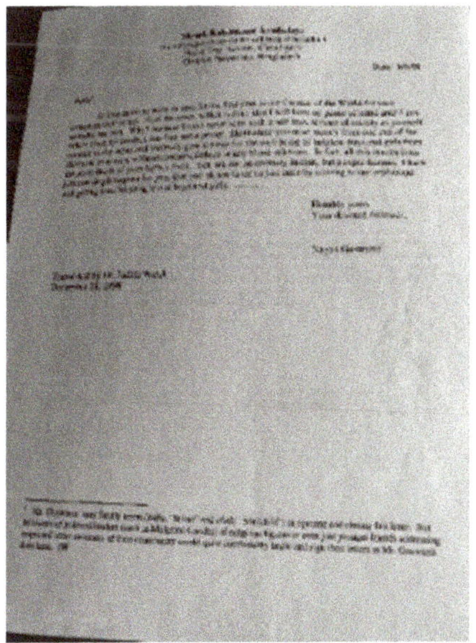

These types of oppressive stories should be shared with every corner. We still remember in 1980s, when we went to meet with LalitaDi, Older Sister Latita, the first female engineering graduate of India, but posted in Dhaka, Bangladesh, where she came to set up the first girl's engineering diploma college, called polytechnic in local jargon, in Bangladesh. LalitaDi was principal of a similar college in India. After some chat she asked, "Sachi, how come you as a visitor are able to meet with local Hindus, while living in Dhaka of Bangladeshi-origin, I am not able to do so? I am not able to meet secular Muslims either," There are tons of tolerant Muslims, but they are marginalized both by secular and anti-secular ruling groups, and Western media. They have been totally ignored by the Left in India, most of whom are from Bangladesh. In 2005 at the annual Bengali Studies Conference of U.S. was held at the Stamford University of Bangladesh. This is a new private university. Sachi was invited to be the keynote speaker. This was a great honor. This was also a time when anti-secular leader was the Prime Minister. With the invitation came online death threat. Sachi simply deleted the threat.

At the Bangladeshi capital city of Dhaka, at huge Islamic Mosque was built in 1980s by an Indian-born Islamist military dictator. He pushed Islam to be the State Religion of Bangladesh, removing Secularism from the Constitution, knowing fully well that most of the people martyred for Bangla independence were minority. Yet his friends and mullahs kept repeating that they want India to be secular. This is true for all countries surrounding India – Afghanistan, Pakistan, Sri Lanka, Burma (Myanmar), Bhutan, and Tibet (China), want India to be "secular" not themselves, and India not to follow the old saying, *shathey shattam samacharet* (Treat demons as it is), or follow "To every action there is equal and opposite reaction." Hypocrisy? To build a big mosque in the middle of the city he needed space. Whose space? He just bulldozed property belonging to Hindu Widows Trust without notice, and without any compensation. Hindu lawyer Haldar went to the court to stop the demolition, and displacement. The corrupt judiciary didn't care to respond. Illegal demolishing of minority Widow Welfare's property began. When attorney Haldar brought a court order, dictator's thugs simply tore apart the order in public, as he told this writer. The work was completed bringing in Islamic glory to him. Now, every day faithful prays five times on the body of kefir's property. Glory? Some say it brings glory, others say it is bad. Many said it would have been legal for the dictator to call the property "Enemy Property" and demolish Hindu widows' homes and businesses!

Once more joy turned into pain while visiting Rabindranath Tagore's home and that of monk-like poet-composer-singer Lalon Fakir, in Shilaidaha of Kushtia District in western Bangladesh bordering West Bengal, India. Lalon was born Hindu in late 1700s who died in late 1800s, raised by a Muslim, maintained a Hindu monk-like existence combining Islam and Hinduism. Rabindranath and Lalon influenced each other as their lives overlapped. At Rabindranath's former home, we got a personal tour by one of the workers being the only visitor during our visit. At Lalon Akhra or Lalon Musical Center, the reception was overwhelming with impromptu Baul folk songs. Bauls are singing minstrels of Bengal, tying villagers together, through their songs, from early morning to sundown, and at festivals.

Their patriotic and nature loving songs wake people up through music, and allowed collecting of alms. This is a noteworthy Bengali tradition. During British oppression, many *bauls*, mostly very poor, were imprisoned for singing in praise of Mother India, notable among them was Charon Kobi (Singing Minstrel) Mukunda Das of Barisal district. In Barisal, there are lots of wonderful places to visit in the city, among them are Braja Mohon College, now an university and one of the oldest colleges of Bengal and India established in that remote coastal area, A. K. (Aswini Kumar) Town Hall, Ramakrishna Mission built with donation from a Parsee or Zoroastrian devotee, the old Kali Bari temple, the Baptist Mission, the Gutia Masjid mosque, the Kirtonkhola River, boat rides, the old landowner Zamindar Bari, the bazar and more.

Charon Kobi (Travelling Poet) Mukunda Das-Established Kali Temple.
The shrine was abused during 1971 genocide.

Sri Sri Sankar Mott (Shrine), Destroyed During Hindu Genocide of Islamic Republic of
Pakistan's Army and by Bengali Islamists.

Ramakrishna Mission of Barisal, Bangladesh, built in early 1900
with Funding from an Indian Zoroastrian

After Sachi's visit to Lalon Akhra, he was invited to at a nearby home. There he ran into a Hindu maid who told the visitor how her family was almost starved to death for being Hindu, as her progressive Muslim Lady boss with half-a-dozen Muslim maids and servants, demanded that the Hindu maid must cut beef. All her Muslim maids objected as they were the one who were hired to cut beef and cook non-veg while the Hindu was supposed to cook vegetables and fish. Hindus do not eat beef and do not touch slaughtered cow flesh. As the Hindu maid cried in desperation, and Muslim maids came to protect her who received verbal abuse, a slap or two. Then the Hindu maid was kicked out of the home. She and her rickshaw-puller husband, an accident victim, and two kids were literally starving for days, until she found a job at a minority family. Are these for visitors to find? We assume she was waiting for someone to listen to her story. Why liberal Kolkata, Delhi, New York and London papers do not write about these? Conservative Dhaka does.

Citation to Sabyasachi Ghosh Dastidar from Lalon Academy,

Kushtia, Bangladesh

A Musical Performance at Lalon Folk Music Center in Honor of Sachi G. Dastidar

A Musical Performance

Musical Performance with Ektara (One Stringed Instrument)

A Celebration with Sabyasachi Ghosh Dastidar, sitting Left

Shilaidaha in western Bangladesh, reminded us of another Tagore landmark in Shantiniketan and Viswa-Bharati University located at Bolpur town in West Bengal State of India, about 100 miles northwest from Shilaidaha, Bangladesh but a world apart.

Rabindranath Tagore's Home in Shilaidaha, West Bangladesh

Rabindranath Home, now Museum

Rabindranath Home Museum

At the Roof of Rabindranath Tagore's Former Home in today's Bangladesh

Rabindranath Tagore build the Viswa Bharati university in the age-old Indian tradition where many classes are held outdoor under shady trees, but with modern curriculum. The morning prayer hall is an experience by itself, in addition to a museum, as well as stores selling local handicrafts. From mid-December, with the beginning of the Indian/Bengali month of Poush, a Poush Mela festival with varieties of traditional music, dance and *jatra* plays make visit pleasurable. Bolpur is in the midst of a rural area. It is a nice escape from Kolkata's urban hustle, now only two hours by train.

A Prayer Hall at Viswa Bharati University

A Museum at Shantiniketan

A Former Bedroom, now a part of the Museum

Viswa Bharati (University), Bolpur, West Bengal State, India

Back in Bangladesh about 75 miles south of Shilaidaha at Andharmanik village in Bagerhat (meaning "Bazar for Tigers" located north of Sundarbans Forest of Bengal Tiger) District, it was at the home of Mr. Gharami, that our sister Didi and Sachi got a unique Bengali welcome with freshly cooked *luchi*, the small flat fried white bread, and *alur dom* or thick potato curry, special welcome food in Bengal. This is the first time we stayed in a rural two-story traditional Bengali wooden thatched-roof building with modern amenities. Few months back cyclone Ayla destroyed many villages, and killed a Hindu schoolgirl in nearby area for whom Mr. Hossain, a Muslin friend helping cyclone victims, sent aid through our contact in the nearby village. We were there to open a girls' dormitory in a very remote corner of the world. It was a festive affair, with banners and decoration. We had a big send off at the bus stop for the Indian border. Pomp, ceremony, music and welcome stayed in our memory forever!

Here are some pictures of opening of a girls' hostel (dormitory) in deeply rural, and poor section of coastal Bagerhat district of Bangladesh:

The New Girls' Dormitory

Opening of Donors' Tablet

A Section of the Early Arrivals

Older Sister Didi, 2nd from left, being Introduced by a Teacher, left.

At each journey to Bangladesh added new experience and excitement to the family. In early 1990s Shuvo, Sachi and sister Mejdi traveled directly from Kolkata to Chittagong, the second-largest Metropolis and the largest port of

Bangladesh. On that trip we would meet legalist-author Mridul Kanti Rakshit. A few years down the road, Rakshit's son was beheaded as the family didn't give away their ancestral home and land free to a Muslim politician. During our visit, we were invited to stay with Mr. Majumdar, an engineer, whose home and surrounding areas were covered with beautiful fragrance of Night Queen flower, that blooms at night once in many years. On that trip we three ended up in Gava (Gabha) Village, the ancestral home of Ghosh-Dastidar family. From the paved Barisal-Banaripara Road we had to walk barefoot on mud-covered road, slipping and falling frequently, finally reaching one of our "family" members. There were only three Ghosh-Dastidar families left in Gava village where the family's written history goes almost to the First Millennium. In seconds of our arrival, we were welcomed as "cousins." In one home the lady of the house was reading *panchali* poem narrative dedicated to Goddess Sitala in her outdoor Pujar Ghar or Shrine Room with an unlettered peasant woman who was holding a copy of the *panchali* that she was uttering diligently as if she was reading that. This is the strength of oral history and powerful memory. Instantly village crowd gathered to take us to homes of notable luminaries of India born in that village. Those homes were taken over by others, although because of the power of oral history everyone calls those buildings by their old residents' names. We crossed bamboo bridges with only one bamboo at the floor level with bamboo handrail. In another trip in 1986, instead of going to a friend's home we went to Ci Hotel in Dhaka City. The hotel was full of foreign guests. To our surprise the hotel owner came and asked us, "Why are you staying here? You are a Bengali, so why can you not stay with family or friends? Don't you see you will be among smugglers? Tomorrow they will leave for India, then we will get another batch. Don't you see what they are wearing?" They were carrying illegal stuff, including their garments. This was true hospitality, warm heartedness. On another trip Sachi was flying back to Kolkata from Bangkok, Thailand. The flight was completely full. It was carrying foreign Nationalities who will reach Nepal on the next leg of the flight after a brief stopover in Kolkata. Finally, it will reach India illegally. Every passenger was wearing the same new leather jackets and pants, carrying same suitcases and carry-ons, same new watches, and more. We realized that this is what the Dhaka hotel owner was talking about. In 1992 Sachi was flying back from a trip to Singapore. It was February, and he always wanted to visit Dhaka on February 21, the Language Martyr's Day or *Ekushey*. Kolkata-Dhaka flights were sold out for months. So, he thought he will take a road trip after he reached Kolkata, that too was risky as all long-distance buses were sold out from the border checkpoint. The flight left Singapore, to stop at Dhaka first, then will head to Kolkata. It was a day before 21st February. He decided to get off the plane in Dhaka, to which flight attendants said it is not allowed. He told them that he has a visa for Bangladesh, and that he was carrying only a backpack, and can just walk out putting them in trouble. They agreed, and asked him to sign a paper that he won't claim any refund for Dhaka-Kolkata portion of the flight, which he was happy to do. And life-long dream of attending *Ekushey*, 21st February, was fulfilled. *Ekushey* was a joyous and colorful event, which is now the World Mother Language Day. On that day in 1952, Bengalis – then majority of Pakistani population – demonstrated for their language to be declared a national language of Pakistan, and Pakistani police shot dead six youngsters starting the process of eventual independence of Bangladesh. On that day the numerous processions with song and music head to Language Martyr's Memorial near Dhaka University. And almost all the neighborhoods, temples, churches and viharas, and many mosques, have their individual celebrations. We visited celebrations in Dhaka University, Sakharipatti area, Dhakeswari Temple, Ramakrishna Mission, and some other places. Sweets were offered in all places. During another trip to Rajshahi University of western Bangladesh, bordering West Bengal, India, with daughter Joyeeta our (Muslim) host, a professor at the university, while chatting at dinner told us how his Canadian-born granddaughter is becoming vegetarian like "Hindu," while a local young school-going minority girl said how at times she gets harassed for being minority, and at times some Muslim girls refuse to play with her. This was something new to us. Hindu and Muslim both were extremely cordial and friendly to us. We realize being a tourist and living as a native are two different things! Teenage daughter Joyeeta was traveling that's why we may have heard stories of those two girls. On that trip we met Prof. Mitra, who had an untimely death. Sachi was asked to write a paper for a book in his memory, that he did. The paper was "One Hundred Years of Banga-Vanga – The Partition of Bengal: 1905-2005," and the book was *Pritikumar Mitra Commemorative Volume*, Eds. Dr. Mahabubur Rahman and Dr. Swaroschish Sarkar, Institute of Bangladesh Studies, Rajshahi University, Bangladesh, October 2009; 285-298. In India, one of the most interesting-yet-difficult places to visit was the very remote Tuichawng village of Mizoram state in northeast India. Mizoram is a Christian-majority state created by the Hindu-majority Indian government bifurcating Assam State. Mizoram is a beautiful hilly region stuck between Bangladesh on west and Myanmar in the east and south. It is basically a landlocked place. A flight from Kolkata takes only 1 hour and 30 minutes, while for most people it takes over three days by bus to reach from Kolkata. Mizoram state still follows a colonial British tradition where they prohibit visit by any Indian citizen without a visa. To turn the Assam district around, in 1885 the Colonial British administration prohibited entry of Indians, including Assamese to which the district belonged, but gave a foreign Christian church responsibility of education and converting, kicking Assamese/Indians out. They were preventing anyone from the same state to enter their state, but not distant foreigners. By the time British was forced to leave India in 1947, vast numbers of Mizos were converted to Christianity, changing their script from Assamese to English. In turn the district of Assam was elevated to a state by Prime Minister Indira Gandhi to avoid a separatist Mizo-Christian war. Newly converted Mizos went for cleansing of remaining non-converted indigenous Hindus called Brus and Reangs driving them out of their own home. This is India! Tens of thousands of Brus and Reangs were living for decades in refugee camps in neighboring Tripura state. Mizoram Legislature declared itself a "Christian State" in secular India. What would have Western press said if a Hindu-majority state in India declared herself a "Hindu State"? A picturesque ride through mountainous road took us to Lunglei in the south. The 100-mile journey took us over four hours. With a quick lunch stop at a restaurant that hang on the side of a 150 feet deep gorge. From Lunglei we headed southwest towards Bangladesh for Tuichawng in an area that is Buddhist majority. We drove through one of the most wretched roads anywhere in the world. The last 40 miles took us four hours! It brought us to a serene, dirt-poor area, with real warmth. Everyone wanted us to be part of their family. Sachi was welcomed to stay with school headmaster Mr. Rajesh. Visiting individual homes, the small bazar, a walk to the Karnaphuli River, climbing small ridges, were more than enjoyable. Then came invitation to join with a group trying to build a school and dorm for very poor kids who have no resources to go to school. Moreover, some villages are only accessible by foot, and it takes hours to reach any school. Thus, the need for dormitories. Visiting such places are very different. Most enjoyable moments are talking and visiting strangers' home, and receiving their warmth. Those who like trekking, there are lots of paths to trek, as those paths are the only way to reach remote villages. This is also a bird watcher's paradise. As of now there are no hotels for people to stay, but we are told that, commercial home rental is fast developing in remote places.

Here are some pictures of Buddhist Twichwang village school in remote and extremely poor area of Christian-majority hilly Mizoram State of Northeast India https://empireslastcasualty.blogspot.com/2013/02/tuichawngmizo ram-india.html.

Mizoram Landscape

Ultimate Truth Preaching Mission School

Welcome to Sachi G Dastidar by Villagers

Setting up Scholarships for Students

Welcome by Secretary Sudip Chakma (left) and President Rajesh Chakma (right) of Ultimate Truth Preaching Mission

Welcome to a Village

Typical Homes in Local Area

Karnafuli River ending in Bangladesh

On our return to Aizawl, the state capital, Sachi saved the day for visiting other places. But that was not to be, as January 11 is a "state holiday" when two foreigners came to convert from their indigenous belief. Is it that different of forced conversion by Islamist conquerors? The state still has colonial British policy of no "Indian is allowed to enter" without a visa called Entry Permit or Inner Line Permit. Pakistan and Bangladesh wiped out of their "Entry Permit" areas, but why not India? How would Americans feel if Hawaii or Alaska established a visa fee for Lower 48 Americans? This is going on in a country oppressed by followers of Christianity and Islam for over a millennium. Seeing this contradiction, Sachi wrote to the Chief Minster, "*Ironically, I was in Aizawl on January 11 … .*" Here is the entire letter:

February 9, 2013

The Hon. Sri Pu Lalthanhawla Chief Minister, Mizoram

Dear Chief Minister Lalthanhawla: Re: Road to Southwest

Please accept warm greetings from me, my family and friends in the U.S. Recently I was in Mizoram and enjoyed the hospitality of the people and loved the spectacular beauty of the land. Having traveled all seven continents and every state in India I wondered why your state is not on the world map of tourism through which many parts of the world have pulled themselves up economically. I was told by many that a visa needed to enter – Inner Line Permit – has been very unwelcoming even to other Indians…….. Ironically, I was in Aizawl on January 11 when the state celebrated Missionary Day holiday as two English Christian missionaries J. H. Lorrain and F. W. Savidge arrived in Mizoram on January 11, 1894 to guide Mizos away from their nature-worshipping Hindu-like belief. I wonder if there is a contradiction as coming of foreigners is being celebrated yet we are restricting countrymen from traveling to the state!

My trip took me towards the Bangladesh border via Lungsen, Matri Chhara (Tlabang) and towards Chakma Autonomous Area. I was moved by the warmth of the people yet I was appalled by the condition of the state road from Lunglei onwards…….

Let me extend an invitation to visit us during your next visit to the U.S. Please ask your office to drop me a line before you leave India.

Best wishes and belated Happy New Year.

Pakistan:

For Indians wanting to visit Pakistan it is not easy, especially if you are Hindu or non-Muslim. Red tape is the problem; plus, the law. At times it takes over six months or more to get a visa. In 1978 I was invited to speak at a famous Punjab university, but the visa never came even after waiting for nine months. Lahore is the intellectual and political capital of Pakistan, the capital of former united Punjab Province of Colonial India. Our second attempt was in 1989. Not hearing from Pakistan consulate in months, as our travel date was approaching Sachi finally rushed to the New York City's Pakistan Consulate without an appointment. Earlier, he couldn't get an appointment by phone or by mail. After some hesitation, the doorman at first asked him to wait outside. Then Sachi was invited to meet the Counsel. The friendly gentleman asked Sachi "Why does a Hindu Indian wants to visit Pakistan?" Sachi replied, "Just for fun, as I have visited other countries! Why not Pakistan?" The Counsel laughingly said he never heard someone going there "just for fun, that too taking a wife and two minor kids. And you are Hindu." He then stamped a tourist visa in Sachi's Indian passport. Shefali, Shuvo and Joyeeta didn't need a visa as they had American passport. This was the other side of the bureaucracy. Sachi had a warm welcome. It was unpredictable. To get a Pakistani visa Indians need family sponsorship from Pakistan, that we didn't have. For a Hindu it becomes extremely difficult as almost all Hindus, Sikhs, Jains, and Buddhists have been cleansed from Pakistan, thus getting a family sponsorship for a Hindu-Sikh-Jain-Buddhist refugee is impossible. One of our Pakistani Muslim friends in New York suggested that we give his family as his "relative's address," that we couldn't do. We had applied early but the visa hadn't arrived in months. Pakistani law says, all Indians must register at police stations wherever they go, immediately at arrival and before departure. We didn't know of all those restrictions and named several cities that we wanted to visit.

They allowed Sachi to visit only Lahore, Rawalpindi, Karachi, and Mohenjo-Daro. Yet, at all police stations Sachi was welcomed warmly with his Indian passport. Duty officers apologized for this rule saying "Sir, you are wasting your time visiting us. Visit bazaars. Visit your friends." At one city, the lady officer asked several foreigners in the que in front to move so that she "Can take care of a Hindustani *mehman* (honored) guest." At another station, the officer stamped "arrival" and "departure" at the same time "to save your time," and at third station, the officer told our friend how to ignore the rules, as Sachi was going to stay overnight with a friend, possibly just outside the city boundary not approved in his visa. And on a stroll at the famous Murry Hill tourist station on top of a hill north of the national capital Islamabad, a shopkeeper seeing Shefali in sari assumed we were Indians rushed to us like a bullet, then introduced him with folded hands, "I work in one of the shops here. We were Hindu too, but I can't say that now. Family converted to Islam," and immediately vanished into the crowd. Sachi ran after him, but he just vanished. Our kids and that of our friends took ride on horseback. Murry Hill was built by the British as a cooling place in the tropical country as they built colonial office in Darjeeling in Himalayan mountains, 400 miles north of Calcutta, then British capital. Near Murry Hill, we went to the ruins of Taxila Buddhist Vihar, built on 6th Century B.C. A cleaner at the outdoor ruins were discarding some bricks from the structure. We wanted to get a broken piece of the discarded bricks. The cleaner was happy to give us one of the broken pieces, and asked, "What are you going to do with that brick? Buddhists built that.

We have no Buddhist left here." We didn't know that we would save that in our Partition Museum in New York thirty years later, as well as another broken discarded brick from the ruins of a 7th Century Buddhist Maynamati Vihar in Comilla City in eastern Bangladesh. We were at Taxila as visitor. The museum had lots of information of one-time Buddhist region of today's Pakistan, where not a single Buddhist exist today. Even in Pakistani Ladakh, that we visited later, there exists no Buddhists or Hindus, whereas in Indian Ladakh it is still a Buddhist majority area.

A Buddhist Shrine in Tibetan-Speaking Ladakh, India

Entrance of a Shrine in 14,000 feet High Altitude Town

A Buddhist Shrine with Buddhist-Hindu Deity

Entrance to Another Shrine

With a Buddhist Monk After Attending his Meditation Prayer; 1986

Visiting the new capital city of Islamabad or the City of Islam, capital of Pakistan, was great, but more interesting was the old city of Rawalpindi, Islamabad's twin city. Before 1947 partition, Rawalpindi was a city of Hindu temples built in Punjabi style. It had substantial Hindu population, if not the majority of the population. Our friend knocked at a stranger's home and took us to the rooftop where we were able to see dozens of spires of Hindu *mandirs* (temples). Spotting a nearby temple, we knocked at the door, when the lady of the house took us to the building which is her home now. Then we stopped at the famous Krishna Mandir which was converted to a school for the deaf, while at the temple sanctum the deity was missing. We offered our prayer with flowers and grass. After returning to Lahore, we were supposed to visit Karachi first and then Mohenjo-Daro, the famous ancient city of Indus Civilization, 3rd Millennium B.C. in southern Sind Province. Our friend from Karachi called us to cancel our trip as the next two days of our three-day trip everything will be closed because of *hartal* or general strike called by ethno-religion-based political parties in Sind, locally called Sindhu province. In life, sometimes one gets only one chance! Historically both the words "India" and "Hindu" have evolved from the name of the river Sind or Sindu as neighbor Persia or Iran liked to call the river Hind and people residing on its shore as Hindu, otherwise called Sindhu.

During another visit, we arrived at Pakistani Kashmir's Baltistan after crossing 14,000 ft. high Khunjerab Pass from Xinjiang-Uygur, China. On our second day on the Chinese bus, the journey stopped as the road went under overflowing river in Pakistani Kashmir territory. We had to climb a high mountain to get to the other side to catch a waiting Pakistani bus. Pakistani travelers on the bus, mostly minor traders, recruited a porter for our carryon bags, as they carried our hand luggage. We were the last to arrive at the waiting bus. The entire bus gave us a cheer, saving the last two seats. They guessed we were Indian. Customs and immigration were at the village of Sost, 70 miles from the international border. We possibly drove over 150 miles of treeless uninhabited high-altitude territory. The picturesque drive was above tree line and without habitation. At Sost, the first inhabited village, we decided to break our journey, as we were extremely tired. Our customs and immigration were done in an open courtyard. All the travelers were Pakistani, but for a European biker couple, and a Chinese Muslim couple heading for religious studies in Pakistan. These we learned as we were questioned publicly in open courtyard. After immigration a young man spotted us and offered to take us to his hotel. We were happy to accept his proposal, and became "celebrities" in his village. After a bit of rest and a cup of hot tea, we were given a tour of the local village, and to private homes. The village was home to Shia Muslim minority. Women working outdoor were quite open and welcomed two strangers among themselves. They didn't cover themselves as in many Muslim-majority nations, or in Jamaica, Queens, New York City. An order for a cup of tea was served by two persons. Soon they learned that we were "Indians." As Indians we became special guests. Some of them were seeing live Indians for the first time. The young man discussed his intention to go to India for higher studies, but that route was closed for many years. Surprisingly, the restaurant was running a 24-hour Hindi news channel from India, in one of the remotest corners on earth. Another day's journey would take us to a government hotel, In Gilgit, Pakistani Kashmir, now called Gilgit-Baltistan after division of Pakistani Kashmir by Pakistan's Government, although officially it is not part of Pakistan. The workers were happy to see "Indians." We bought a bunch of posters from their shop. To figure out local travel options they sat with us as we offered them hot tea. On 14th of August, Pakistan's independence holiday, they suggested that we do not go out as the street is full of people. We went out. There was not a single woman on the street, only men. It was really odd, and very uncomfortable for both of us. This was a new experience. We returned back to hotel. During a city tour, our taxi driver took us to a roundabout with a captured Indian helicopter. He said, "Sir, please take a picture of that Indian helicopter. Taking picture of that helicopter is banned, but we take pictures all the time." At the bazar, shop owners were very happy to see "Indians," one offering cold drinks, but all of them cautioned us to be careful. Traveling is not fun where you are cautioned to be careful every minute. In 2020 Pakistan changed area's status and incorporated into Pakistan in India-contested territory of Pakistani Kashmir. No Western country, no Islamic nation complained about it as they did for India when she changed the status of Indian Kashmir from special status to a regular state of India. Confusing? There are, of course, thousands of people full of hate, who hate their ancestry. But generally, they avoid you, and you don't see them in person, except occasionally as we ran into a Caucasian Muslim convert at a conference in Pakistan, or a book seller at a Lahore bookshop who simply said "I don't carry books of Hindu/Indian writers". At same Lahore, a friend asked for some books by Tagore. We sent him several Tagore's English translated books from India, which he never received.

At Peshawar University Conference on 150th Anniversary of India's First War of Independence from Britain, all the attendees were extremely warm for two "Indians", especially when Shefali wore sari, saying, "This is our heritage," that almost all the attendees mentioned. Islamization has turned wearing of sari underground, although the First Ladies of new Pakistan wore sari, including a 1960s presidential candidate Ms. Fatima Jinnah against the military dictator General Ayoub Khan. At the conference a Western Islamist tried terrorizing the non-Muslim participants, while local Muslims tried to expel him for his obnoxious views. This is the other side of Pakistan-India, Muslim-Non-Muslim relation. A young journalist then sought our help to restore a pre-Islamic Shiv Temple, possibly as old as 600 B.C. Legend has it that Lord Buddha went there with his Begging Bowl. This was a big honor, and Peshawari friends were able to bring the temple back to life. In 2011 the entire city celebrated the first Pathan Diwali Festival of Lights after 1947 partition with huge posters in Pashtu language. (Unfortunately, soon after Diwali true believers attacked the temple, but it was restored back.) On our bus journey to the Indian border Wagah-Atari, we planned to stop in Lahore, the capital city of Punjab Province of Pakistan, for a few days. The historic city dates back to pre-Islam era. The name had roots in the ancient epic Ramayana, and is the current cultural-political capital of Pakistan. On our way to Lahore, we were "kidnapped" by two lady conference participants, to take us to their home in Lahore. Nabila canceled our hotel reservation through her cell phone, surprising us. Prof. Nabila's mother, Didi or Older Sister, welcomed us, "This is your home now." Didi made sure we were at home, and when we rented a car to visit a friend, she personally interviewed drivers to her satisfaction that we were safe with the driver. Didi and Nabila joined us for our trip to Nankana Sahib, the birthplace of Guru Nanak, the founder of Sikhism, and the ancient Indus Valley Civilization City of Harappa. Unfortunately, both were unknown to most locals as those are not lessons at Pakistan history courses. At first the military guard at Guru Nanak Gurdwara temple didn't allow us to enter as in bold letters at the entrance said, "Only Hindus and Sikhs are Allowed to Enter." We had to produce our passports to prove that we have Hindu names, and beg the guard that our two Muslim guests be allowed to enter, which he did. The guard looked us again. Maybe he was seeing a live Hindu for the first time in his life as all the Punjabi Hindus, Sikhs and Jains have been killed or cleansed at India's 1947 partition. Only non-Muslim minority left in Pakistani Punjab are Christians, who had to Arabize their names. Guru's birthplace had a small number of Sikhs from Pakistan's Northwest Frontier Province, now called Khyber-Pakhtunkhwa, some of whom realizing we are heading to India gave us their names to offer prayer at the Sikh Holy Golden Temple shrine in the Indian city of Amritsar, across the border in India, that we did. It was one of the top places on earth where we had the huge Guru Nanak Birthplace shrine to ourselves. Recently, in April of 2020, there was a bit of tension in that town where true believers threatened to attack the shrine, while the military of the Islamic Republic tried to encourage anti-India Sikh terrorists to attack India. In 1989, in Lahore we tried to visit another historic Sikh temple, Ranjit Singh Gurdwara, across from the famous Lahore Fort. That temple had written sign of "Hindus and Sikhs Only," yet we were refused admission even after producing our passports. So, with our Christian host whom we met a day before said, let's have lunch at the parking area across the temple. This was at the height of anti-India Sikh separatism, when some Indian papers accused Pakistan of instigating anti-Hindu and anti-India acts, both are two sides of the same coin, this time by Sikhs, that we thought was Indian propaganda. We sat under open sky, barely 30' feet from the temple entrance.

To our surprise we saw young Sikhs in their 20s and 30s with same uniform of white turban emerging from the Ranjit Singh temple in a military-style single-file march. God knows how many there were; may be 75 or 100 or more. Some of the young men noticed us as Shefali was wearing sari, waved at us. We waved back. Our friend said in dismay, "These are the terrorists we are training. I heard that before, but didn't believe. Now I am seeing through my own eyes." In 2008, after Nankana Sahib tour, next day we headed for Harappa, the 2,500-5,000 BC ruins of the Indus Valley City. Growing up in India, and learning about Indus Civilization, we were excited for our dream come true. Seeing how China has turned around their terracotta statue-famous city of Xian into an economic power house through tourism, we felt dismayed, as there was no visitor. Didi and Nabila were visiting for the first time. At the fork on the national highway, the sign in Urdu was so small that our driver missed it. We were the only visitors which was a blessing for us. A water buffalo ranch has encroached onto the ancient property, and someone has built a grave in the middle of the ancient city. In Xian the entire site has been covered with air-conditioned dome, whereas this ancient site is open to rain and shine. On the upside, we were able to spend as much time as we wanted. This time though we had to pay 10-times higher foreigner's entrance fee as Shefali's pants gave our foreignness, not our look. At the small museum we became a celebrity as we bought a copy each of their booklets. One of the armed men then took us to the corner selling us a copy of a recently-discovered 5,000-year-old 1½" seal of a horse, typical of Indus Civilization. This was a wonderful souvenir for a dream come true. Didi was happy with our find. Some local scholars bemoan the plight as hesitation of Pakistani rulers and Islamists to teach their citizens of pre-Islam roots of their nation.

Here are some pictures of Harappa, a city of Indus Civilization, 2,500 – 5,000 B.C.:

Copy of One of the Artifacts Found at the Site

Introduction at the Entrance

Parts of the Ancient Harappa City

Here are some pictures from Guru Nanak's Birthplace:

Birthpalce of Guru Nanak, Founder of Sikhism

Guru Nanak Janamsthan (Birth Place)

The Gurudwara Shrine

Entrance to the Inner Sanctuary with Our Host Prof. Nabila and Didi, Nabila's Mom

Before the Peshawar conference, from Sust on top of the mountain, our first stop in Pakistani Kashmir, we headed to a picturesque city of Karimabad where we were introduced to the local kings' palace and restaurant. View from the upstairs dining room was spectacular of snow-covered Nanga Parbat (Mountain). The region was suffering from lack of tourists. After a brief stay, we caught a public bus, more like station wagon, to our destination for the night at Gilgit, the capital of Pakistani North Kashmir, renamed by Pakistan in 2020 as Gilgit-Baltistan. Three persons sat on each row of the van. A lady sat at the window, Shefali sat next to her. For some reason of modesty, her husband sat behind her. Soon, they started to chat with Shefali in Hindi. Learning two Hindustanis, meaning Indians in local vernacular, were traveling with them, both wife and husband got excited, and told us many stories about Gilgit. It was like having a private guide. We got down at Gilgit, so did the couple. The lady immediately turned to Shefali and held her hand asking us to stay with them instead of hotel. It went on for a few minutes before they relented. What a welcome! Unfortunately, we didn't write their address down for a "Thank You" card later. After our Gilgit break, we took a day long bus through China-built Karakoram Highway to Abbottabad. Next day our rented car took us from Manshera in the north to Haripur in the east. Many years later we would realize that we must have passed the house where terrorist Osama bin Laden was hiding. Osama was killed on May 1, 2011, two and a half years after our visit. We learned that Pakistan dictator Ayyub Khan was born at Haripur, or the Land of Lord Hari, and established a Pakistani military base there. Ayyub saved the Hindu name of his village, but organized many anti-Hindu pogroms and genocides in East Pakistan, now Bangladesh, killing tens of thousands, without an iota of criticism from Islamic countries, Western democracies, and Indian Hindus. At a mosque there, seeing Hindus for the first time, preacher imam came to tell the story of how the mosque came to exist there. According to him, before 1947 partition, the area was 50/50 Pathan Hindu and Muslim population, but Muslims were gaining strength as partition was approaching. A small water fall was in the area. Hindus started to build a temple using the water falls for religious bath. Some Muslims didn't like the idea of a temple. According to the imam as soon as Muslim neighbors got opportunity some laid some bricks and gave a Call for Prayer. Hindus couldn't fight back, and within months they were all gone, killed or cleansed. He showed us raised circular lotus decorations on the mosque wall, which is very unusual for mosques, but proper for temples. It seemed to us it was an example of a temple converted to a mosque. The hospitable imam offered us hot tea, soon we had to rush for our next site. A day later we joined Peshawar University conference at their Bara Gali Hill Station campus for the 150th Anniversary Conference of the First War of Indian Independence. We learned that we were the only "Indians" as visas for a dozen Indians coming to the conference were denied. Four years later we met Dr. Rizwan, a professor at a university in Delhi, at his home when Sachi learned that he was denied visa for the conference.

At the First War of Indian Independence, 1857, Conference

Journey from Uighur, China to Pakistani Kashmir through one of world's most difficult hilly landscape:

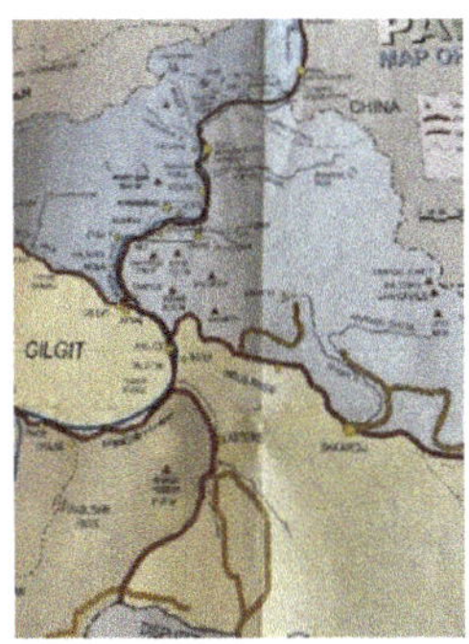

Upper Kashmir: From Xinxiang, China border to Gilgit, North Pakistani Kashmir.

Lower Kashmir: From Gilgit to Peshawar.

This trip resulted in an unexpected benefit of restoration of a pre-Islam, perhaps pre-Christ Hindu temple in Peshawar – the Gor Khattree Shiv Madir. Sachi was asked as Hindu to request top administrators of Northwest Frontier Province, now called Khyber-Pakhtunkhwa, and Federal Pakistani administrators, for repair but the activism was done by journalist Shabbir – not his actual name – and other secular Muslim activists. Just to imagine a place visited by Lord Buddha in 600 B.C. was brought back to life by a tourist gives us great pleasure of travel in the Open World. Very true! After opening, the shrine's key was given to two poor local indigenous Hindus, Mr. Kaka and Mrs. Devi. See https://empireslastcasualty.blogspot.com/2013/05/gorkhatree gor-khuttree-shiva-mandir.html.

One of the Old Structures

Old Temple

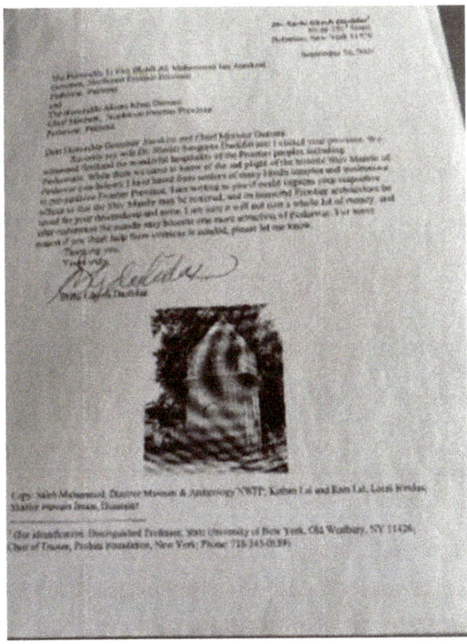

Copy of One of Sachi's Many Letters to the Top Leaders and Administrators

Since 1947 Partition the First Diwali Celebration in 2011

Internationalism:

Surprise comes many ways in travel. In many areas the most difficult part is language, and the other is the socialization with average persons. There are risks involved when you don't know the language. Then again, at times, knowing the language doesn't help either.

One of our greatest shocks was when we learned that rich New York's college student stole an India-made wristwatch from an educator's classroom table where he kept it to manage time. This happened at the very first year. Cost was not important. It was nice looking golden colored wedding gift from an in-law. Sadly, it happened again almost 40 years later in the same class before retiring. This time it was a wristwatch keeping lecture time. This was not in poor Alabama!

We always like to take trips in local transport – bus, subway, trolley, train, ferry boat, cycle rickshaw, or three-wheeler called Bajaj or baby taxi. During a trip in a local bus in Hohhot, Inner Mongolia, China where no one spoke English, all of a sudden, we found a tap on Sachi's shoulder. A young man in his early twenties, said in a packed bus, "Look, I am the only one in the bus who knows English. I want to be friend with you. I am the only Mongol in the bus, others are Hun." He hung around with us, telling stories, for some time as our personal guide. Fearing that he may be harmed by authorities, after sometime we said we

197

have other plans. His story reminded us of propaganda of Indian left parties where they preached "Look how well China has protected their minority Mongol, Uighur and Tibetan tribes compared to India." At Hohhot we learned that at China's revolution in 1949, 95% of Inner Mongolia was Mongol, and 5% Hun. Now it is a complete reverse. When we asked our hotel in Hohhot if any of the workers knew Mongol, they just laughed. We met Mongols at organized villages in poor living condition taking tourists on horseback ride. India created tribal-majority states like Mizoram, Manipur, Nagaland, Meghalaya, Arunachal and Jharkhand where tribal culture and languages are thriving. On a flight from Urumqi to Kashgahr or Kashi in China's far western Uighur Xinxiang Province we were surprised to find the Communist Party's English language daily praising capitalism for economic situation in the West. Whereas the pro-China Communist Parties of India, and other leftists in India, preach just the opposite. Kashghar, with a Sanskrit-based name, felt close to India than China, as this was the first place in China where non-Hun citizens were visible. Long way from Xinjiang we ran into Eric, a Chinese student at a California university, in remote Easter Island of Chile. He came for a short trip, but was having difficulty in walking. So, to his joy, we became his surrogate parents during his visit, taking him around the island on visits to Moais, giving support when needed, taking him to restaurants and gift shops, then bringing him back to the airport for flying to Santiago, Chile's capital, for his flight to California.

In the U.S., in the summer of 2003 we had a one-of-a-kind experience in McLean, Virginia. My eldest sister Pratima or Didi and her husband Naresh or JamaiBabu (Mr. Brother-in-Law) came to visit us from India. This was right before schools opened. So, after New York, we took them to visit Washington D.C. We were supposed to spend the night with our friend Shrikant, an IT entrepreneur, who lived at McLean. We visited him many times, and knew his home well. Sachi knew he had to exit from the freeway, then had to take a left turn to head to his home. As usual we were running late for our dinner. It was already past 8 PM. Our plan was to take Shrikant out to dinner. As Sachi was rushing towards his home, he took a wrong exit, not far from Shri's home, and then seeing a greenlight for a left turn for multiple lanes on an east bound road he passed the entrance sign that he could hardly read in that darkness, with a raised road barrier. We heard some noise from a speaker, and soon we found some machine guns pointing at the car. As soon as Sachi stopped, we found half-a-dozen soldiers surrounding our car from all sides. They asked Sachi, "Do you know this is CIA Headquarters?" Thus, our journey stopped. After Sachi, they checked his wife Shefali's driver's license. Then they asked for Didi and NareshDa's passport. They were not carrying those for safety reason. One of the soldiers said that they could be imprisoned for that. Sachi told them it was his fault as he didn't want them to lose those. Brother-in-law NareshDa produced his Indian driver's license, and both of them gave their date of arrival and the airline. When Didi wanted to get a bottle of water for her medication, soldiers warned them she couldn't do that. They asked us not to listen to music or play the radio. We couldn't talk to each other. The checking process was fast yet it took about two hours. Guards were following their protocol. Finally, one of them came and told us that we are free to go, and gave Sachi a warning saying "If you enter the property again within next six months, you will receive penalty and imprisonment." Afterwards we visited Shrikant many times, but never missed the turn.

Traveling on water always attract us. Thus, whenever we get a chance, we like to touch waterbodies, especially rivers. May be unconsciously our minds were influenced by traditional rituals of worshipping with water, the Ganga River called as Ma Ganga or Mother Ganga, and offering water to ancestors as a yearly duty. One of the most sacred acts in Sanatani is to offer water in the mouth of a dying person. It is believed that at the very dying moment the body feels dry and cringes for water. In India we visited the Ganga River many times in Kolkata where the branch is called Hooghly River, as well as at Varanasi where the water was quite unclean, and in pristine Haridwar at the foot hills of the Himalaya, where the river begins its journey in the plains, from the mountain. Each place has developed separate tradition for thousands of years of nature shrining. At the very end of Ganga, where she meets ocean, the Bay of

Bengal, every year there is a huge celebration at the end of the month of Poush in mid-January, called Poush Sankranti, at a place called Gangasagar or Ganga-Ocean. For centuries, it used to be extremely difficult to get there, through pirate-infested river, roaming of wild animals including Bengal Tiger, crocodiles, cyclones and more. By 1990s travel to reach Gangasagar improved a lot, and soon a rail connection and bridges will make it even easier. We were there for visiting the pilgrimage during Sankranti or End of the Season. It was so distant and difficult to travel in old days that there exists a Bengali saying, *"Sab tirtha bar-bar, ganga-sagar akbar"*, meaning "All pilgrimage places are many times, but Gangasagar only once." There are stories how pilgrims got lost forever while traveling by boat, and on foot as they traveled to Ganga-Sagar beach where River Ganga and Bay of Bengal of Indian Ocean meet, next to the Sundarbans Forest. Transport has improved even more by 2024. A bridge has been built.

Ganga Sagar Beach

To Take a Dip in the Water of Confluence of Ganga River and Indian Ocean

Pilgrims Arriving on Foot

A Long Line to Get into the Temporary Living Area

A Shrine of Lord Shiva

Temporary Living Area

Access to the Ganga-Sagar (River-Ocean) Meeting Site

We also sprinkled water on our head from the other end of Ganga in Bangladesh, and at many of its branches in the delta, as at Sandhya River in Barisal, Burri Ganga River in Dhaka, and have touched the Brahmaputra River at Mymensingh, 75 miles north of Dhaka. We met Brahmaputra further north at Dibrugarh, Assam in India. In Assam Brahmaputra widens to over six miles wide in many places, creating world's largest river island Majuli which sits in the middle of the river. The area is very picturesque and peaceful. Majuli is a pilgrimage and tourist destination for many, but not well known to travelers. In the southern Bangladesh we have floated on riverboats in huge Padma and Meghna Rivers, as well as set foot on Kirtonkhola River in Barisal, and Arial Kha River in Madaripur. Overnight journeys in ships give breathtaking views, and provide hot food from its kitchen. Way back in March of 1985 Sachi wrote about that journey in the American travel magazine *International Travel News*. In America, living in Tennessee gave us access to Mississippi River in Memphis. While living in Huntsville, Alabama we were invited to take a dip in Tennessee River, which was just south of Huntsville city limits, close to our home in southern part of the city. And now living in New York City we have floated more on Hudson River than we were able to touch its water. Hudson was easily accessible at Governor's Island, south of Manhattan than anywhere else. It was also accessible during a high tide when the river flooded New Jersey's Palisades State Park during an outdoor summer party. In warm climate taking a dip in a river is pleasurable. Thus, taking dips in rivers and ponds have become a part of indigenous Indian culture in that tropical climate. We thought we would find similar water use of Nile in Egypt. But there was hardly anyone bathing or swimming in the river while we were there. In Cairo the water was not easily accessible, except at boat landings. We were able to reach Mother Nile at Luxor in Lower Egypt. Further south in Africa's Bahir Dar city in Ethiopia, one is able to reach the river easily, and there were many who were on the river taking a dip. In Brazil we were fortunate to travel on Amazon River for hours. The huge metropolis of Manaus was really one-of-a-kind setting in the middle of the massive forest, and river journeys began from its port. At a lodge in the middle of the forest we were able to jump into the river under watchful eyes of lifeguards. Luckily there were no caiman or snake or piranha. Generally, flesh eating fish and river animals keep people away from using Amazon as freely as the rivers in India. On the southern end of Brazil, we got lots of water from the falls of Iguazu River when our tour boat went through a water falls. The spectacular falls is made of two major rivers, Iguazu and Parana. Most of the park is on Argentinian side, and their parks department has made a good job of constructing miles of raised walkway for visitors to enjoy the falls spread over a long distance. In the Brazilian side one gets lots of moisture from nearby water falls. On the eastern side of the Brazilian Iguazu City lies Paraguayan city of Ciudad del Este, across a bridge on Parana River. At Iguazu City crossing it is a bridge over a gorge, the river flowing several hundred feet below. It was remarkable to see that there was no border check or customs between these two nations. Ciudad del Este advertises itself as a shopping destination for tourists coming to visit Iguazu Falls. At a long distance from Brazil, during our visit to China we made sure that we got a glimpse of their most important river. So, we headed to Baotou in Inner Mongolia, where Huang Ho River was accessible, but hardly anyone was trying to reach the water. In cold climate, jumping into water is not fun. In Asia, the other important river's water we were able to use to offer thanks was Syr Darya at Turkestan Town in Kazakhstan. Just before one enters the historic city, the river becomes accessible flowing a few feet below the street level. In Europe, Danube River was reachable at Belgrade which cuts the city into half. Thus, Belgrade was able to control traffic from Central Europe trying to reach ocean via Black Sea.

Three of the very unique places on earth for visitors are the Antarctica, the Galapagos and the Easter Island. In Galapagos tourist couldn't meet local inhabitants as tours began and ended at the airport, bypassing a small town on the main island, with journey taking place in enchanting boats. Indigenous culture of Easter Island of Chile provided extra charm. In addition, some of the attractive places we visited are, Tasmania, Zanzibar, Lali Bela in Ethiopia, Gaborone of Botswana, Salt Flats in Bolivia, Namib Desert in Namibia, Machu Pichu in Peru, Venice in Italy, Durban of South Africa, Dhaka-Barisal River trip and Arian Kha River in Madaripur, both in Bangladesh, Four-day Karakorum Road trip through Himalayan Mountains from Xinjiang of China to Pakistani Kashmir, Leh, Imphal, Varanasi, Sundarbans and Kanyakumari in India are some of the wonderful places for tourists like us. To this we must also add Tierra del Fuego, the southernmost archipelago of the world, located in the southern tip of South America. Its cold climate, pristine air and penguins give a special flair. One must add the southernmost city of the world, Ushuaia. Ushuaia city center has a big map of Argentine southern province showing Falkland Islands, which

Argentinians call Islas Malvinas, as part of that province. Fishing, and increasingly tourism, are the economic backbone of the region. There is even a train to the Tierra del Fuego national park from Ushuaia. Antarctic is unique as this is the only place where one doesn't find any green of Mother Earth. Everything is covered with white snow with black stone mountains showing up at different places. It is also a place where wild animals, penguins, are not afraid of humans, just as in Galapagos. We hope Galapagos survives in its pristine stage. With growth of population in the main Island, we wonder how long Ecuador will be able to protect those unique animals. During our tour of Galapagos, Sachi became dinner buddy with Favio and Renata, a mixed Catholic and Jewish couple from Brazil. Decades later, we were in touch with each other. Years later we headed to Easter Island of Chile in the Pacific Ocean. It is one of the remotest places from any mainland. Their famous *moais* are awe inspiring. One wonders how did the islanders subsist with so little land to produce food and water for survival, yet they built huge *moais* representing humans. It is baffling as to how one can build such structures without heavy machinery, just as you wonder how those stone temples and pyramids were built in ancient Egypt, or how caves were curved out creating ancient cave statues in Ajanta and Ellora in India. Here are some pictures from our visit to Easter Island:

Visit to Antarctica Created a Penguin Statue at Ushuaia,

Argentina, the Departure Port

Pictures from Easter Island, Chile:

The Moi

Traveling in the Caribbean and Central America was always uplifting. We were frequently taken for locals, unless we opened our mouth. Most of the islands have a mix of Caribbean, African, Indian, Hispanic, European, and in some cases, Chinese ancestries. We crossed border in Hispaniola when we went from Dominican Republic to Haiti and back. We don't think we have ever seen any fortified international border like that. As soon as the bus entered Haiti, within minutes a solid steel door blocked the road without allowing anyone to see the other side. Port-au-Prince, Haiti's capital, looked lot like many Indian cities, especially of Eastern India, with people's color and colorful dresses. On our journey from Dominican, we got an English-speaking friend, who was the physician of the returning Haitian athletes of the Inter-American Games held in the Dominican Republic. In the Dominica Island of the Caribbean, eating tropical fruits gave us plenty of pleasure, but the presence of cricket team from India added extra attention for "Indians." Many thought we came to see a cricket match between West Indies and India. Had we paid more attention to events there, we would have certainly bought tickets. We haven't watched a cricket match in decades. One of the most difficult tourist place must have been El Salvador. Everyone warned us to be extra careful, including the hotel and the long-distance bus company. As we ended our early dinner at a restaurant located at the second floor across from a park in central Salvador City, the restaurant owner in his late thirties, speaking fluent English, with tattoos in his arms, said he must escort us to our hotel because "the city is too dangerous." At the hotel we reached after 6 pm, in bright sunshine. The hotel and bus managers were furious for our lateness. Thank goodness they were cursing in Spanish, but anyone could understand their expression. Someone later said, how did you know that the English-speaking guy was not going for ransom from you. Later, we realized it was very true, but in this case the guy protected us. At Guatemala City the taxi driver stole one of our carryon suitcases. At the police station, they were sure who the thief was, but they couldn't retrieve the bag. In 2019 October during a trip from New York city to Washington D.C. on a bus Sachi was pickpocketed most likely by the bus attendant, but D.C. Police didn't want to question the guy as he went to a nearby store to use my credit card as I got a text from my card. Life goes on. At every country in Central America, we were warned about thuggery, except Costa Rica and Aruba. It is no fun traveling if you have to be cautious of robbery or violence. From San Jose, Costa Rica we had an early morning flight to Nicaragua. Our hotel assured us of security. The taxi driver kept telling us, "If I see a thief, I will immediately take him to Police Station." Truly, Costa Rica was lot more relaxed than rest of Central America. We visited again in April of 2024, but his time with three generations. In the middle of such violence, political turmoil, Costa Rica has survived without an army! Wonderful! At Trinidad we were fully at home as in U.S. and Subcontinent, except it was a bit more Westernized than cities of India, and less lavish than America's. The African-Trinidadian family we stayed with, seemed to know more about Indian food and spices, than we did. Knowing that three "Indians" visiting from America, one Hindu ashram invited us for their service. Their knowledge of Hindu literature, and devotion to Hinduism, was intense. We learned a lot from them.

Here are few pictures from Costa Rica in April 2024:

Travel in two Island nations in South Asia was not that different from Trinidad – all "Indian" looking. This is the first time in anywhere we had to take a ferry from the airport to get to the capital Male of Maldives. Actually, the exit from the airport terminal is the ferry landing. It seemed possibly a third of the residents, and most of the workers were from Bangladesh, but the lingua franca was Hindi. Maldivian language is a dialect of Malayalam, the language of Kerala state of India. Maldives uses modified Arabic script, not Malayalam script. Maldives is a Muslim nation of hundreds of coral islands, with tourism being the backbone of the economy. Maldivians boast as a nation devoid of crime, although there were several military coups in the recent past. China loaned her money for some projects which were barely needed, but now has become an economic burden close to losing sovereignty over parts of her territory. Neighboring Sri Lanka has already given up sovereignty over a new city-harbor project. It was refreshing to see how Sri Lanka is trying to reconcile after a brutal genocidal war against her own indigenous Tamil speaking Hindu (with Christian and Muslim) minority. Sachi's 2017 travel to Jaffna, the heart and spiritual center of the Tamil north accorded the proverbial Tamil hospitality. One of the Hindu monks who stayed through the horrible genocidal war against Tamils by Buddhist-Sri Lankan military, showed us parts of the northern Tamil-majority areas. It was sad to see destroyed Tamil homes and properties, but pleasant to see how life has returned. Visiting children's orphanages of war victims gave us hope for the future. We were told that lots of new homes for Lankan Tamil genocide victims were built by poor India. A Tamil-Christian young girl of militant Liberation Tigers of Tamil Eelam (LTTE) killed young Indian Prime Minister Rajiv Gandhi by a bomb. Was it Rajiv's fault to send Indian Army at the request of LTTE to Sri Lanka to mediate between two warring parties, allowing self-rule for the Tamil minority? And visits to Colombo and the old historic Buddhist city of Anuradhapura introduced us to the pride of Singhalese. Anuradhapura is famous for having relics of Lord Buddha. Many believe that Buddha's message was brought to Sri Lanka by a Bengali named Atish Dipankar. A Sinhala individual told us how closely they are connected with Bengal of Eastern India and with North India. As a Bengali we are able to understand 80% of Sri Lankan national anthem as it is very close to Sanskrit, just as Bengali, Hindi, Marathi, Gujarati, Punjabi, Assamese are close to Sanskrit.

Anuradhapura, a Holy Buddhist Site

Monk, right, Who Survived Sri Lankan Tamil Genocide in Jaffna, Northern Sri Lanka

Destroyed Tamil-Hindu Home

Tamil Islamic Mosque, Colombo, in Sinhalese Sri Lanka, written only in Tamil and English

New Colombo Port Area, Almost Taken Over by China

Returning Home:

For people like us, returning home is a catch phrase, as we have many homes, and as many people consider us as part of them. Persons with mixed culture, mixed habits, and refugees are able to be accepted in many "homes," at the same time they could be unaccepted in many cultures, except for multiethnic and fatalistic India, and multiethnic settler-colonized America. It could be a burden as well. This is especially true when we crossed land borders between Bangladesh and India, speaking the same language, sharing the same culture. Once we were amused to get a tap on Sachi's shoulder. It was right in front of Jagatbandhu Institution, the school Sachi attended, barely two minutes' walk from his south Kolkata home, on his way to Gariahat Bazar for our daily morning shopping. In India and in many developing countries daily marketing for fresh vegetables and fish is a must, as we would argue in the absence of refrigerator such habits grew. He was surprised, as he didn't know the person. Sachi asked, "Can I help you?" He smiled and said, "You must be from outside." Sachi was a bit annoyed, "Why do you say so? Don't I look local?" Stranger laughed and said, "Don't you see that you are the only one walking on the sidewalk, all others are walking on the middle of the street." It turned out that the man lived in New York for two decades, then returned "home" permanently a few years back for his daughter to finish high school and grow up in India. Both father-daughter held American passport. The man should have worked in intelligence service! In 1992, Sachi sought an appointment to meet the local city councilor, a Bangladeshi-Hindu-Indian, member of the ruling Communist Party-Marxist. We wanted to talk to him about our work, and about his homeland going through an anti-Hindu pogrom. Getting an appointment with any Indian politician is difficult. They avoid people. Older brother, Dada, a medical doctor, was able connect us, as he had a big following among the locals. The councilman asked to meet at the Party Office in Fern Road, across from Jagatbandhu school. Accidentally, it was December 18 when they were offering prayer to Stalin. Stalin's picture was decorated with a big marigold garland. There was only a small number of party full-timers present at that early morning hour. The Councilor was very modest, who fled to India a few years back, and rose in Party through his dedication. All of them denied knowing about anti-Hindu pogroms in their homeland, although the Councilor said that his older brother with his family came to India recently and are residing with him. This was during 1991-1992 anti-Hindu pogrom in Bangladesh, but the councilor denied that his older brother's family fled because of the pogrom. We asked Party workers, if they know that Stalin was notorious mass murderer. Stalin killed my best friend Jay's great-grandfather. They denied knowing any of that. Ironically, India's southern Tamil Nadu State's head is named after murderous Stalin. He is also one of the most sectarian rulers of India, like some other Indian states.

Kolkata takes pride in leading Bengali and Indian nationalism during British colonialism, yet first with Congress, then with the Communist rule of West Bengal, Bengali language and culture were losing to English. It was also losing to Hindi language, India's National Language, and culture in natural intermixing of cultures though Bengal opted not to teach Hindi in school. Each year some noted writers and scholars organize a parade of Bangla Language and Culture with big banners and signs. Over the phone our friend introduced to one of the organizers, Dr. Rahman, a Muslim and a history professor and Bengali writer, who then invited us to join the parade starting from Deshapriya Park in southern Kolkata, barely a kilometer from our home. Sachi asked him how we will recognize each other in that crowd. He boldly said, "We'll figure it out." Sachi went there few minutes before start, stood almost at the front of the line, before elementary school girls and drummers had arrived, taking note and flicking his camera. A man behind him tapped his shoulder, "You must be from New York, right?" Sachi asked, "How did you guess?"

"Didn't you realize that you came before time, then were taking notes and pictures? Which other *Kolketia*, Calcutta resident, does that?"

Next day he invited Sachi to the infamous Calcutta Club, a one-time "Whites Only" club, near Maidan, the green space that acts as the lung of the congested city. The club still maintains some old rules. After Sachi entered to look for Rahman, Sachi was told he couldn't enter the Club with his ordinary Bengali outfit to which he refused to move. He was cheered by other workers. One worker with East Bengali/Bangladeshi accent was wearing dhoti. Sachi asked the guard, as to why the dhoti clad man is not being kicked out. He replied, "Mr. Jaga is a worker, you are a visitor." Unfortunately, Sachi had a similar experience at Romania's capital Bucharest.

At a high-end restaurant, in a big hotel, Sachi and his friend were told that their sneakers make them ineligible for a drink in that hotel. In 1993 when Sachi met Kolkata's Communist-Marxist Mayor Chatterjee, a Bangladeshi-Hindu-Refugee-Indian, at Kolkata Corporation Headquarter Sachi told him of the racist colonial traditions still being maintained in his socialist city. This was in the era of the Marxist-Communist rule. Mr. Rahman was a member of the club; thus, he could invite others there. As he entered the Club, he said "Meeting you earlier. I was afraid that you may challenge their rules." We had our tea and *singara* (samosa) at the Club. Later at his home Rahman introduced his wife Ratna, a Hindu, their daughter and her husband, Bishnu, a Hindu, and their baby. As India changes some new leaders are adopting colonial British-style apartheid, anti-India, anti-indigenous, anti-Hindu acts. In 2010s a new oppressed-group-dominated government of Uttar Pradesh Chief Minister Mr. Mulyam Singh Yadav approved new restaurants where Indian outerwear, sari, was banned, but not in the U.S. outerwear *The New York Times* reported, "Where Night Life has a Spice," on June 25, 2006. Sachi protested to Mr. Yadav about such colonial, racist standard. We wonder what the Indian independence leaders, including our grandma, grandpa, two uncles who together spent 17 years in British oppressor's prison for India's freedom would have thought about such slavery. Here is the article and our protest. We didn't receive any response from Mr. Yadav.

The New Times Article

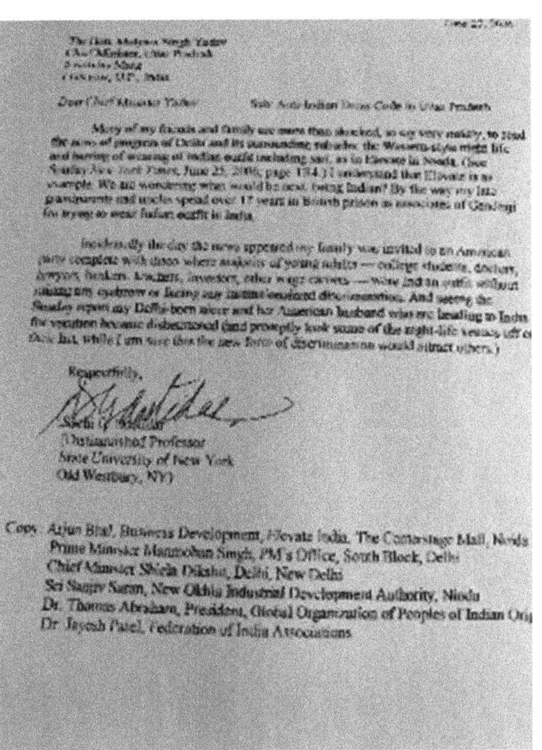

Protest Letter of Sachi with Copies to Many Leaders

Bridging many cultures has other benefits too. Because of our trips across Bengal border, a friend introduced us to Mr. Annada Sankar Roy, a famous writer, scholar and a top British Imperial Civil Service (ICS) bureaucrat who served many east and west Bengal districts before 1947 partition. His famous poem "You adults become angry if your baby breaks a glass doll, yet you are breaking a country apart" became a symbol of failure of politicians to keep India united. He loved Bangladesh and India, and a well-known figure in both Bengals. Hearing we have returned from Bangladesh, he ordered us to come to him immediately for a briefing. This became a routine that we will visit him before our departure and immediately after return give him a briefing. Friendship started when Sachi was in his thirties, and Mr. Roy, was in his seventies. His wife was a sari-clad White-American-Bengali, and author of children's book in English. In 1986 when we had our kids with us, she read her books to them, presenting her books. Mr. Roy was an individual who provided shelter at his home for secular Muslims who were attacked by Islamists, and fled Bangladesh. He was also one of the very few secular Hindu Bengalis who was keenly aware of minority plight in Bangladesh, and protested. As Hindu minority is vanishing from Bangladesh, he wrote an article there in a journal, "I am Afghan, but Hindu," telling readers that Bangladesh can soon become like Afghanistan, once a Hindu nation, but no one would believe now. He became a strong supporter of us for visiting our homeland. And, in 1994 when we released our tribute to Calcutta, now called Kolkata, from the South Asia Forum in the U.S. headed by Dr. Mohsin Siddique of Washington D.C. and Sachi of New York. Mr. Ray came to release the book along with the U.S. Consul General of Calcutta. Our book was named *Calcutta 300 Kolkata – Memoirs of a Diverse City: Overseas Tribute to Her on Her Tercentenary*. At that time name Kolkata was not officially adopted yet. Over a dozen nationalities wrote their tribute.

"Calcutta: 300: Kolkata. Memoirs of a Diverse City: Overseas Tribute to Calcutta on Her Tercentenary," Released in Kolkata by Annada Sankar Ray and U.S. Consul General in India

Paribartan (Change) Journal

"Pathan (Afghan), Yet Hindu" by Annada Sankar Roy

220

"A Collection of Light Verse" by Chandrahas Ray and Lila Ray, presented to our kids, 5th and 6th Graders, in 1989. (Lila Ray is White-American-Indian.)

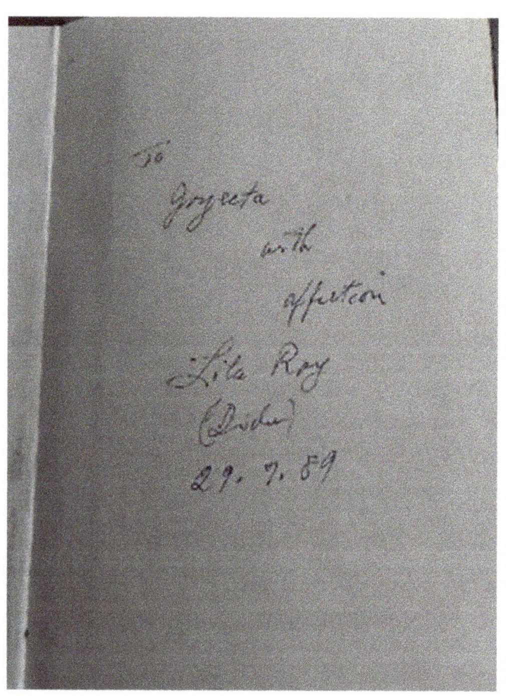

To Joyeeta with affection, from Didu (Grandma) Lila Ray, 29.7.89

*With Noted Philosopher, Writer and Civil Servant, Mr. Annada Sankar Ray
at his Home*

For Children of All Ages: A Visit to the Zoo, Poems by Lila Ray

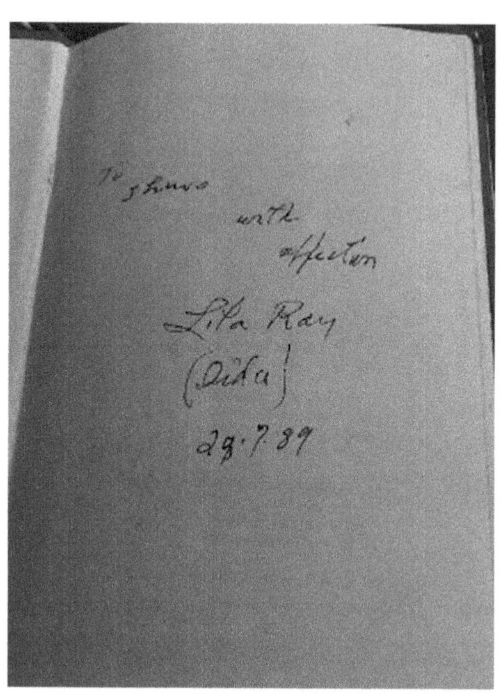

To Shuvo with Affection, Lila Ray (Didu or Grandma); 28.7.89

"Calcutta 300 Kolkata" was in honor of Calcutta's tercentenary. The book was published by South Asia Forum of New York and Washington D.C. The release was held at the former residence of the famous Bengali-Indian writer Sarat Chandra Chattopadhyay, in Ballygunj, now an event space. The book had authors of fourteen nationalities who called Calcutta home, and of several faiths, who wrote stories about their beloved city. During one of our visits, Mrs. Lila Roy, whom we called MashiMa or Maternal Aunt, doctors came to home as they found a health issue. Every time Sachi tried to leave the room giving the family private space, each time Mr. Roy waved at Sachi to sit down. MashiMa was American, but except for her skin color she was Indian and Bengali by all measure. She spoke to us in Bengali. She presented our kids her two children's books, first reading to them. Dr. Siddique and Sachi decided to look for a publisher in Kolkata so that the book will be available in India in affordable price. Quite a few well-wishers gave us leads to various publishers. This was a time of unchallengeable power of Communist rule in West Bengal State and in City of Kolkata. This was an era of one-party rule of West Bengal. It taught us how the reality and propaganda vary. In a city that was in decline due to communist rule, it revealed how a region can go down socially and economically. All private publishers were eager to get the job, while the government publishers had no interest at all. One editor of a government-funded Bengali daily said in dismay, "If you want real result and timely commitment, please look for a private publisher. The private sector cost will be a fraction of our cost, besides, even after requesting a meeting with a public printing office, the manager may not show up. And there is nothing I can do even as the editor of the government publishing house." On the contrary, every private publisher was eager to get the business, and often said, "Please get the job done here in Kolkata. It will create jobs here." The editor then referred us to another government publication office in Chitpur Road in downtown Kolkata, who published many government publications, including school texts, school award books, and government journals. After Sachi arrived, he was asked to wait as the manager didn't arrive yet, and Sachi took the opportunity to read many of their publications. He was excited to see a district award booklet. As he went through the booklet, it struck him to be too patriarchal and anti-women as all the award recipients' names appeared with only father's name, i.e., like Sachi, son of Bibhuti Bhusan, with mother's name totally absent. He went to another booklet from another district, and it had the same format. Our meeting with the manager was cordial, and he said that their government cost will be many times higher than the private sector. This was baffling to us. The manager gave Sachi couple of publisher's names. As he was leaving, Sachi showed him the mistake of the booklets with only father's name as guardian of a student. The Marxist guy got furious, saying it was their tradition. He was joined by a few other male workers, with the lone female worker supporting Sachi in feeble voice. This was a real lesson of reality and rhetoric.

Two important journalists, Mr. Ghosh and Mr. Dhar, both Bangladeshi-Indians who wanted to help our project but communal and self-destructive politics of West Bengal prevented them to help. We realized interest of all neutral journalists increased because of our family's intense connection with their homeland as well as our Kolkata book project was a Hindu-Muslim, India-America joint effort. Here are letters from journalists Ghosh and Dhar.

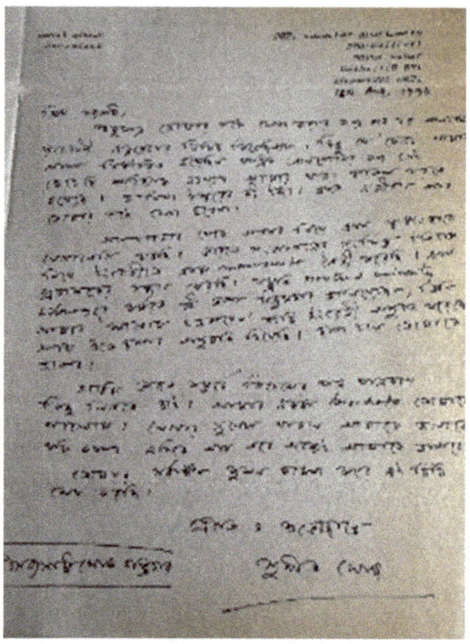

Letter from Journalist Ghosh

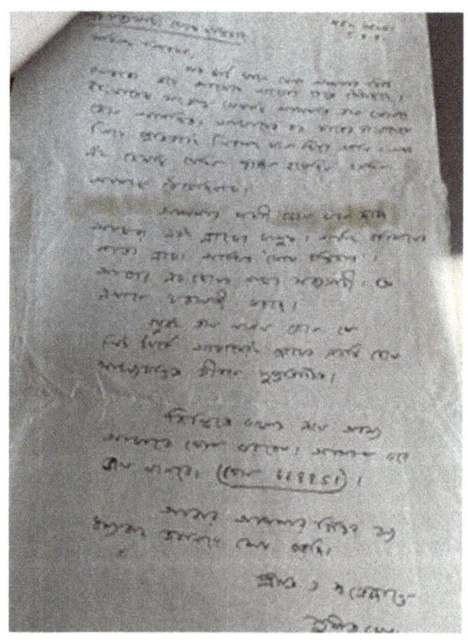

Letter from Journalist Ghosh

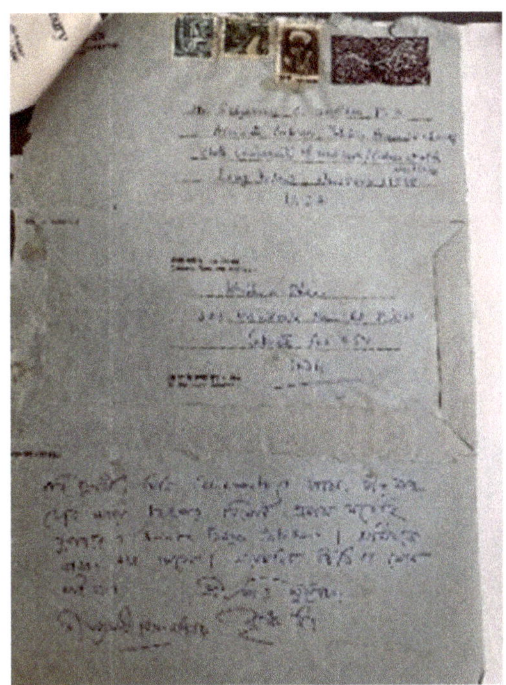

Letter from Journalist Dhar

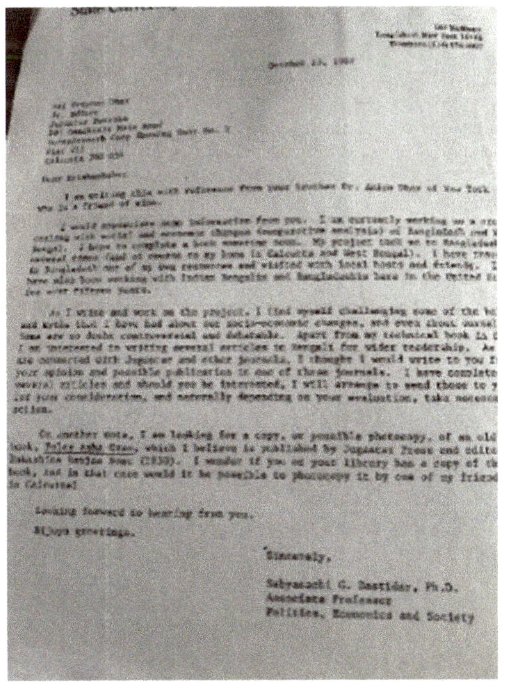

Sachi's Response

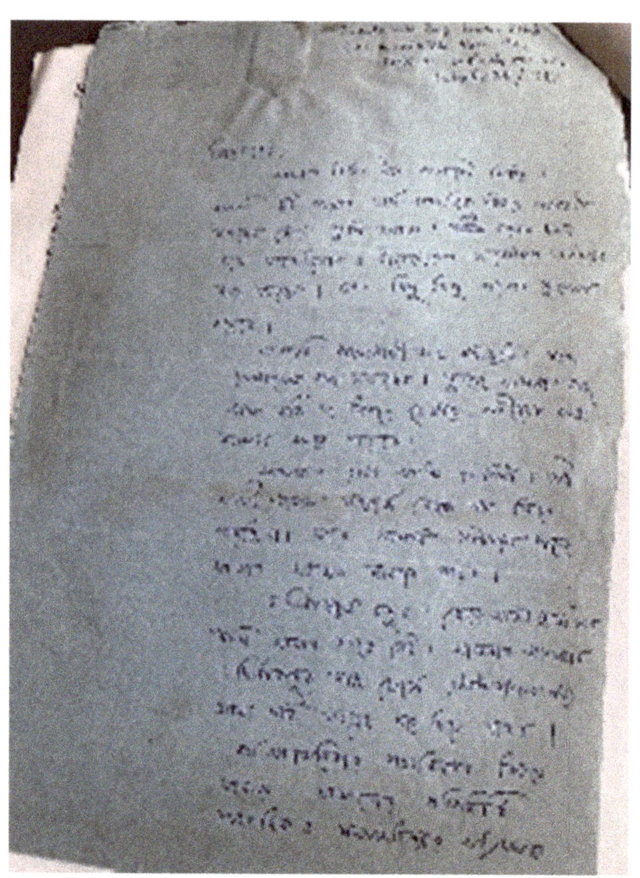

Letter from Journalist Dhar

"Calcutta-300-Kolkata" book project taught us many lessons. Our proposed book project was mentioned by several publications including *The Statesman* daily of Kolkata as did American weekly India Abroad. Response was remarkable from diverse nationalities.

Last time Sachi saw Mr. Annada S. Roy as he fell ill, and his helper piled up his entire library for discarding. He asked Sachi to come back to take some books. But his next visit was too late. One of his books Sachi has, *Bidagdha Manas* (Suffering Mankind), Dey's Publishing, Kolkata; 1997. Here is the last book we collected from him, and a handwritten note from Mr. Roy telling Sachi how those minorities living in Bangladesh has to organize and people like us have to help them.

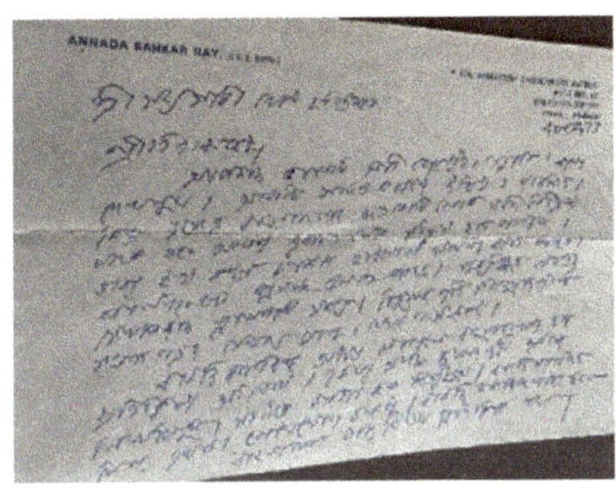

Hand Written Note from Mr. Annada Shankar Roy, ICS,
to Sabyasachi (Sachi) Ghosh Dastidar

Unknown to Sachi Mr. Roy knew Mr. Prasanta Chandra Mahalanobis, founder of the Indian Statistical Institute, a famous person in India and abroad. In 1970 Mr. Mahalanobis wanted to establish a new way of creating cheap housing using modular method, but wanted to start brainstorming with a young person. Out of many applicants, he selected Sachi. It was a very big honor, but Sachi couldn't accept the offer as he was planning to join his doctoral work in the U.S. Mr. Mahalanobis then gave Sachi an offer that he couldn't refuse, but making Ma unhappy. Sachi will keep working for the Calcutta Metropolitan Planning Organization (CMPO) as usual, but will spend breakfast and dinner with him. The Institute will provide Sachi food and shelter. So, he had to live on Barrackpore Road campus in northern suburb. Sachi went to work from there and returning back, and on Saturday he will head home, as in India people worked from Monday through Saturday, with Saturday being half-a-day of work. This routine continued for several months, until his plan to join Florida State in 1971 August was finalized. His boss at the full-time work, Mr. Badal Sarkar, the Chief Town Planner of CMPO, was happy that Mr. Mahalanobis chose Sachi to be his assistant, and was happier that Sachi didn't quit his job as a junior planner. Mr. Sarkar chose Sachi to be his assistant, among many other applicants. Mr. Sarkar or BadalDa, Older Brother Badal, as everyone called him, was world famous playwright, actor and director. Planning was his day job, but passion was acting, directing and writing, He was from an interfaith, Hindu-Christian family.

He introduced us to his plays. Until Sachi finished college, watching plays and even going to movies was beyond our ability. All of those waited till he had a job. So, when BadalDa would have a new play, Sachi would buy 12 to 16 tickets, for his brothers' and sisters' families and friends. For the first show BadalDa had a captive audience, and Sachi had secured seats. It was great experience! At CMPO Sachi became friends with draftsman, Sandip, a Bangladeshi-Hindu-refugee, who was a connoisseur of art, culture and stamp collection. He would stand in line for the First Day Cover of every stamp released by Indian Post Office. Sandip and Sachi would go to pay birthday homage to the Bengali poet Mr. Kazi Nazrul Islam at his house on CIT Road in central Kolkata. A long line of people carrying flowers, stretched several city blocks was a norm for devotees to touch Nazrul's feet, who was otherwise invalid and not able to communicate. At CMPO Sachi met Tapan, a Kolkata native and a geographer, with whom our friendship still continues for over 55 years. He is one of the families in Kolkata who have been holding annual autumn Durga Puja festivities for 380+ years in the northern Baghbbazar neighborhood of Old Kolkata. From the festival in 1969 we have supported to keep their tradition alive. Late 1960s was the time of the Left to raise its militant head. Many of our friends, all Bangladeshi-Indians who didn't live in East Pakistan (Bangladesh) and fled to India, joined in hoards the Communist Party of India, Communist Party-Marxist and Communist Party-

Marxist-Leninist, commonly known as Naxal, Socialist Unity, and more. In 1960s we supported them. Like the Islamists from whom they fled, their target in West Bengal was Hindus. They started attacking the bureaucrats, for no reason. Just kill them, was their attitude. Our brother-in-law NareshDa started receiving death threats from terrorists. He was an official of a public tea company. No one could figure out why he was a target. Sachi offered him service as his bodyguard. For few months, Sachi accompanied him to his office at Dalhousie Square, from where Sachi would walk to his CMPO office. Sachi accompanied him back home, which made Sachi leave office on time, not working extra hours or hanging out with friends. End of the Communist rule in West Bengal came a few decades later, closing over 50,000 factories, and cleansing of educated, young, and uneducated poor, who fled to other states and to overseas.

One of the sad parts of Indian politics has always been tinged with sectarianism, especially that hurts eastern and northeastern states. One of the true racist Indian laws was the Nehru-Liaquat Treaty between the Congress Party Government of India headed by Prime Minister Jawaharlal Nehru and Muslim League Party Government of Premier Liaquat Ali of Pakistan that prevented settlement of East Pakistani, now Bangladeshi, Bengali-Hindu refugees in India, killed and cleansed from East Pakistan, but allowed full settlement for similar Hindu-Sikh-Jain refugees from West Pakistan, now Pakistan. Noted Indian Freedom Fighter Dr. Shyama Prasad Mukherji resigned from the Indian Cabinet on April 8, 1950, as did another Bengali Minister Mr. K. C. Neogy, for Nehru's racism, protesting one of the most racist laws ever enacted in India, especially targeting Hindu Bengalis who fought against British colonial oppression, and oppressed first by the British, and then by Pakistani and Bengali partisan Muslims. Federal Indian Government also passed a Freight Equalization Law affecting West Bengal and eastern India which provided raw materials for Indian industry from eastern India with subsidy for industries elsewhere, but not the other way, draining assets from the east and northeast. Mr. Ranajit Roy cautioned India, eastern India, and West Bengal of the upcoming economic disaster in his book, *Agony of West Bengal*, and *Dwangsher Pathey*

PaschimBanga (West Bengal on Its Way to Destruction) which was criticized not only by Nehru's Congress Party, but also by the rising left of West Bengal, the Communist Party of India, Communist Party of India-Marxist, Socialist Unity Center, and many more left parties. Even the nationalist Bengali papers of West Bengal didn't realize how wealth transfer was going to work from eastern and northeastern states of India to the west, north and south India.

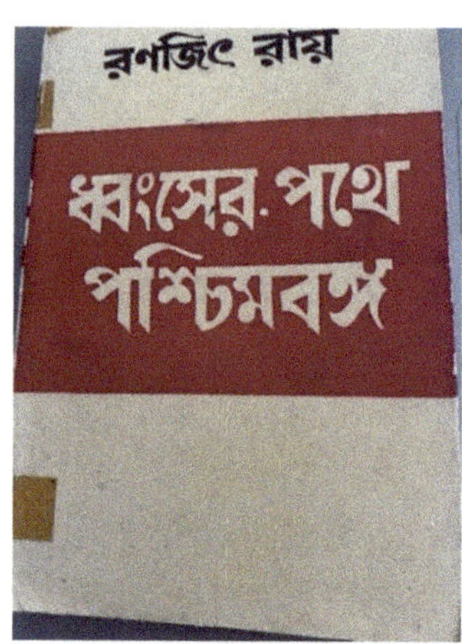

"Dwangsher Pathea Paaschimbanga" (West Bengal on its Way to Destruction) by Ranajot Roy. The book predicted correctly as to the future of West Bengal State but despised by then ruling Congress Party and future ruler Communist Party of India-Marxist.)

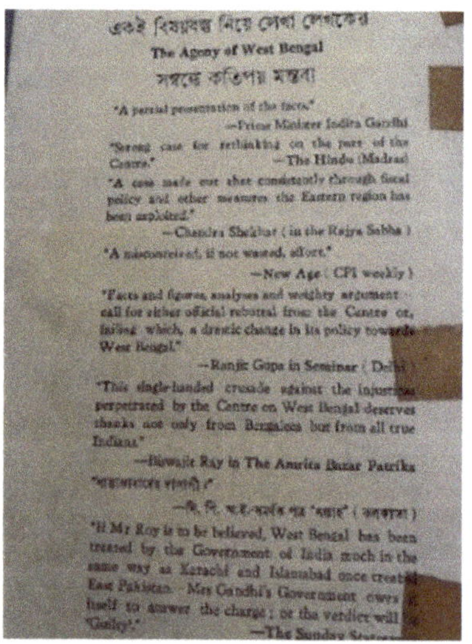

Some comments on the Book

Indian Northeast:

One of the regions that is always overlooked by tourists in India is her northeast. There are many reasons. Among them are poor infrastructure, distance, time from major cities by air, train, and bus. Transport is always full, plus long-time insurgency – funded by India's neighbors, British colonial racist laws prohibiting entry of Indians. It is a nightmare unless one is an illegal visitor. Laws for Indians against buying land, investing and settling down, adds to parochialism. Fear of illegal Bangladeshi settlers, lack of hotels, and tourist infrastructure adds to the problem. Then there is the fear of unknown. Only recently, possibly after a new Indian party came to power in 2010s, this area is opening up to tourists and investment. In our travel through Assam, Arunachal, Nagaland, Manipur, Meghalaya, Mizoram and Tripura, we found the area to be spectacularly beautiful, friendly people, and soothing to our eyes. Unfortunately, sectarianism and democracy in India have steered peoples to further subdivision, and separation, often funded by foreigners. Thus, Assam's identity crisis gave rise to five separate states with five separate identities. And in each of those states there are potential for many more sub-identities.

A Village Home in Arunachal

A Community Area in Arunachal Pradesh State

In 1986 elementary students Joyeeta and Shuvo came for a stay of six months in Kolkata, India and receive the warmth of their family, especially of grandma Thakurma and Uncle Barro-Jethu, Oldest Uncle, a medical doctor caring for the very poor. Kids joined a local St. Mary's Christian school near our home, while Sachi worked at the Indian Institute of Management. We headed to Manipur and Assam in far northeast. Manipur's capital Imphal, an ancient city, sits on Loktak Lake in the middle. Surrounding are Changi, the Mapithel, and the Mulian ranges of Eastern Mountains separating India from Burma (Myanmar). As one lands in the airport, it has a spectacular view of the Imphal City, and the valley. During monsoon, the lake becomes twice its size collecting waters from the mountains. Manipur had one of the oldest and longest monarchies of the world, stretching for over 2,000 years, until monarchies were abolished in India by Prime Minister Indira Gandhi. There are lots of places to see in Imphal, among them a bazar, where all the sellers are women. World's propaganda won't believe this. There was a new edible water creature of the lake that we thought of buying, but the ladies just laughed at us. Manipur's neighbor Myanmar is an attractive place, especially because it has had a long cultural connection with her Bengal neighbor. Our fathers worked in Rangoon, as did our uncle ChhotoKaka, Young Uncle lived there in post-independence India. After General Ne Win overthrew the civilian government in 1962, he deported all

"Indians" or Indian-looking citizens to India. India accepted them – Hindu, Muslim, Sikh and Christian. This is a illogicality of India. Uncle's house was next to a park. After many tries, we couldn't locate that. Possibly it has a new address, and new name. Rangoon is where the last Mughal Islamic emperor was imprisoned by the British, where lies his grave and that of his wife, revered by many Indians. Many of Rangoon's (Yangon) Buddhist Viharas have spectacular architecture. It takes days to see them. Yangon has British Colonial look as is downtown Kolkata or Mumbai. A few of the Hindus, mostly Bengali, stayed after mass deportation, or couldn't be deported. During our visit one old Durga Mandir temple was celebrating its 125th Anniversary in 2013. The crowd welcomed with warmth, and invited to another site where the Ramakrishna Mission (RKM) center was established before Burma's separation from India, but was shut down by the military dictator. Now it is open with a Buddha statue. The RKM Center and its hospital for the poor was closed by dictator Ne Win. The newly reformed government has asked RKM to return and open their hospital in the devotee-free city. A Bangladeshi Hindu at the Durga Mandir introduced to the history of the temple. He invited for a Burmese-Bengali sumptuous dinner at his home. One of the most punishing journeys anywhere in the world must be the Yangon to Bagan train ride. A pleasure trip became a punishment. The train track follows Irrawaddy River. The distance was about 500 miles. It was basically a tourist train, but tourists were fooled. For a 12-hour nonstop journey the train was "only six-hour" late. There was no provision to buy food on train, or before departure. Because of train's late arrival we missed our morning tour at Bagan, located on Irrawaddy River. Train trip's misery was compensated by the exceptional city with 10,000 Buddhist temples. Trip to the city was very special. Its bazars are worth visiting. Flying is the best alternative. One can take boats to Bagan from Yangon. A little further north on Irrawaddy is the second largest city of Mandalay, a onetime home to many "Indians" and "Bengali" natives. At many bazars there were many jewelry stone sellers, telling visitors that it costs less in Myanmar, than overseas. Actually, during our first attempt to visit Burma in 1980s by Sachi and Shuvo, we were given a visa by the

New York Consulate, and then stamped passports at the last minute saying we "must spend at least $100 dollars a day."

He told that "there is no way one can spend so much money in Burma." He also said, "You can buy gems with extra money." Seeing that stamp of daily spending, we immediately asked the Consul to cancel our visa and return our money, to which he agreed, but asked us to come back. Every time he gave us a date and time, he was absent, but we weren't allowed to talk to anyone else. Finally, we gave up. He won. During our trip from Kolkata to Yangon and back, the flight was full. It was a pleasant surprise to see so many Burmese traveling from their nation with little connection to rest of the world.

Brochure of the 125th Anniversary of the Durga Bari Temple of Yangon, Myanmar (Burma); 2013

Front of the Shrine

At a Buddhist Temple in Burma (Myanmar)

In Assam, a stop at Kaziranga National Park was extraordinary, and a must see for any tourist. It should have been one of the most visited sites in the world. From Jorhat airport a taxi brought us to the National Park through a pristine green landscape of Assam State of Northeast India. The park is famous for one-horned rhinos. But more importantly, one can ride an elephant for sightseeing. There are sightseeing trips on the backs of elephants, as well as on jeep. So, we took the early morning ride on two elephants, one with a long tusk, the other with no tusk. Joyeeta and Sachi took the no tusker while Shefali and Shuvo took the elephant with a huge tusk. After lunch it was time for another trip by jeep through marshes and thick forest. Those were fantastic trips. In the evening came the Park boss to chat with Joyeeta and Shuvo. Joyeeta demanded him another ride next morning on the elephant with big tusk. So, next morning we had another elephant ride. We saw wild rhinoceros, water buffalos, deer, boars, monkeys, ducks, eagles and many other wild birds, plus so many beautiful flowers and trees. Here are some pictures of Kaziranga Game Reserve, Assam, India:

Trip through Kaziraanga National Forest, Assam State, India; 1986

Wild Rhinoceros

Taking a Tour on Elephant Back

A Family of Wild Water Buffalos

Standing with Our Elephant Friends

Leaving for the Tour

We were so impressed that we wrote a letter to Assam's Chief Minister. Surprising us, he replied back. Getting replies from top officials in India is a big honor. Here is our letter and Chief Minister Mahanta's reply:

Sachi's Letter to Assam Chief Minister Mahanta

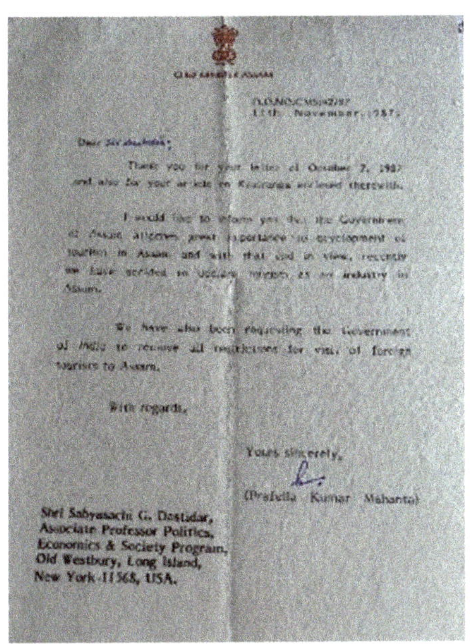

Chief Minister Mahanta's Reply

Visit to Kaziranga was followed by a trip to the old Kamtapuri Mandir (temple), near Guwahati, Assam in Northeast India.

In the Mandir Complex in Guwahati, the State Capital

A Temple in Assam

An Entry to a Palace in Northeast India, 1986

Kaziranga was so enchanting that Sachi wrote an article in April 1987 for the *International Travel News*. Its wildlife experience was similar to wildlife experience in Tanzania in Africa in 2015.

Women Carrying Water, as in Many Parts of the World, on Road to Selous Game Reserve, Tanzania

Selous Game Reserve, Tanzania

Mid-Day Resting of Lions at Selous Game Reserve, Tanzania

Selous Game Reserve, Tanzania, a Bird Carrying a big Bone

Dar es Salam is a nice city with immense traffic, for a city of that size. That congestion reminded us of congestion of Dhaka, Bangladesh. Zanzibar Island tour was a tour of mixed African, Arab, Persian, Indian and European cultures. Who could imagine that Sachi's student's mom would come to see us at Stone Town of Zanzibar City. Mom told us stories of Zanzibar, and what to see and what to avoid.

Dar Es Salam, Tanzanian Capital

Zanzibar Street

Zanzibar Island Market Area

While walking down through Stone Town, we were invited to chat by an Indian-origin shop keeper whose family migrated from Kutch region of western Gujarat State of India 350 years ago. The man spoke Kutchi, Gujarati, Hindi, Swahili and English as his first language. There are many persons of Islamic faith as well as Christians in Zanzibar. In the mainland our reserved trip to the famous

Selous National Park posed some problem as the tour operator, an African woman, couldn't accept a few of our $100 notes, as they were not issued in the same year. We were in deep trouble, as she didn't accept credit card. After a closed-door discussion with her assistants, she agreed to offer us the tour, mostly on trust. We had to send her the money after our return to the U.S. This was a big risk on her part. She said, "We felt like you won't cheat us. My father was Gujarati Indian," yet that was a big risk with 80% of unpaid fee. It was a big honor for someone completely unknown trusting with a huge loan. As soon as she got the funds, she told us that she knew she could trust us, and invited us for a second visit. This was a National Geographic-type experience driving through the park with deer, monkey, elephant, giraffe, fox, boar, hippo and so many birds and animals. We realized their raptors must be very strong as one was flying with a big animal leg bone to a treetop. We were getting restless as we didn't see any lion or tiger after driving for hours. All of a sudden around 2 PM in the afternoon, the van stopped and the guide whispered, "Look to your front." And there it was, a huge pride of 15 lionesses and one lion! They were taking a midday nap, mostly on their back, with legs up in the air, in deep sleep, except for the lion, who was dozing. The guide then pointed out to a carcass saying, "These lions must have killed that buffalo to fill their stomach. Now they are sleeping." Our balcony at the forest lodge had a great view of Rufiji River full of hippos and crocs. Residents were careful to go to the riverbank for fear of attacks from crocs. So, although it is a tropical country, no one was jumping into the river, as in India.

In the neighboring Ethiopia, it felt like another India. Many of the men and women looked like Indians, especially women's outfit looked like sari, and men looked like Indians. Christianity reached Abyssinia, now called Ethiopia, well before it reached many parts of Europe, which Ethiopians reminded us. This is the only culture which was able to resist Arab-Islam or Euro-Christian transformation. Baher Dar, Axum and Lalibela were great places to visit if one is interested in history and culture. There are other places to visit for natural beauty.

Shrine at Axum, Ethiopia

Axum, Ethiopia

Nile River, Bahar Dar, Ethiopia

Bahar Dar, Ethiopia

Lali Bela, Ethiopia

Bet Mariam Church, Lali Bela, Ethiopia

Church Design, Lali Bela

More of Secluded Northeast India:

Back in northeast India, after Guwahati, Assam's capital, we headed to Shillong, Meghalaya State's capital. It sits on Garo-Khasi-Jayantia Range inhabited by Garo, Khasi, and Jaiantia tribes, where the British built a capital for Assam, as it was cooler than the plains. They often compared the area to Scottish Range. With restrictions on Indian educators, British was able to Christianize many locals, and changed their local Eastern script to English script. This trip was a disaster for us as Indian Prime Minister Rajiv Gandhi planned to take a trip to

Bangladesh for a South Asian Nations' Conference, leaving Shillong by helicopter. It was very special for the locals as Meghalaya was being put on world map. Shillong didn't have an airport. Its closest airport was in Guwahati, the largest city in the Northeast. Every hotel room was booked. Finally, at a restaurant a local Bengali came to rescue, and took us to a hotel slightly off the road. We were glad for his help. For centuries Shillong had large number of Bengalis as it is adjacent to Bengal. In India every region has populations of adjacent groups for millennia. There are lots of Garo, Khasi and Jaintia peoples in Bengal. But as India's and Hinduism's pluralistic democracy influenced India, and as Muslim separatism succeeded, so rose regional, sub-regional and sub-sub-regional sectarianism, very close to a form of racism. We planned to meet our friend Khona's uncle in Shillong. Few years back Garo Christian thugs murdered her uncle, a noted doctor, for being a Bengali Hindu, but the family lived in the city long before the arrival of murderers. Their family home goes back to 1800s long before Garos migrated into the newly built capital. Still, once a new district is made with an ethnic plurality, some minorities in India become empowered to murder others. This is the other side of unknown India and "Anti-Hindu" mind.

Now, many of the northeastern states see tourism and industry to develop their economy, and create jobs. There are lots of nice places to visit all over the world. So, we told a minister, unless they get rid of visa, and Inner Line Permit for Indians and foreigners, and unless states allow other Indians to live, invest and buy property, why would anyone care to come to their state, invest or visit? There are tons of hassle-free equally-magnificent places in India and overseas. Why would one spend extra time and money to visit natural beauty with restriction, when the same is available across the border, and they are happily welcoming visitors. It will be impossible to be economically successful with all these man-made barriers where one feels unwelcome.

Because of our travel in the Subcontinent, especially traveling with family, we were lucky to come in contact with scores of individuals who were eager to bridge a divided region, convulsing with pain of partition. They are many of them. Among them are Dr. Mohsin of Washington D.C., Mr. Lokendra Kumar Sengupta, an Indian nationalist from East Bengal imprisoned by the British many times, Ms. Mahasweta Debi, a writer and activist, the family of Dhirendranath Datta who was the first to propose Bengali to be the national language of Pakistan when majority Pakistanis spoke that language, Dr. Mamoon, a historian of Dhaka University, Prof Dr. Anupam Sen of Chittagong University, Prof Nabila of Pakistan, Buddhist monk Rev. Bodhipal Mohathero of Bangladesh, Christian activist of Bangladesh Teddy Rozario, Gen. C. R. Datta of Bangladesh Liberation Force, dean Dr. Khan of Peshawar, Pakistan, Mr. Sib Narayan Roy, a leader of India's atheist movement, promoter of Bengali language in India and editor of Jiggasa, and his fellow movement members Abdul Malek of Bangladesh, and Prof Dr. Ghulam of London, Oxford History Prof Dr. Tapan Roy Chowdhury, history Prof Dr. Amalendu De, journalist Mr. Shabbir of Pakistan, Indian Parliamentarian Dr. Tharoor, a former Deputy Secretary General of the U.N., Mr. Sudhindra Adhikari of Kolkata, a Christian thinker and an Indian nationalist, Mr. Khurshidul, a former communist activist of Bangladesh and a free thinker, Buddhist monk Bimal Bhikkhu, a Bangladeshi refugee in India, to name a few. There are others. We couldn't meet the real ambassador to humanity and promotion of democracy in his native Pakistan Mr. Dhirendranath Dutta. He, his brother and son were brutally cut into pieces in 1971 while alive by the Army of Islamic Republic of Pakistan devoid of humanity. Their bodies were never found. No Pakistani was held responsible. Neither West, nor Muslim-majority nations sought any punishment of murderers and for genocide, nor the refugees living in India. We were honored to meet his surviving granddaughter Aaroma at our home in New York and at her home in Bangladesh. Shockingly, Mr. Datta's home and homestead became a target of confiscation of indigenous Hindu minority assets in Bangladesh through Pakistan's "Enemy Property Act" (Bangladesh saved the same act to confiscate indigenous assets with slightly different name, "Vested Property Act") of a person who promoted democracy and stabilization of Pakistan, and helped the Bengali identity of East Pakistan. See YouTube for Aaroma's interview at Partition Center's Ispad1947 channel.

Aaroma Dutta

Here is a gift (to Sabyasachi on January 11, 2008) from progressive Mahasweta Debi, a Bangladeshi-Indian, of her journal Bartika, critiquing Communist-Left Front's aggressive move to take over peasant land by killing 17 peasants in Nandigram, Medinipur district. Left was planning to give the land to a foreign industrialist. During a trip to Nandigram to help a school we were stopped by local activists from entering the village. We entered after lots of negotiation.

"Bartika"

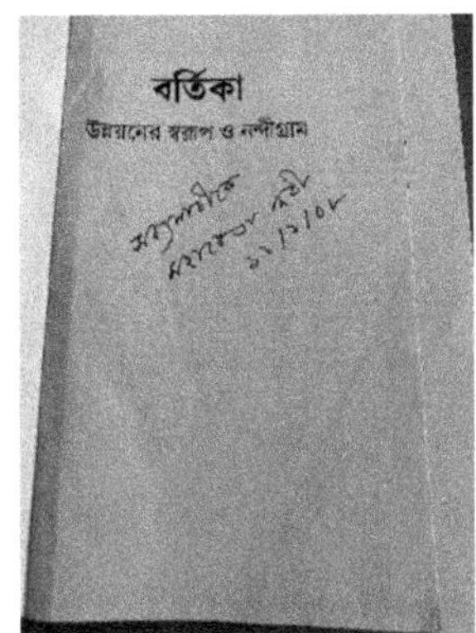

Post-Partition Kolkata:

In 1998 Mr. Lokendra Sengupta wrote in Bengali, which was translated in English by Sachi's colleague Prof. Dr. Judith Walsh the following, especially about our humanitarian work.

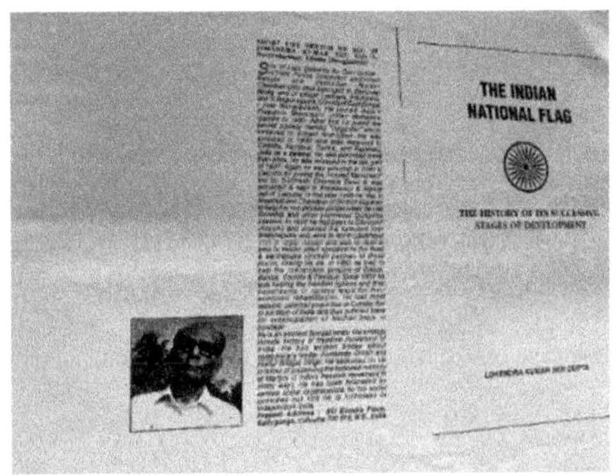

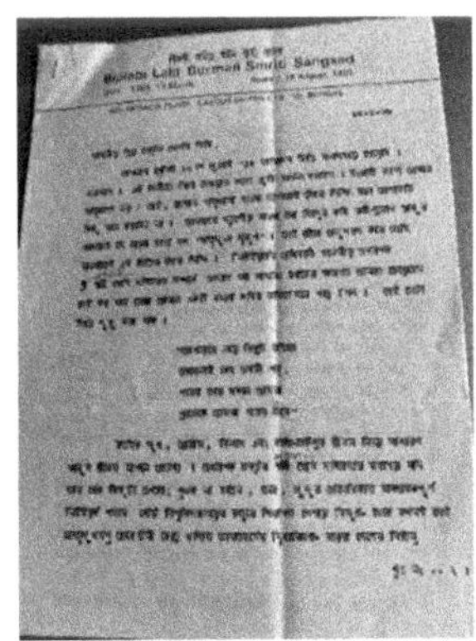

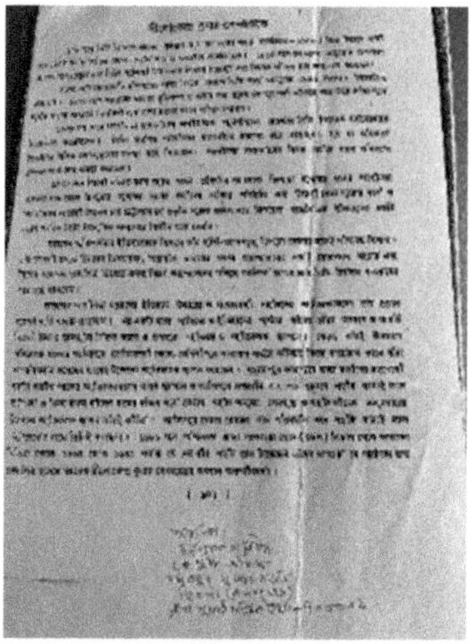

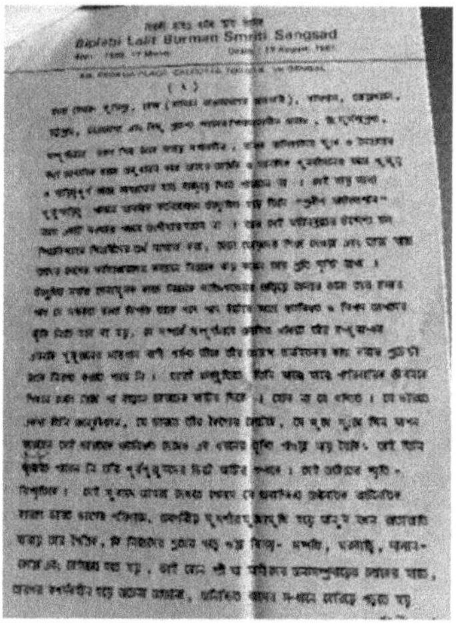

(১)

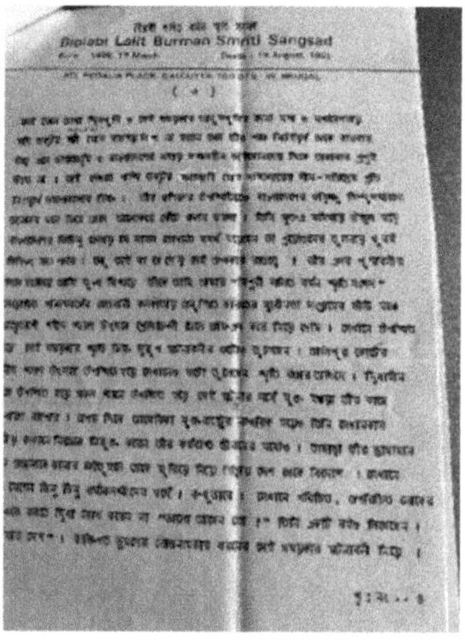

(৮)

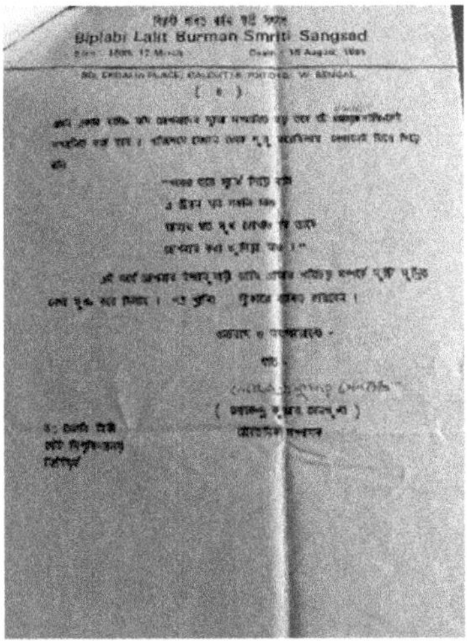

Biplabi Lalit Burman Smriti Sangsad

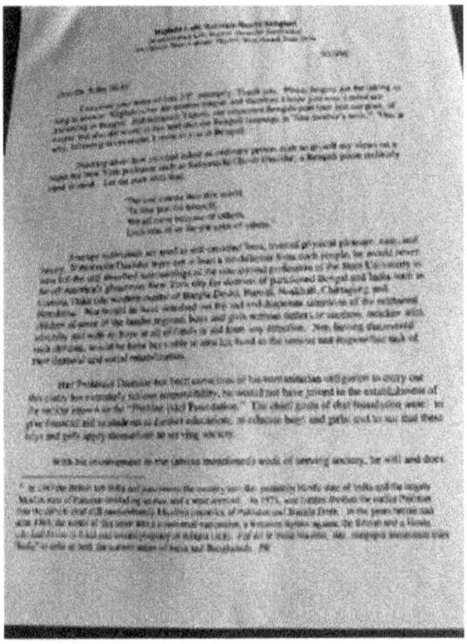

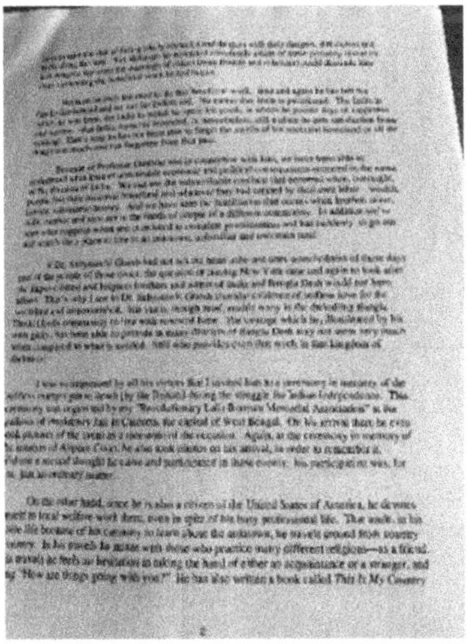

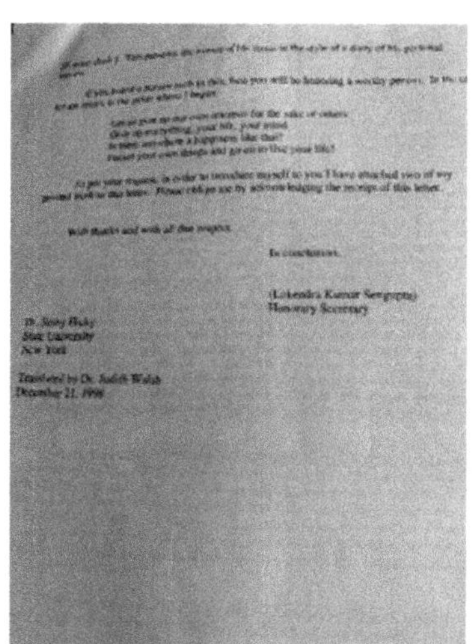

Here is a booklet we received from Mr. Sengupta and about a dozen anti-British Indian Freedom Fighters, almost all East Bengali or Bangladeshi Hindus. They introduced our work getting invitation by the ruling Left. All Indian Freedom Fighters were demoralized as West Bengal, run by Communists, didn't introduce any historical information on colonial British oppression, or settler-colonial Turkik, Arabic and Persian Muslim ruler's abuse of India. A booklet of Indian Freedom Fighters published in Kolkata, with pictures of Indian Freedom Fighters hung by colonial British Adinistration was presented to us.

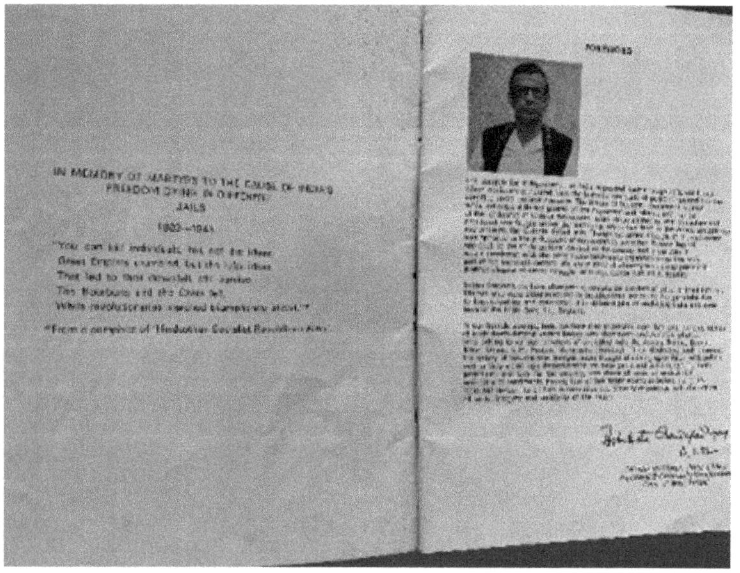

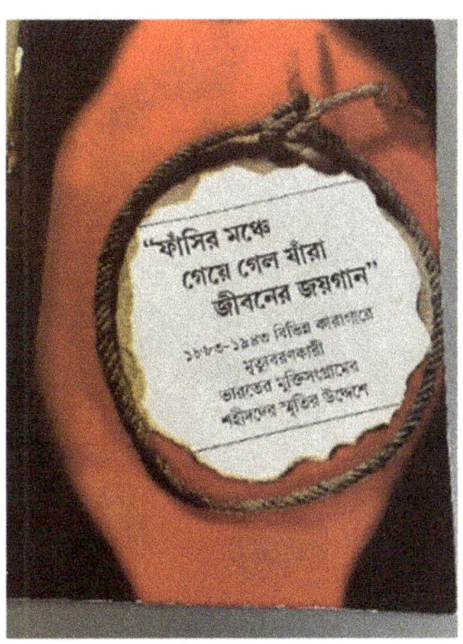

"Those who Sang the Song of Victory of Life Headed to British Execution by Hanging"

Some of the Martyrs of British Execution by Hanging for Seeking India's Independence

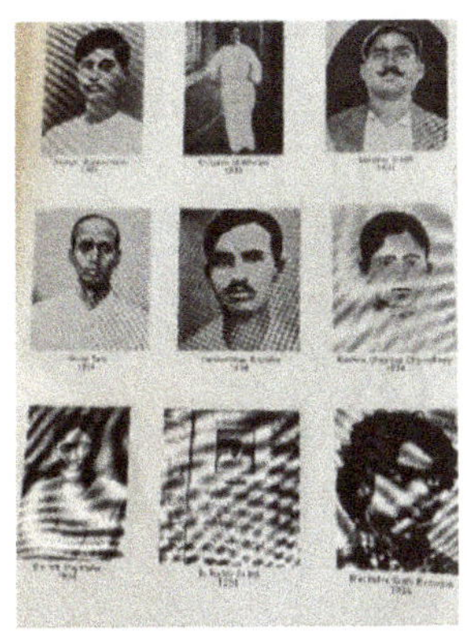

Some of the Martyrs of British Execution by Hanging
Who were Seeking India's Independence

In India rarely the politicians ever respond, much less meet a constituent. Before decline of Kolkata as an international stop, her airport was the most important stop in India. Thus when Pan Am started its "Around the World" route

Kolkata was its stop, not Mumbai or Delhi. So when older brother MejDa flew to America in 1950s, he flew out of Kolkata airport. After coming to America two decades later, we realised how difficult it is to go to Kolkata for a short visit. So we wrote to many airlines, and two of them, Scandenavian and Singapore, responded favorably. Sachi wrote to Indian authorities. Some Federal authorities replied, as well as one of the Communist-Marxist's Bengal parliamentarian Mr. Somnath Chatterjee.

Here is Hon. Chatterjee's letter:

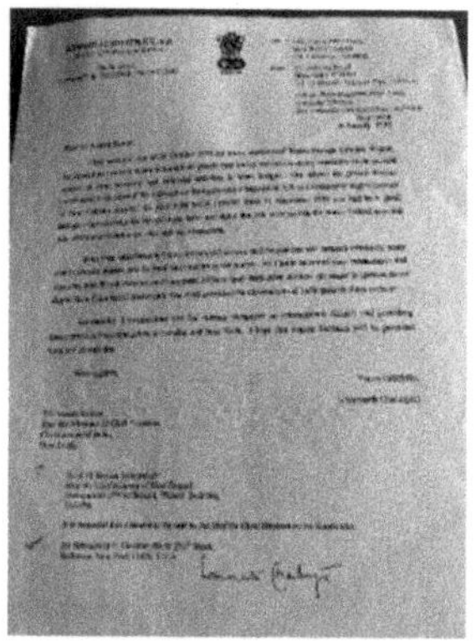

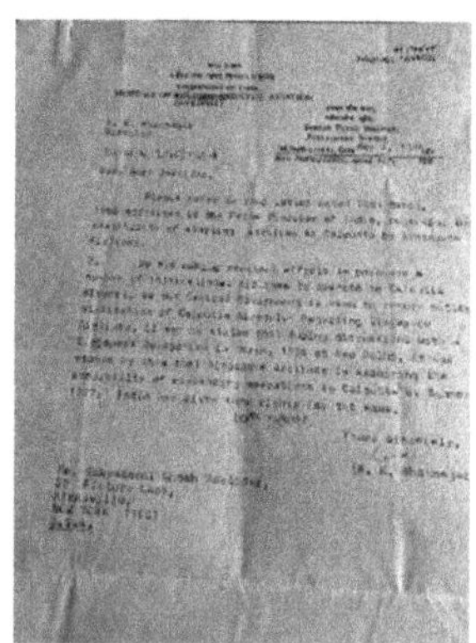

Dr. Amalendu De, as a young man in East Pakistan (now Bangladesh) fell in love and married a Muslim girl, Nasima Banu, in 1950s. They had to flee to India because he didn't convert to Islam and Ms. Banu was happy with that. De became an eminent historian. As a leftist he wrote many books as to the future of minority non-Muslims in Muslim-majority nations, and on democracy in developing nations. The "narrow-minded Hindus" warmly accepted their marriage, but not by the "broad-minded Muslims" and her educated family even after 50 years of marriage. Here is a letter Dr. De wrote to Prof. Dr. Hicky of New York:

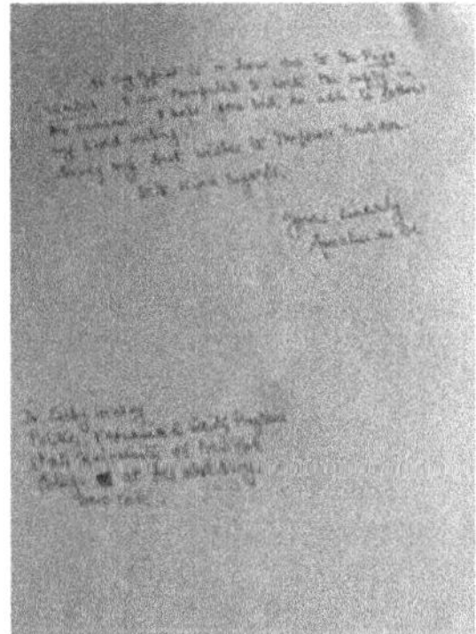

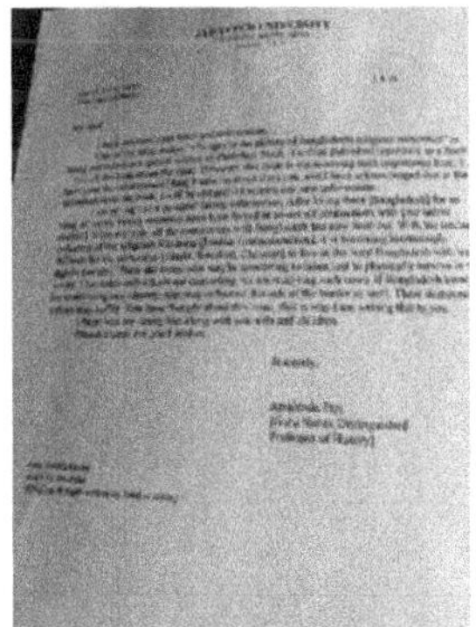

English Translation

It is really surprising that so many very important people started connecting with us. We were unaware of such a suppressed emotion on the part of Bengali intellectuals, almost all East Bengali or Bangladeshi-Indians. Here is a letter from an eminent writer and thinker of India, Mr. Santosh Kumar De, a letter in Bengali and its translation, and emotional appeal in Bengali trying to reach us during our visit to India.

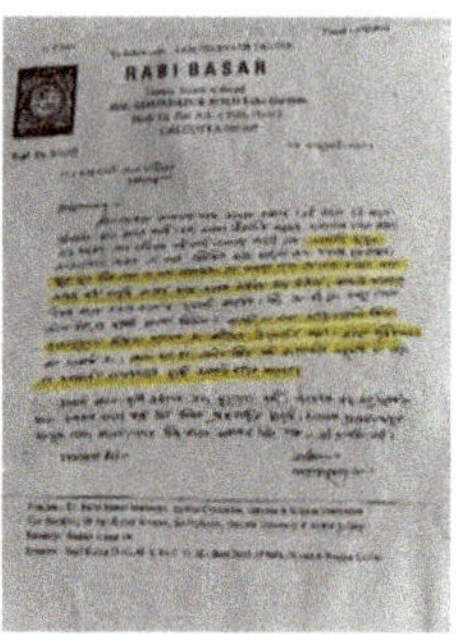

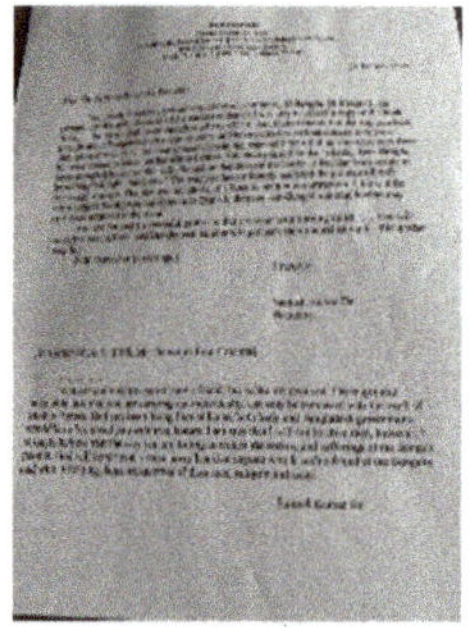

A Bangladeshi-Buddhist monk, Rev. Bimal Bhikkhu "kidnapped" us from our meeting in Kolkata to visit his new monastery east of Baguihati, just south of Kolkata International Airport. It was being developed as a student dormitory mainly for Buddhist Chakma tribal refugees who were fleeing their homeland in Bangladesh, the Chittagong Hills District, which was being forcibly colonized by Bengali Muslim settlers who were being given free land and transport by

Bangladesh Government with financing from intolerant nations and monarchies, as per monk's presentation at the U.N. No plains Indians were allowed in Chittagong Hills during British era. Pakistan and Bangladesh both nullified the law, but not the tolerant-fatalist-coward democracy of "Hindu" India. It was wonderful to be with Chakma boys. On our way we passed a famous Muslim Darga shrine of a non-native who was able to convert many Hindus into Islam. We were given a wonderful welcome by the keepers of the shrine where we offered prayer with flower, and they offered us *prasad* or blessed food. Several hundreds of feet from the monastery a truck blocked the road, and no request from the Buddhist monks – who were also carrying supplies – didn't budge the workers. As we threatened to move the truck ourselves to the side, the driver obliged. Several residents told us that this is a new norm of harassment by the Muslim shrine. Seeing is believing. The monk presented us a booklet he presented at U.N. conference for protection of indigenous peoples. Has anything changed since his 1993 speech? Nothing.

In many ways Kolkata is a remarkable city. Most major Indian cities are majority-minority, that is, the majority linguistic population of the state is minority in their major cities. Thus, Kolkata is where majority population is not of West Bengal origin. City offers schooling in at least a dozen languages. In 1960s the Board of Education in Kolkata listed possibly dozens of languages in which one could take School Final exam. It will be like New York City or Houston offering K-12 education in dozens of languages as medium of instruction. The city is home to a diverse group of people. In early sixties, Kolkata's population was almost half Pakistani-Bangladeshi-Hindu-refugees. City has been home not only to many Brits, but also Armenians, Jewish, Chinese, Tibetan, Nepali, Burmese, and other nationalities. One of her major river ports is called Armenian Ghat (steps) and a football club is Armenian Club. There are lots of Jewish institutions in the city. One road is called Synagogue Street, and another Ezra Street. As a young college student Sachi worked on Ezra Street, and later became friends with one of their descendants of Ezras living on Long Island. During a 2017 trip to publisher Firma KLM, he visited a famous Kolkata institution: Elias Meyer School & Talmud Torah of Calcutta (See https://empireslastcasualty.blogspot.com/2019/01/elias-meyer-school-talmud-torah-of.html). Besides a warm, impromptu welcome, the world, especially the anti-Jewish world would be happy to learn how a Jewish school is educating majority Muslim students.

Majority Muslim Students of Jewish School, Elias Meyer School & Talmud Torah of Kolkata

Noted writer Achintya Gupta of Kolkata, Sunit Ghosh of Delhi, history professors Dr. Mamoon and Dr. Salahuddin of Dhaka, Mr. Surjangshu Bhattacharya, a Bangladeshi-Indian refugee and President of Headmaster's Association of West Bengal, Mr. Rai Mohon Pal, a Bangla-Indian refugee from Comilla and Editor of Indian Journal of Civil Liberties in Delhi, the Head of Victoria Memorial Museum of Kolkata, and many more invited us to meet with them.

Here are some of their letters of invitation:

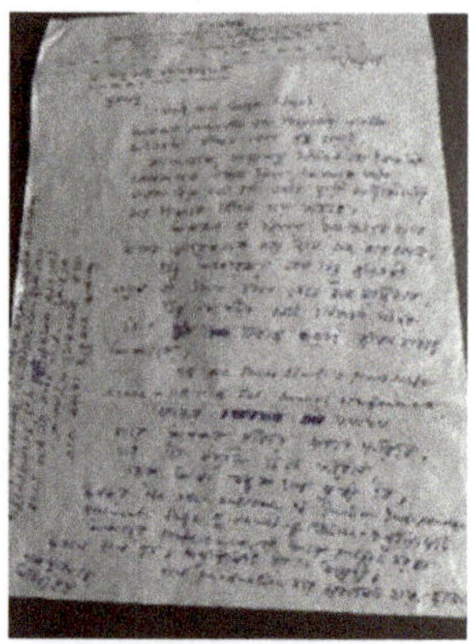

Letter from Achintya Gupta

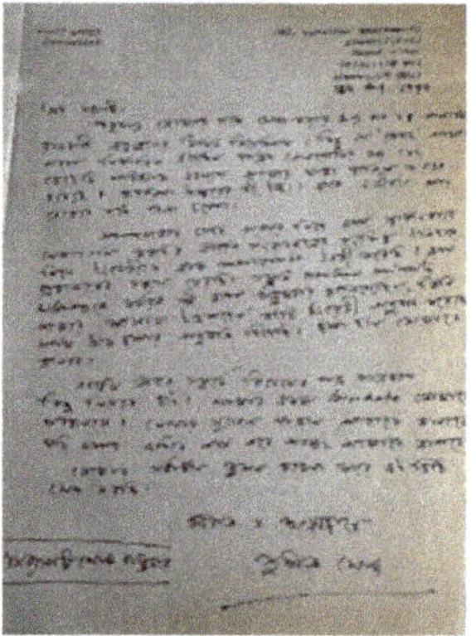

Invitation from Editor Sunit Ghosh

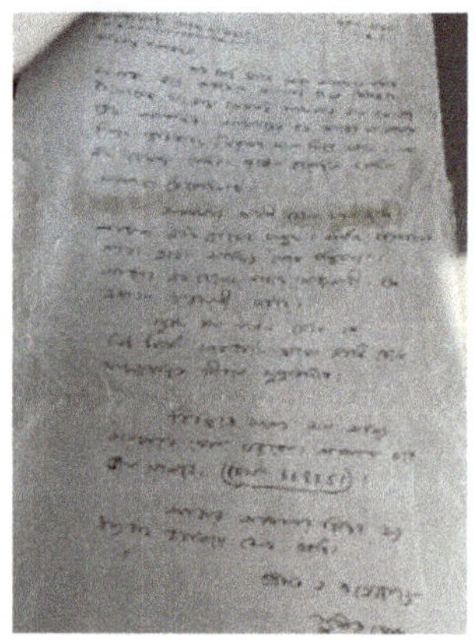

Letter from Sunit Ghosh

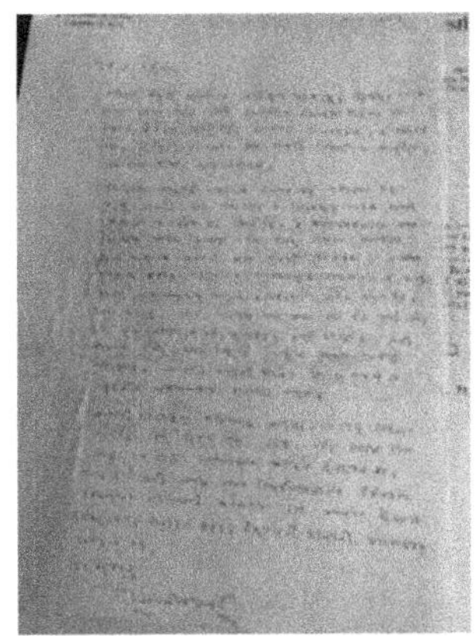

Letter from Dr. Mamoon

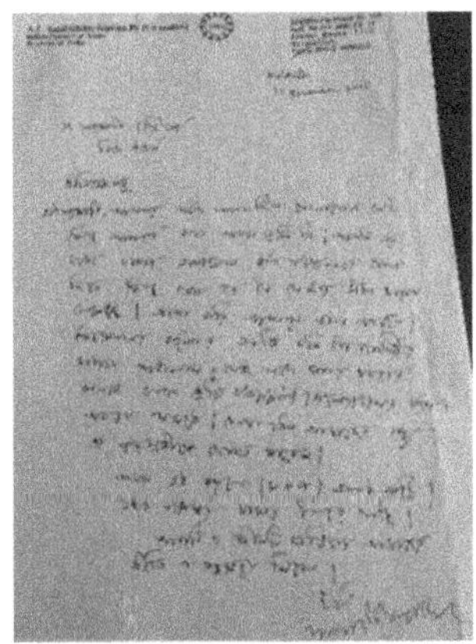

Letter for Dr. Salahuddin

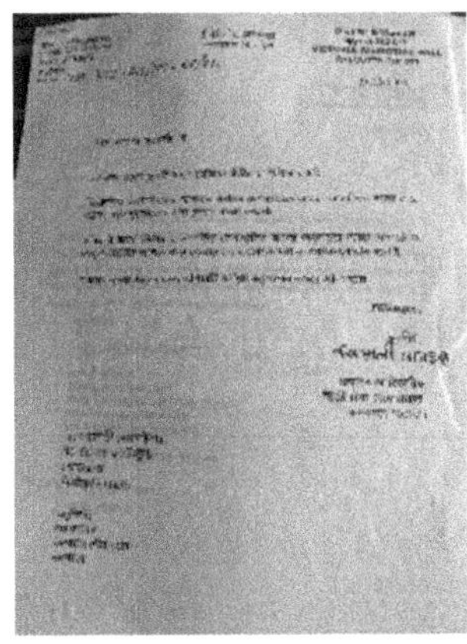

Letter from the Head of Victoria Memorial, Ms. Sengupta

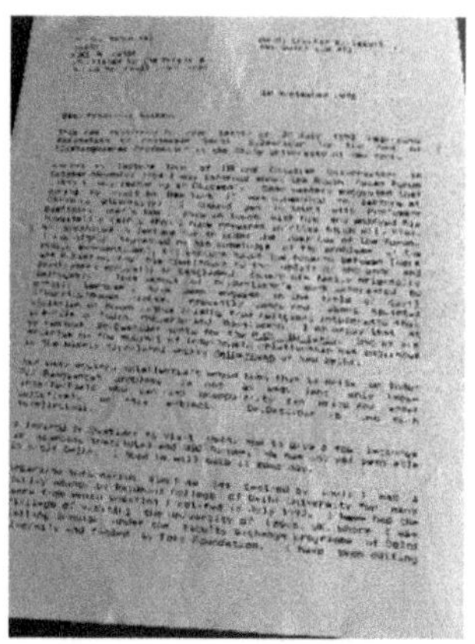

Letter from Mr. Rai M Pal to Prof. Dr. Selby Hicky, p 1

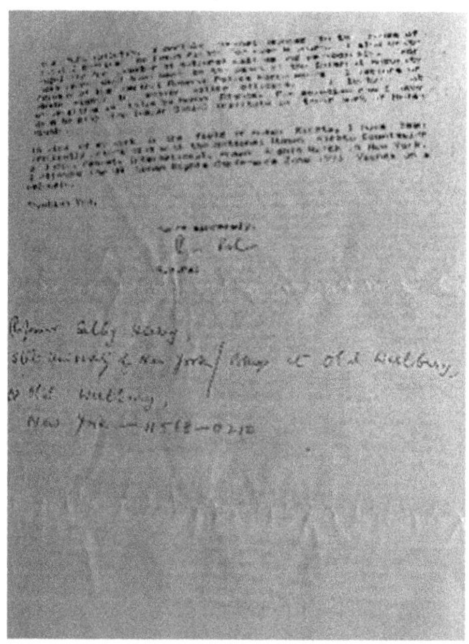

Letter from Rai M Pal to Prof. Dr. Selby Hicky, page 2

Fortunately, or unfortunately, during our travel we would often run into people believing in us more than our capability. Thus, in Pirojpur, in southern coastal Bangladesh one persecuted minority Hindu father thought we had the power to influence national administration to force them to arrest a gang of Muslim terrorists who kidnapped his daughter, then abused her, and finally murdered her by dumping her injured body into a canal. Killers were roaming free when we were at Pirojpur. The daughter was the first in her family to finish college. She was from an oppressed-group of peasant family. What can one say to a grieving father when the State does not arrest because the abuser is from the majority community? Situation is at least many times worse than black Americans in America highlighting the Black Lives Matter movement with Whites marching with them. Many secular Muslims are protesting these. During and after the 1992 anti-Hindu pogrom we received many letters and notes. This is sad, very sad! Here is a letter from Bangladesh giving first-hand and intimate description of anti-Hindu pogrom. This gentleman had inside knowledge of people engaged in ethnic cleansing and taking over Hindu minority property, free of charge. Here is the letter handwritten in Bengali:

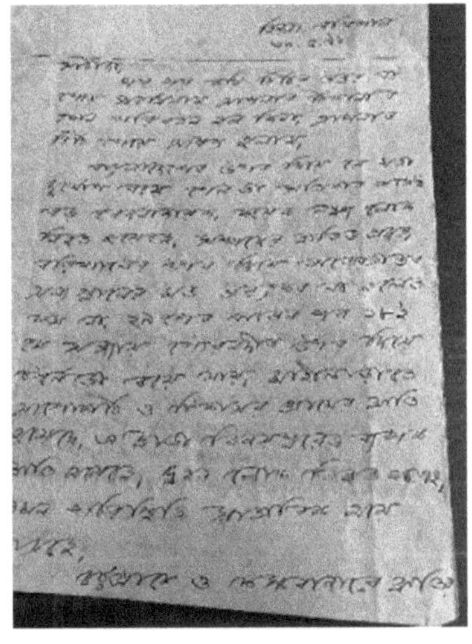

Trip to coastal areas like Pirojpur, Bangladesh must be the opposite of visiting European and Western cities; socially, culturally, economically, and politically. Lack of material comfort was compensated by the warmth of the local residents. Welcome to the area has always been accompanied by conch blowing, ululating, and garlanding with home grown flowers. During one visit we didn't realize that the host had given us their bedroom, while they slept in the living room floor. If we ever looked for hot tea, there were half a dozen volunteers to bring six cups. First time we went to southern Bangladesh was to assess building a school. Local indigenous minorities and secular Muslims had come under attack in that area by terrorists for a long time. As a matter of fact, a local Member of Bangladesh Parliament acted against Hindu minority when he killed them by the hundreds, torched homes, and violated many women, during the extermination campaign against Hindus and secular Muslims in 1971 genocide by the Army of Islamic Republic of Pakistan, and its Bengali Islamist allies, while the world, the oppressed and Indian-settler Hindus looked the other way, except Prime Minister Indira Gandhi. The killer politician was sheltered by Pakistan after Bangladesh independence in 1971. During secularist pro-independence party rule in 2008 War Crimes Trial convicted him. Eventually, Probini of New York built a school, and by 2020 the school became a vibrant place with an ashram, health care center, dormitory, a temple, vocational training, guest space, and so much more. This is where we made our life's one of the best journeys with Rev. Monk's "Kandari," meaning warden, boat on a day-long journey to Uzirpur village in Barisal district of costal Bangladesh, near our ancestral home. Monk also urged us to help a school at the nearby Swarupkathi island where cyclone Aila demolished a school. At that Martyr's Memorial Girl's school at Swarupkathi, a farm area in 1971, Army of Islamic Republic of Pakistan and its Bengali Islamist allies corralled, then killed 135 Hindu minorities trying to exterminate them from Islamic Pakistan. Why didn't the world protest? Why didn't New York and Kolkata protest? Silence is support for atrocities! Here is the first school we built at SriRamKathi, Pirojpur, Bangladesh:

Probini Foundation Built a new Brick-&-Concrete Building,

Replacing this old School Building

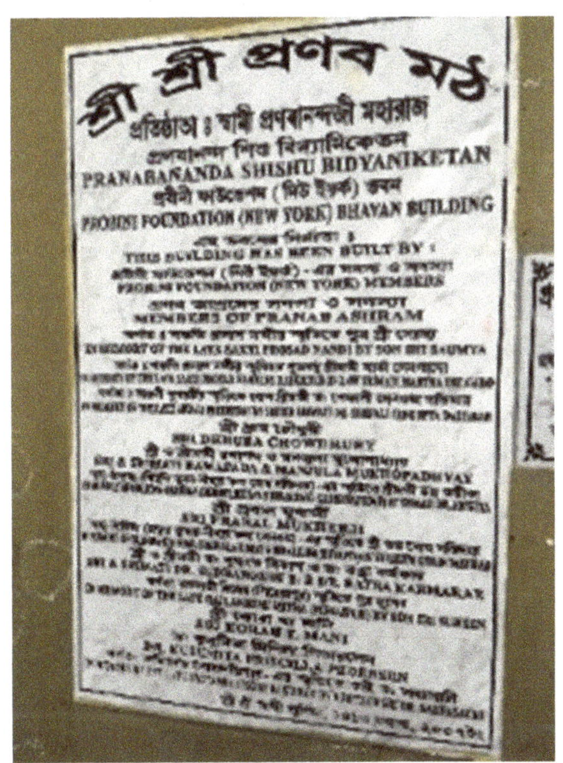

School Builder's Tablet at Sri Sri Pranab Moth Monestary

Probini Foundation Built School at Pirojpur, Bangladesh

Sri Sri Pranab Kandari Boat School, 2019, for all Residents

Dastidar Picture Hanging in Room with Deities, Shocking Dastidar Family

The Boat School

An Honor Citation from Pirojpur, Bangladesh

It was wonderful to see the turnaround of the Martyrs Memorial School from nothing to a place to live, learn, visit and offer prayers to the martyred. Here are pictures of school after a hurricane destruction of classroom and dorm without roof, and later building after reconstruction.

Classroom after Storm Destruction

Dorm Room Without Roof. Can one Imagine its Plight during Tropical Monsoon?

Rebuilt Probini Building

List of names of 135 Hindus Murdered. Many Bodies were Dumped into the River for not to Trace them

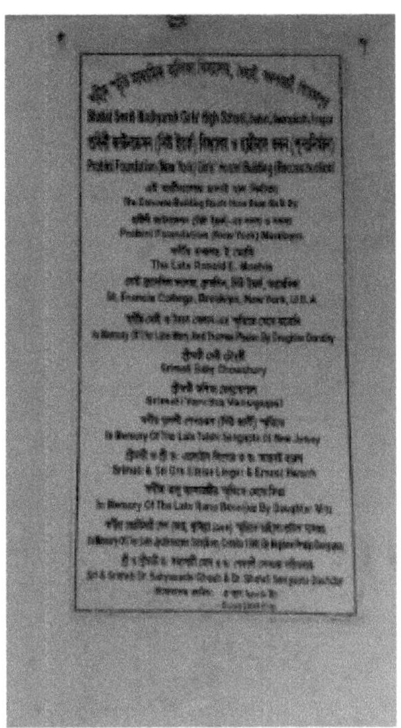

Builder's Tablet of Probini Foundation of New York with Donors Names

Our parents always believed that miracle can happen today in Koli Yuga, not just in Satya Yuga or the Era of Truth. During a trip from southern coastal district in Bangladesh, we were heading towards Jessore-Benapole Bangladesh-India border crossing, heading to Kolkata for a flight to New York. Bus from Pirojpur District stopped at the Rupsa River ferry, before Khulna City. At the ferry we were told that the Khulna District Transport Association is observing a strike. As a result, no public transport was available. Walking 40 miles was out of question, as was taking cycle rickshaw as we'll have to change every few miles, besides there is always the threat of pro-strike ruffians who could easily beat up the rickshaw driver and its passengers. Our friend, monk Sunil, who had traveled with Sachi to "protect" him, found a "Press" van who was willing to take Sachi to the border at ten times the usual fare. The van came to deliver daily papers, and was planning to return back north. Generally, during strikes press and ambulance are allowed to move.

Sachi was given the passenger seat in the front, his carry-on was hidden between front and second row, and at the trunk area sat two helpers sitting on their knees facing front. The driver was telling stories of the local area. Sachi was enjoying the greenery of Mother Earth. The road was empty in the world's densest nation. Midway, around Daulatpur or Dighalia, we saw a street barricade, and the van slowed down, hoping that they would remove the barricade seeing the "Press" sign on the windshield. This was not to be. A mob came running to the van and tried to pull the driver out of this seat while some others tried to push the van on the roadside ditch. The driver whispered in a hurry, "This is the end of my trip. I hope this is not end of me!" Initially seeing the mob, he asked Uncle Sachi to remain quite as Sachi's accent may give his identity. As the man was being dragged from his seat, while the engine was running, Sachi couldn't remain silent and hollered, "Why are you beating him? He was giving us a ride for our urgent trip?" We don't know why, but the mob stopped beating the driver. On the opposite side of the road emerged a young man, possibly in his mid-twenties, short, skinny and handsome, but not looking like a leader. He asked the mob to stop pushing the van, and asked Sachi, "Sir, are you a journalist; or, a writer?" Sachi nodded his head. Then the boy ordered the mob, not to beat the driver and not to push the van into the ditch. He then waved the driver to leave. The driver and helpers kept asking, "What happened uncle? We've never seen such a thing. We were afraid for our lives too." As they dropped Sachi off at the border, three young men, all Bengali Muslims, said with folded hands, "Namaskar, Greetings, Uncle Kaku, have a wonderful journey." This time we came from Pirojpur. On an earlier trip north from Pirojpur, monk Sunil took Shuvo and Sachi to the best journey of their lives to Uzirpur village in Barisal District by a boat named Kandari, as mentioned earlier. We were heading to a poor area of the 4th World nation, but 1st World in terms of warmth. Scores of people welcomed us with traditional Bengali *baran kula*, welcome wooden plate with a flat basket full of grains, soil, water, grass, lighted lamp, touching our forehead, chest and lower body. There was welcome *dhunuchi naach*, dancing with bucket full of smoldering cocoanut husk and incense, a traditional dance at festivities, ululating and putting vermillion dots on our forehead. In this poor area, our foundation has built a school and an orphanage. During our trip we were told that villagers have built a home for the widows and abandoned women named after Shefali, and a Sanskrit college building named after Sachi, surprising us. They have hung Shefali's picture with world, Indian, Bengali luminaries, and deities, and put Sachi's profile in a marble tablet at a school honoring us. During a walk, they showed us a big surprise, a baby goat, that was to be sacrificed for visitor's honor. We said we will be honored to let the goat go free. They obliged. What an honor!

Opening of a New School Building at Uzirpur with Computer Class

Shefali's Picture Hanging with Deities and Luminaries

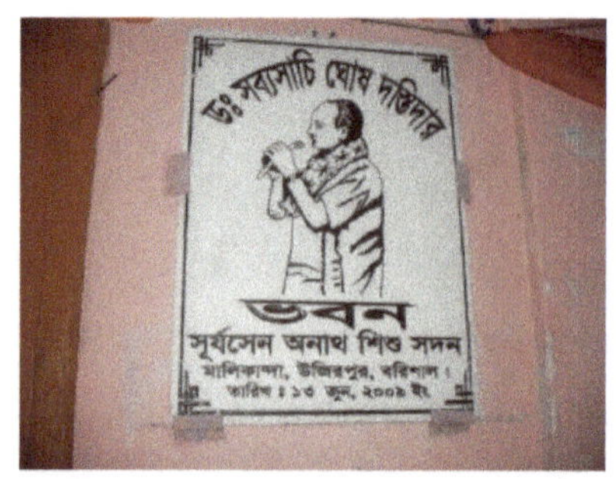

Dr. Sabyasachi Ghosh Dastidar Bhavan (Building) of Surya Sen Anath (Orphan) Shishu (Children's) Sadan (Building)

Mahatma (Great Soul) Dr. Sabyasachi Ghosh Dastidar Sanskrit College Bhaban (Building); Foundation Laid by Dr. Sabyasachi Ghosh Dastida, January 8, 2008

Africa's Light:

Beautiful Sky of Tanzania

Who would have thought one would find personal connection in distant Botswana, in addition to the charming landscape and wild animals that the nation is famous for? At the bus from Johannesburg, South Africa we ran into Omphile, a student at Chicago, heading home for a break, and father Kenneth. They became our impromptu guide. Omphile's mom gave us a ride to our hotel at Gaborone, Botswana capital. They came to see us next day at the hotel. One of the workers at the hotel counter said, "Sir, I have read your writings!" We were speechless. At one of the tourist attractions of the city, a Krishna Temple, we were welcomed by the temple priest, a Botswana-African-Hindu. The other African-Hindu priest was from Zambia. Some volunteers were making flower garlands for an upcoming parade. The temple folks introduced us to the head of one of the largest Botswana industrialists, Mr. Moon, whose invitation to meet days later we couldn't keep as we were heading to Namibia. Namibia was a wonderful place. During a trip from capital Windhoek to Swakopmund and Walvis Bay through National Geographic fame Namib Desert, the van driver, a native Namibian, started talking to us in Hindi that he learned at a nearby mine where lots of Indians work. These peoples are very smart! We know many African countries are economically poor, yet most of us don't know that they offer amenities. At the hotel in Windhoek, the Namibian capital, Mr. Clark, an Englishman, became our companion at the breakfast table. Clark is a pensioner or retiree, as we say in America. He said after visiting 12 countries, including America, for post-retirement settlement, he found Namibia to be the best place for retirement. Who knew? Namibia, a former German colony, also faced white oppression. Yet, she has bent over backwards to include former oppressors in Namibian society, appointing into offices, making them candidates of the ruling party of liberation, and more. South Africa's African majority is actively pursuing for a multi-racial society, in spite of horrible oppression by white segregationists. We witnessed the progress. In Durban we were invited to an Indian prayer service where a white South African was a force. He was sharing an apartment with a South African-Indian. This would have been unthinkable just a few years back. Hindu temples there had South African and Malawi African priests. Apartheid wouldn't have allowed that. We stayed at an

"Indian/Asian" neighborhood as Apartheid mandated it, but is a mixed community now. We visited Pietermaritzburg Railway Station where Gandhi was kicked off the train for riding in First Class reserved for "Whites Only", beginning his political journey.

An Indian neighborhood where Gandhi lived was burned down during anti-Apartheid struggle. Mr. Rooplal still mourns for the loss of their home. Unknown to us was the women's participation in workforce. We witnessed more women in police force to roadwork in South Africa than we've found in America, Europe, China, or India! Bravo! For our daytrip to Lesotho through the mountain, starting before sunrise and ending late at night was led by a female African driver, Joy. She exposed us to a traditional Zulu home, where grandma heads the family, with a central domed room in the yard for family gathering.

Johannesburg, South Africa

Apartheid Museum

Mandela Museum, his Former Home

Free School for Children

View From the Seaside

Three African-Hindu Priests at a Cape Town Temple

Train Station where Gandhi was Kicked out of First Class being a Colored Individual

Playing with a Lion Cub at a South Africa National Park

On the other end of the world, Sachi was heading from Melbourne, Australia to Davenport, Tasmania. Australians are known for free spirit and athleticism. The ferry takes all night, from evening to early morning. At dinner table he met with many individuals, mostly families, and some single travelers. People gave him tips for sightseeing in Tasmania famous for Tasmanian Devil. Locals suggested places where Sachi can see Devil and other wildlife. At breakfast, he met a lady whom he met earlier. He asked information about buses to Hobart, the capital of Tasmania, where he had a hotel reservation. The lady said, "Why should you take a bus, when I have a car? I am going to Hobart. I can take you there." Sachi didn't know what to say, but politely declined. She was adamant. When Sachi suggested that he should pay for gas, she refused. Only a coffee and snack at the gas station was all she accepted. She even made a detour of driving him through the town of Launceston in the middle of the island. Watching many wild animals, it reminded him of our camping in South Dakota in the U.S.

The Australian Symbol of Success

Downtown Sydney

Sydney, Australia

At the University with a Professor

On Tour with a Host Professor

At an Australian Landmark

On Overnight Boat from Melbourne to Tasmania

In South Dakota we camped at a site with a view of a large meadow. The park was almost full in that hot summer. We woke up early in the morning with noise coming from the meadow. Wow! What an experience. A large herd of wild bison were having breakfast with grass, thus the noise, as mentioned earlier. A few were as close as 30 ft. from the tents, but they ignored the campers. All the visitors stood for a long time till the buffalos moved away. One of the greatest treats on a camp site came in western Colorado in the Great Rocky Mountains. At a remote site by the side of a stream with beautiful view, we were the only campers. A forest ranger came and made sure we are fine at the site. An hour later he brought some firewood for us. No payment was accepted. And then again, after dark he came around to make sure we are enjoying our camping and safe. That was fun, for sure.

A Fossil in Stone Collected from a Rocky Mountain Park Store

Censored in India:

Any story of travel in India will be incomplete if one doesn't point out the censorship that is part of life in colonized India as well in a post-colonial India, especially about its religious heritage. India is the only country, besides Nepal, of surviving indigenous faiths, which hasn't been converted to monotheism of Christianity, Islam, Buddhism or atheism. From America to Arab World, from Australia to Afghanistan, or from Peru to Poland, from Pakistan to Philippines the indigenous shrines have become irrelevant or destroyed with pride of the conquering cultures. Thus, a destroyed shrine brings pride in Afghanistan, Arabia, Peru, or Pakistan, except for the intellectuals, historians, and marginalized secularists. Unfortunately, there is censorship in discussing the past in many nations. When Taliban destroyed 1500-year-old Buddha statues at Bamiyan, Afghanistan, how many Muslim-majority nations condemned that? How many communists condemned Chairman Mao when his army colonized Tibet and destroyed Tibetan shrines and viharas? Is it that different from Taliban's destruction of Buddha statue when Afghanistan was a pre-Islamic Buddhist and Hindu nation? When a Muslim friend of ours said in public that the Kaba Shrine in Mecca, the Holiest site of Islam, belonged to a pre-Islamic Hindu-like Arab faith, he was publicly scorned as a heretic and kefir. Why others from Muslim-majority nations couldn't rise up and defend? Or, from the West? This censorship has extended in post-independence indigenous-majority India. In 1995 as we traveled to Gour, Pandua and Murshidabad, the former capitals of non-native Persian-speaking Muslim kings of Bengal, it revealed many atrocities against Hindu majority by minority Muslim rulers, especially where mosques were built by destroying Hindu temples. The greatest example was Adina Mosque, which many locals called Adinath Mandir or Temple of Lord Shiva. Next to that was a grave of the queen which was Saraswati Mandir or the Temple of Goddess of Learning. Our visit was during the Communist-Marxist rule of West Bengal. To promote censorship, the appointed boss told us not to take any picture in that tourist attraction. That is India! Soon appeared some local boys as unofficial guides giving us tour and oral history of the area, and guiding our picture taking.

A few miles south, in former Non-Native Muslim ruler's capital, in Murshidabad, our Bengali-Muslim guide told us the local history of how terror-

ruler Murshid Kuli destroyed hundreds of Hindu shrines as per Islamic doctrine. Nevertheless, he got scared of Mother Kali, the Black Mother, after building the mosque. He then built a Temple of Ma Kali, next to the mosque so that the devotees attending the mosque can see the Mother. And according to our guide's oral history, as self-punishment Mr. Murshid asked himself to be buried under the open steps of the mosque so that dirt from devotees' feet fall on his grave as penalty. Our guide said, "At least Murshid expressed his sorrow that most other terrorists do not."

Thus, when one travels in India, there are hundreds, perhaps tens of thousands of such examples. The people claiming to be secularists instead of confronting oppression they have engaged in censorship. They are all for teaching white oppression of African-Americans in the U.S., but not British-Christian oppression in the Subcontinent, or Islamic-Settler oppression there. Should Germans and Europeans censor Nazi atrocities of Jews and Gypsies?

Here are a few more examples of censorship of atrocities in India by minority rulers in India. Incidentally, our last name Dastidar was given as honor to our ancestors by a Persian-speaking Islamic ruler of Bengal.

Kuttab Minar of Delhi, India:

The first Islamic victory tower in Delhi, a national park, built by destroying 29 Hindu and Jain temples. The engraved sign exists from British colonial times. One doesn't have to be anti-something, but should learn as a matter of history, and move on. Yet, one complication of the issue becomes if one group thinks it is their duty to destroy other cultures and shrines. Unless tolerance and equality are promoted from all sides, a peaceful resolution was difficult in the past 2,000 years. It is a good thing that in the U.S. one can learn about Black and Native Indian American oppression by settlers, not censoring that, and move forward. President Biden apologized on October 25, 2024 for Native Indian American oppression. Thanks.

Kutub MInar, the Islamic Victory Tower in India of 1,100s AD

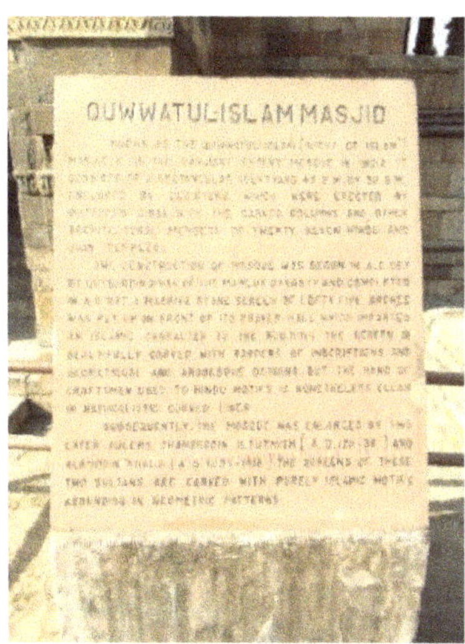

Inscription of Destruction of 29 Temples to build the
Victory Tower Existing since British rule

Varanasi Shiv Mandir:

Varanasi is one of the holiest sites of Hinduism and its ancient Shiva Temple was demolished by a Muslim ruler. A mosque was built on top of the temple. These days one cannot even enter Shiv Mandir with a pen to avoid taking pictures of the mosque.

Varanasi Ganga Ghat Steps

Mathura: Birthplace of Lord Sri Krishna:

A Krishna Temple was destroyed by colonizing minority Islamic rulers to build a Muslim Mosque on top of that. An old British-era tablet inside the complex tells visitors as to how many times attempts to rebuild the temple was crushed by Muslim rulers. Now one is not allowed to take a pen in case one writes down the inscription that existed from British colonial era.

The Temple

The Islamic Mosque seen from the Back, next to the
Hindu Temple, left, Built on its Wall.

Not until one is fortunate to visit around-the-world, one may not learn about the beauty, one's own history, and at times, pains associated with beauty.

Let us pray for a tolerant, uncensored culture, as the U.S. is trying. God save the Nations!

Chapter 3

Public Policy Of India & America

Public Policy of Partition-Affected Suicidally Fatalistic Hindu India and the Partition-Crushed Christian-Settler-Established Militant America

Introduction:

As United States is the first Republic of the world, her constitution, national goals, Declaration of Independence, separation of power, decentralization, balancing secular ideas and Christian traditions, support for decolonization of European colonized nations, her growing inventive mind, economic and military power, and settler colonization by welcoming the world's poor have justifiably influenced the entire world. For centuries, people from Europe and from Northern hemisphere looked America as their final destiny. After 1964 when the new policy was enacted allowing colored Africans, Asians, and South Americans to come for studies as well as migrate to the U.S., many of them including non-Christians started entering the nation bringing their values, good and bad. Whether candidate Trump's platform of barring Muslims migration, or, occasional attacks on Jews, Hindus, Muslims, Buddhists, Sikhs, Asians and Africans, are the consequence of the change of immigration policy and demographics will be debated for long. This has influenced both the New World and the Old World. However, this is a democracy determined by settlers, not by indigenous people. If the Navajos, the Cherokees, the Seminoles, the Utes, the Mohegans, the Mohawks were socially, culturally, demographically, and politically powerful, and were able to read and write their languages, and ruled their lands, would we be reading, writing and speaking in English now? It is also true for Aztecs and Incas of South and Central America. If they were ruling the regions, would we be able to take their land for settler colonization? This is true from Canada to Chile via Central America and the Caribbean. Would the Native Americans have given up their languages, religion if they ruled Americas? If

291

Aztecs or Incas were able to overpower Spanish conquistadors how would Central and South America look like today? Like Asia and Africa? The New World was dazed not only by England, but also by Spain, Portugal and France. With this came European Christianization of the indigenous cultures, by giving up their own indigenous Sanatani-(Hinu)-like nature worshipping beliefs. Monotheism has no room for diversity. This is similar to Islamization and Arabization of regions from West Africa to Middle East to Indonesia. After Enlightenment and Reformation in Europe, religious tolerance rose, and politics changed dramatically. The European colonization of Africa also brought along French, English, and Portuguese colonization and Christianization. Colonization of Asia was different as Asia was already developed more than Europe; thus, Christianization didn't have mass appeal, except Islamization which was able to spread rapidly with is militancy, and monotheism. In the New World we were able to overwhelm the indigenous peoples as some monarchs and kings did that on other nations of Europe, Asia and Africa before the Age of Exploration. There were monarchies of Greece, Hun, Persia, Byzantine, Ottoman, Tsar, Arab, and the Mughal who colonized foreign territories in earlier era; most of the time with brute force. One finds those cultures in Central Asia, Southeast Asia, Indian Subcontinent, North and East Africa, and the Balkans. Then there is Arab-Islamic colonization. This colonization spread from Arabian Sea to the Mediterranean Sea via North, East and West Africa, to Indian Subcontinent and to Southeast Asia via Bay of Bengal. In many ways they have done a lot better job of colonization than the Christian-European colonization, because once they colonized a land, they were able to completely wipe out local identities of nature-worshipping, and deity-symbolized pluralistic faiths. Arab-Islam colonization of new lands was able to stop any discussion of their past heritage, even if there were forced conversion, atrocities, killings and kidnappings, or conversion with love. Lord Jesus Christ's pacifism and Prophet Muhammad's armed militancy created these narratives. Christ didn't kill anyone with his own hand, and how He was punished we know very well. Newly colonized Islamic peoples gave up their own identity for Arabic one. This is even happening today as they migrate in tolerant U.S. Converts demonized and destroyed artifacts of their own parents and forefathers, without any repentance. Even in 2024 we may not only find such unfair examples from Afghanistan, Pakistan, Bangladesh, India, but also from Iraq, Syria, Mali, Nigeria, Mozambique, Kenya, Sudan, Ivory Coast, and other Afro-Asian nations where some "non-believers" still exist. Moral lessons, religious doctrine, multiple marriage, easy divorce, forced conversion, brutal oppression, brought Arabic culture to distant regions. It is their great success. At times Arab-Islam was able to convince advanced cultures that theirs's were inferior than distant culture was a very big achievement! And, this continues even today. Locals easily give up their indigenous identity, as we often find Bengalis giving up their rich identity for Yemeni identity. The advanced Persian, Byzantine, Coptic-Egyptian, Malian, West and North African, Punjabi, Sindhi, Afghan, Baloch cultures succumbed to the Arab-Persian invasion, wiping out some of those rich cultures. In Africa only the Abyssinian Christian Kingdom survived the onslaught of Islamic invasions as well as onslaught of European Christianity after Middle Ages. It is the only country in Africa that retained its own script and ancient rituals. During a visit to the holy city of Axum in Ethiopia which holds the Arc of Covenant, local residents reminded visitors how there is only Orthodox churches in the city, but no mosque or church, although Ethiopia is across the Red Sea from Arabia, and the two nations were connected culturally, religiously, and economically for millennium. How Ethiopian Christianity was able to save their tradition from Arab and European invasion, our guides told us many stories. This is a unique example in Africa, just as Indians are the only people to save their indigenous identity in the world. Good or bad is a different issue. The Arc of Covenant is locked in an Ethiopian church, accessible only to a lifelong ascetic monk, who then grooms another monk to give that right to the next generation. Ethiopia has had a large number of Jews, known as Falasha. We felt Ethiopian lifestyle parallels lifestyle in India and tribes of Americas. There are lots of similarities with indigenous India in their appearance and clothing. At times, some Ethiopians thought we were local. It was nice to see how Ethiopia survived colonialism in Africa from Arabia and Europe.

Poster in an Ethiopian Church

Display at an Axum City Park

Ethiopian Church Saving Ancient Christian Works

Ethiopian Church

Ethiopian Church at Lower Level

Centuries Old Amharic Bible

Church Decoration

Bible Study

A Relatively "New" Centuries Old Palace

Ethiopia is the only country in Africa who was able to save its script. Many old cultures lost its language or script, or both, such as Farsi, Sindhi, Pakistani Punjabi, Pushto, Baloch, Malay, Sumatran and others. Under pluralism of Hindu-majority India, even very small groups of a few thousand people in a country of over a billion and a half allow teaching, reading and writing in its own languages and scripts. We found that while traveling in Arunachal Pradesh, India near Myanmar (Burma) border where handwritten posters demanded education of a tiny group of a few thousand peoples who migrated to India hundreds of years ago from Thailand. Even in the tolerant U.S., language teaching doesn't mean teaching in that medium from K-12 grades. It will be like in America we were offering instructions in languages who arrived in 1700s, but not in English.

Indigenous Rural Home in Arunachal Pradesh (State)

A Remote Tiny Thai-Indian Community Demanding Instruction in Thai Language

In another remote corner of India in a Christian-majority state some folks were trying to revive a language and a script from which that group emerged centuries ago. Yet in post-1947 Partition era in Pakistan, the largest linguistic group after Bengalis, Punjabis willingly gave up their own language for Urdu developed during the British colonization in Northern India. Punjabi Muslims were able to force other Pakistan nationalities like Sindhi, Baloch, Pashtun, and

Kashmiri to give up their languages and scripts for a new Indian Urdu language possibly because Punjabi Muslim elites had inferiority complex about their mother tongue and adopted a distant Urdu as "their" language written in Arabic script. After 1947, in the new Pakistani Punjab Province one female Muslim legislator proposed to adopt Gurmukhi script-based Punjabi as the official language, but her wish was wish only. Urdu is basically Hindi of India but written in a foreign Arabic script. Punjabi Hindus and Sikhs in India continue to use Punjabi written in Gurmukhi script. What would be the reaction of Islamic nations, the UN Human Rights, Organization of Islamic Countries, and the free Western and neo-colonial press if India forced Hindi on Indian Kashmiris, or for that matter to Punjabis, as Pakistan did? This forceful subjugation of smaller Pakistani minorities, and rejection of their own Punjabi identity created the Bangladesh genocide when Punjabi military and elites tried to force Urdu language on the majority Bengalis while trying to change its thousand-year-old script and literature. Opposition to the new script, linguistic oppression and killing of Bengalis on February 21, 1952 created the Language Movement in East Pakistan, resulting in Independence Movement in 1971. Pakistan's Hindu Genocide and extermination of secular Muslims in former East Pakistan, now Bangladesh, resulted in independence movement. Not one Muslim-majority nation condemned the genocide. Even the U.S. and many tolerant Western nations supported the genocide. New converts to new religion associated with brutal force and political power felt better with Arab identity, than the old tolerant indigenous ones. One of the attributes of any conversion is to make the indigenous cultures feel inferior to the new one. This is also true for conversion to democracy, Westernization, Communism or more. Pluralism and equality are accepted in democracy.

Colonial British-Christian and Colonial Persian-Arab-Turkic-Islam in India:

If pluralism and colonial Britain-introduced democracy has survived in a large and diverse country like India, with millions killed by the British and Muslim colonizers, and during 1947 Partition of India, it has to do with the basic tenets of tolerance, fatalism, diversity, cowardice and pluralism of "Hinduism" or indigenism. India didn't follow Islamic and Christian world's intolerant conquerors who were able to destroy other cultures and beliefs simultaneously convincing converted natives that they were inferior than Arabs or Europeans. Even the Marxists tried to convince others that their monotheism is better than indigenous pluralism. This is not to glorify Indianism or polytheism, but to acknowledge the survival power of extremely suicidally fatalistic, tolerant, decentralized, pluralistic beliefs.

In 2017 at a forum organized by Saudi pro-secular group in Washington D.C. a Princeton University history professor reminded the attendees why and how India and its indigenous tradition remains to be the only culture and religion that was not Islamized even after 800 years of Islamic oppression, intolerant and brutal rule, with thousands and thousands of temples, libraries and ashrams destroyed, hundreds of thousands, perhaps millions, of people killed by invaders, or settler kings. In 5,000-year history of Subcontinent, lots of new ideas for humankind evolved from there, as well as many baggages, among them inflexible racism-like caste. The word "caste" is a word from Europe. Many suggest that some of the hardening took place during foreigner's Islamic rule, and during the British-Christian rule, together for 1,000 years. All the Islamic rulers used foreign languages for their communication, as British did. Many of them dreamt of their ancestral homes in Persia, Uzbekistan, Turkey, or England. How much of this caste hardening took place during the rule of settler kings? It is difficult to quantify. Although Western press and neo-colonial Indians have projected India as a monolithic caste-based entity, but it is not true. As mentioned earlier, caste and tribe difference, regional and linguistic sectarianism varies from region to region. In Bengal where resistance to British colonialism was severe versus non-Islam colonized Assam and Northeast India, casteism was ignored. Non-Islam colonized South India versus Islam-converted West India – which is mostly in Pakistan now, caste influence was different. Bengal and eastern India, on the other hand, was influenced by cast-eliminating and gender empowering Vaishnava movement of the 1400s and the anti-British diversity-embracing nationalist Indian independence movement. Today, in some region's caste issue is present whereas at other places it is rare or non-existent, as in Assam. Even in those areas caste becomes less of an issue in urban areas, colleges, universities and in factories. In many regions politics has more to do with their native district, tribe or political party than birth or caste. Even in caste-dominated politics of Tamil Nadu state oppressed-groups representing DMK or Dravida Munnetra Kazagam party came to power driving out many of the privileged Tamils to other parts of India, but rarely mentioned in the Western press. It is true that in many rural areas of India, there are deep-rooted sectarian prejudice, but there has always been push against caste prejudice during Indian independence movement and before that during Hindu Renaissance in 1800s when everyone fought against British oppression. Justifiably, British, Islamic and Christian converters have exploited divisions instead of reformation preached by nationalists.

To divide Indians, Colonial Britain reintroduced the Portuguese word "Caste" to divide "Hindus," not to improve the oppressed population, but introduced religious Muslim-Non-Muslim divide in late 1880s as India wanted to be free. Because of Portuguese origin, the word is recent in Indian culture. It is also worth mentioning that in Indian/Hindu epics individual's rank was decided on knowledge, not by birth. Even in 15th Century, recent by Indian standard, Sri Chaitanya reaffirmed a casteless society for all to start life at the foot of God as "das" or "dasi," meaning male or female "server" raising through knowledge to priesthood, yet rarely neo-colonialists or pro-colonialist mention these. We have been to Hindu services led by Caucasians, Africans, non-Indian Asians, South Americans, Christians, Muslims, Oppressed Hindus, and Jews when not a single indigenous Hindu had any problem, unlike neo-colonial sectarian journalism. It does not mean that everything is fine. It is not, but changing. There are many deities, saints and sages who came from different orders, high or low, and followers didn't see any problem except exploiters. Indians have been thoroughly brainwashed by Britain promoting divisiveness instead of bringing together like Sri Chaitanya, Guru Nanak, Raja Ram Mohon,

Ramakrishna, Gandhi, Michael Madhusudan, or Nazrul Islam, in recent time. In 2020 at a Fulbright Award recipient meeting in America Sachi came across several female Fulbright recipients from India, mostly graduates from Delhi. One of them started talking about casteism at their campus. When Sachi mentioned that in his college five decades ago they knew who got special admission based on Scheduled Caste and Scheduled Tribe quota – British created designations retained in India, but not in Pakistan or Bangladesh – yet no one showed any difference towards anyone. They studied, played, and ate together. They slept in the same room.

Not only that, when those classmates came to stay at our Kolkata home, no one in his traditional family treated anyone differently. She replied, "It is true. We don't differentiate." When asked "Why is that in your mind?" She replied, "For Americans." One can argue, even in America, Canada or Australia, if families live in the same village or in the same neighborhood, doing the same job, and marry with similar families for 400 years, 600 years, or for 1,000 years, we too may develop that "group" differences based on money, type of work, importance of those families, or those villages. And, if some of those jobs paid little while others paid more, we too could develop an idea of high and low. In any city or suburb, including New York City or Long Island, almost everyone can name high or low neighborhoods, and for college admission high and low demand based on job prospect. Pre-marital sex and open sexual culture of the West, and multiple marriage and child marriage in Islamic tradition of the East, and easy divorce and pre-marital living in the West, and three-*talak* divorce in Islamic East have countered generational family differences of low or high. Even in 2024 overwhelming majority – possibly over 90% marriages in India, Pakistan, Bangladesh, Nepal, Sri Lanka, Afghanistan – are within one's language, region, sub-region, religion, sub-religion, tribe, ethnicity, tradition, group, family, sub-group, and more. Deviation is quite common in urban areas, and in college campuses. We know hundreds, perhaps thousands, of such examples. When there are mixed marriages, it rarely becomes news in the media. There are examples from pre-colonial ages. Premarital sex and easy divorce of Western model is being promoted by the Bollywood movie industry in India, including alcoholism. In 2024 alcoholism is possibly more common in India than in America. Ganja or weed was there in India for millenniums, however, now it has entered the minds of young via Western practices.

Again, the same anti-privileged DMK Party of Tamil Nadu State of India elected a privileged group person as head of elected governments, but was ignored by free partisan press. DMK government also opposed teaching of Hindi, the official language of India, which is also the link language of India, but not opposed to teaching colonial language English in schools, although millions of Tamils find jobs in other parts of India speaking Hindi. India has elected a small minority Tamil as a President of India that no Indian questioned. India elected minorities – Muslim, Sikh, and tribal – as head of the nation. Is that a good policy? How many of India's neighbors elected to high offices of their indigenous minority? Will Americans treat equally if a state that doesn't teach English? Or, elect someone president or senator who doesn't know English? Not to be outdone, when Communist Party of India-Marxist (CPM) came to power in West Bengal State in 1970s they removed teaching of English, Hindi, Sanskrit – the mother language of Bengali – from their school curriculum, thus cutting off students from Indian and the world literature. They also cut off Bengalis from their past literature and history since most of their literature had to do with Mother Nature. Ancient literature was written in Sanskrit before Second Millennia. Indians have to go to America and Germany to study their ancient literature and religion. Bengali grammar is determined by Sanskrit. Our friends and family living in West Bengal objected to that Communist policy, but authoritarian anti-majority policies of Marxists had no room for discussion. Nevertheless, Sachi congratulated the education minister, Mr. Ghosh, as he himself studied in Bengali medium, for teaching in Bengali medium as the norm. Sachi was also a product of his parent's post-independence self-confidence and pride. His parents studied in British era. Dad went to engineering school in Britain. Dad even worked for the British military during WWII. Dad wrote to Sachi only in English, but took offence if Sachi wrote back in English. Baba used to say, "I had no choice, but you have choice because of your grandparents' sacrifice. Honor them, and all the people killed, tortured and jailed by the British." Thus, Sachi always wrote Dad in Bengali, and Baba replied back in English, using his typewriter. This was very much Indian nationalism in Bengal. In a big surprise, in 1980s, Sachi received a postcard from the education minister Ghosh expressing his appreciation of Sachi's support of their education policy. A reply from a Left minister was never heard of. A few months down the road in 1986 Sachi invited his friend Tapan, his wife and kids to a musical performance by Russian Gypsies at the famous Rabindra Sadan auditorium of Kolkata. At the end of the program the Culture Minister Fadikar of the Communist Party-Marxist, wearing western outfit – which was rare for Communist and Congress political leaders – spoke only in English which was neither understood by the Gypsies, nor by the children taught in Bengali medium to whom our U.S.-educated grade-school kids provided translation to our friend Tapan's kids. This is bad! Sachi wrote a protest note to Hon. Fadikar that was not replied as Sachi himself studied in Bengali medium at Jagatbandhu Institution in Kolkata. All protests were ignored. (See Editorial of the largest-circulation Bengali weekly *Desh*, December 4, 2002, p 5). We also know so many talented Americans who studied in non-English schools in Europe, South America and Asia. So, studying in one's mother tongue is normal. All our West Bengal friends said, "Didn't I tell you that all Party elites send their kids to private English-medium schools. Our kids are supposed to go to sub-standard Bengali medium schools."

It is worth mentioning that after Communist Party-Marxist-led Left Front came to power in 1977 several changes were made in West Bengal education system. Among them were only Bengali-medium classes to be offered at lower grades. Then, Hindi, the Official Language of India at the Federal level, and lingua franca of the Subcontinent and beyond, was dropped. English the language of colonizers and international language was dropped from the lower grades. They also removed teaching of Sanskrit, mother language of almost all Indian languages. Removing Sanskrit was to please anti-Hindu groups in Hindu-majority West Bengal run by people who ran away from their Muslim-majority homeland of Pakistan/Bangladesh for India. Contradiction? Hypocrisy? Till First Millennium most of India's literature, music, theology, science, shlokas and mantras were written in Sanskrit. Actually, translation of Ramayana from Sanskrit to regional languages created literary renaissance in all Indian languages. During Communist rule of West Bengal Schools run by Hindu organizations had to follow Bengali-only law, but not Christian- and Islamic-run schools. Those schools could keep English medium teaching. Was that anti-Hindu, anti-majority communalism of the communists? Many years later, in 1993, Sachi was working on editing a book on Calcutta's tercentenary. He was working with Dr. Mohsin of Washington D.C. on behalf of South Asia Forum that both of them jointly founded. While in Kolkata he sought and received an article by Mr. Chatterjee, then Mayor of Kolkata, a Bangladeshi-Indian who fled from his Muslim-majority homeland. Getting through the dreaded Bengali bureaucracy was easy for reaching the mayor. We were happy to receive a Bengali essay on Calcutta from the mayor. We also received a tribute on Kolkata from the New York City Mayor Hon. David Dinkins as well.

We sought an article from West Bengal Communist-Marxist (CPM) Chief Minister Mr. Jyoti Basu, a Pakistani-Bangladeshi-Hindu-Indian who chose not to live in his Muslim-majority homeland. To reach his office Sachi had to get leads from CPM party activists. Locating someone from the Party was eased by the presence of his oldest brother Dada, a medical doctor serving the very poor. At the *Laal Baari*, the Red Building, also called Writers Building, the office of the Chief Minister, he was able to get an appointment to meet Mr. Basu. After many checks he was at his secretary's office, where sat a Party official as well. They all checked his credentials and then the book proposal. After some discussion among themselves, he was asked for a written letter requesting his appointment. He promptly wrote a letter in Bengali, with his university business card attached to it. The secretary returned back his letter saying "You must write in English." He objected saying that "State's official language is Bengali and you don't even teach English in schools, so why is this hypocrisy?" It didn't move the Party functionaries and State bureaucrats. Seeing that he is running out of time, he wrote a second letter in English. But his time the functionaries came back and said, "It must be typed." Again, he protested by arguing that not even 1% of state population has typewriter, so why this barrier? This arrogant attitude, hypocrisy, double-standard, anti-Hindu policy to cover their anti-Muslim original lifestyle have pulled India back from progress. Incidentally, both Chief Minister Basu and Kolkata Mayor Chatterjee are Bangladeshi-Indians who chose not to live with their Muslim-majority in Bangladesh for safety of India while calling all non-Communist Indians as communal or anti-Muslim. When Mayor Chatterjee went to visit his home in western Bangladesh, their government appointed a Hindu minority bureaucrat to be the mayor's guide. CPM rule instituted many anti-Hindu or anti-majority discriminatory policies. One of them was not allowing the Ramakrishna Mission, a Hindu order of monks, not to offer English-medium instruction in their schools, but no restriction was placed on Christian or Islamic schools. To continue teaching in their schools both in English and in vernacular languages in West Bengal, the Ramakrishna Mission had to go to the Indian Supreme Court to declare itself a "non-Hindu" entity.

We wonder what would Americans, Brits, Norwegians or Italians do if their most prominent local Christian organization has to go to Supreme Court to declare it a non-Christian entity for it to be treated equally with Jewish, Muslim, or Jain minorities? The Left leaders who chose not to live with Muslims in their Muslim-majority Bangladesh and Pakistan homeland, to cover their anti-secular credentials, added another trophy. On April 30, 1982 their anti-Hindu thugs in atheist-ruled state beat, then lynched, doused with gasoline, then set on fire to over twenty Hindu monks and nuns of Ananda Marg Order in broad daylight at Hindu-majority Kolkata's prestigious Ballyganj area's Kasba or Bijan Setu Bridge, about 150 yards from where Sachi grew up. In spite of many pictures and videos in social media, not one person has been arrested or convicted either by the Communist-Marxist government, or by the post-2011 anti-Communist Trinamool Administration of Ms. Mamata Banerji, who herself was tortured by the communists when she was in opposition. (See *Maron yagyer pariprekshitey kayekti prashna* [Some questions in light of the killing spree], A.C. Haramatmananda Avaduta, 527 VIP Nagar, E. M. Bypass, Kolkata; and *empireslastcasualty.blogspot.com/2009/07/hindu-monks-and-nuns-killed-in-india-by.html*). We wonder how many editorials have been written in Kolkata, Delhi, New York, Washington, or London papers of Ananda Marg mass lynching in broad day light? Can one imagine anti-Islam mob killing of Islamic preachers in Saudi Arabia, Iran, Pakistan, Bangladesh or Egypt, and not one killer would be arrested? Or, dozens of Christian preachers lynched and burned to death in America, Argentina, France or Italy, and not one killer would be arrested, and media censors that? These are the contradictions of public policies between the largest and the strongest democracies. Sadly, there is a disease of Indian/Sanatani mind, especially of their intellectuals. People who chose not to live with Muslims in their Bangladesh/Pakistan homeland, identify themselves as "secular" or while calling one "communal" who believe in Muslim-Non-Muslim cohabitation.

This is of serious concern for the oppressed. Personalities supporting fake narrative includes noted professors, award winners, laureates, journalists, column writers, and more. A noted U.K. history professor of four decades while visiting New York came to know about minority plight in his homeland. The professor was a Pakistani-Bangladeshi-Indian-British-Hindu-refugee. He moved from East Pakistan to India, then to U.K. Professor was surprised to learn of oppression, and shared his shock with a famous writer-professor of Kolkata, Ms. Nabaneeta. Ms. NabaneetaDi, Older Sister Nabaneeta, wrote about Oxford History professor's confession in a Kolkata journal as how the professor, a close friend of her, was "shocked to learn of oppression and cleansing from his homeland when he visited the home of Sachi and Shefali in New York" while reading Sachi's book, *Empire's Last Casualty: Indian Subcontinent's Vanishing Hindu and Other Minorities* (Firma KLM, Kolkata, 2008). The U.K. professor wrote about his atheist family of East Bengal, now Bangladesh, but chose not to live there after partition (see *Bangalnama* (East Bengali story), Ananda Publishers, Calcutta; 2008). During his visit to Bangladesh in 1980s, then the military dictator provided the professor a helicopter to visit his village in Barisal District, not far from our ancestral home. The first time he saw Sachi, he immediately asked, "Aren't you from Gava?" the ancestral village going back to almost first millennium. This is very typical Indian culture of identifying with an ancestral village. In some regions, families add the name of the village as the first name, sometime as middle name, while others as last name. Bengali Muslims do not keep common last name.

There are exceptions. Thus 10 children may have 10 different last names, but not of Hindus, Buddhists or Christians. Our Dastidar was an honorific title given by a Persian-Muslim ruler of Bengal, which was added to the traditional Ghosh. Ghosh is common among many families belonging to many "professions or castes" as defined by the British. One noted Muslim poet and freedom fighter, Mrs. Sufia Kamal, hearing Sachi's name immediately asked like U.K. professor "Are you from Gava?" and then gave an oral history of Sachi's family. Finally, in the village of Gava, a surviving Ghosh Dastidar family welcomed us as their cousin, one who was 23 generations apart from son Shuvo. Locals showed us how many Ghosh Dastidar homes are occupied by confiscators. Our millennia-old Pancha Ratna (Five Jewel) Mandir temple stood with demolished deity. In its property stood an Islamic Mosque. As we were touring the village with sister Mejdi, and Shuvo, three poor, bare-chested peasants rushed from the paddy field, and begged us, "Uncle, please do not allow folks to occupy your properties, and don't allow them to change the name of our Lakshmipur-Gava union. It is your ancestors who named Lakshmipur, Home of Mother Lakshmi, the Giver of Prosperity and Wealth. Now, some people want to change that." See https://empireslastcasualty.blogspot.com/2008/02/gavabangladeshhome-of-ghosh-dastidar.html.

Pancha-Ratna (Five Jewel) Hindu Temple, Gava, Bangladesh, 1991. A Tin-shed Mosque on the Back, was Illegally built on the Temple Property

Mrs. Ghosh Dastidar, in White Sari, Offering Prayer with Local Hindu Peasant Lady at Gava Village

Old Memorial of a Ghosh Dastidar Ancestor

Pre-Partition Famous Gava High School, 1991

On one of our trips to Gava from Barisal City, we came across a sad yet remarkable event near Nimtola village. A flow of humanity, almost all of oppressed high-quality gifted minority, were walking from every direction towards a village. Some were arriving on small boats in nearby canal, and many others came even sitting on top of buses. Our volunteer guide, a monk trainee, found out that it was the day when the *sraddha* or last rites is being done of a Hindu monk who rose from the a very oppressed group. Shuvo and Sachi paid their tributes for the monk, or swami. It reminded once again, how some oppressed minorities have survived in spite of oppression and forced conversion by English-Christian and Persian-Islamic converters. Here are a few of those pictures:

People Riding on top of Cars

Site for Commemoration

Devotees Walking Miles through Paddy Fields

310

People, Hindus and Muslims, walking to Offer Homage to the Monk

Sad, dehumanizing story from Indian Bengal can go on and on. NabaneetaDi, Older Sister Nabaneeta, is a wonderful storyteller, a professor, who kept us awestruck as he told her story of growing up in India, how she was dumped by her elite husband for a Western woman, and how she raised her two daughters. NabaneetaDi in typical Indian tradition didn't remarry. Those daughters were by her side when she breathed her last in 2019. At one of her daughter's *griha-prabesh* or housewarming in Brooklyn, the mother-daughter duo arranged for a German Hindu priest to do a beautiful *arti* lighted lamp celebration with dozens of layered lit *diya* lamps.

Rule of Left Communists in West Bengal and Kolkata reminded us of a famous Bengali proverb, *"jei jaai lankai, sheai hoi rabon"* meaning "Whoever goes to Lanka becomes (Demon King) Ravan," or in other words Power Corrupts, or Power Makes You Oppressor. According to Indian belief during the epic rule of Lord Ram, the demon King Ravan ruled Sri Lanka who kidnapped Ma Sita, Lord Ram's wife, starting the tales of pre-Buddha, pre-Jain Ramayana. Communist Party of India-Marxist, came to power by calling all opposition groups "communal", or anti-Muslim but all of their leaders fled Muslim-majority Pakistan/Bangladesh for the safety of Hindu India while preaching to live with Muslims. They blamed Congress Party leaders for following British-censored colonial history. Yet, they barely taught the history of Indian independence, Bengal Renaissance, Hindu Reformation Movement, and Indian Renaissance in

India's West Bengal and Tripura states' text books when they ruled those states for over three decades. Revisionist text books don't include man-made genocide of Prime Minister Churchill that took three-to-seven million lives in Bengal in 1942-43 in a man-made Bengal Famine when Bengal had bumper crop. British destroyed over 60,000 boats in the world's largest Ganga-Brahmaputra Delta while tens of thousands of tons of grain were shipped to Britain. Communist rulers didn't add a line of oppression, genocide, mass extermination, destruction of temples, schools, ashrams, etc. by the British or pre-British non-native Muslim rulers of Bengal or India. This is censorship of modern era, that many in the Western press also follow. Even in formal celebration of many Indian Freedom Fighters – including places in West Bengal where we were invited by formerly-imprisoned Freedom Fighters, where British and Muslim League Party actions were barely mentioned. Is it because Left didn't take part in India's independence movement? During Quit India Movement of 1940s, all Congress Party members were imprisoned by the British Colonial Administration. Muslim League Party and Communist Party members remained free. Even the Martyr's Memorial in Alipore Jail in Kolkata is not accessible to the public, which didn't include a single Muslim or communist.

This is just the opposite of what we found in the U.S., Bangladesh, South Africa, Germany, or in the Baltic Nations. By 2020 the sectarian anti-communist Trinamool Congress Party who came to power by ousting communists, hasn't made any change, except using "anti-Delhi/India" rhetoric, to cover its failure in development, controlling sectarianism, or promoting pluralism. Ruling Communist Party-Marxist also banned books they considered anti-Muslim, as *The Koran and the Kafir: Islam and the Infidel* by A. Ghosh of Texas, 1983; a Bangladeshi-Hindu-Refugee-Indian-American. Soon the ruling Congress Party at Delhi also banned the book in India. Communists attempted to ban the festival of Saraswati (Sarasvati) Puja in schools, a millennia-old tradition of welcoming Mother of Learning and Education encouraging kids to learn. They banned loudspeakers in Hindu puja festivals, but not Islamic mega speakers preaching at the middle of the night. After 2001 anti-Hindu pogrom in

Bangladesh, writer Dr. Taslima Nasrin's book *Lajja* (*Shame*, Pearl Publishers, Dhaka; 1993); a novella depicting the plight of a Hindu minority family in Bangladesh was banned by the pro-Islamist rulers of Bangladesh. Communist rulers of West Bengal and Tripura states also banned the book. Such is Indian and anti-Hindu hypocrisy of Hindus. Unlike the U.S., truth is censored on partisan basis. In the U.S., the other side fights back. In sectarian anti-indigenous India, it is not easy as states are controlled by sectarians.

Koran and Kafir by A. Ghosh

It is worth mentioning that after Communist Party-Marxist came to power in West Bengal and in the City of Kolkata, there were many attempts to improve urban lifestyle. One of those was to prevent smoking in public buses although that was a law for ages. During summer, there was a 15-day program to improve the quality of public transportation, among them was to enforce "No Smoking" laws in public buses. Most public buses in Kolkata are owned and run by private individuals. There were big banners all over the metropolitan area. As Sachi got into a bus from Gariahat More stop to Dharmatala near downtown, the ticket collector, called conductor, started smoking as he came to him to collect his ticket. Sachi objected to his smoking. The man replied, "Who are you to remind me? Government does that propaganda for their publicity......," and he continued to smoke and insulted others who objected to that. Sachi wrote to the person-in-charge listed in posters with his ticket, with bus and registration number. To his surprise he got a reply back in a day or two. This is not U.S. This is remarkable in Indian politics. A few days later, this time on a Kalighat to Sealdah bus route, also in southern Kolkata, he ran into a similar situation. Now the conductor loudly and publicly stated that there is "Nothing you can do, as the Minister of Transportation is elected from my district, and we own him with the money we give him." This time the letter wasn't answered.

From his personal experience he found that elected leaders in America – from the locals to higher levels – are more accessible than in India, more specifically than in Communist-ruled West Bengal, from 1970s to 2010s. In both nations if you push hard doors opened, but in case of Kolkata or West Bengal "Party Cadres" created a shield that was often difficult to break. This is personal experience. We always wondered after President Trump's polarization, if U.S. is heading in that direction. During one of our trips to Kolkata, some of our friends suggested that Sachi visit a Bangladeshi-Indian Communist Party-Marxist (CPM) minster who represented the Durgapur constituency. Durgapur was created in 1950s as an industrial hub by West Bengal's post-independence Congress Party Chief Minister Dr. Bidhan Chandra Roy that was turned into ruins by the communist rule. New York's Probini Foundation was helping schools for the poor in Durgapur. So, we had an easy time to get the telephone number of the elected communist assemblyman from Durgapur. At the Mahakaran Bhavan or Secretariat Building his assistant asked Sachi to meet at "MLA Hostel" in Hungerford Street in mid-Kolkata, not far from American Consulate. So, he appeared promptly at his appointed time of 7:30 pm. Doorman allowed him to enter the building. The apartment door was opened by a stranger, whom Sachi assumed was a "Party Cadre" who graciously asked Sachi to take a seat. At the other end minister's wife was cooking fish that one could smell very easily. After few minutes the minister appeared and told Sachi how sorry he was that he is unable to discuss West Bengal's industrialization, and his assistant will give Sachi a call the next day. That call never came. This was very similar to the situation when he went to talk to a journalist of the CPM's Bengali paper at the party headquarters at Alimuddin Street of Central Kolkata after 1992 anti-Hindu pogrom in Bangladesh that Sachi witnessed firsthand, but the journalist wrote a fake report. Sachi arrived at the appointment time surprising the journalist. Seeing Sachi he said he is too busy and will give him a call back "tomorrow," that never came. A few days after assemblyman's Hostel trip Sachi headed to Durgapur by train. It was a 2-hour trip from Howrah Station. Arindam, Nirmal and Jayanta came to pick him up at the station to take him to the school for the destitute that they started. At the station they said "We have our elected legislature, who is a minister, is visiting Durgapur. Let us take you to meet him." He agreed, but had no idea who that was. It is worth mentioning that in India candidates running for elective office do not have to live there, unlike America. They have to be nominated by political parties. So, when the elected leaders came to their constituency, they often stay in "Guest House," not in their home. As soon as Sachi saw the man he realized who he was. With his folded hands he said, "Namaskar. Greetings. Here we meet again as you didn't have time to sit down with me as your wife was busy cooking fish. It smelled very good. I never received a call back from you. I wonder, will you have time today?" The minister laughed and said he will be too busy all day before returning to Kolkata late afternoon. During a trip to Durgapur city in 2022, the group gave Shefali and Sachi a surprise reception for helping them for 20 years. Twenty years ago, they had seven students. Now it has grown to over 1,600 poor and orphaned students, with many schools, medical facilities, and over 120 teachers.

Dance Reception by Students

Singing Reception by Students

Marching Reception by Students

See http://empireslastcasualty.blogspot.com/2022/10/probiniparti tion project-ispad-honored.html. In that same spirit in 2005 during a visit to New York City at the Annual Bengali Convention at Madison Square Garden the head of Communist Party-Marxist, CPM, a Pakistan-Bangladesh-Indian-Hindu, claiming to be atheist, Mr. Biman, when asked about the Kolkata Metro in comparison to NYC Subway, told visitors that "I never take the Metro as I have a chauffeur-driven car given by the Party." After 1991 and 1992 Bangladesh anti-Hindu pogrom that Sachi personally witnessed by visiting village after village, he narrated his experience to the famous Bengali poet Mr. Rahman of Bangladesh when he was visiting Dastidars at their New York City home. Mr. Rahman was staying with his daughter at Bronx. Mr. Rahman was known as a secular, tolerant poet. Sachi told him a very touching story of an elderly Hindu man, a hermit-like teacher, in eastern Comilla City's old Abhoy Ashram who was beaten so badly that his left hand couldn't be fixed and remained permanently crippled, yet he refused to leave his homeland for India. Soon appeared a poem by Mr. Rahman with title "Shudhangshu Jabey Na," or "Shudhangshu Won't Go" that became very symbolic after the pogrom. With his pen he was encouraging Hindus to stay in their ancestral homeland. Mr. Rahman, a Muslim, is asking Hindu minority to stay in their homeland, but were refugees encouraging Hindu minorities to flee from their home, leaving their ancestral land, to colonize India?

Abhoy Ashram, Comilla, after 1992 Pogrom

The Old Ashram After 1992 Pogrom, Bangladesh

Remains of Hindu Aunt's Home, one of Hundreds in Southeastern Bangladesh During 1991 Pogrom

Once for Sachi's work he sought an appointment with a one-time Mayor of Kolkata, and a former Minister of West Bengal Government under Communist Party of India-Marxist (CPM) rule. He too was from Bangladesh, whose father was a noted lawyer of eastern Noakhali District of Bengal Province of British India. During 1946 Noakhali anti-Hindu genocide, thousands of Hindus were murdered and tens of thousands of mothers and daughters were abducted and forcefully converted under the rule of Muslim League Party of British India's Bengal Province. His parents were ordered by Islamic killers to dig a grave so that his family could be buried alive. When Sachi asked about the Noakhali genocide, he simply ignored the question. It is said that all members of his extended family – mother, father, brothers, sisters, grandpa, grandma, cousins, etc. dozens, possibly 27 members – were hacked and burned to death. He didn't express any sadness!

This reminded us of hundreds of illegally-occupied refugee colonies of post-1947 West Bengal State where tens of millions of refugees found shelter. Thanks. From 1997 many "Hindu Refugee Colonies" in West Bengal started to observe 50-year of existence since partition of Bengal in 1947, and publish commemorative journals, but without mentioning their pain. Almost all of these colonies' lands were illegally confiscated from West Bengali Hindus, called *Jabar-Dhakhal* or Forcibly Occupied, were run by activists. Articles after articles talked about how glorious their life was in their native East Bengal and highlight their struggle in refugee colonies, but no one mentioned why they fled their home of a thousand year, and why no one protested! No one ever wrote about how they lost their mom, dad, brothers and sisters, how homes, land, and ponds were confiscated, how their grains were set on fire or looted, and how fish in their ponds were forcibly caught or poisoned, and how temples, ashrams, schools and libraries were torched. Yet all of them said as they were atheists, they have no hatred about their killers, or against Muslim League Party who cleansed them, but their hatred was for Congress Party, Hinduism and Mahatma Gandhi who fought for India's independence and opposed partition, and gave them shelter in India. This was a narrative we all believed in 1950s, 1960s onwards. To show their brevity, even a mother wrote how she witnessed losing her family, including her children, but she doesn't shed tear because of her ideology. Is that humanism or de-humanism? Is that tolerance or intolerance? Is that "anti-living being" mind? From childhood we were told to defend our family as a cow does to protect her calf, a pigeon protects her den, or even a mother snake defends her little ones in a pit. But an Indian mother doesn't shed tear for her children? A daughter doesn't dream of her mother? What kind of mind is that?

With our passionate trips with entire family even when the kids were toddler, our parents, elder brothers and sisters became extremely happy, sharing many stories, even showing us a postcard that Sachi's father kept with him from the Muslim occupier of dozens of homes of our extended family of uncles, aunts and grandparent, many ponds and acres of farmland offering 600 rupees, possibly around $100 dollars then, when the value would have been in hundreds of thousands, perhaps millions. No one responded that letter. The Muslim occupier just moved into our properties of hundreds of years protected by Enemy Property Act of Pakistan which allowed confiscation of indigenous Hindu homes and land without paying a penny by declaring the family as "Enemy of the State." With the rise of Pakistani-Bangladeshi-Hindu-Refugee-Indian-run Communist-Marxist (CPM) governments, Sachi's dad and oldest brother Dada would often ask him to meet one of our uncles from the village who was an activist of CPM, Mr. Ghosh. Last name Dastidar was added by some creating a double last name when a non-native Persian-speaking Muslim king conquered Bengal in 1400s, and depended on our Ghosh family for ruling the region. The king gave "Dastidar" an honorific title with Persian root. Since then, many in the family use double last name Ghosh Dastidar, while some others write only Ghosh. Our father and mother used just Ghosh, except for formal or celebratory occasion, but insisted that his children use that to remind our connection to our homeland. Mr. Ghosh lived in Karaya Road in southern Kolkata, close to our home. When the colonial power Britain banned Communist Party in 1939 Mr. Ghosh hid with our parents at our Lakhsmankathi village home in east Bengal, now Bangladesh. Our father insisted that Sachi talk to him about our village as Sachi was the first person to visit our home since 1947 partition.

Uncle Kaka was a trade unionist and a bachelor. In India there is a tradition for people to sacrifice their life for the good of the nation, that includes remaining an ascetic bachelor or bachelorette, when the entire nation becomes one's family. This is like the lifestyle of swamis (monk) and swaminis (nuns) in ashrams, or priesthood for Catholics. However, Catholic priests are allowed to keep connection with the family, while Hindu swamis and swaminis break all connections with family, as the world becomes his/her family. They give up their family identity for the entire world. They do their post-death rituals beforehand, as they won't have any relatives. Desire for sex is controlled in Indian and Eastern cultures since the day one is born. After each trip to Bangladesh, dozens of freedom fighters of Indian independence would come to meet with us, hear stories of villages, almost all bachelors and bachelorettes, and almost all refugees in 1980. Uncle got elected to the Indian Parliament with CPM ticket from north Kolkata. Communists ruled West Bengal from 1977 through 2011. They held power in a coalition government from 1967 through 1969. When Uncle was elected, it was impossible to meet with him. Sachi tried but failed. In 1990s as Sachi was working on his book on partition, our eldest brother Dada insisted that Sachi visit him in his government apartment. Dada met him in our Bangladesh village. In India it is very common to just walk into someone home without prior notice. As most people live with other family members, there is usually someone to answer the doorbell. All bachelors end up staying with a brother's or sister's family, and uncle too was staying with such a family, as a lady brought Sachi hot tea soon after his arrival. This time there was a hermit-looking guard outside his third-floor apartment who sat on a chair. The guard hinted to knock at the door, and a lady opened the door and asked to wait at the living room. Soft-spoken Uncle came and asked some questions. Initially he said he didn't know Lakshmankathi village, and couldn't remember if he hid at our parent's home during communist ban. He asked Sachi a few more questions and thought Sachi was confused with someone else. Sachi apologized, and then said "I am sorry that my dad Bibuiti-Bhusan, or your MonaDa gave me wrong information, but he is no more." There was a big change in him. Uncle immediately recalled everything, and asked Sachi to stay. After some discussion, he heard from Sachi as to how difficult it is to visit Kolkata from overseas after communists came to power with closing of factories and businesses, as airlines left Kolkata for other cities of India.

Over 50,000 factories closed through labor strikes during CPM rule, and the state changed from one of the leading Indian industrial states to one of the backward. We told him that we have been writing to various air carriers to connect Kolkata. Hearing this he was very happy, as he served on Transportation Committee of Indian Parliament. Later he asked Sachi to send his correspondences to Comrade Chatterjee, a CPM Member of Parliament from southern Kolkata constituency. Sachi sent his letters to Mr. Chatterjee, who breaking many Indian elite practices, replied to Sachi's concern.

Mr. Ghosh died in 2001 at the age of 87. Communist Party-Marxist wrote in their paper the following obituary:

"Sunday, July 1, 2001 Comrade …. Ghosh, he died at Calcutta on 1st July at the age of 87. As a student, … Ghosh joined the anti-imperialist movement and became a member of the Communist Party in 1937. He became a whole-time worker of the Party and organized jute workers around Calcutta and developed the Party in the 24 Parganas district. For the past six decades, … Ghosh worked devotedly in the working-class movement in West Bengal and the country. He was a prominent leader of the AITUC (All India Trade Union Congress) and one of founding leaders of the CITU (Centre for Indian Trade Union). He was the President of the West Bengal state committee of the CITU till his death. Comrade …. Ghosh played an important role in the struggle against revisionism and in the events leading to the formation of the CPI(M) when he was based in Delhi. A leader reared in the finest Communist tradition; … Ghosh was one of the stalwarts of the Left movement in West Bengal. His was a determined voice in defense of the working class and for the rights of the states in a federal system. These concerns were effectively voiced by him while he was a member of the Parliament. Comrade … Ghosh was a bachelor. His entire life was dedicated to the Communist movement and marked by staunch adherence to Marxism-Leninism."
Source: cpim.org.

Here are some of the letters produced after Sachi's discussion:

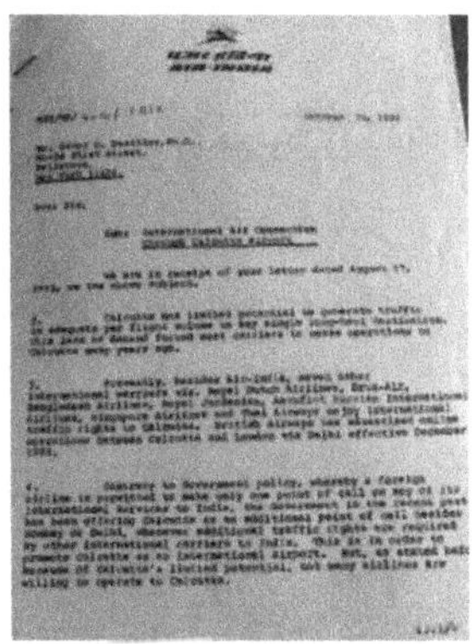

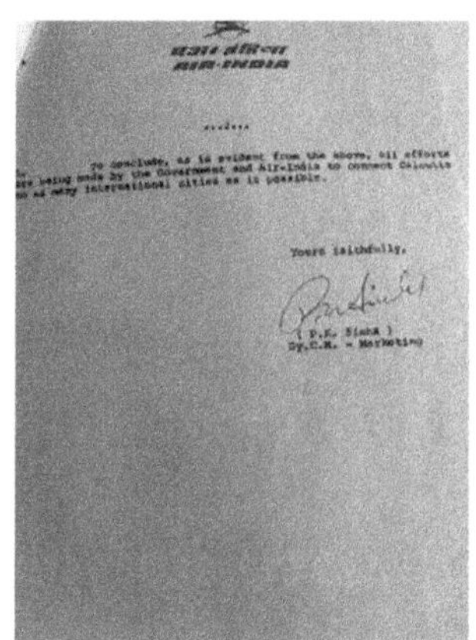

Letter from Air India, 1993

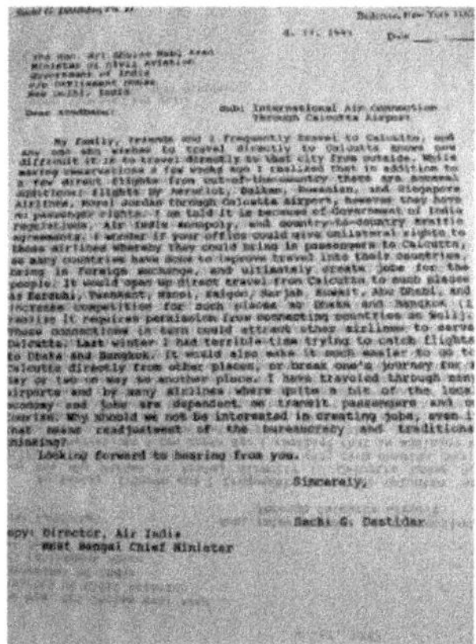

Sachi's Letter to Hon, Golan Nabi Azad, India's Federal Minister of Congress Party

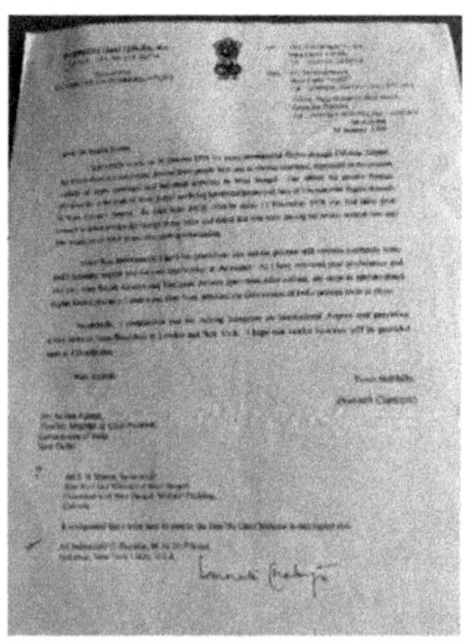

Reply from Minister Azad's Office

It is worth mentioning the mixed role of communists during Indian independence movement against the British colonizers. Communist Party of India (CPI) was banned by the British in 1939, but the ban was revoked after 1940 Hitler-Stalin Pact. During the Quit India Movement (QMI) in 1942 of Gandhi-led Congress Party, the pro-partition secessionist Muslim League Party and Communists Party supporters were free for politicking while all the workers of the largest, secular and pro-united India Congress Party were arrested and put in British prison, including Sachi's maternal grandparents and uncles. However, "When the Congress Party conditionally supported the British Government during the Second World War, the CPI came forward with strong criticism of this policy of the Congress. ..... But when Hitler invaded Russia, it altered the whole international situation. The CPI on the initiative of Russia supported the (colonial) Indian Government in its war efforts. In turn, the Indian Government lifted ban from the party.... Now the British Government in India used the Communist Party as a counterpoise to the Congress. During QIM, the Communists helped the (British) Government.... On the industrial front the Communists tried their best to keep the workers out of the national unrest during the period. .... But after the end of the Second World War, the CPI realized that it had lost the good faith of the people and during post-independence period, they worked hard to gain their lost ground..." writes Soma Banerjee in "Short Essay on the Origin of Communist Party in India" via Internet.

Western Neo-Colonialists and Indian Pro-Colonialists:

Westerners' neo-colonialists and Indian pro-colonialist project that the objectionable and inhuman caste practice exist only among Hindus, but not with those converted to Islam or Christianity. Castes is like racism that became institutionalized in some regions of the Subcontinent – not everywhere – in the second millennia when India was ruled by colonial powers. Some blame it on 1,000 years of colonial European-Christian and settler-colonial Arab-Persian-Islamic rule of India. Others see that as inherent problem of millennia-old tradition failing reformation even when suggested by sages and reformers. Caste discrimination is quite serious among some Muslims, including among

Pakistani Punjabis, the majority of Pakistan, and among Pakistani Kashmiris, as well as with many other non-Hindu groups. Although Islam should have brought equality among their followers, yet Army of Islamic Republic of Pakistan and Bengali Islamists murdered over 3 million Bengalis only in 9 months, in their Hindu genocide and secular Muslim extermination campaign. Pakistani Islamists did that supposedly to "inferior Bengali Muslims." Not one Muslim-majority nation protested, or even asked for trial of those mass murderers. Is that because most of those killed were kefir Hindus or kefir-called secular Muslims because of their tolerance for others, thus they can be considered as kefirs in Islam? Even killers of Bangladesh's Father of the Nation Sheikh Mujibur Rahman were sheltered by Muslim-majority nations, unfortunately, even by freedom-loving West sheltered killers. Why do our lives not matter to the East and West? What kind of public policy are these? Democratic or anti-democratic? Why did President Nixon's America, and many European nations supported the Hindu genocide? U.S. sent her 7th Fleet to the Bay of Bengal to prevent Mrs. Indira Gandhi's effort to stop the genocide and liberate Bangladesh. Hypocrisy of pluralistic, tolerant nations?

"In my mind, India is nation of nations where national, sectarian, regional or narrow-based parties and ethnic states fight against 'Delhi' in a pathologically dysfunctional manner to hide their own incompetence and sectarianism. From distance I sometimes wonder if India's neighbors too are fighting against 'Delhi' like Indian states, as ethnic cleansing from their nations suggest with no reaction from leaders of those nations, and leaders of various regional/ethnic/linguistic /religious groups in India. Their populations are warm to each other as our experience suggest. Why reality and rhetoric do not match? Once our family was welcomed by a family in Pakistan while their boy was staying at our home in New York as he had no place to stay," as written by Sachi in his paper. This is nothing unusual. On many college campuses in India or in America, Indians, Pakistanis, Bangladeshis, Nepalese, Sri Lankans live as roommates, just as Tamils, Marathas, Oriya, Manipuri, Telugus, or Bengali Indians, Hindu or Muslim, Jain or Christian live as roommates. All neighboring nations of India – Pakistan,

Afghanistan, Bhutan, Nepal, Tibet, Burma, Sri Lanka – cleansed Hindus, Buddhists, Jains, Sikhs, plus Muslims and Christians from two nations, for India as they didn't fit into their narrow national identity. But India did not cleanse their minorities. Let us quote from Sachi's essay "Independence and Partition Commemorative and Mujib Remembrance; August 15, 2020," now in blog; http://empireslastcasualty.blogspot.com/2020/08/subcontinentpartition documentation.html. "I appreciate Mr. Khurshedul Islam's suggestion as to evaluate how far we have come since British-created divide-and-rule policy starting on October 16, 1905 by dividing Bengal Province into Muslim Bengal and Hindu Bengal when there was no such demand from Muslims or Hindus, and then giving money to a North Indian non-Bengali Muslim to start a separatist Muslim League Party in Bengal."

"Let me look back at what happened since India's Bengal, Punjab, Assam were partitioned in 1947, and Kashmir in 1948."

"With that Pakistani Punjab became a place devoid of Hindu, Sikh, Jain, and losing many of her Christians for India. She (Pakistan) lost her Hindu-Sikhs from Sindh, Pathan and Baloch areas."

"Indian Punjab lost most of her Muslims, but not all. (And not from other 28 states.) Thank goodness most Muslims stayed in India, though most supported pro-partition Muslim League Party as British started an apartheid voting system in India for Muslims and Mon-Muslims."

"Pakistani Kashmir's 20% non-Muslims vanished altogether. My friend Bal Gupta of Atlanta lost 26 members of his family. Should we care about that? It is great that Indian Kashmir has retained her Muslim majority, although some Muslims are agitating, while their Hindus, Sikhs and Buddhists are not."

"Bangladesh/East Pakistan lost 50 million Hindus from 1947 through 2001 Census, plus many Chakma and Buddhists. Can our displaced minorities return back? Incidentally, our Big Powers are pushing Bangladesh to ignore 71 Genocide, but still are protesting Nanking massacre though the number of people killed is very small compared to Bangladesh killing by Pakistan. And because of Nanking Japan, China, North and South Korea have not normalized their relation. Why this hypocrisy?"

"In 1947 India's West Bengal lost some Muslims but quickly many more returned increasing its share of state population."

"Burma declared herself Buddhist-Burmese, and after 1962 coup deported millions of local Hindus, Muslims, Christians to India. I had classmates who were deported to India. Why didn't revolutionaries and pacifists protest? A new form of racism?"

"Sri Lanka declared herself Buddhist-Sinhala and expelled Tamil Hindus, Muslims and Christians to India. My NY Tamil neighbor's parents were deported although they were Sri Lankan."

"China after occupying Tibet cleansed tens of thousands of Buddhists to India. Did we protest? Did our Left or Right protest?"

"Years later, after Tibet's occupation, China marched her army through the Indian territory of Eastern Ladakh in 1962 occupying an area slightly smaller than Bangladesh. So, what did we do?"

"Many Indian states are divided because of ethnic sectarianism."

"Bhutan claiming to be Buddhist-Bhutanese monarchy recently expelled over a quarter of her citizens, the Nepali-speaking Hindu-Bhutanese. Many of our Nepali neighbors in New York are those refugees. Our reaction?"

"Nepal during her Hindu monarchy expelled her plains' Hindi-speaking Madhesis to India, though India is the only country which allows Nepalese to work without any paper. And now the communist rulers of Nepal have come up with a new map including parts of India. Surprise? Are they following the same "anti-Delhi" policy of communist rulers of Indian West Bengal?"

"In 1971 Pakistan killed over 3 million Bengali Hindus and secular Muslims when Bengalis formed the majority of their nation, yet no Army mass murderer or *babus* (bureaucrats) have been arrested. Why? Why no nation in the Subcontinent but Bangladesh, and no Muslim-majority nation demanded trial of mass murderers? Their followers also murdered the Father of the Nation Mujib and his entire family including babies. Why haven't we asked for trial of those murderers living in the U.S., Canada, Britain and in Muslim-majority nations? Why our lives don't matter? How can we move ahead forgetting our history? We admire the courage of our transformative leader Bangabandhu or Friend of Bengal."

"Time is long past when people sharing a generic Indian culture to come together, not at the cost of one another but for prosperity of all. This must be at equal footing for all. I find that spirit side-by-side with intolerance. All nations need to be equally tolerant, secular and pluralistic, not one standard for one, and another for others."

"I am speaking from what I found from my visits from Kathmandu, Nepal to Kanyakumari in Tamil Nadu, from Karakorum Mountains in Pakistani Kashmir to Jaffna in Sri Lanka and Chittagong in Bangladesh, and from Varanasi, Uttar Pradesh to Rawalpindi, Pakistan to Maldives, and from Tuichwang, Mizoram, India to neighboring Bagan in Myanmar. If Mizoram and Bagan were in Europe or South America the journey could have taken a few hours instead now it takes days from Mizoram via Assam, North Bengal, to Kolkata. Just to get a visa for Mizo's border Myanmar one has to travel to Kolkata, a 3-day journey by bus for most average citizens, or, visit illegally crossing the border. From Pakistan to Myanmar, Bangladesh to Sri Lanka, and to distant states of India, my family has been invited by strangers to their home. This is wonderful, heartwarming, and life changing. One poor family invited us to stay with them who had only a torn sari on the floor as bed and a roll of hay as pillow."

Post-1947 Partition and Independence:

After independence of India loyalty of Muslims towards a united India was always questioned. Before partition in British controlled apartheid-like election of Muslim and non-Muslim electorates when Muslims voted overwhelmingly for partition and creation of Islamic Pakistan, and non-Muslims for united India. With secessionist Muslim League Party remaining part of Indian politics, they remained a constant reminder, unlike in Muslim-majority Pakistan where pro-secular Congress Party was wiped out overnight. Muslim League party still operates in India, but hardly any cleansing of Muslims took place from India. Good thing. Cowardness do not follow the saying, 'To every action there is an equal and opposite reaction,' only possible in fatalistic India and untaught indigenism. Cleansing, pogrom and genocide of Hindu, Sikh, Jain, Buddhist minority continued in Pakistan, then in Bangladesh, formerly East Pakistan, till today without any repercussion from refugees, or from Indians or Hindus, or from the rest of the world. The Communist Party of India was tolerated by the British colonial power, at times banned, depending on communists' support of colonialism. Thus, as mentioned earlier, during Quit India Movement, Communists and Islamists were allowed to roam free in India while all Congress Party supporters were put behind bar in 1942, including my grandparents, and uncles. Even after freedom from British oppression when Communist China occupied Tibet, left parties in Bengal and India remained silent as colonial China cleansed tens of thousands of Tibetan Buddhists to India. And, this is India who never learned to fight back even for land which was part of India, from 100 years to 1,000 years back. Later in 1962 when China marched its army into Indian Ladakh region, Indian elites remained silent. China's action is similar to Putin's action in Ukraine. Thus, when China attacked Indian soldiers in their occupied Ladakh border in 2020, this time Communist Party of India-Marxist leader Mr. Surjakanto Mishra openly said "aamra chiner dalal noi," meaning "we are not" – read no more – "the agents of China" (see daily *Kolkata24x7*, June 18, 2020), implying they were agent of China before.

Comparing two democracies of U.S. and India should be easy, but it is just the opposite. In America with its primary system, it has become a democracy, although democracy run by minorities. Very few people vote in the primaries. At times the percentage of people voting is in single digit. Then there are many candidates for each position. However, once an individual gets the top vote in primary, one gets to run for the office. In our New York City School Board election in 1996, when Sachi ran for election, and was elected to the Board, there were possibly low teen percentage of voters who voted in the election. Then there is money. Candidates in rich countries are able to raise funds to conduct election, without depending on foreign funding. Thus, wealthy are able to run for election better than poor candidates. In poor countries like India running for office gets complicated for money, bringing corruption and illegal funding. Extortion has come to play a big role in Indian politics. In the U.S. those are legal. In addition, some people often gossip as to how money from non-democratic monarchies, West, or East, are playing role in buying candidates. This also happens in other democracies. To avoid foreign funding of elections in late 2010s Indian Government put restrictions on receiving funds from foreign countries when it came for criticism from Western press, but the same press took opposite position and criticized when they found U.S. candidates received funding from Russia and Arab monarchies (see *NY Times*, March 15, 2022.) Similar press also criticized Indian Government for not allowing foreign funding for Christian Mother Teresa's organization which also converts indigenous population, but the press didn't see any problem when New York-based Probini Foundation that helps the poor and the orphaned faced the same problem, but many are managed by minorities. (Even in 2024 donation to orphanages and schools were not allowed to be accepted in India and Bangladesh.) The press saw India being anti-conversion or anti-Christian in Mother Teresa's case, but not as anti-Hindu in Probini or Partition Center's case.

If U.S. has been able to make the nation run by the "Rule of Law," as the nation produces millions of lawyers each year, with each district, county, state and the Federal Government enacting new laws each year. In India law rarely guides one's life. In April 11, 2022 the *Statesman* paper of India disclosed that it takes 30 years to resolve a court case. How can a democracy survive if it takes 30 years to evict an illegal occupier when elected representatives' term is for two or four years?

Thus, arrives thugs, political parties, criminals, guns, extortionists, and more. Illegal gun is entering India too, while gun has created a murder culture in the U.S. In India, two more tools were developed by the rulers: open mass killing of Hindus, and dropping voters from electoral rolls. We know quite a few people who were dropped from the electoral rolls in India, assuming those voters won't vote for the regional or state ruling parties. Ironically, the anti-Communist Trinamool Party, who ousted the Communists in Indian West Bengal state, is following the same tool as they too have dropped voters. And to keep the opposition out of reach, they too have started mass oppression of opposition, and promoting colonization of the state through illegal Bangladeshi settlers. (See daily Anandabazar https://www.anandabazar.com/editorial/ouropini on/caawaragainstbengalis/cid/1343571, May 11, 2022.) Unlike America and Europe, in India, especially in Pakistani-Bangladeshi-Hindu-Refugee-Indian-ruled West Bengal and Tripura states one becomes Indian citizen through bribing police and bureaucrats, not through the process one finds in the West, without any role by the federal government. If America was India all our 11 million "undocumented" aliens would have become U.S. citizens within years of arrival, and voted in our election, and some would have become local and federal lawmakers.

*Ex-Communist-Marxist Chief Minister Mr. Nripen Chakraborty (left) of
Tripura Holding Sachi*

*With Hon. Dasarath Deb (left), Deputy Chief Minister of
Communist Party-Marxist Tripura, India*

*Communist-Marxist Ex-Chief Minister Nripen Chakraborty,
After his Expulsion from the Party*

Indian public policy has been influenced by her independence struggle, trying to accommodate an extremely diverse population, group pressure, minority pressure, sectarian politics of states, incompetence, timidity of her liberators from British oppression, the Congress Party of India, murder of the Father of the Nation Mohandas Karamchand Gandhi by a Hindu fanatic, Prime

Minister Mrs. Indira Gandhi by Sikh bodyguards, and Prime Minister Mr. Rajiv Gandhi by foreign Sri Lankan Tamil Christian Minority. Thus, the first Prime Minister of India, Jawaharlal Nehru, on one hand wasn't able to protect Hindu-Sikh-Jain-Buddhist-Christian-Parsee minority population of Pakistan – West Pakistan and East Pakistan – but felt obligated to protect the Muslim minority in India who overwhelmingly voted in pre-partition colonial India for a separate Muslim homeland called Pakistan, and against a united India. In a hypothetical situation if a minority group came in power in the Southern U.S. and became an independent nation, and drove all the Protestants out from the South but if the majority in rest of the U.S. were Protestants, would there have been any reaction from rest of the U.S.? Some Muslims who migrated, not fled, to Pakistan called themselves Muhajir, the armed militants who went from Mecca to Medina to convert non-Muslim Arabia to an Islamic one, even by force and killings of non-believers. In Indian East Punjab there were some attacks on Muslims, as attacks on Hindu-Sikh-Jain-Non-Muslims continued in West Punjab, now in Pakistan, cleansing over quarter of the population. Sikh militancy, which came to power with arms to protect the indigenous minority under Islamic rule, fought back. In Bengali eastern wing of Pakistan, a third of the population came under attack with loss of over 49 million from her 1941 and 2001 Census (see *Empire's Last Casualty: Indian Subcontinent's Vanishing Hindu and Other Minorities*, 2008, and *Bengal's Hindu Holocaust: Partition of India and Its Aftermath*, 2021). On the other hand, at 1947 partition, Indian minority Muslims were about 12% of the population, even after massive migration of Hindu-Sikh-Jain-Buddhist-Christian Pakistani, Bangladeshi, Sri Lankans, Burmese, Tibetans, and other refugees, the share of Indian Muslim population has risen to 14% by 2011 Census, instead of going down. This is theoretically impossible unless there was huge Muslim migration to India. How cleanser and cleansed moved to India? Were supporters of atrocities and victims of atrocities of WW II were treated equally in the West?

One would argue that one of the problems of Western journalism in India is that they are Delhi focused, and meeting and talking to some folks in Delhi.

They assume it is "India." When one talks to "Indians" in India or in America or elsewhere, those Indians see through their own experience in their own state, for example, Tamil Nadu in the South, Gujarat in the West, Manipur in the northeast, or Odisha in the east. Many Indians overseas may have no idea of "Delhi," politically, culturally or emotionally, or beyond their town or village. Many of those folks or their families may not have visited Delhi or other parts of India at all before traveling overseas. Sometimes, experience of those individuals is based on their experience in their own state, and of effects of public policy of those states, not of the federal government. This was true for many who were influenced by one tolerant nationalist policy in pre-independence India, and then post-independence intolerant politics of Islamic Republic of Pakistan in East Pakistan, and other intolerant sectarian politics of states and nations. Sachi didn't know Hindi, the official language of India until he spent months at an elite, caste-politics-influenced university in Delhi in 2013. One self-critical professor called the institution as "White elephant." Bengali and Hindi are sister languages forking from Sanskrit, it was easy to learn Hindi. Yet a tolerant public policy of India allowed him to get a federal job in 1970 without knowing Hindi. It will be like getting a U.S. federal job to work in Washington D.C. without knowing English.

India is going through another dilemma of her school and college education. Schooling existed in India for millennia, mostly based on *pathshalas* and *bidyaloi* (*vidyaloi*) or schools to higher education run by monks (swamis), nuns (swaminis), or by educated families. Some were free. Some were residential. In most cases boys went to those schools, but others were for girls or coed. Families played some role in this process. There were many universities in old India as well, and most famous of them was Nalanda Vishwavidyalaya (University) in modern-day Bihar State in Eastern India. There were several others going back to the first millennia. See https://www.thestatesman.com /education/listancient-indian-universities 1503075194.html on ancient Indian universities.) Nalanda was destroyed by Islamic conqueror Khilji. He destroyed many other sites of kefirs including Bodh Gaya where Buddha received his spiritual fulfillment. The process of education got disrupted with second millennial colonial rule of Arab-Persian Islamic rulers, and later by the British-Christian colonial rulers. It is the British who introduced the modern, Western education in early 1800s with the opening of Presidency College in Calcutta (Kolkata). Schooling was later spread throughout its colony. Schools run by Christian institution came with Britain's colonization which exist even today. Colonial Britain didn't allow teaching of Indian literature by giving them "religious" branding. It is true that world's only surviving indigenous culture's literature came from Vedas to yoga to meditation to songs and dances were all tied to Mother Nature, represented by many deities, animals, plants, seasons, water, sea, oceans, mountains, valleys, and more. Thus before 15th Century almost all literature was based on these. Moreover, printing didn't develop until 18th Century. So, colonial masters didn't include teaching of any of literature of Ramayana, Mahabharata, Vedas, Upanishads, yoga, meditation and more.

This was their way of disconnecting natives from their past heritage and literature. In some cases, colonialists allowed teaching in local languages, but didn't encourage teaching Sanskrit, the mother language of most Indian, South Asian, and Southeast Asian plus some Western languages. After 1947 independence, Pakistan and Bangladesh eliminated teaching of Sanskrit altogether, but many Indian states did that too. They followed colonial policy. This is a big tragedy of post-independence India. In case of Bengal, India, the leader of Indian independence movement, initially Congress Party, tried to decolonize the curricula, but not the private schools or schools run by Christian and Islamic missionaries. When communists came to power in West Bengal, they immediately dropped English, Sanskrit, and Hindi from West Bengal schools, although it was reported in papers that the ruling elites sent their children to English-medium schools, as mentioned earlier. In June of 2022, the Communist Party-Marxist appointed a minority Muslim as head of West Bengal unit who was sending his kid to Bengali medium school. Surprisingly, Bengal's ruling nationalist Congress Party, anti-nationalist Communist-Marxist Party, and anti-Communist Trinamool Party, all were officially for teaching in local languages. Yet, for the past 75 years kept English to be the language for tests in Kolkata City Corporation, not Bengali. This is true in most of the regional states with local languages. Corporation hires many non-technical low-paying jobs for their work, many of whom come from villages offering education in vernacular languages. In 2022 one Bengali nationalist group, Bangla Paksho, marched on the streets for Kolkata Corporation to allow tests in Bengali (see daily *Kolkata24x7*, January 1, 2023).

Post-Colonial India and Post-Civil War America:

Post-colonial India is inheritors of many streams, rivers and movements. Some of these are the result of, (a) world's longest nationalist struggle for independence and decolonization, (b) suicidal fatalism of Hindu mind, (c) only surviving nation of indigenous believes, (d) pluralism of Traditional Religion (Sanatana Dharma or modern non-local term Hinduism), (e) inordinate tolerance of Hindu mind, (f) identity problem of "Indians," (g) identity problem of polytheistic "Hindus," (h) rule for thousand years by Arab-Persian-Turkic Islamic, and European-Christian colonizers, (i) rise of British promoted Caste racism, as opposed to deities (symbolism) belonging to all colors and peoples, (j) rise of sexism as influenced by Islamic and European colonizers, (k) religious rituals in temples without any discourse, sermon, or *khutba* telllng the meaning of rituals, (l) not teaching the history of minority and foreigners' oppression of the majority, and (m) not teaching of traditional beliefs, thus one has to come to America or Germany to learn about Hinduism-Jainism-Brahmhoism of Monotheistic Brahmo believe, and many more. Added to this is the language, tribe, caste, sub-caste, regional, sub-regional differences were strengthened by the British-created divide-and-rule policy, and India's fatalistic acceptance of oppression by Farsi-speaking settler-rulers of the Islamic Mughals. Colonial era is the inheritor of Indian Enlightenment, Hindu Reform Movement, Indian Renaissance, Bengal Renaissance, and renaissance in various regions. Renaissance varies widely from region to region, some with none. Some supported colonizing oppressors, especially after conversion.

One can easily argue that the American independence and Indian independence have no similarity expect that both the colonies were ruled by the British Empire. America was a settler colony, where indigenous peoples didn't matter. American rebellion against the British gave rise to the first Republic of the world, a new political system that the world would follow. And India was a colony ruled by a handful of European Christians where the natives had rich millennia-old culture, economically affluent, yet weak in arms and militancy. India's independence was followed by independence of Third World nations of Africa, Asia, the Caribbean and a few countries in South America and Oceania. In America, the native population was small in number. India was a high-density nation with huge population, and higher income than the colonizers. Some claim that their old Sanskrit language is the mother of Indo-European languages developed thousands of years before British arrived.

Another Indian language, Tamil of southern India is equally old. India was already a country with decent standard of living, when the British arrived. Thus, British was able to enrich their economy with huge amounts of wealth transfer. In April 18, 2020 Dr. Nazrul Islam writes in *The Daily Star* (Dhaka, Bangladesh) that "$45 (forty-five) trillion dollars of wealth was transferred from India to Britain between 1765 and 1938"! A YouTube historical video reminds of that. The earlier Islamic colonizers of India didn't transfer too much wealth to their motherlands, as they were settler colonizers, much like European settlers in Americas. We still remember, while visiting Fergana Valley in Uzbekistan in 1999 to look for Indian Mughal Emperor Babur's home, Shefali was mobbed by all the sellers of a bazar – women, men and kids. Everyone wanted to take pictures with a "Hindustani" lady, offering her gifts of apple, bread, fruits, and hug. In all over the old world, India is known as Hindustan – the land of the Hindus, as pre-British region used to be called. It is believed that the river Sind which became Indus in English, came to be known as Hind in Persian, and those who lived there in that ancient civilization were known as Hindu, and in lower part of the river people are known as Sindhu from where the word evolved. The Sind land became Hind in ancient Asia and Africa, to Inde and India in Europe. In all Egyptian bazars we were welcomed as "Hindustani" with folded hands saying "Namaste," Welcome. An Uzbek-speaking European diplomat traveling with us in Uzbekistan, seeing the spectacle, said "I will suggest back home to send an Indian lady as our diplomat here to get popular support." In Osh, Kyrgyzstan, at the western end of Fergana Valley, we ran into a Bengali-Indian visiting professor on teaching assignment from India. Osh is so remote that when one resident learned we are from the States; he came running to introduce two young American college graduates who were teaching English there. We went to Fergana to look for Babur's home, the first settler Islamic king of India, but there were no locals. Babur is said to have dreamed of his favorite Fergana fruits – watermelons, persimmons, apples, and more. True to his dream we found scores of street-side melon vendors that was unique to that region. It was a true delight, but realized the limitation of our stomach. After lots of search we were able to find Babur Museum in the small town of Andijan.

The museum was locked, but we could see through the iron gate the persimmon tree in the yard. Seeing two "Hindustanis" were trying to get into the museum, someone took it upon himself to find a key to the locked museum while we waited next to the museum. He ran around for half-an-hour through Andijan while we were made at home by locals speaking Russian and Uzbek, but mostly through sign language. Afterwards we went to a nearby town of Namangan where the large bazar was located. During another trip to Uzbekistan's capital Tashkent, almost 350 kilometers west, we again got a royal treat at the new Museum of Amir Timur, also known as Timur Long or Tamerlane. He killed millions of people. We vaguely remembered Timur's horrific anti-Hindu genocide in India. Public policy in post-independence India is to censor colonizers atrocities – Islamic and British, rather than learning from that history, and moving on. Censorship is not good for any culture. If Americans followed India's public policy, she would have to censor slavery, racism, war against Native Americans, and American Civil War, rather than teaching those as a part of history, and not promoting anti-white or anti-black policies in our society, and learning how to avoid that. Again, if India was Germany, she wouldn't have taught Holocaust or built Holocaust Memorial right at the heart of Berlin, as well as in other cities. In Tashkent, the capital of Uzbekistan, at the heart of the city used to have a statue of Lenin. It was replaced by a statue of Amir Timur on horseback, and a sparkling new Timur Museum was built next to the statue. This was just a few years after the fall of Communism, and it showed the world how superficial was the communist ideology. Germany created a different remembrance.

Berlin

Berlin Jewish Memorial

Berlin Jewish Memorial

After collapse of the Soviet Union all the Former Soviet Republics pushed for pre-Soviet identity, at times pre-Islamic, as in the case of Kazakhstan and Kyrgyzstan. Hearing our plan to visit Timur Museum, one Uzbek professor asked us, "Why visit that? He was a mass murderer." It was eye opener. We were to visit after Fergana. As we were heading to Tashkent, from nowhere appeared a local English weekly newspaper with an article describing how Timur murdered tens of thousands of "Hindus" in Delhi when those natives didn't convert, then making a "mountain" with their body parts. But no one in India, Pakistan, Afghanistan or Bangladesh, with same heritage and culture, will be told of these. Some literature is available, but almost underground, like Dr. Radhashyam Brahmachari's *Falsehood Shrouds the True History of Agra and Delhi* (Tuhina Prakashani; 2014) or M. A. Khan's *Islamic Jihad: A Legacy of Forced Conversion, Imperialism and Slavery* (felibari.com), and many more. Many hypocritical activists would brand these historians as anti-Islam, or something like that, yet the same critiques will not live with their neighbors in their Pakistan or Bangladesh homeland, and would appreciate how "America is teaching Black history." We got another surprise at the Timur Museum ticket counter.

The cost of admission was 10 times higher for Central Asia's former Soviets than for Uzbek citizens, and 100 times higher for foreigners. It was shocking. So, we expressed our surprise in broken Russian, "Ochin daroga!" or "Very expensive!" The young lady looked at us, and was surprised, possibly shocked.

She asked "Hindustani?" We nodded. Our driver said in Russian "Hindustani Amrerikii." She then converted our driver and us to local, and said, "Can't you see I am Hindustani too as my ticket office is decorated with posters from India? I like Indian movies? I like Indian dress. I like Indian food." We presented her an American and an Indian coin exciting her.

Before the rise of modern states, people migrated from one region to another, often sheltered by kings and emperors. At times there were maltreatment, while another ruler treated fairly. After sometime, those migrants became "local." Thus, one found different European nationalities in different regions, until two World Wars made European states ethnically pure. State diversity is still common in India. Some European states with heterogeneity are now facing new challenges. And after the Soviet collapse, many of the ideological traditions –from social equality to forced assimilation of cultures and religions to supremacy of atheism – gave way to killings, ultra-nationalism, partition of nations, dictatorships, war, and more.

India's experiment in political democracy came from her millennia-old religious democracy or pluralism practiced by indigenous peoples. People may worship one Mother in Tripura in eastern India, but the same Mother may be worshipped in Kutch in the western India by a different name but using same Sanskrit slokas, whereas Himachal in the north may revere a tree whereas Tamils in the south may worship an animal, thus protecting all life forms. People learned to tolerate this, and to tolerate diverse ideas and cultures. And India was a place that was geographically defined by the Himalayan Mountains in the north, Baloch Desert in the west, Naga Hills-Arakan Yoma Mountain range in the east and the Indian Ocean in the south. For millennia people intermingled, intermarried, and developed a pluralistic religious practice embracing diversity. It is represented by a line in a poem of Rabindranath Tagore, "In the body of Bharat (India) Saka, Hun, Pathan, Mughal peoples and others have become one." Before the arrival of the new religion Islam, almost all the invaders of India became part of India, and their faiths became part of pluralistic Hinduism. The invaders came from the Greece, Central Asia, Persia, China, and from Southeast

Asia. But coming of followers of Islam to India was very different. They came to India either from the west via the Arabian Sea, or from the northwest crossing Hindu Kush Mountains. Hardly anyone realizes that Hindu Kush means "Hindu Killing." Thus, you cross that Mother Nature's barrier to kill Hindus, i.e., Indians. Very few Afghans of present day hardly know that they are one of the inheritors of ancient "Hindu" religion and culture, just as very few Pakistanis realize that fact. During a visit to Lahore, Pakistan's cultural and intellectual capital's old downtown Lakshmi Bag or a Place of Mother Lakshmi, the Goddess of Prosperity, a Punjabi Muslim shop keeper told us that it was so named because it was owned by "foreigner Indians," not realizing that before ethnic cleansing, those shop owners were Punjabis like himself! Plunder, forced conversion and destruction of indigenous edifices were the goals, as the followers had done in lightning speed spreading from Morocco on Atlantic Ocean to Indonesia on the Pacific Ocean. This was really a great achievement. Religion was promoted, My Way or No Way! Monotheistic ideology, supported by deadly force and terror was great attraction to many, no doubt. That's why it spread like wild fire. It was not the pacifist preaching of Christ, Buddha, Jain, Chaitanya or Shiva. And one of the real glories was that once converted, new converts were able to forget their past, their identity, and no tears were shed as their families, ancestral homes and shrines were destroyed.

How many Arabs cry for their past Pagan, Qureshi, Christian or Hindu-like nature worshiping? Or, Turks for their Christian heritage? Or, Pakistan for their Sanatani heritage? In Pakistan, and in rest of the true believer's world, the indigenous faith is constitutionally barred from many offices, and now (2024) in Afghanistan they have created a law which prohibits friendship with "Hindus," their ancestral faith, although Afghanistan is almost 0% minority. How many articles have appeared in Western and Indian press about that? This is another form of racism. There is no compassion for some lives in the Western and Indian press! Some lives can be sacrificed, as they have no lobby or money. Even worse is that brave Muslim secularists in Muslim-majority nations do not get protection through Western media. This is serious. In order to retain a hold on to its colony, Britain started a new divide-and-rule policy by partitioning Bengal in 1905 into Muslim East Bengal and Hindu West Bengal when there was no demand from Muslims or Hindus for dividing Bengal. Britain started a Muslim League Party in Dhaka, Bengal, now Bangladesh, paying a non-native, who didn't know the local language, huge sums of money to start that party. Naturally, the non-native didn't have any emotional connection with the land. Earlier in 1800s Arabs sent missionaries to Bengal to start an anti-local Arab-based extremist Wahabi movement, who ignored all connection to Mother Nature of Bengal and India. Thus, once converted, their connection to the land, its water, flora and fauna, name and outfit became irrelevant.

Even in the year 2020s destruction of temples, deities, Hindu homes and forced conversion is daily occurrence in many places, at times even in Hindu-majority India, yet ignored by the free press of the West and East, surprisingly not by secular press in Muslim-majority Bangladesh. Still, we believe, there is no difference among West Bengalis and Bangladeshis, or among Indians, Pakistanis and Bangladeshis (and Nepalese and Afghans and Sri Lankans and Burmese.) If the two Bengals – East and West – who have no difference, mirror image of each other, then why all the non-Muslim minority is being ethnically cleansed from Bangladesh bringing its Hindu from over 33% of the population in 1947 to a mere 7% in 2024 – creating the largest ethnic cleansing anywhere in the world with over 50 million people missing from 1947 through 2001 Census, i.e., in just five decades, and possibly 60 million cleansed by 2025, with over 3 million killed. Minority population in Hindu-majority West Bengal has increased from 18% to over 30% in the same period, in spite of mass migration tens of millions of persecuted refugees from East Pakistan-Bangladesh to West Bengal. (See *Empire's Last Casualty: Indian Subcontinent's Vanishing Hindu and Other Minorities*, Firma KLM, Kolkata, 2008; and *Bengal's Hindu Holocaust: The Partition of India and Its Aftermath*, Garuda Prakashan, Delhi, 2021.)

One may question, what is the difference within the same ethnic population? Answer is very simple: faith. Bengali East Pakistan/Bangladesh is Muslim majority, and India's Bengali West Bengal is Hindu-majority, as created by the British. One experiences sharp decline of minorities even when the minority gave disproportionately their lives for independence of Bangladesh in 1971.

Destroyed Deity, 2019 – almost Daily Occurrence (Source: Social)

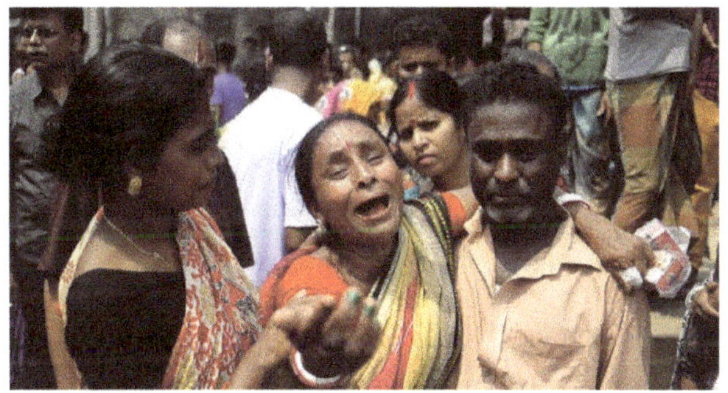

Pogrom 2019: Regular Event (Source: Social)

Destruction in Northern Areas, Fall of 2021 Durga Puja Pogrom in Bangladesh (Source: Social)

But saying this about our homeland one automatically becomes a pariah, a reactionary, a hardliner, a communal, similar to racist or fundamentalist in America and more. No rightminded American says such things to African-Americans protesting against lynching, slavery or discrimination. Are those people reactionary, hardliner, racist or fundamentalist? Or, when a Jew protests against Nazi atrocities against Jews and Gypsies, are they racist, fundamentalist and reactionary? Or, when a German Christian protest such atrocities, is she a racist and reactionary? Palestinian Gaza and Israel war has exposed liberal U.S. contradiction. When we lived in Ireland, we found many museums of Anglo atrocities against Irish Catholics. It was wonderful experience compared to fatalistically tolerant and forgetful of history of indigenous India. During a visit to Belfast, Northern Ireland, a huge wall separated minority Catholics and majority Protestants in the city. In India seeing no wall separating majority and minority, it felt 100 times better. British promotion of Islamic separatism succeeded in minority cleansing in Pakistan, Pakistani Kashmir and Bangladesh. Yet, hardly anyone talks about the indigenous minority with roots in pre-Islam era, and what happened to them. Visit to Northern Ireland in 2010s was lot more open than in early 1990s when the streets had many barriers possibly because of the effects of Bloody Sunday.

Here are some pictures from Belfast, Northern Ireland 's Catholic-Protestant wall divide. Walls were covered with murals:

KMA

Are those Irish remembering their past are hardliners, communal, racist, or fundamentalists? We certainly do not think so. Or, are Tibetans not allowed to protest ethnocide of their families by atheist China? Or, are Uighurs and Mongols supposed to hide their pain and misery? And, Armenians not allowed to talk about their genocide by Turkish monarchy for fear of offending present-day Turks? Should African-Americans not mention slavery?

Minority Rule in Democracy?

One of the serious issues in Indian democracy is the toleration of majority of "Hindus," and linguistic majority "Hindi" speakers. They do not have a singular identity, but are very tolerant, and do not or did not oppress others. As a matter of fact, they welcomed others, although Hindi in central, northern and western regions were oppressed by colonizing Islamic rulers, east was also oppressed by non-local oppressors. Thus, there are hardly any old Hindu-Jain-Buddhist shrines left in Pakistan and Afghanistan, and affected in central and western part of India and Bengal. If one has to find wonderful architecture of Indian

Civilization one must travel to southern India, especially to Tamil Nadu and Andhra Pradesh, or to Odisha (Orissa) in the east, and Assam and Manipur in the northeast. Rajasthan in the west where strong rajas or kings saved their heritage fighting foreign rulers. They have left imprints with the population. In India all the distant states from Delhi, whether Tamil speaking Tamil Nadu and Malayalam speaking Kerala in the south, or Kashmir in the north, or Tripura in the East maintain their separate identity, and a form of racism using faith, caste and language! Then there is West Bengal, a state declined economically, but acts with superiority complex. Northeast is dominated by Assam, but with complex identity issues, at times acting for self-defenses, and at other times for self-destruction. The leadership in Northeast has acted at times against indigenous Bengali Hindu minority, at other times against Bengali Muslim settlers from East Bengal/ East Pakistan, at times against Assam tribes, and at times against Bangladeshi Hindu refugees, at times Christian converted tribes against Bengalis and Hindus. British colonizer's action to convert parts of Assam to Christianity complicated even further, as mentioned earlier.

Now Nagaland, Mizoram, and Meghalaya are three Christian majority states. They were raised from districts, like U.S. counties, to states. It will be like making Brooklyn a state to make a Brooklynite-majority state in America. India still follows her colonial master's policy. As India is governed by a weak political system, there have been no effort to change such colonial discriminatory laws. Did Britain create laws where English people couldn't enter in parts of Britain? Of course, not. However, India has survived because of her fatalistic tolerance, pluralistic identity and corruption. So, when we visited our extended family in Nagaland, we were welcomed at the airport by their friend taking us to his home in Kohima, the state capital, in picturesque mountain area. No Non-Resident-Entry form was needed, even at police check points. This is when family ties help. This was also the reason why illegal Bangladeshi Muslim settlers have increased in many states. Nagaland, at the border of Myanmar, was in the midst of separatist warfare funded by India's opponents, but we had no trouble in visiting them. Tu, a young architect, graduate of a Kolkata's university, became our impromptu guide. He took us to homes of former cannibals which were decorated with skulls. Tu was struggling with his Hindu past and newly-introduced Christianity. We had no problem reading Naga as they were Assamese language written in English script, result of British Christianization.

Once we visited Assam state's northeastern city of Dibrugarh to visit a Buddhist center where our Probini decided to help the students at the orphanage. The monk, called swami or *vaante*, came inside the security zone with garland to welcome us. It was close to Arunachal Pradesh border of northeast India where British had also imposed travel restriction of other Indians, including Assamese to which the district belonged. Next day Sachi decided to visit the pristine rolling hills of Arunachal state. The driver knew what to say to the police for us to visit areas. It is a picturesque area which could create easily many jobs and prosperity through tourism. Again, we came to an area, recently settled, where school kids in uniform were walking with some papers. Our guide-cum-driver took us to a small public office where the officer seeing a newcomer was excited, and introduced him to the students. They told us that they were India-born kids of East Pakistan-Bangladesh-Buddhist-Chakma tribal refugees carrying Indian Citizenship certificate. Some local Arunachal tribes, who live far away from that remote unpopulated hilly region, went to Indian Supreme Court to drive these refugees out of Assam, or deport to Bangladesh. Supreme Court said before they can decide of their foreign-born parents, state must issue India-born kids their citizenship papers. This is the first time we saw such a document. In many areas of India many kids do not have birth certificates. It is worth noting that after decolonization, both Pakistan and Bangladesh removed such British restrictions in their nations, but not India. Did our media write or talk about it? Of course not. When India tried to remove that restriction in Indian Kashmir, how many times it was written and broadcast? Why is this double standard? Chakma were 97% majority in Chittagong Hill District of Bengal Province of British India, later in Pakistan, and then in Bangladesh. Why Britain gave that area to Islamic Republic? One of Bangladeshi ruler, General Zia, just decided to ignore all the British rules, and lifted almost half-a-million Muslim peasants from the plains to Chittagong Hills, making locals half of the population in their homeland in just a few weeks. Zia didn't bring any landless Buddhist or Hindu peasants from the plains to Chittagong Hills. Why? This is another example of anti-indigenous racism in a country born with millions of Hindu lives. Many locals said Zia took examples from China as how they colonized and marginalized indigenous homelands of Uighurs, Inner Mongolia and Tibet.

Bangladeshi Buddhist Tribal Chakma Refugees Living in Arunachal Pradesh in the Northeast India. Indian Citizenship papers to Boys and Girls were Delivered on that Day. An Assam-Bengali Manager is Standing in Front and Students with Citizenship Paper on the Background.

Buddhist Orphanage in Dibrugrah, Assam, India with Monk in Center

Students at the Buddhist Orphanage, Assam,
India Supported by Probini Foundation of U.S.A.

Again, as Sachi traveled to Mizoram at the invitation from Ahimsa (Nonviolent) English School in the remote southern part of the state, the contradiction in Indian immoral politics was exposed. Mizos are a small minority in India with a population of less one million in a nation of 1,300 million. Majority was identified as of indigenous tribal faith in 1890s. When the British left India they had converted about three quarters of the population. Non-converted indigenous Hindus are called Bru and Rehang. Soon, after creation of a separate state, Christian activists cleansed Brus and Rehangs, about 20% of the population, from the state to refugee camps in the neighboring Tripura state for almost two decades until the formation of Bhartiya Janata Party government when they were able to bring some of them back to their homeland in 2010s. Not all have returned yet. There are daily demonstrations by Mizo (Christian) Student Association in their capital Aizawl against return of their minority indigenous Hindus. The school that invited Sachi is run by even a smaller Buddhist Chakma tribe. Just across the border in Chittagong Hill district is the home of Chakma tribe who was colonized by Muslims of Bangladesh. Many of them were driven out to India as homeless refugees, now living in Indian states of Assam, Arunachal, Tripura, Mizoram, and more. Their Mizoram village was the most difficult to reach among all the seven continents that Sachi and his family visited. In a modern India the last 40 miles through hilly terrain took over four hours in a private car. It was a small Buddhist area, and locals complained of neglect by majority Christian community https://empireslast casualty.blogspot.com/2013/02/tuichawng-mizoram-india.html. It is difficult to verify complaints, but this is a popular belief, and they are extremely poor even by poor India's standard. Now the community is trying to buy a property or land to build a hostel for Buddhist and other tribal students in the capital, for students to complete high school, but majority Christians won't sell any property to minority non-Christians. It is hard to believe. One group for the minority non-Christian emailed us in December 24, 2021, "All have said, it is not possible to buy and own a land in Aizawl (the state capital). The Mizo (Christian) Students Union is a strong and aggressive student body in Mizoram and they don't allow the Chakmas (Buddhists) to buy land in Aizawl and Lunglei (the second largest city). We have been facing the racial discrimination since time immemorial and our leaders have faced so many struggles with them to get our rights......".

"Our children need to study in different fields to fight with them. We have no lawyer, doctor, engineer, Civil Servant, and not having a post in higher rank to fight with them!........" Another note said, "At Aizawl, we have the following problems. 1. Communal hatred and feeling occurs between the Mizo peoples (Christian) and the non-Mizo (non-Christian) peoples most of the time. 2. The Mizo people do not sell house site to the non-Mizo (non-Christian) people easily, if they sell, they used to sell with higher rates and having so many difficulties in changing ownership. There's not a single Chakma house in Aizawl (the state capital) till today. 3. Ragging has happened in commercial hostel and schools. 4. The Mizo people however, they do not deny to give the houses as rent to the Chakma people. We can live without fear and worry in rented building as the owner gets monthly rent from the non-Mizo. 5. We have religious issues in Aizawl, Mizo people are Christian and the Chakma's are Buddhist, and they only like us if we convert to Christianity......." So, what was their solution? Their solution was to find a space in Hindu-majority Assam's capital, another 12 to 16-

hour by bus, as opposed to 6 to 8-hour journey to the capital Aizawl. The suggestion, "At Guwahati: We only have permanent and peaceful solution. 1. Guwahati is the best and safe place for the Chakma students. 2. There's no discrimination and communal problem in Guwahati for the Chakma students. 3. The houses are easily bought in Guwahati. We can also buy flat other than the whole house building. 4. Rented house maybe at higher rates. 5. There are no religious issues in Guwahati and no conversion campaign. Moreover, Chakma students are free to adjust with Hindu brothers and sisters as the Hindu people follow the 'right to freedom of religion'. In Mizoram, everything is dominated by the Mizo people. The Chakma people do not have much constitutional rights in Mizoram.......... Best regards, ..." What was quite reveling was that indigenous Buddhist-Hindu minority constituting over 20% of population has no right in Hindu-majority India's Christian-majority area, but equal rights in Assam where Buddhist minorities constitute less than 1% of the population. Why the free press of West and East do not cover this?

Against Indian Constitution Mizoram State Assembly declared herself as a "Christian State," and one day on January Sachi had to cancel his travel plans as everything was closed for Missionary Day holiday, when first Christian missionaries came to convert them from indigenous faith. Sachi wrote to the Chief Minister regarding the state holiday, as mentioned earlier. We wonder if someday an American state or a Canadian province will celebrate their non-Christian arrival for its change of identity. Or, how would "media" report if one non-converted Hindu-majority state declares herself as a "Hindu State" in India, although India's case is problematic as every nation around India has driven out their indigenous non-converted citizens to India, making India a "Hindu Nation" by default? Neighbors have created identities with ethnic cleansing, indirectly supported by democratic nations with silence.

Here are some pictures from remote southern Twichwng village, Mizoram State, India:

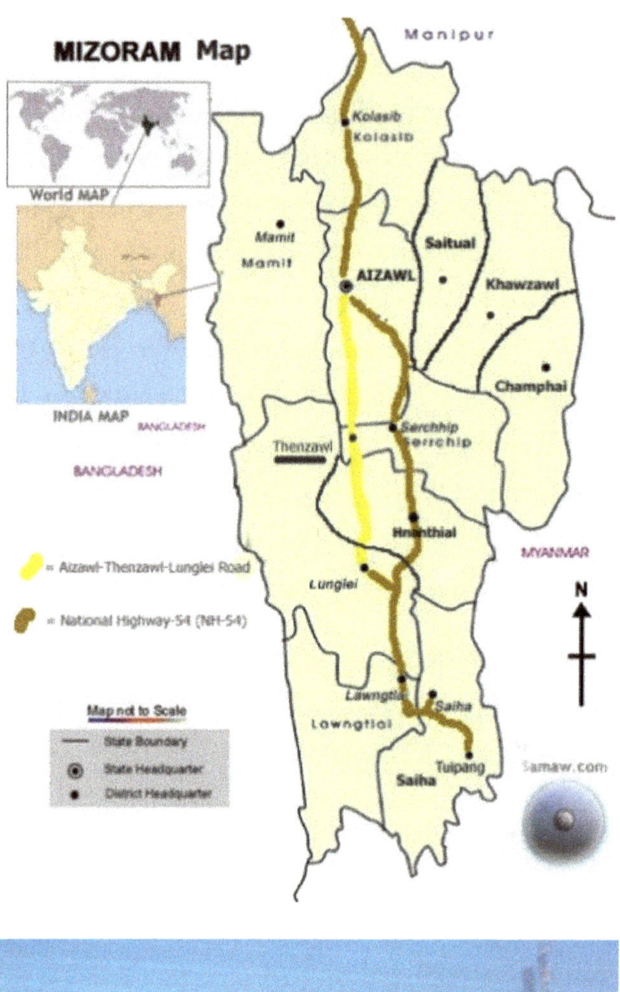

Homes in Precarious Location

Welcome by Locals

School Builder's Tablet done by Locals

Welcome to Sachi G. Dastidar by Local Buddhist Chakmas

Welcome by Locals

The Hon. Sri Pu Lalthanhawla
Chief Minister, Mizoram
A/14, Zarkawt, Aizawl, Mizoram, India

Dear Chief Minister Lalthanhawla: Re: Road to Southwest

Please accept warm greetings from me, my family and friends in the U.S. Recently I was in Mizoram and enjoyed the hospitality of the people and loved the spectacular beauty of the land. Having traveled all seven continents and every state in India I wondered why your state is not on the world map of tourism through which many parts of the world have pulled themselves up economically. I was told by many that a visa needed to enter – Inner Line Permit – has been very unwelcoming even to other Indians. (I received the permit from Mizoram House in Delhi while at work at Jawaharlal Nehru University.) Tourists told me that there are choices in this world and people like to avoid extra hassle. Actually I was in Burma (Myanmar) before my trip to Mizoram to enjoy similar beauty from the other side of the border. Ironically I was in Aizawl on January 11 when the state celebrated Missionary Day holiday as two English Christian missionaries J. H. Lorrain and F. W. Savidge arrived in Mizoram on January 11, 1894 to guide Mizos away from their nature-worshipping Hindu-like belief. I wonder if there is a contradiction as coming of foreigners is being celebrated yet we are restricting countrymen from traveling to the state!

My trip took me towards the Bangladesh border via Lungsen, MatriChhara (Tlabang) and towards Chakma Autonomous Area. I was moved by the warmth of the people yet I was appalled by the condition of the state road from Lunglei onwards. I witnessed a large number of trucks rumbling towards the Bangladesh border for creating a fence. People told me of the rationale for the fence. However, if the connection with Lunglei is not quickly improved, and Bangladeshi Chakma areas are cut off economically I am afraid that the region may become a virtual prison without any prospect for economic improvement. I wonder if you can secure funds to rebuild the road and bring prosperity to the area and the state. Let me extend an invitation to visit us during your next visit to the U.S. Please ask your office to drop me a line before you leave India.

Best wishes and belated Happy New Year.

Namaskar,

Dr. Sachi G. Dastidar

(Distinguished Service Professor, Politics, Economics & Law Department, State University of New York, Old Westbury, NY 11568; dastidars@oldwesrbury.edu; Founder, Probini Foundation; Chair, Indian Subcontinent Partition Documentation Project)

Copy: Gov. Sri V. B. Purushothaman, Raj Bhavan, Aizawl 796001; The Hon. Sri Nihar Kanti Chakma, Mizoram Government;

Letter of Protest to Mizoram Chief Minister

We found a serious problem of India, especially in her border states of Kashmir, Nagaland, Mizoram, Tamil Nadu, Kerala, West Bengal, Punjab and more. After Tamil Nadu rebelled for India's national language for colonial English, then Mizos bordering Burma and Bangladesh tried for secession with support from external groups. After that Nagaland tried to secede, also with foreign help. From 1947 India's Kashmir's problem was created by Islamists and neighbors devoid of toleration and secularism.

Dilemma of New Democracy in New World, and New Democracy in Old World:

Settlers in America kept their wealth in their new homes, putting deep root into it, developing the nation not just exploiting it. The new nation allowed not only to bring their relatives and neighbors to colonize the new land, but also use their skills and develop new ones. The new nation also convinced new settlers to give up their culture and identities for the new Anglo-Christian culture. As all the immigrants were Christian, the debate over religion in America was not an issue, although some Christians were fleeing persecution in Europe. American Constitution of 1700s made sure of freedom of religion. Indigenous religions didn't come into play, nor did the religious beliefs of Africans forced to come here. We wonder, if in the U.S. the indigenous Nature-Deity-Animal worshipping tradition of Native Americans still existed, and if they were the rulers of the nation, would they have incorporated those traditions into our constitution? The first non-protestant immigrants, Catholics and Jews, faced some difficulty in late 1800s. Modernity, Middle Age's Christian Reformation Movement and Enlightenment, American Revolution, and French Revolution helped ease the role of religion in American life. This was not true in Europe as evidenced by Irish partition, Nazi extermination campaign, Cyprus partition, Balkan war and partition, and more. One advantage Europe had was that she can ship some of their citizens to New Lands.

Officially, most European nations including monarchies, identified their National Church as their symbol, but in reality, those churches wielded limited power. As a result, many of the newly independent nations of Africa, Asia and the Caribbean included "Secularism" or equal treatment of religions. Exceptions were all the Muslim-majority nations, including India-partitioned Pakistan, and now Bangladesh. Muslim-majority Turkey after her revolution was different, yet hardly any Turk thinks their nation of Christian heritage. Sadly, even in Bangladesh, which gained her independence with the blood of millions of her Hindu minority removed "secularism" from its constitution, with hardly any protest from the West or Muslim-majority nations, promoted by two India-born

Muslim dictators who were proud to say that they were "Indian." They also added a preamble in Arabic, not in Bengali, in a nation born out of a Language Movement so that they are able to read and write in their own mother tongue which was prohibited by Pakistani Islamist rulers! Indonesia is an exception among Muslim-majority nations as its Constitution recognizes several religions as State Religion. Malaysia was most likely a Muslim-minority nation, yet declared herself an Islamic nation, pushing the Chinese-majority Singapore out of the country. During a trip to Malaysian part of Borneo Island, devoid of Malay Muslims, the local tour operators asked us to ignore the call for Islamic prayers from "official" mosques. Many of the local tribes have taken to Christianity leaving their traditional nature-worshipping Hindu-like beliefs. Now on Indonesian part of Borneo Island, some are being Arab-Islamized. All the Buddhist-majority nations in Asia declared themselves as "Buddhist," and all the Muslim-majority nations declared themselves as "Islamic," Communist nations declared themselves as "atheist," and Israel declared herself as Jewish State. Nepal was a Hindu nation from time immemorial, but recently declared herself as an "atheist" nation after Communist Party came to power removing its monarchy and bringing largescale invasion of non-native religions. Communist rulers recently banned "conversion" from Hinduism as tons of money from the rich were buying poor to change their faith, and identity. Conversion is great as long as it is not sold with money.

In Bengal terms emerged as Bread (*paoa ruti*) Christian and Beef (*gorur mangsho*) Muslim as some poor Hindus were tricked to eat those inauspicious foods, and told the victims that "You have eaten '.......' thus you cannot go back to your faith. Now you change your identity." One note worth mentioning is in Indian Subcontinent "secularism" often means "atheism," or the absence of religion. Thus, in India taking Oath of Office with Bhagavat Gita, one of the Hindu Holy books, is looked down upon, as "Hindu communalism" or "racism" of Hindus, in many states, especially in Bengali-run West Bengal and Tripura states where millions of Hindus fled from Islamic Pakistan and Bangladesh. Irony? The same leaders never objected even once while in their Pakistan and Bangladesh homeland where there were State Religion, and officials took oath with Koran, the Muslim Holy book.

That leaves us with India, a very imperfect society, with the only surviving polytheistic indigenous faiths of the world. Incidentally, there is no word called "Hindu" in any Indian scriptures, as mentioned earlier. It evolved as a geographical term used by Persians to describe "Indians," that was finally adopted by the English via Greece and France. The role of neo-colonial Indians and pro-colonial outsiders have been to turn the society to a monotheistic polity, unlike Buddha and Jain of 6th Century BC, Sri Chaitanya and Guru Nanak of 1400s, Rani Rashmoni and Raja Ram Mohan of 1700s, Vidyasagar or Ramkrishna of 1800s, and Gandhi or Shyama Prasad of 1900s, who tried to improve the basic practices. Within Hinduism it has monotheistic ideas introduced by Buddha, Jain and Ram Mohan. In Hinduism they all believe of a superpower, male or female, or joining both. Even European Christians like Anthony Firingee, Mother Teresa and Syrian Orthodox created bridge between two practices. Two of them lived in Bengal in 1800s and 1900s respectively. Our theologian and interfaith activist friends in New York tell us that a famous Catholic priest from Vatican became a "Hindu" monk after years of preaching in India creating a bridge between two religions. Diverse opinions are accepted in Hinduism. For monotheism we have to wait and see how much diversity is acceptable. In Mexico some Aztec practices like "The Day of the Dead" have been incorporated in Catholicism, as Aztecs have given up on their religious practices. During a conference in Mexico's Puebla City, we witnessed the excitement of The Day of the Dead festivities.

The Day of the Dead festivities in Puebla City, Mexico:

CELEBRACIÓN
DE MUERTOS 2018

Puebla City

In 1966-1967 for Sachi's architecture thesis, he met Mother Teresa and visited the Mother House in Entaly area of Kolkata, before it became a tourist attraction. Sachi planned for the 1967 final year architectural design thesis to work on her proposed center in Diamond Harbor area south of Kolkata, but had to abandon that. In early 1998 he visited the Mother House again to pay tribute to her after her death, as well as met Archbishop Henry D'Souza of Kolkata at the Cathedral. Mother died in late 1997. Sachi wrote a letter to Rev. D'Souza with copies to Indian Prime Minister Gujral, and West Bengal Chief Minister Jyoti Basu. Here is a copy of the faded letter to Archbishop:

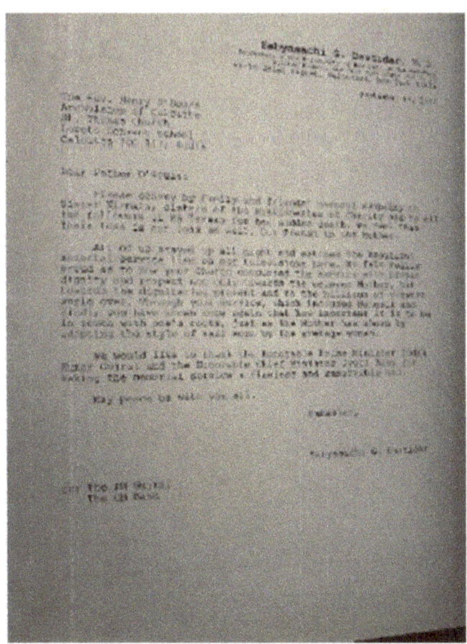

After Mother Teresa's death Monju, Shefali and Sachi visited her Missionaries of Charity house in the Bronx, New York City to offer condolences.

364

Paying Homage at Bronx

Shefali Writing Homage with Monju on Back.

In Kerala State of southern India, Christianity existed before it reached Europe. It is said that Saint Thomas came to the west coast of India in AD 26, and many families took to His teaching. He was buried in Tamil Nadu State of southern India. In typical Hindu style, many Hindus offer prayer at that holy site like Christians. The Kerala church followed strict Orthodox guidelines, but was "Indianized" that some fundamentalists may not like today. When new Christian missionaries came to India from Portugal, after the era of exploration, seeing the "bad Christian practices" the new colonizers destroyed many old churches and its papers. (See PBS documentary on Christianity.) Portuguese colonizers also destroyed many Hindu temples, and built churches on top of those destroyed Hindu temples, especially in Goa State of India, formerly a Portuguese colony. This is the problem of true believers. Islamists destroyed tens of thousands of temples, churches, viharas and ashrams in the world, from Turkey to Turkmenistan, Arabia to Algeria, from Cairo to Chittagong. As mentioned earlier, once the destruction takes place, and takes new name, people's identity changes, like change of DNA. Once victims give birth to a new generation, willingly or unwillingly, with a different name, people start to forget their past good or bad, atrocities or love. Women were extremely vulnerable as they depended on their husbands for survival. This is even true today with dependent mothers from ISIS controlled territories in the Middle East, or Taliban controlled Afghanistan, or in absolute monarchies. Do pilgrims think anything but glory while doing Haj in Mecca's Kaaba Shrine – one of the five pillars of Islam – that was once a non-Islamic temple, and its deities of local tradition were destroyed? Writer Salman Rushdie has a price on his head for writing about it. Even secular India under Congress era, and West Bengal under Communist era refused to shelter him, although he is Indian. Iranian religious leaders put a bounty on his head, and in 2022 there was an attempt on his life in our secular New York, of all places! True! Religious beliefs? Sectarian rulers of Communist West Bengal didn't allow Bengali writers like Dr. Taslima Nasrin, Salim Samad, Salam Azad, Mr. Haq and many more to stay in India's secular and "intellectual capital" Kolkata/Calcutta, although the ruling elites chose not to live with Muslims in their Bangladesh homeland for "communal" India. Indianism or indigenism were not a colonizing force. They welcomed outsiders who were destroying their faith and culture, creating an untenable model, much like indigenous peoples of Africa and Americas experienced. While visiting a school for the poor that Probini Foundation supports in Durgapur, West Bengal on a Christmas morning, we saw a picture of Jesus Christ with Mother Mary for festivity organized by the school of Ramakrishna Mission Order, one of the largest monastic orders. It will be like seeing a celebration of Mother Durga during a festivity in a mosque in Arabia, or in a church in Italy. Maybe they celebrate that, but we haven't seen yet.

Old, New, Dependent, and Non-Existing Public Bureaucracy:

It is not uncommon for neighbors to develop bad relations with each other. And, in New York City one million people live in basement "illegal apartments." When a renter complains against his neighbor of "illegal apartment," police immediately punish the home owner but not the complainer of "illegal apartment resident" or the same neighbor with "illegal apartment." Building Department even gives violation on buildings or wall when it was built according to earlier laws, thus not being a violation. To prove City or State's wrongful assessment, one has to spend tens of thousands of dollars, lot more than making wrongful changes suggested by the State or City. One good thing in the U.S. is that at least at grassroots level some of these can be solved by individuals, but not in Subcontinent. In India and in many other nations, even confiscation of homes and land can hardly be resolved by the court. In India a lawyer can drag on a case for 20 or 30 years, not solving in 2 to 3 years. This is huge structural problem. And, even after court verdict, it can simply be ignored. In the U.S. too it can take a long time to resolve an issue. And, if politicians politicize it, even courts can be influenced.

In India many have given up faith on the judicial system. Again, it varies from state to state. Federal Government in Delhi is lot better than many regions. In addition, judicial system was politicized in partition-affected states. Tens of millions of Hindu minorities were driven out from Pakistan and Bangladesh to India, without any protest in India from those ethnically cleansed Hindus, although they daily demonstrated for the oppressed around-the-world, and against "capitalist" democracies. Bengalis mostly found shelter in Bengali-majority West Bengal, and Tripura states bordering East Pakistan/Bangladesh. Within days' refugees became voters in India. Did they need any paperwork? They needed bribe, political connection and false data. As Hindu homes, properties and land were confiscated in their homeland of Pakistan and Bangladesh with the help or racist Enemy Property Act of Pakistan allowing declaration of indigenous Hindus as "Enemy of State" and confiscating their thousand-year-old property without paying a penny. Luckily refugees became "Indian" overnight by confiscating land and homes of West Bengali Hindus who gave them shelter. It is known as *"jabar-dhakhal"* or "forcibly occupied" property. If one went to a court in West Bengal for eviction, it could have taken decades. And even after a positive verdict police may refuse to enforce the law.

This is a general norm, although unbiased. This became acute, and institutionalized in some states. Result has been disinvestment in some states and cleansing of educated as well as uneducated from those states. Noticing people keeping unused homes and apartments locked rather than renting to someone earning a return on investment, and solve housing problem Sachi wrote his observation of his own Fern Road neighborhood of southern Kolkata that was published in 1983 by the Indian Planning Commission's publication, Yojana. In his crude estimate close to 20% of housing units remained vacant and unrented in a city short of housing!

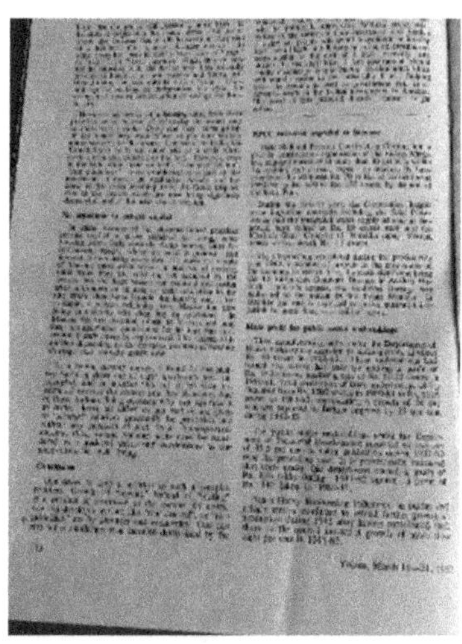

Yojona, the Planning Commission Journal with Sachi's Article

In July of 2022 a friend of ours in New York who had apartments in her hometown of Kolkata, two more at her husband's work place in Mumbai and Delhi, all in India, decided to sell the property in Kolkata for fear of illegal confiscation by neighbors, but not in Mumbai or Delhi. She rents the apartments in Mumbai and Delhi, but not in Kolkata for fear of illegal confiscation. Finally, Sachi wrote a letter on September 21, 2023 after visiting Kolkata to all the political and moral leaders of West Bengal – Governor, Chief Minister, Chief Justice, Speaker of Assembly, Leader of Opposition and to the Mayor of Kolkata, hoping some positive result.

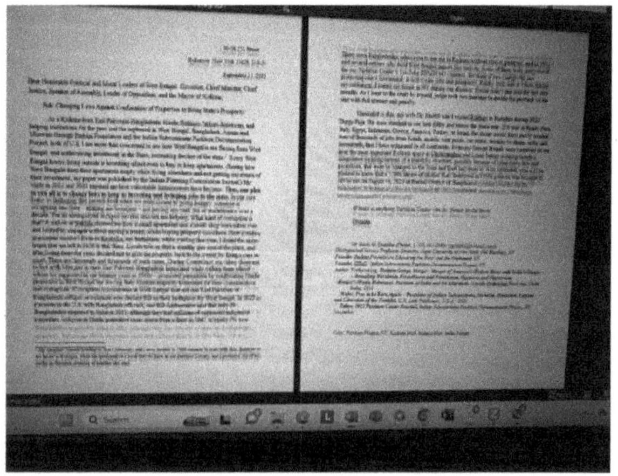

In America, one can struggle, and then mistakes can be corrected, but rarely in India. In New York, again, we were falsely accused of parking in a street that we never heard of. We paid, then continued our paper work for days, resulting in the refund of $35 dollars that we already paid. Shefali was lucky and persistent. That is not possible for everybody. It costs lot more than $35 dollars in her time.

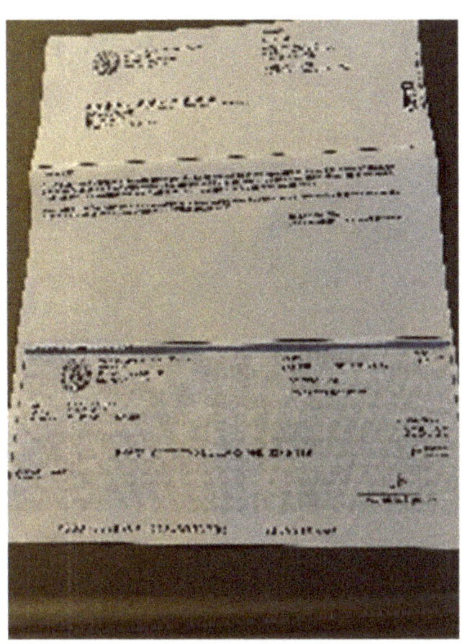

False Ticket that was Finally Reversed

It was reveling to us when we found out in September of 2022 in that same Kolkata neighborhood when Sachi wrote in 1983, that one new building was built in a former garden with six apartments, but no one lives there. It is very common in India, especially in West Bengal, to buy an apartment but keep it locked for fear of confiscation by renters until one retires and moves back to the city. No one is able to evict "renters" even if they don't pay rent, but homeowner has to pay everything. Thus, a Kolkata resident will be poorer by 20,000 rupees monthly rent for 12 months in a year for 25 years when the owner will move. It means loss of 6,000,000 (6 million) rupees than someone living in other states of India. It is no wonder that West Bengal, one of the richest states of India at 1947 independence and partition, is now (2025) one of the poorest states of India. In addition, even if home owner gets a positive verdict after 30 years, there is no way one can be evicted as police or paid enforcers won't enforce the law. Still illegal occupier may ask for hundreds of thousands of rupees to move out. This is another side of post-colonial democracy.

A New Apartment Building in Kolkata where no One Lives

Then there are other aspects of rule of law. If the judicial process takes decades to solve, naturally citizens give up faith in the system. In 1990s, American Ashok took his expectant wife to Kolkata for delivery. Local doctors mistreated the expectant mother who died with the unborn. In fatalistic India people would have just blamed the couple's fate. Ashok was not fatalistic, and went to the court. It took him over 12 years to get a verdict spending millions of rupees. No one knows if his U.S. connection speeded up the process. Recently, the daily newspaper Bartaman Patrika of Kolkata disclosed on February 22, 2022 that a verdict for killing a boy in Bowbazar neighborhood of Kolkata took "only" 15 years. This is also true in many other developing nations, pulling them backwards. In the U.S. illegal occupation or non-payment of rent could be resolved in relatively short time, but in India it could easily take decades. Again, it varies from state to state, and their corruption. In India bribery and minor thuggery has entered public mind, but not the murder and gun violence of the

U.S. Grabbing someone else's asset has corrupted some states. Bangladesh and Pakistan were corrupted as they confiscated indigenous Hindu properties through Enemy Property Act by declaring minorities as "Enemy of the State." In turn, it has created a parasitic mentality, also called "*pargachha*." In India excuse for failure of states is the distant "Delhi Government." This is not that different from the U.S. except Americans are aware of "tax" that Indians are not. March 13, 2022 news report on daily *Sangbad Pratidin* reminded us that an Indian independence freedom fighter Mr. Narayan Das Mahanta, an indigenous Hindu minority of Patua village of Kishorganj Subdivision of Mymansingh District of Bangladesh received his pension from Indian Government after a 15-year fight. He didn't get pension either from Pakistan or from Bangladesh to which he belonged; https://www.sangbadpratidin.in/kolkata/freedom-fighters-wi-fe-gets-pension-after-long-fight/. Mr. Mahanta spent time in British Colonizer's Cellular Prison in distant Andaman Islands before 1947 partition of India. Why Pakistan or Bangladesh didn't give its minority a pension?

In West Bengal, India, the rule of law was so politicized that many murders and mass murderers were never tried. In addition, in West Bengal, Hindu refugee elites who fled from their Muslim-majority neighbors, to prove that they are "secular" started persecuting India's Hindu majority without any repercussion. This is a suicidally-fatalistic disease. There are many examples of that. The most grievous one is the killing of dozens of Hindu monks and nun in the heart of Hindu-majority Kolkata without a single arrest and prosecution even when the anti-communist party came to power; https://empireslastcasualty.blogspot.com/2009/07/hindu-monks-and-nuns-killed-in-india-by.html. There are lots of pictures available in social media. Mother of Sai family of Bardhaman District was forced to eat rice, she was cooking for her sons that was drenched with her sons' blood murdered by communist thugs. No one took the killers to the court. Police didn't act. In another atrocity, thousands from oppressed groups of East Pakistani-Bangladeshi Hindu-refugees who took shelter in an island in Sundarbans Forest were killed by state police and Left activists. No one was arrested. Ironically, the state was headed by East Pakistani-Bangladeshi-Hindu-Communist Chief Minister Jyoti Basu, who chose not to live in his Muslim-majority homeland but supported Hindu killings in India, https://empireslastcasualty.blogspot .com/2009/08/marichjhapiwest-bengal-india-communist.html these are other painful contradictions. Same is true about 1971 Islamic Republic of Pakistan's genocide of 3 million Bengali Hindus and secular Muslims for which not a single killer has been convicted in the past 50 years, at home or abroad. Muslim-majority nations, as well as democratic Western nations gave shelter to those mass murderers, and didn't ask for justice. Canada sheltered one of the open terrorists, but in 2023-2024 was questioning India for going after a Sikh terrorist. All Western nations, including the U.S., U.K. and Europe are fighting terrorists and funding anti-terrorism. Poor Third World nation is not allowed to do that? Again, the verdict in Bangladesh of a February 25, 2009 of mass killing of 74 persons took until February 25, 2022, thirteen years later. The verdict was ready on January 25, 2020.

Baba, Sachi's dad, always dreamed of his rural Lakshmankathi village home in Bangladesh. He always dreamed of going back. So, without telling his adult sons and daughters, as is common in Indian family-based culture, bought a piece of land with his village-style pond and a hut, in southern West Bengal in Baruipur village, a short train ride from our Kolkata home. Eventually everyone knew about it. But, in parasitic and dependency-based culture that the ruling Left promoted, whom Baba supported like all refugees, fell into that trap. Soon, the day laborer Dad hired when worker had no job for months, learned from politicians to demand ownership of the property. And, all the fish in the pond, and vegetables grown in the property would be gone. The laborer would be defended by gangs when Dad wanted to talk to him. During a visit in 1980s he invited kids and grandkids. Luckily, he was able to sell the property before confiscation.

Relaxed Chat in December 1975 at Baruipur Village, India

Relaxing Under a Tree in December's "Cold"

A Beautiful Pond similar to Dad's Bangladesh Home

Dad's Lakshmankathi Village Pond, Bangladesh; 2023

Kids' Corner, Baruipur

The Pond Before Confiscation

The Village with Private Granaries

Baruipur Village Path with Farmers Carrying Harvested Grain on their Head

What about compensation? That is another subject for discussion.

Moreover, in case of India, one must figure out how to address the indigenous peoples, the Hindus, the Jains, the Buddhists, and the Sikhs, the Brahmos and the Vaishnavas, who were oppressed by invading monarchies, by Muslim settler kings, and the oppression by the ruling British-Christian monarchy. This has to be done without being anti-Muslim, anti-Arab, anti-Persia, anti-English and anti-Christian. It is similar to what U. S. has tried while discussing slavery, anti-African, anti-Jewish, or anti-Native American oppression without being anti-White, anti-Black, anti-Semite, anti-Muslim, anti-Hindu, or anti-Indian American. It is similar to German example of discussing Holocaust, and campaign for extermination of Jews and Gypsies, without being anti-German. Indian neo-colonials argue that there are lots of ill treatments by Hindus on Hindus, especially caste oppression. But the same activists are unwilling to discuss if the caste racism and oppression was created in the second millennia during colonial Farsi-Islamic and English-Christian rules. And they are unwilling to point out that in old Indian stories there are many "oppressed" who rose to be a prominent divinity like Lord Krishna, or that many oppressed people rose to become monks, and Hindu saints like Hari Chand and Guru Chand of Bengal. All ordained monks and nuns have to give up their identity and family connection when they are ordained. "Caste" is a Portuguese term exploited by the British to promote division in India as India's anti-colonial movement got strength in early 1800s. This doesn't fit their propaganda. Britain promoted "reservation" in India for "tribes" and "oppressed castes." Thanks. But they didn't do the same for the oppressed groups in the British Isles, or in the New World.

No one ever reminds us that because of their exploit Mr. Jogen Mondol, a leader of India's oppressed Hindus before 1947 partition, joined with Mr. Mohammad Ali Jinnah and his Muslim League Party in promoting Partition of India. (See Debesh Roy, *Barisaler (Barisal District's) Jogen Mondol*, Dey's Publishers, Calcutta; 2009.) He was the first Law Minister of Pakistan. It is one of the most important historical betrayals in the modern world history. Mr. Mondol soon gave up being the first Law Minister of the minority-cleansing Pakistan for the safety of "reactionary Hindu India." In his resignation letter, he documented thousands and thousands of oppressed Hindus killed in barely 36 months in his East Pakistan homeland through Islamic pogroms and genocide. No American, English, Canadian, European, Islamic countries have ever asked for return of oppressed-caste and oppressed-minority peoples back to their homeland in Pakistan, Bangladesh, or Afghanistan. Why not? Mr. Mondol submitted his 20-page resignation letter from Islamic Republic of Pakistan's Cabinet on October 8, 1950 from the safety of India detailing case after case of mass Hindu killing, including his own oppressed neighbors. We have personal attachment to that land as our grandparents are from the same area of Mondol.

We have deep link to the area where we have built schools and dormitories for the poor. In a normal democratic nation, Mr. Mondol would have been imprisoned or expelled for causing deaths of tens of thousands of minorities. But this is fatalistically-tolerant Hindu India. So, what did the Honorable Minister Mondol do after seeking the safely of Hindu India he denigrated and despised during Partition? Immediately without delay he ran for India's Parliament for a seat reserved for oppressed Hindus where he chose not to be a citizen of. Shocked? Suicidal Hindu fatalism? Is this what a Western diplomat called "Too much democracy" in a forum where we were present. This is India where he claimed citizenship the very next day of his arrival, but supported partitioning of the land! Pakistan Founder Mohammad Jinnah and Muslim League Party didn't drop any tear for the departed Hindu who helped create Pakistan! Does U.S or France allow a politician to run for office the next day one arrives who was opposed to U.S. or France and minister at another nation? On the week the New York, London, Kolkata and Delhi papers were shedding tears for Indian Kashmiris or Indian Muslims after the new uniform citizenship laws in India was enacted in 2019, not a word was said about oppression or cleansing of families from Bangladesh, Pakistan, Pakistani Kashmir or at times, from Indian states like Kashmir, West Bengal, Mizoram, Tamil Nadu and more. On the other hand, those families who sacrificed for India's independence won't be accepted there? Our families sacrificed for India's independence but will not be accepted there? The families who confiscated our homes and properties will be given rights to colonize our new home? Why our lives don't matter? Why is this communalism? How many editorials have been written in the West or in Muslim-majority nations asking for arrest and prosecution of 1971 killers of 3 million people in 9 months in Bangladesh? Is this because most of those murdered in cold blood were Hindu minority or Muslim secularists? Why didn't world object when these mass murderers held high offices in Pakistan and in Bangladesh? Even the liberal press which went after Kissinger and President Bush Jr., for Iraq war, didn't see anything wrong with our killers. Why not? Bangladesh has been begging for return of convicted killers from the West and Islamic countries, without any luck. Why? In 2020 Gambia, an Islamic nation on the west coast of Africa, and

Member of Organization of Islamic Countries, brought a charge in the International Criminal Court against Myanmar for Rohingya displacement. Bravo. Grateful. We wonder how many Gambians would be able to point to Bangladesh in the world map. Still, thanks to Gambia. Yet, we are not sure why Gambia couldn't bring any charge for the 1971 genocide by Islamic Republic of Pakistan, and her Islamic Bengali allies? And, Gambia couldn't make another complaint for constitutionally discriminating against indigenous pre-Islamic peoples of Pakistan, by not allowing them to hold some posts. Why not? Why didn't Gambia or Saudi Arabia or Turkey or Iran or Pakistan go to the World Court or International Criminal Court or Islamic Court in Mecca for arrest and prosecution of ISS members for their extermination campaign against Yazidis? Yazidi lives didn't matter? Why? As long as we have such hypocrites, anti-kefir mentality in the 22nd Century as in 6th Century, we will not be able to see justice in humankind. Holding onto double standard is a bane in democracy, but not necessarily harmful to politicians. There are huge number of activists in Muslim-Christian-Buddhist-Hindu-majority nations asking for fair treatment of citizens.

Early Life in America and India:

In the first part of our lives in America in 1970s Sachi went to more churches and synagogues than temples. He loved that. This was due to our friends Jay and Tom, of Florida and Tennessee, and since 1980s in New York influenced by our friend Rev. Arlene became a close friend of the family providing Christian sermon at the wedding of our daughter Joyeeta, and son Shuvo. In addition, priests also provided traditional services. Since 1990s we were invited to many Christian services in our neighborhood by an India-American minister. 1970s started migration of Indians. Since then, many Hindu-Jain-Sikh-Buddhist temples, and Islamic mosques, with Indian regional identity, have been built giving ethnic groups space for socializing. In America and in many parts of the world words Hindu and India are interchangeable. Thus, Kali Puja in New York is an Indian festival, not Hindu festival, which is just fine, but Kali Puja of Black Mother is also celebrated in Bangladesh, Nepal and more. In India we grew up in refugee families in mixed refugee-native neighborhoods, where role of religion was next to nothing, except for seasonal Hindu festivities of Durga Puja of Mother Goddess, also known as Autumn Festival, or Saraswati Puja of Goddess of Learning, Lakshmi Puja of Goddess of Prosperity, and Kali Puja of the Black Mother, killer of demons. These are mostly festivities rather than religious events. Then there is Diwali, the Fall Festival of Lights, and Holi, the Spring Festival of Colors. Even in India, if one asks a Hindu the meaning of these festivities, most would explain in terms of nature, and festivity of culture. These festivals were more like America's 4th of July, Thanksgiving, and Christmas, which to many are festivities than religion. This is true of all Indian festivities which are connected with Mother Nature than religious preaching. Even in religious part, it is mostly rituals connected with regions, its flora, fauna, and in case of Bengal, her gifts of bountiful fish of rivers Ganga, Brahmaputra, Jamuna, Surma, Meghna, Karnafuli, Hooghly, Damodar, Ajoy, and more. Having animal products in Hindu-Jain-Buddhist-Sikh religious rituals is unthinkable, but then there is flexibility, diversity and tolerance in Hinduism. In religious rituals the priest says fast Sanskrit shlokas from holy books that few understand, and attendance during those services is usually a fraction of attendees of its social-cultural programs. Usually, festivities are held past mid-day, while the religious services are held mostly in the morning.

Though the cultural practices vary from region to region, or sub-region to sub-region, all are generally welcome, including from other regions and religions, not much different from Christian services in America. In Bengal, the largest mixed Muslim-non-Muslim society of the world, large numbers of Muslims, Buddhists and Christians actively participate in "Hindu" festivals, but not now in partitioned Pakistan and Bangladesh. In Bengali-Hindu-majority City of Kolkata, all neighborhoods of majority religious and linguistic groups have their own celebration of various festivities, at times creating their own identity. Generally, non-Muslims are not invited for Muslim religious rituals. Sachi was told that it is forbidden to offer Islamic *namaz* prayer by non-Muslims. We were also told that it is a punishable act, but not the post-prayer exchange of greetings in Arabic. Only once Sachi was invited for a Muslim *namaz* prayer at the home of

Dr. Alam. The prayer service was arranged for his departed wife. In Hindu festivities everyone can participate, like Christian services. Once I wanted to go to Saudi Arabia, but wasn't allowed. I understand it is open now (2025).

In early 1980s when our kids were toddler, we suggested to some of our close friends with kids to start a Bengali language *pathshala* free school. Hearing the proposal Swapna and PrabalDa, PurobiDi and SaktiDa immediately formed a group, with Bhaskar and Nita. We called that Nassau County Bangla Pathshala (school), later came to be known as Nassau Pathshala. Soon many other families joined the free Sunday language school. Pathshalas are traditional schools for language, literature, science and math run generally by a learned person, at times by priests, or casteless monks, open to all, irrespective of identity or religion. Some schools run by religious scholars were called *toll*, also open to all. For millennia traditional *pathshala* and *toll* schools educated children in the absence of formal Western-style schools; then some headed to formal schools or *bidyaloi (Vidyalaya)* or universities or *biswa-bidyaloi (Vishwavidyalaya)* in pre-colonial era. These *pathshalas* and *tolls* not only educated villagers, at times with free boarding, as our grandparents did in today's Bangladesh. In Bengal with the advent of English education, hundreds of schools were opened in remote areas by educated families. In 1800s, and in early 1900s almost every town and village had schools established by English-educated families, in the spirit of "educating my village." Generally, the teachers were either ascetic monastic, or lived in wealth-free lifestyle. Initially, our Long Island *Pathshala* was held on Sundays at parents' homes on a rotating basis. Then we rented a daycare center at a university campus as our students increased, and finally in a Square Hall on Long Island. Now there are many *pathashalas* in the Indian-American and Bangladeshi-American communities. Our *pathshalas* started a music class, mostly teaching popular patriotic songs. During a winter break in Kolkata, as Sachi was walking down Chitpur Lane of Old Kolkata lined with Indian musical instruments, he found a store with one portable harmonium, a popular instrument, and decided to buy not knowing who would play the instrument. At the *pathshala* he tried his luck. Wow! Not only he was able to play on his first try, soon he became a regular player, surprising himself. It must have been a gift that he got free of charge from the music teacher of his elder sisters. His parents couldn't pay for a third student, but he was allowed to sit next to his sisters, as their music teacher gave lessons. What a nice fringe benefit!

In New York we got introduced to Hinduism by default. Our Sunday Pathashala was a new idea in America. Our kids got busy with many social-cultural activities at Sunday school, religion was not part of it. For example, our Nassau Pathashala took part in marching with a bilingual banner on the first India Day Parade in New York City on August 15. We participated in local events. Occasionally there were write ups in local papers. One Guyanese Hindu Monk while visiting New York decided to call Pathshala for more information. His last name was associated with a village in Barisal District, now of Bangladesh. Those with intimate knowledge of history of India, Bengal and Barisal are aware of Dastidar last name. Sachi was quizzed by hundreds of Hindu refugees in India about his last name. In America too he was quizzed. Among them were the Oxford University History Professor Dr. T. Roy Chowdhury, and the famous Bengali poetess and Bangladesh Freedom Fighter Mrs. Sufia Kamal, both of Barisal District. Besides, one Dr. Akkaraju Sarma, a Tamil, wrote to the Indian Subcontinent Partition Documentation Center (ISPaD) in 2018 "Namaskarams (greetings) and we wish you all a safe July 4 holiday. In my opinion, these (Partition Center) documents are going to be seen by readership (probably for the first time by many years) thru ISPaD publications. That is important for readers as well as researchers on USA diaspora to be aware of. On a somewhat lighter note, with Dastidar last name meaning 'keeper of seals-documents-etc. in a Royal setting', as coincidences have it, you have a role at ISPaD, and with both hands (Sabyasachi – full first name meaning someone able to work equally well with both hands, like Lord Arjun)! Hari Om, Akkaraju Sarma, MD, FAAFP." (See ISPaD Newsletter, December 2018.) Besides, a close friend and Partition Center Journal Editorial Committee Member and Partition Center Board Member Professor Dr. Alireza Ebrahimi, frequently reminds of our Persian connection. The famous journalist, and a writer of many Bangladesh freedom songs and verses, Mr. Abdul Ghaffar Chowdhury, during a meeting at the home of Morshed in Queens, New York City asked Sachi if he was from Barisal, like him. Possibly he knew all people with last name "Ghosh Dastidar" come from Barisal District of Bangladesh, as he is a native of that district.

We always thought that a monk in New York City was a Hindu refugee from Bangladesh, but we could never find that out as Hindu monks and nuns, swamis and swaminis, have to sever all ties to their birth family for the "world family." They never reveal their former family, and birth place. They are casteless. Actually, before being ordained as monk, they have to do their last rites as they won't have their family to do that. When Sachi's mother visited U.S. in 1987, Swami Brahmananda of Guyana came to New York, and graciously accepted invitation to stay with us in Hicksville, Long Island. Soon, Ma realized that Swamiji, as they are called, knew every corner of our ancestral village, our family history, and realized that the monk must have been from nearby villages or from our family, but Ma couldn't find his family identity and that of his village. Ma and Swamiji talked for hours discussing family, spirituality, meditation, yoga, religious tradition, rituals adding joy to both of them. Swamiji introduced us to the Guyanese community in Queens who were planning to build an ashram, a branch of Bharat Sevashram Sangha, a Hindu monastic order in New York, originated in Bangladesh near Ma's home.

Swamiji's New Center in Toronto, Canada

At Swamiji's New Meditation Center Funded by Guyanese and Caribs

Swamiji Took us to Visit Lake Ontario

The Guyanese group immediately drafted Shefali and Sachi into their committee which was headed by the first Hindu monk of Guyana, Swami Vidyananda, an amiable man. They built the first center of Bharat Sevashram Sangha, Center for Serving Bharat, as America Sevashram Sangha (Center for Serving America), in Jamaica, Queens Borough of New York City. A Hindu monk fighting for India's independence, imprisoned by the British oppressors many times established the monastic order – Bharat Sevashram Sangha – in Faridpur District of Bangladesh, to serve all natives – Hindu and Muslim – during natural calamities and British-created famines, Muslim-Hindu riots, and for educating boys and girls.

In some ways our journey to find ourselves started with a Hindu monk's brutal murder in Bangladesh in 1985, after liberating Bangladesh with their

Hindu lives. To the killers "Hindu Lives Do Not Matter." Dastidar family was in New York, when a monk sought his help. We visited their founding headquarters at Bajitpur village in Madaripur district in 1999. The founding monk was oppressed by the British colonizers in early 1900s as he sought India's independence, and imprisoned him many times. There are many stories how sacred power freed him from British prison. Although we have no records, but it is most likely that our maternal grandpa Girindra Nath Roy Chowdhury of the same area, a noted lawyer of British era, and an Indian freedom fighter, knew each other, as well as East Pakistan leaders from the same area Mr. Mujibur Rahman, the founding Father of Bangladesh, of grandpa's Gopalganj subdistrict and Bengal Premier Mr. A. K. Fazlul Haq of Barisal District of Dastidar family. The monks and devotees at the ashram in Bajitpur extended a warm welcome to all of us, and reminded us of our ancestral connection. If locals were secular, Bajitpur could have become a tourist attraction creating thousands of jobs, as in many places in Europe, Asia and Africa.

Home of Swani Pranavananda, founder of Bharat Sevashram, in Bangladesh

Steps to a Sacred Pond

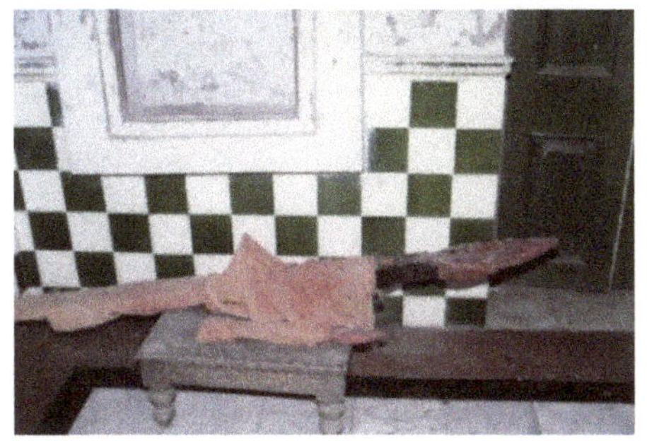

A Sacred Boat Langar Navigator

A Shoulder Carrier at the Museum

One Sevashram Building

Ashram Yard

At the Shrine

With Mr. Prasanta of New York, left; 1999

Prasanta Offering Prayer to Swami Pranavananda

After slavery was abolished, Britain brought large number of Indians as indentured laborers to Guyana and the Caribbean, and elsewhere. These hardworking Guyanese were always eager to establish connection with India and Hinduism, and two unwise Hindus like ourselves were drafted to be Guyanese. We felt it was great honor for us. Soon our son Shuvo, a teenager, and two of us, decided to embark on a tour of Trinidad and Guyana in mid-1990s. For us Guyana felt very much like India, especially like deltaic Bengal. For its people – East Indian, African and Native Indian – seemed to us to be very enchanting, and felt "home" like India and America. On a day when Shefali wore her sari, the local bus refused to accept money for our tickets, but asked for mementos of India. Luckily, we were carrying a few Indian coins, and the bus conductor and driver started debating who should have the bigger coin! They gave us a ride to an ashram which we were going to visit, away from the end of the line, but refused to accept extra fare! A young man named Ram, 6' 5" tall nicknamed Palm Tree, at the ashram told us that his parents would like us to visit their home. It was an unbelievable experience. Ram's family was farmer deep inside Amazon rain forest. The only access was by boat on Berbice River.

We took an early morning boat going south towards Amazon Forest from the coastal town of Rosigel. The region was full of cow and rice farms, much like rural India. The boat stopped for a minute every kilometer to pick up milk left in a jar by cow owners that the lone boat operator measured, recorded in his book, then poured in a huge container as he went south towards Amazon Forest. The river narrowed as it went further south. After about two hours he dropped us at Ram's home. It was a wooden two-story structure with a front veranda, about 25 yards from the river. Ram's parents, brothers and neighbors were there to welcome us. Word of our arrival had spread through the forest, and soon many ladies started arriving rowing their own dinghies. Women wanted to know everything about their ancestors' homeland: food, flora, fauna, pujas, festivities, saris and sweets. Men took us up for a tour of the nearby jungle, and cow grazing clearances. One of the boys took us to catch minnows in a pond, that resulted in a small number of tiny minnows and baby shrimps, but a large number of parasites entered our body that took months of treatment. Hosts told us that the river was so pure that they drink that water, but made arrangements for green coconut water from local trees for their new cousins. Three decades later we would have the opportunity to walk on the Brazilian side of the Amazon, but the Guyana walk was not meant for tourists. Our journey from Guyana to Surinam ended at Guyana side of the Courantyne River as the new military regime in Surinam changed policy by not allowing Americans to enter via Guyana. We headed south on Courantyne River marking boundary between the two nations towards Fort Nassau, in the middle of northern Amazon Forest. Our stop at the Native Indian village of Orealia was remarkable for several reasons: people bathing on the river showed us injury marks from earlier piranha bites, a native food stall sold only Coca-Cola, all the homes had exotic animals as pets, and indigenous Indians showed warmth towards "Indian-Indians" as they refused to recognize us as "American."

Welcome to Amazon Forest Area of South Guyana

Taking a Boat to the Amazon Forest Area that also was Collector of Cow Milk at Each Stop

Collecting Cow Milk, with Shuvo on the Back

A Rural Path in Amazon Forest Area of South Guyana

A Hindu Shrine in Guyana

Welcome to a Bharat Sevashram Shrine in Georgetown, Guyana; 1996

In 1995 we had a different kind of welcome by a Surinamese in the Netherlands. Joyeeta and Sachi arrived at Amsterdam for our journey ahead to Germany and Scandinavia. We arrived without any hotel reservation. It was a holiday and all nearby hotels were booked solid. Sachi was driving from hotel to hotel, before the days of Internet reservation. At a boutique hotel in the middle of the old town we stopped to look for a room. A man at the counter showed us the "No Vacancy" sign. As we were asking for suggestions, an Indian lady emerged from the back, and asked us in Hindi, "Are you Indian?" Sachi nodded. She then said in Hindi, "Don't worry. I'll give you our special family room. I am from Surinam. I can only speak Hindi and Dutch. I can't read Hindi, but all Indian families speak Hindi at home." She was sad to know that we couldn't visit her homeland because of military rule. On the same trip we got a different welcome at a Belgium village. We headed south from Amsterdam towards Antwerp, Belgium. After crossing into Belgium, we decided to stop for coffee and snack. It happened to be a bar with lots of folks enjoying themselves with drink. After ordering, Sachi asked if the bar accepts US dollar, which it did not. Before he could produce his credit card, one of the bar patrons asked us where we are from, hearing that we are from the U.S., the patron asked the bar cashier not to accept our money so that they can treat the guests by wishing, "Welcome to Belgium!" No amount of insistence on our part changed the group's mind. They gave us many travel tips to Belgium, and for our next destination to Germany and Scandinavia, especially to the divided Berlin and its Brandenburg Gate and viewing tower for East Berlin. In Guyana people have many mixed marriages – racial, religious and ethnic. What is wonderful is that it rarely causes any tension when families arrange marriages between Hindu and Muslim, or Hindu and Christian, or Christian and Muslim, Indian and African or tribal, though all share some rituals as "Indian" not "Hindu," just as exchanging garlands as sign of marriage in indigenous custom is now regarded as "cultural" tradition in Subcontinental marriages in the U.S. Sadly, in spite of genuine efforts by many leaders, some politicians have fallen into the British-inspired trap of divide-and-rule race-based politics.

In the Subcontinent inter-religious and inter-regional marriages pose many problems, especially between Muslims and non-Muslims, because Islam dictates conversion of non-believers to recognize a marriage. People see this rational as dictatorial, negative, humiliating, and dishonoring of other faiths, and supremacist. If all the mixed Christian-non-Christian marriages in Christian-majority areas were forced to change their identity by a minority religion, how many would have tolerated that? All the mixed Hindu-Muslim or interfaith marriages in Muslim-majority Bangladesh, couples had to flee to India when one didn't convert to Islam. If everything was equal, why would one flee to poor India? Dr. De, a Hindu, an Islamic history professor and an activist of the Communist movement, and Mrs. Nasima, a Muslim school teacher, and former East Pakistani national, openly describes how they had to flee to Hindu India in 1950s once they decided to marry. A Muslim fleeing to Hindu India that many in the West describe as anti-Muslim! Even 50 years after their marriage the bride's liberal politically-active family hasn't reconciled. (See YouTube's ispad1947 channel for their interviews.) There are mixed couples in Brooklyn who came to America after first finding shelter in India. While Mr. Mazumdar, a noted playwright of Bangladesh, survived keeping his non-Islamic name, yet had to legally convert to Islam when he married his Muslim girlfriend in Bangladesh. (His family home was burned to the ground during 1946 anti-Hindu genocide in

Noakhali, ironically by the maternal uncle of his wife in British India, long before his marriage. See YouTube's ispad1947 channel for interview.) There are other couples with similar experience as Mr. & Mrs. De, but refused to give video testimony. Engineers Biswas-Orb couple, married in 1990s, living in Queens, experience in not that different from Dr. & Mrs. De. Dr. & Mrs. De, now in their 80s, were both very vocal about the hypocrisy of the press, and how one cannot live under religious rule.

In many Islamic countries, including Pakistan, formerly India, one may get death sentence if a Muslim converts to another religion, or even one asks questions about ill practices of the faith. So, what has our democratic world done? What has the atheist world done? And their press? So, in a country like India with a millennium of recorded oppression of the majority, and dismemberment, what is she supposed to do? Ask for more oppression as many in the world is asking for? Or, more dismemberment as some are openly asking for? Or, complete conversion to a non-Indian culture? Incidentally, one of the hardline Islamist parties, Jamai'at-ul-Ulma-I-Hind (Association of Indian Ulma Religious Preachers) of India did not recognize Pakistan because all of India was npt converted to Dar-ul-Islam. And, this is inside India. If there was a party in the U.S. which does not recognize freedom of Whites, what would be the reaction in America? There are some in the Christian fundamentalist movement who want India to be a Christian nation, but their goal is not through the brute force. As per "free media" what should be the goal of public policy in India? Same media does not ask for transferring Protestants of Northern Ireland to make it Catholic only place. Or, they do not propose of transferring Protestants from Britain to Ireland to unify with Britain. Democratic nations didn't object of drawing boundaries, or transferring population in different parts of Bosnia, Croatia, Serbia, Kosovo, Ukraine or Baltic states to create monoculture states. Erdogan's Turkey was at forefront of showing disdain for Indian democracy and for showing Islamist intolerance, yet completely cleansed Northern Cyprus of her indigenous Greek-Christian minority. Hypocrisy? Dishonesty? Of course, not. Did Turkey not witness Armenian genocide, or witness marginalizing of Kurds?

Why Kurds couldn't have equal rights like the majority? Why liberal West couldn't help such a large minority? There are many such hypocrisies from Africa, South America, Asia and Europe.

Here are some 2023 pictures from Cyprus:

Northern Partitioned Islamic Cyprus; 2023

Mosques have been Built in many Places, as in the Back

Guyana was not the only place with special welcome for us. During a visit to the Island of Guadeloupe in the Caribbean in 2016, we were checking into our hotel. This time Sachi was wearing an Indian "Hawaiian shirt" with Bengali *Kalka* flowery design. A short, skinny Indian man asked, "Indian?" Then he started to speak in English in an Island where no one spoke anything but French. Dr. Jean S Sahai, a historian and an activist, was "trying to preserve slave history of Indians in the Caribbean." We didn't know that France also brought Indian slave laborers to work in the Caribbean in post-slavery world. Next day, he took time off to be our guide to historical places on the island, from a Hindu temple built by an Italian-Guadeloupian couple, to Slave Museum, to the dock where Indian laborers first landed, to the beaches, to the African market, to Paris-style restaurant, and more. In 2018 Dr. Sahai sent a paper, "The Guadeloupian Model" for Partition Center's 2018 Journal. Guadeloupe has heavily mixed population of African, Indian, Carib, and European nationalities, as in French Martinique or English-speaking St. Lucia in the Caribbean.

Dr. Sahai on Right

Italian and Afro-Caribbean Established Center for Meditation

Memorial for Indian Slave-Laborers on Port Landing

In St. Lucia, our Indian-origin taxi driver took us to a small hamlet with "Indian shop keepers," though they were mostly African-Caribbean. Identity there was more fluid as in America. He lamented how some locals were trying to bring back "Hindu" festivals of Diwali, the Festival of Lights, and Holi or Phagwa as known in the West Indies, the Festival of Colors, from Trinidad. In heavily mixed Martinique an Indian-looking fruit vendor on the waterfront bazar was hesitant to take money from Shefali saying in French, "I am Puducherry, Tamil" area of southern India. She was several generations removed from her ancestral land, but still holds memory of her land through the oral tradition, extremely important in migratory culture. Puducherry or Pondicherry was a French colony in India, and now is a Tamil city-state in India. Our rudimentary French helped us to communicate with her.

St. Lucia of the Caribbean

Entry to the Market Celebration with Saleswoman from Puducherry,
Former French Colony in Southern India

Waterfront Area with Offices and Hotels

American Inspiration:

So, what kind of democratic policy should India and Third World nations have adopted? Inspired by America, where the indigenous peoples were absent from power, land gone, tradition wiped out. Should that be the model? Or, French model, which inscribed freedom with non-religious constitution, yet freedom in colonized lands in Africa was gone, and in spite of efforts, native languages were wiped out. Or, should she follow the model of the former Socialist Republics of Soviet Union to East Germany to Yugoslavia where tens of thousands of citizens were killed by the State, or should she follow the model of the Peoples' Republic of China where millions of Chinese were killed by Peoples' Army as well as ethnocide and colonization of minority areas of Tibet, Xinjiang, and Inner Mongolia? Or, should she follow the models of Islamic Republic of Pakistan where the pre-Islamic indigenous peoples are constitutionally barred from top offices, and people going back to their ancestral religions are prohibited by commandment? Why or why not? What about Islamic model, as India is close to Muslims through geography, culture, colonization and demographics? Was there democracy under Islam? Under Islam followers and kefirs are not, and cannot be treated equally. Thus, hardly any of the 53 Muslim-majority nations of 57-member Organization of Islamic Nations have equal rights to non-Muslims, even for pre-Islam minorities, except Indonesia, and two places under autocracy. In Muslim-majority nations, most monarchies are relatively tolerant to their religious minorities, from Jordan to Morocco to Oman to UAE. In UAE, we saw a long line to enter a newly established *mandir* (temple). And in Oman we were taken to a centuries-old Hindu temple in its capital city, as well as to mosques. It was also a nice experience when at a grocery checkout an Omani clerk spoke to us in Hindi, as we looked "Indian."

Centuries Old Hindu Shrine at Oman

Entrance to the National Mosque

Old Abandoned Buildings

Entrance to a Hindu Temple in Muscat, Oman

A Typical Muscat Neighborhood

When plurality of democracy is brought in those society, why it becomes intolerant towards their minority from Egypt to Pakistan, from Chad to Afghanistan, from Somalia to Bangladesh, must be discussed by the majority in those places. However, West, Americas, and India and the East have failed by giving shelter to tolerant debaters – which they should – but demand nations to protect those intellectuals in their own countries. Revolution or change cannot be done from outside. One can create pressure, nothing more. Sheltering nations must do more than giving shelter in exile for Egyptians, Turks, Pakistanis, Saudis, Bangladeshis, Somalis, Cubans, Russians, and more. Turkey's 1923 Ataturk Revolution created the first true secular state in a Muslim-majority nation, yet almost all of her Christian minority vanished. In 1971 Bangladesh was the second Muslim-majority nations to revolt for a secular constitution from the Pakistani Islamic structure. Yet, after the murder of the Father of the Nation Mujibur Rahman, killers reverted back to discriminatory Islamic structure, and *attack* on her secularists and indigenous minority, and minority cleansing continued, along with the small Buddhist and Christian community. Genocide of the Islamic Republic of Pakistan of her Hindu-Sikh-Jain-Buddhist minority and tolerant Muslims are not discussed in the world. Double standard? India can't follow her colonial master England, who was able to transfer huge sums of wealth from Afro-Asian nations without paying a dime, and bringing a new form of racism through her divide-and-conquer policy. Ironically, post-independence rulers of India, Pakistan and Bangladesh didn't ask for reparation from their British masters. British colonial model cannot be followed today as the era of open colonialism is over. French, Spanish and Portuguese models cannot be applied in Third World countries either. Should colonialism continue?

West and East must come up with ideas of returning families like ours back to our homeland, with return of our illegally and immorally confiscated ancestral property through Enemy Property Act of Pakistan and Bangladesh. (Bangladesh renamed it to Vested Property Act, with everything remaining the same.) This law allowed only indigenous Hindu minorities to be declared as "Enemy of the State", even by a newcomer Muslim who could confiscate homes, homesteads, hearths, shops, ponds, paddy fields, barber shops, factories, businesses, temples without any notice or paying a penny. Why the Indians, including secular

Calcutta's Muslims, Communists, and Western press and politicians haven't protested even once? Why they didn't support even once researchers like Abul Barakat, Shafique uz Zaman, Azizur Rahman, Avijit Poddar, M. Taher Uddin, Md. Shahnewaz Khan and Subhas Sengupta (see *Impact of Vested Property Act on Rural Bangladesh: An Exploratory Study*, Prepared for Association for Land Reform and Development, Bangladesh; March 1996, *or An Inquiry into Causes and Consequences of Deprivation of Hindu Minorities in Bangladesh through the Vested Property Act*, PRIP Trust, Dhaka, 2000, or *Deprivation of Hindu Minority in Bangladesh: Living with Vested Property*, forwarded by Justice Mohammad Gholam Rabbani, Pathak Samabesh Book Publisher, Dhaka; 2008) or Mridul Rakshit's *Law of Vested (Enemy) Properties in Bangladesh*, Vol. I, M. K. Publishers, Chittagong, 1985; and Vol. II, Chittagong, 1991? What kind of racism is that? Is that communalism of the communal Left, and Right, and by elite nations? Is the Enemy Property act different from Nazi law of confiscation of Jewish properties in Europe? So why has the West, East and India not protested against Enemy Property Act?

Sanskritik Sampradayikata (Cultural Communalism) by Badaruddin Umar, Bangladesh

That reminds us of questions about Israel and Palestine. Pakistan, all Muslim-majority nations, members of the Organization of Islamic Countries, and Left denounce Israel about Palestine on daily basis. 2023-2025 Hamas-Israel war reminded us of that. We all are sympathetic to Palestinians as well as to Israelis. But, what about others? Hundred times more indigenous minorities have been cleansed just from Bangladesh/East Pakistan than Palestine, although every life matters. After powerful Christian-majority nations ignored the plights of Hindus, Sikhs and Jains for decades in Pakistan, Christians came under attack there so much so that they Arabized their identity for survival, others fled to "Hindu" India. Attack on Buddhists and Christians in Bangladesh started after 1971. Our Pakistani friend Mervin had to take a different name given by his parents, as many of his siblings, except one who was able to keep his original Punjabi last name. In Bangladesh, a trend grew among Christians to Anglicize their names from Bengali name. Such is the pain of West's ignorance and media partisanship. Why Pakistan and Saudi and Gambia are so concerned about Palestinians, and now Muslim Rohingyas of Myanmar, but not for Pakistan's pre-Islam indigenous citizens cleansed from their own nation? Why this partisanship? Why couldn't Saudi Arabia, Kuwait, Libya, Pakistan, Gambia and Afghanistan give Palestinians shelter, as India gave shelter to – Pakistanis, Bangladeshis, Afghans, Chinese Tibetans, Sri Lankan, Bhutanese, Burmese, Nepali and many more? Hypocrisy or racism? On 17th of December 1999 on our flight from Bishkek, Kyrgyzstan to Delhi, India we were pleasantly surprised to find so many citizens of Muslim-majority nations – from Iran to Afghanistan to Arabs – heading to India with Indian passport.

Apparently, Muslim-majority nations from Arabia to Algeria, and Sudan to Saudi didn't give them citizenship. We developed comradery as our flight was delayed by "only eight hours" for a two-hour flight. We waited in a heatless, chair-less departure lounge in below freezing temperature entertaining ourselves with stories of our lives. There was no food, water, or announcement. You just stood. Recently, a boat full of illegal Muslim Rohingya migrants from Myanmar were not allowed to dock at Malaysia and was heading back to Bangladesh, that was stopped by Bangladesh (May, 1, 2020; *New York Times*). A British Minister called Bangladesh Foreign Minister Dr. Momen to allow Rohingya's to return. Thank goodness that Dr. Momen asked Britain to take those people into his country. (See *Daily Prothom Alo*, and *Daily Observer*, April

28, 2020). Bravo. The problem was created by the colonial British Administration. Many Rohingyas actively participated against independence of secular Bangladesh in 1971 in collusion with Pakistan and other nations. Very recently this group even murdered an entire Hindu Rohingya village of 99 people. (See *Statesman*, May 23 2018, and Amnesty International video on the Internet.) Islamic stalwart Saudi Arabia is forcing Bangladesh to accept Rohingyas living illegally in Arabia, and no Muslim-majority nation accepted them. At the same time anti-India, anti-Hindu groups in India and overseas campaigned for India to accept Rohingyas living in Saudi Arabia, although they killed an entire Hindu Rohingya village, and killed secular Muslims and helped racist Islamist forces during 1971 Bangladesh Liberation war. Hypocrisy? No humanity? Why some lives not matter? This is the world politics at its best! Unfortunately, the only two officially secular Muslim-majority states of Syria and Iraq – besides Turkey and Indonesia – are in horrible state after the Iraq War and genocide for fake reason.

How many nuclear weapons did we find there? Many Christians, Yazidis, Sunnis say they were better off under a dictator in Iraq. Muslim-majority Indonesia is a separate case altogether as she recognizes five religions as State Religion, and is trying her best to delicately balance her Hindu past with Islam of today. Way back in 1989, then again in 1991, first in an essay in weekly *Desh* magazine of India, then as a book *Ai Bangla Oi Bangla* (This Bengal, that Bengal) I raised the issue of dishonesty and lies. West Bengal State's ruling coalition of Communist Party, Communist Party-Marxist, Communist Party-Marxist-Leninist, Socialist Unity Center, Forward Block-Marxist led by East Pakistani/Bangladeshi-Hindu-Refugee-Indians who chose not to live with their Muslim neighbors in their homeland took citizens for demonstrations in Kolkata against Israel on a daily basis, but never against the Islamist terror that made them homeless. Such is the partisanship and extreme racism of elites in India. As Left fell from power, and as secular open-mindedness spread, the same followers have now turned against them for their communalism.

National and Regional Public Policy:

For India's public policy democratic West and free press should also insist on tolerant, secular constitution not only of India, which they must, but also of Pakistan, Bangladesh, Iran, Afghanistan, Sri Lanka, Myanmar (Burma), China including Tibet, Bhutan, and all other nations with religious supremacy and cultural-social discriminatory laws like Enemy Property Act, and state religion. They also need to treat minority linguistic population equally, as in India. China officially recognizes three other minorities by writing in their currency, unlike India where sectarian states could decide which language to teach. Asking one party to be tolerant, and the other to be intolerant in a partition-affected land is wrong policy, especially for partition-victim India. It could only be expected from a fatalistic people. This disobeys the law of physics, "To every action there is equal and opposite reaction," and, a very old Sanskrit proverb, "*Shatthey shattam samacharet*," or "React to evil as it is." Do we treat rape victims and rapists equally? Violence victims and killers at par? Yazidis and ISIS equally? Why didn't the West and Islamic nations ask the same of Muslim-majority Pakistan to protect her minority and create conditions to bring them back as we are demanding of Myanmar for taking Rohingyas back? Why Gandhi's love for peace and non-violence failed in East and West Pakistan, Afghanistan, Burma, Sri Lanka and more? In Pakistan it failed again in 1971 genocide that even democratic nations and dictatorial regimes ignored completely. What kind of democratic norm is that? Why some lives do not matter? Can double standard survive? Why Christ's Message of Peace didn't influence Pakistan, Iran, or Arabs? Why U.S. can't influence them? Why couldn't West control ISIS funding from their friendly nations? What about U.S. stand on Israel-Hamas-Palestine war?

In India, since its partition-massacred and partition-displaced 1947 independence, her genuine attempt to create an inclusive, secular society, as envisioned by pre-independence leaders were led for an anti-indigenous society. If India remained democratic and secular, it had nothing to do with Western polity, but only to her pluralistic, tolerant, traditional and secularistic faith. Locals never followed "To every action there is an equal and opposite reaction," or a common saying in Sanskrit, "React to evil as it is." New hypercritic narration was promoted by extremist elites, contrary to their lifestyle. They in turn influenced other elites, and stopped teaching any pre-15th Century Indian literature, as Indian literature existed thousands of years B.C., with song and dance, involved with deities who represented different aspects of life, Mother Nature, flora and fauna, rivers and trees, oceans and mountains, love and passion, as all of these represented different aspects of indigenous "Hindu" beliefs. Teaching of epic Ramayana, Mahabharata, Vedas and Upanishads, Yogas were of course out of question. One has to go to America, England, or Germany to learn those. The same group of elites barred the song "Vande Mataram" or "Glory to the Mother" which led India to independence from becoming India's national anthem, pleasing separatist supporters who opposed the song's imagery association with the Mother, the Creator, and India's freedom. The Indian Congress Party, which acceded to this was vehemently opposed by Muslims, voting for partition-favored Muslim League Party in pre-independence British- instituted apartheid-like elections.

This was the beginning of both Congress and Communist parties started to receive support from Muslim League supporters who chose not to migrate to Islamic Pakistan, but supported partition of India. Indigenous people are easy to divide as they are pluralistic with no common tradition that binds them together, but tolerant of other faiths. Thus, in schools and colleges people like us had no institutional way of learning India's 5,000 years of literature. We learned little bit from our parents as a part of oral history. And unlike Christianity, Islam, Judaism or Buddhism where placees of worship also had sermons on the life of its preachers, Hindu services were brief rituals in Sanskrit by a priest that hardly anyone understands, and rest was festive regional celebrations. Thus, learning about old literature, stories, poems, fiction and non-fiction, yoga, meditation had no room for average students. Even in Bengal where life and literature transformed and expanded exponentially in local language from 15th Century by Sri Chaitanya and his followers, present day

ISKCON literature, yet hardly anyone in Bengal knows the history. That is not true with Muslim Bengalis who feel very proud of their non-native Islamic preacher Shah Jalal who converted them to Islam, though Jalal had very little influence on the literature of Bengal or India. Bangladesh's secular administration renamed the main airport after Shah Jalal. Kolkata created a culture of self-hate, and tried converting them to atheism. But the same atheists wouldn't go back to their homeland to live with their Muslim neighbors, while condemning their Indian shelter givers. Irony? Hypocrisy? Racism? Increasingly, Indian Left came to symbolize that. In 2013 Sachi lived on a campus in Delhi. As he was working on his book *Empire's Last Casualty: Indian Subcontinent's Vanishing Hindu and Other Minorities*, a junior professor invited him to meet with History Department professors.

He was honored to meet with prominent Indian historians. Surprisingly, all the professors were Pakistani-Bangladeshi-Hindu-Refugee-Indians. Discussion revolved around "There are bad people everywhere." True. Soon the discussion revealed that bad minority Muslims have destroyed Hindu temples in Hindu-majority West Bengal, and in other parts of India even after 1947 partition, whereas there is not a single example of bad Hindu minority destroying a single majority Muslim Mosque in Bangladesh or Pakistan, not that one wants to see that, commented a lady professor. Nevertheless, they avoided the reality. The discussion also revealed that hardly any minority has left Hindu-majority West Bengal to go to Muslim-majority Bangladesh they wanted before 1947, although many things are lot better in Bangladesh than neighboring West Bengal, and surrounding Northeast India. All agreed that the narrative they teach is not correct. After demolition of Babri Masjid in India's Uttar Pradesh State in 1992, hundreds of Hindu temples were demolished in Bangladesh and in Pakistan, as were tens of thousands of homes, shops, cremation areas and businesses. During that pogrom Sachi traveled from village after village with secular Muslims looking into minority plight, as well as destruction in Indian West Bengal. In Hindu-majority Kolkata, minority Muslims destroyed many Hindu temples in many areas, including Metiaburuz and Khidirpur of Hindu-majority Kolkata, India that this writer visited, but didn't find a single case – not that he wanted to see it – where Hindus destroyed mosques of majority Muslims in Bangladesh. Sachi was witness to a Muslim Mosque damaged in Beleghata in eastern Kolkata. Sachi also visited many villages in 1991 during another anti-Hindu pogrom in Bangladesh, when his student's home in Chittagong was burned to the ground by locals shouting "Allah hu Akbar; God is Great" in Arabic. He also visited scores of villages and temples destroyed to humiliate minorities. What kind of fun is that? There are lots of courageous people in Muslim-majority Bangladesh, Pakistan and Afghanistan who are against this, but they are extremely marginalized. In India and the U.S. some who claim to be open minded and liberated, have become supporters of intolerance, oppression of pro-secular forces in intolerant societies, as long as they are living in safety. During a Bengal Studies Conference in America, after the demolition of Babri Mosque of India in 1992, one very prominent Bangla Muslim thinker told privately to a tense Bangladeshi group that "Bangla Muslim have destroyed too many Hindu temples, in retaliation. So, if Hindus retaliated in India as in Bangladesh, would a single Mosque be standing in India?" Many believe that Babri Mosque was built by Islamic King Babur on top of a very important temple of Lord Ram. Many revisionists say, "There is no proof, because it was built 500 years ago." Then when one says, "All right, would you then agree to demolish those mosques built on top of kefir's shrines which have been documented by destroyers?" The answer is, "Of course, no."

This is extremist hypocrisy. My own family's 300-year-old Kali temple of Black Mother Goddess Kali was demolished during 1950 pogrom. Do I have any right? Then there is the mosque that sits on top of Mathura Krishna Mandir (temple) at the birthplace of Lord Krishna, where one is not allowed to even take a pencil into the shrine to prevent taking pictures of a history board standing at the entrance since British colonial days which tells people how many times the mandir was destroyed by Islamic rulers. Then there is the Varanasi Shiv Mandir, and diaries of many Muslim kings from Babur to Genghis to Akbar to Aurangzeb who tell proudly how they destroyed thousands of temples of indigenous majority Hindus, Jains and Buddhists. Varanasi is considered by many Hindus, Jains and Buddhists as holiest of the holy places. It is one of the oldest continually lived cities of the world. Many Hindus believe that if one dies there then they will have *mukti*, liberation, from re-birth. So, for millennia many have traveled at old age to die there. That is where a Muslim Emperor Aurangzeb demolished the mandir to build a mosque on that site. Wasn't there other land to build a mosque? And from where call for prayer had to be given for believers. At a weak moment of declining Islamic rule, some devout Sanatanas built a Shiv Temple sharing a wall of the mosque. Today if you visit the Shiv Mandir, you won't be allowed to enter with your phone or camera, in case you take a picture of the wall. This is India. Majority cannot talk about minority oppression. America and Germany are just the opposite.

Learning about slavery or Nazi genocide is not censored. Another reality of Hindu mind is also to accept filth amongst themselves. This is sad. Very sad. During our 2013 visit we were excited to be in that ancient city, walking the same path someone took 5,000 years back, or walking through Bangali Tola, or Bengali Quarters, where for generations people spoke Bengali in a Hindi-speaking state. Sachi looking forward to walk on the famous Daswasamedh Ghat, the famous steps on the Ganga River that have existed for 5,000 years or more. He walked past the *smasan*, wood-burning cremation area on riverbank, that has been in existence for thousands of years. Just to realize that you are walking the same path that people walked thousands of years ago – as in Rome in Italy, Xian in China or Lalibela in Ethiopia or Machu Picchu in Peru – was exciting. Sachi was distressed seeing some smut on beautiful *ghats* – steps to the river – and some pollution of Mother Ganga. He was told by some friends that after a new government came to power in 2010s, they are trying to make the city and the holy Ganga cleaner. We will believe when we see that. On the other hand, one must give credit to pious majority for tolerance as there were huge banners of Islamic preaching and Christian messages right next to the holy mandir visited by millions of devotees each year. We wonder how many Hindu, Buddhist or Jewish banners are there next to the Kaba in Arabia, or in Karbala in Iraq, or next to the St. Peter's Basilica in Rome, or at Tiananmen Square? Lord Buddha was at Sarnath, eight kilometers from Ganga, now a part of City of Varanasi, to give His first sermon to His five disciples, after His nirvana. Lord Buddha preached under a tree. That sacred site is now adorned with banners in many languages of Buddhist nations. Buddha is considered to be the last of the twelve Avatars, reincarnation, of Lord Vishnu, Father of Creation. Lord Mahavir and the last Tirthankara of the Jain religion were there too, as was Guru Nanak, the founder of Sikhism. So, history tells us that even in 600 B.C. Varanasi was a holy place when Buddha and Jain visited. Even that far back Buddha traveled from Lumbini to Gaya to Bodh Gaya to Varanasi to Gwalior and to so many other places, without train, bus, airplane or speed boat. It also tells us that distant travel was common in India millenniums ago. Gaya to Varanasi is about 250 kilometers connected by rivers. Here is Varanasi:

Mosque is Hidden Behind the Temple

Evening Aarati Light Ceremony

Islamic Mosque

Attracting Other Groups through Hebrew Poster

Banner for Islamic Meeting

A Christian Church

Attracting Religious Groups with Korean Ad

It is worth mentioning that many true believers believe that visiting Varanasi brings in surprising blessings. We never believed that. Yet Sachi got a real, real surprise. Near the Shiva Temple one has to keep everything – cameras, phones, video cameras, bags, and more – outside the temple so that one may not take pictures of the mosque and temple. Generally, everyone keeps their assets at flower shops from where one buys flower, sweets and fruits to offer to Lord Shiva. There are hundreds of these shops in lanes from all directions to the temple. Shopkeeper work as devotee's safe deposit box, often containing hundreds of thousands of rupees at no cost. As Sachi returned to the shop in mid-morning he got a call from his wife Shefali from New York as she wasn't able to reach him for days. As Sachi finished the call, he got a tap on his shoulder, asking "Are you Sachi of Koklata? I am AkhilDa." AkhilDa, Older Brother Akhil, is an architect a few years senior in Sachi's undergraduate architecture college, then a classmate at his graduate planning program in India whom Sachi last saw in 1969, 44 years ago in Kolkata. Kolkata is a day away by train from Varanasi. Hearing our conversation, the shop keeper jumped up and said "It must be the blessing of our Baba," Father Lord Shiva. We tried to figure out the probability of that miracle, but couldn't. Was it a blessed miracle that you meet someone after 44 years as you get a 60 second call after many days from his wife who couldn't reach before for days! Shefali was also a graduate classmate of AkhilDa.

AkhilDa, 2nd From Right with Wife, on Left, and Grandson

Connecting with the Past:

If one gets a chance, one must visit Gaya, a holy city in Bihar State of eastern India. Gaya is the place where Lord Gautama came to meditate under a bodhi tree to obtain His Nirvana or Enlightenment to become Buddha. Next to the tree existed a pond from where a poor and oppressed girl Sujata brought water for Him, the first drink after several days of fasting and meditation. Muslim invader Bakhtiar Khilji and others, destroyed the temple built by Buddha's followers millennia ago. Khilji cut the huge banyan-like bodhi tree under which Buddha sat and meditated. Killer Khilji then filled the pond from where Sujata brought Buddha the first drink. Only in late 1800s British Administration found the remains of the temple and began its restoration. Khilji also destroyed many Hindu-Buddhist sites in Bihar and Bengal, including the pre-Islamic Buddhist Nalanda University.

This cannot be learned in India, except by hearsay or by accident. Why not? India censors her history lessons. During our visit we realized that Gaya must have been famous for spiritual reasons in B.C. that is why Lord Gautama Buddha came there to meditate, a long distance from His home. We still wonder how He traveled in the absence of modern infrastructure and automobiles. How long did that take? How brave, dedicated, and courageous one has to be? Hindus believe in offering food and water to the departed and to ancestors to bring peace from Heaven. One is required, like Lord Gautama, to go to the banks of Falgu River in Gaya to offer the departed rice balls with other condiments called *Pinda*, with *bel* or wood apple leaves, flowers, and water. After Ma's passing on December 14, 1999, older brother Dada asked Sachi to go to Gaya to do *Pinda Daan* or Offering of Pinda food to Ma on behalf of the entire family. On his next visit Sachi went with his older sister Didi to Gaya. It was about 4 to 5 hours' train ride from Kolkata. As soon as you set foot in Gaya, you realize how Indians and Hindus are uncaring of their heritage and old architecture. You see a crumbling structure, and the taxi driver would say, "Just ignore. It is only 1,200-year-old Temple of Mother Sita," or "No body visits that ruined building. It is an Ashram from 1,500s," and so on. We thought that in 21st Century people are eager to save historic places, religious or not, but our experience says a different narrative. One of the customs at *Pinda Daan* ritual is astonishing, in terms of finding family tree. Gaya has thousands of *pandas* or agents who keep track of family trees. As you move in your vehicle or walk towards the *ghat* steps to Falgu River, hundreds of agents will surround your vehicle, asking for your family name. They have divided the entire world by agents. Thus, when you tell them you are from Bengal, the crowd thins out. Then naming the district makes it thinner; further down to police station, then down to village. Then when one's village name is found, one has to give the family name. At that stage, there remained only two agents of our historical ancestral book. Then we had to decide whom Sachi and Didi are going to choose for Ma's name as they will be offering *pindas* with blessed soil and grass ball to be listed in agent's book. Sachi chose the man where his older brother Dada had listed his name when he offered *pinda* to our father in 1980s. It was a 3" to 4" thick book-like covered writing pad, with listing of ancestors going back to many centuries. We couldn't believe that we were seeing a book where many centuries back our ancestors signed in their own hand! That is one special gift to any traveler. We are sure foreign visitors of any religion can open a new book in Gaya. It was even more jarring to think how people came to this place that far back. They could only travel by boat or on foot.

It could have easily taken them from Lakshmankathi village of Barisal District to Gaya seven to ten days or more by boat in Indian rivers. Then they had to return back. Bravo to their devotion! Our brother Dada gave up his favorite fruit mango forever that he offered to God and to dad Baba during *Pinda Daan*. Sachi skipped that part of offering one's favorite food. Gaya was rebuilt hundreds of years after demolition by Khilji. India is the only place where the entire population didn't become a part of Dar-ul-Islam. Thus, these atrocities are openly visible and remembered, yet new India censors these. If one opens her eyes, one can find such ill-fated examples from Mecca to Jerusalem to Damascus to Istanbul and to my own village. When you are fully changed – religious or political – you find justification for those, just as colonizers justify colonizing and destruction of indigenous North and South Americans.

Bodhi Tree Garden of Lord Buddha, Gaya

Didi with Priest on the Bank of Falgu River Offering Pinda or Symbolic Food to Ma and Ancestor. River is visible through Banihan and Bodhi trees.

Fallen Three Leaves from the Holy Bodhi Tree

We strongly believe that Subcontinental has no memory. As we cremate our dead, leaving no memorial for our ancestors, we have become a people with no link to our past, and as a result we have forgotten to remember our history, although some think otherwise. We have given up *tarpan* or Remembrance Memorial Service, a week before the start of autumn Durga Puja festival of the Mother who saved us from the demon. Do we mourn for our families when they are killed by terrorists? How many Hindus and secularists worldwide have ever stopped for a minute to remember millions of Hindus murdered by the Army of Islamic Republic of Pakistan in 1971? Not one. Or, killed by the British colonizers, including Churchill-created Bengal Famine of 1943-44 when he took the bumper crop away, then destroyed boats killing 3 to 7 million Indians. Or during pre-British Persian-Turkic rule when tens of thousands of Indians were killed. In 2017 a group from New York led by Shyamal wanted to do a *ganosraddho*, mass last rites, in Dhaka for Hindus killed during Pakistan's genocide of 1971, but he was not allowed to hold that event in Bangladesh by so-called secularists. Why? When Stitangshu tried to do the same in 2020, there was resistance, even in America.

We are sure that they would also have faced harassment in Hindu-majority West Bengal run by Bangladeshi-Hindu-refugees. And, how many American Indian religious groups and temples have come forward to help Shyamal and Sitangshu? Please guess! Question was raised when a Long Island High School history teacher, James, revealed on April 28, 2020, during a presentation that while talking about Indian partition many history books talk of parity or equal victimization and displacement. James revealed, only after research he realized that it is a false history. Before his research he didn't know that almost all non-Muslims were cleansed from their Muslim-majority homeland of Afghanistan, Pakistan and Bangladesh, whereas very few Muslims fled from Hindu-majority India for Pakistan, Bangladesh or Afghanistan. Immediately after 1947 partition there was a slight drop of Muslims from 13% to 12% of the population in India, as Muslim-majority Pakistan and Bangladesh moved out of Indian census data. Some Muslims went voluntarily to Pakistan to create an Islamic State like the founder of Islam – thus they called themselves the Islamic Fighter or Muhajir, not refugees, associates of the Prophet. Muslim share of Indian population has increased steadily to 14% or more, in 2021, in spite of tens of millions of Hindus,

Sikhs, Buddhists, Christians and Jains were cleansed for India. Information is hidden in history books. Statistically, population share should have gone down below 14%.

Democracy and Public Policy:

Democracy demands many things including a well-informed people, equal treatment for all, and no persecution. In case of South Asia, one more element must be added to that: censorship of one-sided faith-supported killing and cleansing of its indigenous minorities. No individual and no nation were held responsible for that. In a hypothetical situation, if slavery continued in the South and if it succeeded in partitioning America, would free Africans and anti-slavery White Northerners treat slave-holding South at per with themselves? We don't think so. We even expelled South Africa from the U.N. during apartheid, stopped trade with them. Should Israel and Europe have treated Nazis as innocent citizens, if we did not defeat the monster? The world went to war with them. We also gave our lives to defeat ISIS. So why is this double standard when it comes to some other lives? In our case, just as we fought against ISIS Islamist terrorists, why aren't we fighting similar terrorists in the Subcontinent? Should we consider lives of Westerners more valuable than Easterners? Why we are not protecting secularists there? Should we come up with deconstructionism of what is taught in holy books? During British rule attempt to protect secularists didn't go anywhere. We need to deconstruct real issues as well as issues made up by neo-colonial press.

One of the real tragedies of British-Indian partition is ethnic cleansing of minorities of Pakistan, Bangladesh and Afghanistan. Bangladesh gained independence through Pakistan's 1971 Hindu genocide. Not a single Muslim-majority nation condemned that. As mentioned earlier, even "civilized" West didn't demand trial of killer soldiers. Why? There was hardly any reciprocity of cleansing. It was a one-sided affair, except Sikhs in the western Punjab fought back in 1947. We believe it was because Sikhs who emerged in the 15th Century as a militant defender of indigenous beliefs. They helped Hindus and Jains to fight back for self-defense, that Bengali Hindus in the east didn't have, leading to one-sided oppression without any repercussion and retaliation. Bengali Hindus fought against the British Colonial power, but with the rise of Muslim League Party in the east their resistance and self-defense vanished. There is rarely any parallel to this self-vaporization in human history.

Routine Torching of Indigenous Minority Homes in Bangladesh

Source: Social Media

British-created castes have many dimensions, among them is the family or village identity. Many indigenous families identify with village they lived for centuries or more, as is the case of our families, and natives in the U.S., Mexico, Peru, Egypt, Ethiopia and more. In many Indian cultures village names get attached to one's name, as with Tamils, Marathas, Kannadigas, Punjabis, Telugus and more. These attachments have created many identities, including family, language or caste. Again, even after conversion to Islam and Christianity, racist caste division has remained in many places. Democracy and pluralism allow keeping such identity, from the U.K. to U.S.A., from Brazil to Botswana, and from India to Indiana. In some state politics caste can be a big and abusive force, whereas not much in many states. In Bengal, since the days of nationalist movements, caste has become a non-issue. Assam and Northeast never had caste division. In early 1968 we were graduate students at Institute of Technology, about 100 kilometers southwest of Kolkata. On some weekends Sachi used to visit his parents taking a commuter train. On one trip a family of oppressed peasants, all men, dressed nicely in *dhuti* (dhoti) and Bengali shirt were chatting about their visit to a boy's family, a possible match for their teenage daughter. The father of the girl sat next to Sachi, then started to chat with hm. Sachi enjoyed talking to them. They were to get off at Panskura Station, in the middle of rural belt of Medinipur District, over an hour's ride from Kharagpur, and 90-minutes southwest of Kolkata. Long before Panskura, the father of the family started inviting Sachi to be an overnight guest. Before leaving he told Sachi that in his dream "Mother Kali wished me to have a son-in-law like you." It was a wonderful family. Few days later he got a letter written in Bengali about the desires of the family. At the Institute one senior classmate KhitiDa picked up the letter, and seeing rural handwriting opened the letter before telling Sachi. Then half-a-dozen friends at Acharya Hall came to Sachi to share the letter, and proposed to negotiate a marriage proposal. Realizing the seriousness of the proposal, cooler heads prevailed, and no response was made. Everybody realized that even in rural Bengal, the caste differentiation wasn't serious in 1960s.

As mentioned earlier, over thousands of years, many malpractices entered into Indian mind, at times as a result of foreign invasion, at times for their own slavery, and at other times based on regional and geographical issues. Since Lord Buddha and Lord Jain, 600 B.C., there have been efforts to rectify malpractices, including caste, gender, tribe, color or sub-regional imagery. Yet, this was not a monolithic religion, or a mono-culture nation. Many deities rose from the oppressed, including the most popular Lord Krishna, a cow herder. Many saints also rose from the oppressed, like saints Hari Chand and Guru Chand of Bengal. Then there are women. Many women are the most popular deities. In Bengal almost all the festivals have to do with Female Power: Ma Durga, Goddess of Strength – when no God could destroy the demon there emerged the brown mother with four kids who went to war taking them along; Ma Kali, the Black Goddess demon Killer, a reincarnation of Ma Durga; Ma Lakshmi, the brown-colored daughter and the Goddess of Prosperity, Ma Sarasvati, the light-skin daughter and the Goddess of Education and Music, and more. Possibly the most influential person of Bengali life has been Khona. Khona was a super genius whose verses guided life in India. Khonar Bachan or Tale of Khona, describes through poems and couplets telling farmers what to plant and when. Or when and how to welcome a bride and groom, how to design one's home, what kinds of plants are good for homesteads and forests, and what medicine to take to fight diseases and viruses, and how to treat people of other faiths, and so much more. In a way Khona is the day-to-day mother of life in India. Unfortunately, Khona's fame made his stupid husband to disfigure her, yet couldn't stop her teaching. Fortunately, not one in a million knows about Khona's criminal husband, but only her as a genius. Ma Durga's family had all skin colors within the family, as is common in many Indian families – brown, light, dark, and yellow, thus trying to break skin color consciousness. Worldwide we need to follow Her symbolism. Thus, when Indira Gandhi became Prime Minister of India, there was no theological or cultural opposition. Once Sachi wrote in a paper, why it has been relatively easy in the Subcontinent with roots in indigenous tradition to elect women as head of the nation without much fuss. Image of the Mother plays consciously and unconsciously. Thus, besides India, Indian/Hindu-culture-based Muslim-majority Bangladesh, Pakistan and Indonesia elected women as Prime Minister, Buddhist Sri Lanka, and an atheist Hindu-majority Nepal has a woman as the head. Even Hindu-dominated Guyana in South America elected an immigrant Jewish woman as its President decades ago.

We need to discuss openly, how to challenge anti-democratic, horrific, oppressive teaching in all religion's beliefs, and politics. There is a worldwide censorship of that, even in democratic West. As mentioned earlier, saying that a preacher's parents were kefir or non-believers, brings prison, or worse in many countries. Talking about love life may bring death penalty. Talking about caste and color racism energizes some. Some non-offensive publications were banned in many nations including Indian states, and some Third World nations. It is good to have censorship of fake news. How can democratic nations challenge partisan politics? Many books have been banned without any repercussion from the Free World.

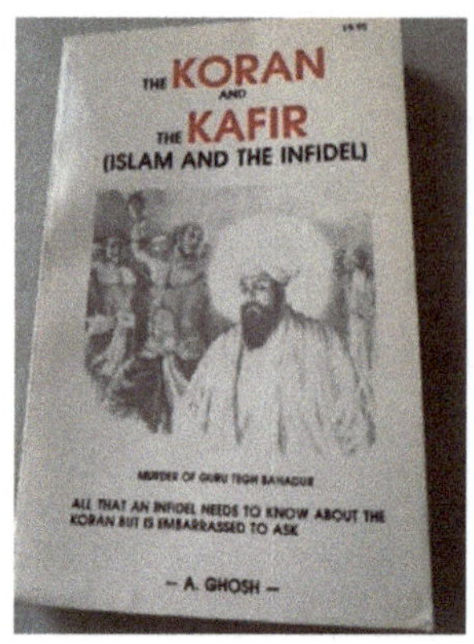

Author A. Ghosh, a Pakistani-Bangladeshi-Hindu-Refugee-Indian-American, with book banned by Indian Congress and Communist-Marxist Governments, along with Pakistan.

Shahriar Kabir's 3 Volume Book on Anti-Hindu Pogrom in Bangladesh in 2001, there was Attempt of his Assassination. Kabir is from a Muslim Family. He was Nominated in 2022 for Nobel Peace Prize but Imprisoned by Nobel Laureate Yunus Government in 2024

Three Volume Shariar Kabir's, a Muslim, book on Oppression of Hindu Minority in 2001 in Bangladesh

Book Banned in Muslim-majority nations, with $25 million Bounty for his Assassination by Islamic Iran, and Attempted for Assassination in New York, U.S.A.

Lajja (Shame) by Dr. Taslina Nasrin with Story of 2001 Bangla Anti-Hindu Pogrom. She was banned from her homeland, and in Left-run and Right-run West Bengal State of India, for the truth. She found shelter in India "reactionary" Delhi, but not in Progressive Bengali-speaking West Bengal, India.

No ban was ordered when derogatory write up appeared *"Sri Krishna: Story of a Ruffian Avatar."*

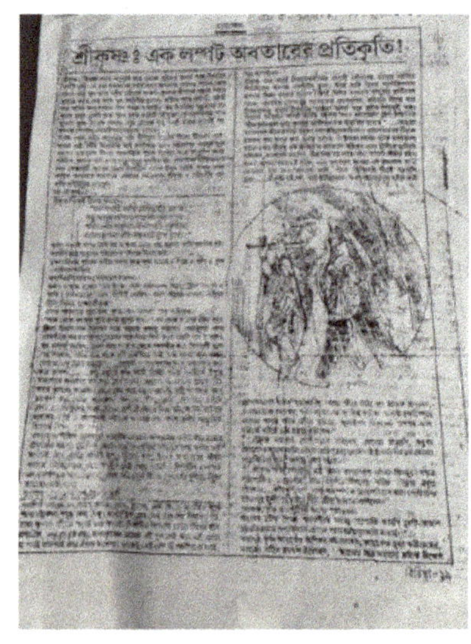

It was a great honor for Sachi to nominate Mr. Shahriar Kabir, a Muslim, and Mr. Rabindra Ghosh, a Hindu, both of Bangladesh for Nobel Prize in Peace in 2022, which was accepted by the Nobel Peace Committee on December 14,

2021. A New York Paper, *Bangalee*, edited by Mr. Kaushik Ahmed, found that out from unknown sources and published a report on that causing sensation among pro-secular groups in the Subcontinent. Here is the report with pictures of the nominees. Both were targeted for killing, and earlier Mr. Ghosh's home in Chittagong was completely destroyed by so-called tolerant citizens. Kabir was imprisoned by the new Bangladesh 2024 government.

For Nobel Peace Award Proposal (Left, Kabir, and Right, Ghosh)

শাহরিয়ার কবির ও রবীন্দ্রনাথ ঘোষের নাম প্রস্তাব

শেষের পাতার পর

এবং রবীন্দ্রনাথ ঘোষ। আর তাঁদের নাম প্রস্তাব করেছেন নিউইয়র্কের বিশিষ্ট মানবাধিকার কর্মী ড. সব্যসাচী ঘোষ দস্তিদার। তিনি নোবেল পিস কমিটির একজন মনোনয়নকারী বা নমিনেটর। ড. দস্তিদার সাপ্তাহিক বাঙ্গালীকে জানান, তিনি মনোনয়নপত্রের সংক্ষিপ্ত ডিসকোর্সে তাদের দুজন সম্পর্কে উল্লেখ করেছেন, তারা দুজনই বাংলাদেশের মূল আদর্শের জন্য লড়াই করছেন। এই মূল আদর্শ হলো একটি সেক্যুলার এবং সর্বধর্মের প্রতি সহনশীল রাষ্ট্র গঠন। তারা দুজনই বাংলাদেশের সংখ্যালঘুদের জীবন রক্ষার জন্য নিজেদের জীবনের ঝুঁকি নিয়ে লড়াই করছেন। সর্বোপরি তাদের মূল এজেন্ডা হিউম্যান রাইটস প্রতিষ্ঠা।

ড. দস্তিদার জানান, শাহরিয়ার কবীর এবং রবীন্দ্রনাথ ঘোষের নাম প্রস্তাব করার পরপরই নোবেল পিস কমিটি জানায়, উক্ত প্রস্তাব গৃহীত হয়েছে। তিনি বলেন, প্রতি বছর নোবেল শান্তি পুরস্কারের জন্য বিপুল সংখ্যক নাম প্রস্তাবাকারে পাঠানো হয়। কিন্তু সব নাম গৃহীত হয় না। এইসব গৃহীত নাম থেকে লং লিস্ট শর্ট লিস্ট শেষে চূড়ান্ত সিদ্ধান্ত হবে।

উল্লেখ্য, ড. সব্যসাচী ঘোষ দস্তিদার পঞ্চাশ বছরেরও বেশি আগে বরিশাল থেকে আমেরিকায় আসেন। এলাবামার এএন্ডএম ইউনিভার্সিটি, ফ্লোরিডা স্টেট ইউনিভার্সিটিতে শিক্ষকতা ছাড়াও দীর্ঘদিন নিউইয়র্ক স্টেট ইউনিভার্সিটির ওল্ড ওয়েস্টবারি কলেজে পড়িয়ে সম্প্রতি অবসর গ্রহণ করেছেন। এছাড়াও তিনি ফুলব্রাইট স্কলারশীপে কাজাখস্তান, আয়ারল্যান্ড, ইন্ডিয়ায় বিভিন্ন ইউনিভার্সিটিতে ভিজিটিং প্রফেসর হিসাবে দায়িত্ব পালন করেছেন। ড. দস্তিদার আমেরিকায় থেকেও বাংলাদেশের মুক্তিযুদ্ধের মূল আদর্শ রক্ষাসহ মানবাধিকার রক্ষায় কাজ করে চলেছেন।

তিনি বলেন, মানবাধিকার এবং সংখ্যালঘুদের রক্ষায় শাহরিয়ার কবীর এবং রবীন্দ্রনাথ ঘোষের যে বিশাল ভূমিকা তা আজ আন্তর্জাতিকভাবে স্বীকৃত। সে কারণেই তাদের নাম প্রস্তাব করা হয়েছে। এবং সেই প্রস্তাব গৃহীত হয়েছে।

Destroyed Bangladesh Home of Rabindra Ghosh

AL men demolish minority right group leader's house in city

Staff Correspondent

LOCAL Awami League activists demolished the under construction tin-sheds of a rights activist at Kalunagar under Kamrangirchar in the capital and looted valuables and construction materials from there early Sunday.

The victim, Rabindra Ghosh, president of Bangladesh Minority Watch, said that the attack was launched to grab his land and as he declined to pay the amount demanded by the attackers.

Rabindra, now residing at RK Mission Road in the city, said that he bought two kathas of land at Kalunagar Mouja under Kamrangirchar in 2010 and local influential had several times threatened him to evict from the land.

'On Sunday, sometimes after 1:00am', he alleged, 'the attackers attacked the under construction buildings, demolished them, beat up the workers staying there, took away their mobile phones, cash money, construction materials, tins and timbers from the house.'

He said he was not on the spot then.

'Those who attacked and destroyed my building are ruling Awami League men,' he said.

He alleged that he began construction works on his land in the first week of March and erected two tin-shed buildings.

Rabindra's wife Krishna Ghosh lodged a case with Kamrangirchar Police Station on March 25 naming seven local people and 50 to 80 unidentified others for the attack, destruction and looting.

The accused named in the case are Md Lokman, Md Shahidullah, Md Jinu, Siraj, Ismail, Maksudur Rahman and Md Siraj, all residents of Kamrangirchar.

Kamrangirchar Police Station officer-in-charge Shahin Fakir told New Age that they arrested Md Siraj. 'Drive is on to arrest others.'

National Human Rights Commission chairman Kazi Reazul Hoque expressed his concern and condemned the attack.

One of the accused, Ismail, told New Age that Rabindra's wife Krishna lodged case against Awami League men and claimed that he was not involved in the attack or demanding toll.

Local ward councillor Nure Alam, also vice-president of Kamrangirchar thana AL, told New Age that Rabindra had been constructing tin sheds grabbing and filling a canal. 'Local people resisted it and foiled his illegal activities.'

See *https://empireslastcasualty.blogspot.com/2018/05/why-is-rabindranath-ghoshs-home-in.html*

Mr. Rabindra Ghosh Receiving Citation at Chittagong, Bangladesh from the Indian Subcontinent Partition Documentation Project of New York, September 2022

Mr. Shahriar Kabir Received Citation at Kolkata, India from the Indian Subcontinent Partition Documentation Project of New York, Presented in September 2022 by Prof. Dr. Sujata Ghosh Dastidar, head of Calcutta Girls' Orphanage,

During the 2001 pogrom an important New York media didn't see any problem of killing of oppressed minority and secularists of the majority community. Shockingly, Sachi received four large envelopes with plea for help and other documentations, but with four different Muslim names in Bangladesh. Together, it must have cost someone's monthly income to send those documents in desperation. Our assumption was that to stop spreading the news of atrocities, those were sent from different addresses, however, we never met the senders during our dozens of trips to Bangladesh. Here are envelopes of those mails:

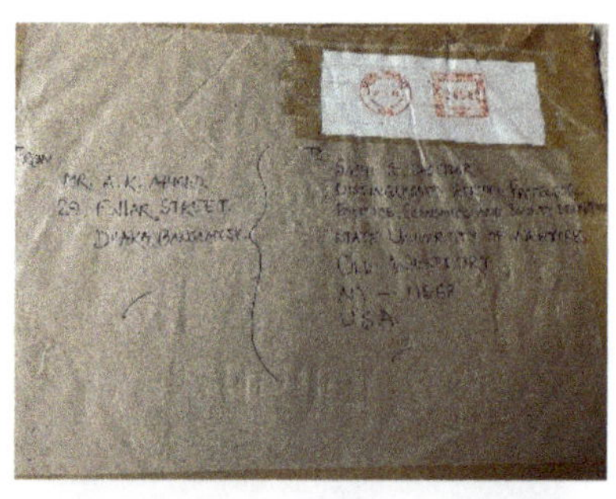

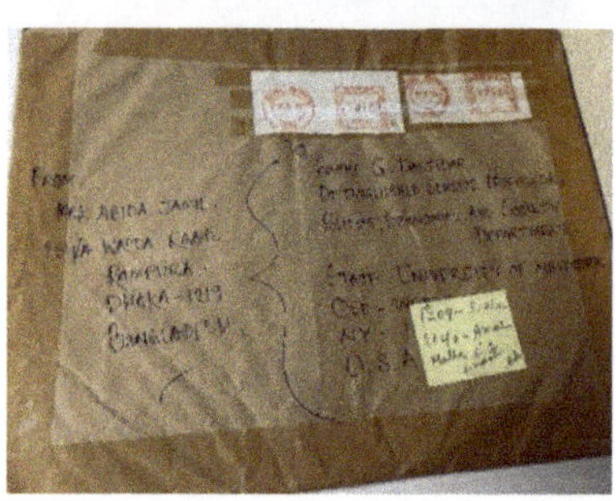

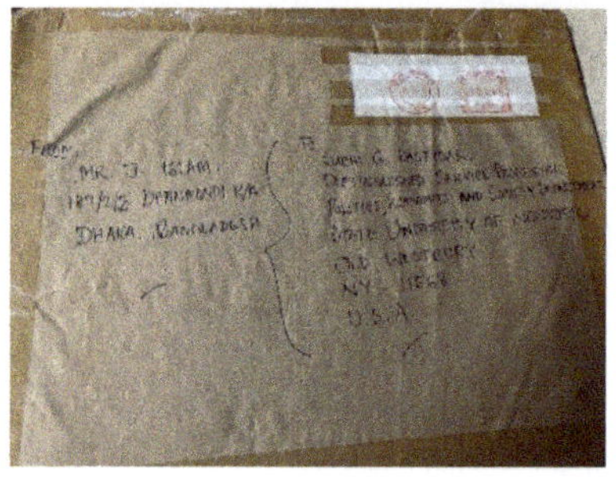

Why hasn't West and the free press objected to the killing, cleansing and destruction? In April of 2020 there were reports in papers that an Islamist killer of Bangladesh Founding Father Mujibur Rahman, Mr. Mosle Uddin, was hiding in Kolkata, India as a Hindu Dr. Datta for 25 years. After Uddin's death, he was cremated in Hindu tradition with the host doctor's kids giving last rites. A Bangladesh daily *Bhorer Kagoj* published that report on April 24, 2020. A learned Muslim, Mr. Mohamed, with his pictures in that paper wrote "This is a real punishment for him if he was really cremated as a non-Muslim. He identified himself as a Hindu. Is it not a more punishment than hanging to death? We are waiting for the real news. And if he is really in the hands of Bangladesh Govt, hang him ASAP." Why a religion has been able to incorporate such hatred without challenge from the West, our free press, and from within? This reminds us the struggle in the U.S. for our First Amendment of Free Speech, and Second Amendment of Gun Ownership. With the rise of complete lies through the Internet, even attempting to undermine U.S. Presidential Elections, lies about Ukrainian war, and partisanship for Israel-Hamas-Palestine war, we are seeing how free speech can become free lies with very serious consequences. Most countries now have tools to control speech. U.S. is trying too. If we continue to promote a gun-murder culture, and economy of some large settler nations like Argentina, Australia, Brazil, Canada, or Mexico improve, we may have difficulty in attracting new migrants here. A few non-settler nations like China, Egypt, India, Iran, Nigeria, Russia, and South Africa may play a role in attracting migrants if they open their door to migration of diverse ethnicities.

In 2021, largescale atrocities took place during Fall Puja Festival of Mother Durga, when thousands of shrines, neighborhood celebrations *pandal* pavilions, homes, businesses, shops were destroyed, and minorities hacked to death. Why did West and East censor that?

Documentation Published in New York by Karmakar of

Bangladesh Hindu Buddhist Christian Unity Council - USA

Destruction of Temples, Homes and Businesses

Destruction of Deities, Continuing for Millenia without
Protest from the World and Media

A Hindu Monk Providing Help at a Site in 2021 where Hundreds of Homes were Torched

In rural areas forced conversion of minorities is common, even with rape. In many Indian languages we use the word "*chhowab*" or "blessing," possibly derived from *Arabic*, meaning blessing from God Allah for converting a kefir. Average Muslims deeply believe that if one converts a kefir or non-believer one moves one step closer to Heaven. Thus, rape or forced conversion never had negative connotation in the minds of many, instead of feeling just the opposite. We know secular Muslims are fighting for change. This change has to come from within. Any time one comes forward to discuss these issues, one immediately receives death threat. How many intellectuals from Egypt, Algeria, Iraq, Sudan, Iran, Somalia, Pakistan, Afghanistan and Yemen have found shelter in Europe, America, and Asia? Getting asylum is very humane, and necessary.

Simultaneously, we need to find ways to keep them at home. On the contrary how many Hindu critiques of "idol worshipping India" have found shelter in Iran, Egypt, Pakistan, Bangladesh or England? Caste oppression must be condemned. Yet the same media fail to tell their readers that in pluralistic India and pluralistic Hinduism, many Indian states are run by oppressed population, and many Presidents and Chief Ministers have come from oppressed groups, and that in 2020 the Prime Minister of India is from an oppressed and minority group, and in 2023 the female President is from a poor tribe. Is disinformation being there because of money coming from certain sources? That divisiveness is also exploited even in America. When Sachi was elected to a School Board in New York City in 1996, he was requested by some Indian parents for school holidays for Diwali and Holi. Sachi thought it was improper for a secular country to have religious holidays, although New York City school had Christian and Jewish holidays, later Islamic holidays were added by Mayor de Blasio. In 1980s New York City Mayor Koch when asked about additional religious holidays in schools, he said that he didn't want to "Indianize" our schools as Indian schools have holidays for possibly ten religions, even when there was not a single student of that religion. We support that position. So, when Sachi was approached by immigrant parents, he expressed his position.

One school in eastern Queens was probably Hindu-Jain majority in 1996. Yet in the same divide and conquer policy, a new Mayor gave Islamic holidays but not for Hindus alienating many, but in typical fatalistic style, they complained to themselves. In the same divisive spirit, de Blasio promoted giving Islamic food, but not Jain vegetarian food, or non-beef Indian food. We think it is extremely bad decision to introduce religious food in a secular body. Even if a Christian does a slow slaughter in Islamic style, still the food will not be accepted by many. Why should a secular institution introduce itself to another form of bigotry? If a Latin says that they won't take food cooked by a non-Latin, why should New York City give into that? Or, if Whites say, they won't accept Asians as teachers, should NYC schools accept that?

So, on April 15, 2020 a letter was sent to the mayor, with copies to Speaker Melissa Mark-Viverito; Councilmen Rory Lanchman and Mark Weprin; Assemblyman David Weprin; and NY Senator Tony Avella.

Dear Mayor De Blasio: Sub: Religious Holiday in Public School writing after reading newspaper reports from here in New York as well as from the Subcontinent about adding only Islamic holidays while ignoring Hindu faith. As the first person from the Subcontinent to be elected to NYC School Board (in 1996 in District 26) I was approached by many parents for not only religious holidays but also of religiously proscribed food – vegetarian and non-vegetarian – of Islamic, Hindu, Sikh, Jain, Buddhist and Vaishnav traditions. (I served Community Board 13 for many years.) As I believe in separation of Church and State in a secular country, I argued with my constituents that religion is a private matter and public school should not get involved with it. Even in 1996 possibly one of the schools in my district was Hindu majority. (At the request of my constituents ...did raise the issue of Hindu holydays to.... then councilman; however, ...shared.... personal belief with him.)

Now that you have expanded religious holidays in public school, (we) would request you to look at the needs of the large Hindu minority as well. With cheers and jeers, triumphalism and taunting – here and in overseas – ignoring Hindu holydays has added another complexity, especially with the Hindu minorities from Bangladesh, Pakistan and Afghanistan. (.... know of at least 9 Hindu temples in New York City run by Bangla, Pakistani and Afghan Hindus.) They are institutionally discriminated in their homelands and now many of them feel unequal again in New York, as do other Hindus. (Many Hindus feel that their nonaggressive, tolerant attitude is seen as a weakness. Even NYC witnessed attack by Muslims when a Hindu-Muslim couple, married in a Muslim-majority nation, wanted to give their son Hindu last rites; see NYT 10.4.08, and a petition by Hindus to Mayor Bloomberg seeking action, 10.02.08.)

In October of 2022 NYC Mayor Eric Adams declared Diwali Holiday for 2023 year, initiated by Hon. Jennifer Rajkumar, New York State Assemblywoman.

Can You Address Past Oppression?

Then again, how do you delegitimize destruction of shrines of Hindu, Christian, Sikh, Jain, Buddhist, Muslims, ashrams, libraries, viharas, and schools as legitimate by destruction of deities at Kaaba when it existed as a temple of Pagan Arabs. Many Muslim friends talk about reformation in Islam. By asking for reformation Dr. Taslima Nasrin lost her citizenship and ability to return home in secular Bangladesh; or writer Salman Rushdie getting million-dollar bounty on his head for a pious Islamic regime in Iran, and attempt of his life in New York on August 12, 2022. This is easy to followers of monotheistic beliefs. Why has West not pressured secularists' return a precondition for working with partisan nations? Hypocrisy? Why no Islamic nation condemned when Islamists bombed Syria killing 46 people during 2020 Islamic Ramadan? We wonder if a Jewish group did that, what would be the reaction of world press? And how many Muslim-majority nations condemned Taliban when they destroyed 1,500-year-old pre-Islam Buddha statues at Bamiyan, Afghanistan? The destruction started on March 2, 2001, and continued till April. Taliban used dynamite, rockets, and anti-aircraft guns. Very few Western or Indian press reported that Taliban also destroyed 144 Afghan Hindu and Sikh temples (See *Indian Abroad*, April 2001) which were their ancestors' shrines. When nations condone such acts through silence, possibly with underground funding, how can the world restore tolerance before all non-believers are gone? Our parents weren't able to set foot on their homestead after they were driven out. Who should be held responsible for that?

In India, many think if it offends religious minorities, as opposed to linguistic minorities, one behaves differently. Thus, when a Muslim woman Shah Bano sought compensation from her husband Mohammad Ahmed Khan as per Indian law, and when Indian Supreme Court ruled in her favor on April 23, 1985, Congress Party Prime Minister Rajiv Gandhi immediately appealed to the Supreme Court to reverse the decision. Sadly, Supreme Court acquiesced giving a black face to "secular" India. This sort of racist or communal politics has been pushing different groups further apart, even after partition which witnessed the largest ethnic cleansing in the world. Who mourned our death, our cleansing? Moreover, Shah Bano case was a verdict against easy divorce by Muslim men by just saying *talaq, talaq, talaq,* and against multiple marriages. This is still not acceptable in the U.S. Multiple marriage was banned for Hindus and for other groups, why not for others? Is that secularism of India? Why not be consistent? Multiple wives are already banned in many Muslim-majority nations. What's the problem with India? After many try a non-communal anti-three *talaq* divorce was passed in 2019, with praise from many, but criticized by a section of "Western liberal press" as "Hindu communalism," but not allowing the same in the U.S. Hypocrisy? Thus, stopping discrimination in America is racism? Or, promoting anti-Semitism is pro-Jewish communalism? This hypocrisy in democracy is dangerous. The West Bengal State's ruling Communist Party-Marxist government found money and devotion to install a statue of Ho Chi Minh in Kolkata. Great! They also renamed the Harrington Street to Ho Chi Minh Street at U.S. Consulate, mentioned earlier.

However, they didn't have money or devotion to install a memorial for Hindu monks and nuns brutally murdered in broad daylight at Ballygunj in Kolkata, under their rule or for Dr. Shyama Prasad Mukherji who saved them in partitioned State of West Bengal. In typical communal fashion the party head of West Bengal and a Politburo Member, a Bangladeshi-Indian, chose not to live with Muslims in his Muslim-majority Bangladesh homeland but curses Dr. Mukherji who gave him shelter, but praises who cleansed them. In interview with Sachi in 2015 the Politburo Member exposed hard-core racism during his visit to New York City. The letter was written on August 15, 2005, the Indian Independence Day, with copies to Mrs. Tulsi Sengupta, Chair of U.S. Cultural Association of Bengal/ 25th Bengali Convention Head; Mrs. Dhriti Bagchi, Kallol Club of NJ; Chair, Bengali Association of North America; Dr. Hore, 26th Bengali Conference; Chief Minister of West Bengal; The Hon. Nilotpaul Bosu, Member of Indian Parliament (Bangladeshi-Indian Present at the Convention), Calcutta Newspapers, etc. It reads:

The Hon. Biman Bosu Calcutta 700 016, India

I am writing this after my brief discussion with you at the Banga Sammelan in New York City as a large number of Bengalis in the diaspora was shocked and offended by your statements. As a result, I thought I will write this note. If there is any discrepancy, kindly let me know.

I had approached you for an appointment. You asked me to meet you at 10 AM on Saturday, July 3, 2005, at Vidyasagar Stall. I am sorry that you were not there. When I met up with you yet again you asked me to come afterwards. At that meeting I discussed our projects of helping orphans and poor get education in West Bengal, Assam and Bangladesh, like the Vidyasagar project in Purulia and the possibility of collaboration. Afterwards [we] asked, "Bimanbabu, it is great that you are always protesting injustices around the world and in remote corners of non-Bengali India. When institutions like those which our foundation supports in Bangladesh come under attack lots of people from New York, the U.S., Bangladesh and around-the-world condemn such acts by intolerant extremists. Would you be kind enough to lend moral support to us and to those victims?" You rudely replied, "There has not been any attack on Hindus in Bangladesh. {I did not raise the issue of Hindu killing.} Hindus are persecuted." As [we] expressed our shock, (there were others present who were stunned at your extreme communal position, especially when you have chosen not to live in your Muslim-majority homeland), you replied, "It is attack on Awami League [pro-independence pro-secular party of Bangladesh.] Thus, Hindus are attacked." [We] said "even then why should you condone it? Why not protest such killings?" Then [we] asked, "if what you say is true, can you show [us] one single all-Muslim all-Awami village, of which there are thousands, where the village was torched, girls and wives raped and mosques destroyed?" To which you said, "There will be killings there. Likhey rakhun (please write down) 3rd july 2005-e aami ekatha bollam (I said this), and ran inside the Vidyasagar Stall away from us. Right before that you told us that your parents and ancestors are from Bangladesh, but now you cannot consider that your ancestral land because you "need a passport and visa." To which I said "so do we to get to India. And if that is the reason not to call your land your home then a large number of peoples attending the Conference from whom you are seeking help – many among us holding U.S. passport, our children and grandchildren born in the U.S. – cannot be considered Indian or West Bengali, then why come to us? And if visa-passport requirements are so offensive if West Bengal Government and your Party are proposing to get rid of such requirements for us?" You did not reply to us.

I am looking forward to hearing from you.

To our surprise, this letter was printed in the Appendix of a book of Hon. Tathagata Roy, *Ja Chhilo Aamaar Desh* (*How was my Homeland: A tale of exodus of minorities from Bangladesh*, Mitra & Ghosh Publishers, Kolkata; B.S. Aswin 1423 [2016]). On May 1, 2020, daily *Anandabazar Patrika* had a news about Mr. Basu and four CPM leaders holding vigil on April 30, 2020 in the midst Covid lockdown in front of Ho Chi Minh statue, without any mask made mandatory by the local state government. During Vietnam War slogan of CPM was "*Aamaar naam, tomar naam, Vietnam Vietnam,* (My name and Your name is Vietnam and Vietnam.)" The Politburo Member told the gathering in New York that as a poor man, he lived in a housing provided by the Party, and never rides the public transport in Kolkata as he has a car with chauffer provided by the Party, thus is unaware of the complexities of public transportation in that city. When we visited another CPM Politburo Member Mr. Nripen Chakraborty, Bikarmpur, East-Pakistan-Bangladesh-born, he was already expelled from the Party. He was sent to build the Party in pre-independence era when Tripura was a Princely State run by its king. He served as Chief Minister of Tripura. He was the other friendly face of Indian bureaucracy, opposite of what we faced in Kolkata at Chief Minister Jyoti Basu's office. On Thursday, June 9, 2001 a call from a stranger in Tripura, Sachi was able to meet with the Principal Secretary, Mr. Ajeer Vidya, a Buddhist from north India's Hindi area, who immediately invited Sachi to a party that evening, and then introduced Sachi to the Deputy Chief Minister Mr. Aghor Deb Barma, a Tripura tribal communist, to talk about a project. Hon. Deb Barma in turn told how to meet the expelled Nripen Chakraborty. Like many Indian nationalists in pre-independence era, Mr. Chakraborty had a very simple living as a bachelor. His government housing was in poor condition, with pigeons flying into his bedroom as he fed them from his bed. A policeman was on duty, while a cook did the cooking, bringing us a cup of tea before asking, as is common in local custom. Sadly, Chakraborty asked for money to feed Muslims in Bangladesh. When asked him "Why not Hindus who are oppressed there?" He had no answer. When Sachi met Deb Barma later, he said, "May be Nripen Babu is going insane." May be! Hon. Deb Barma introduced to a group belonging to a Tripura tribal organization, whose office was also located in the same government building. For a long time, Tripuri tribes or Tripuris identified themselves as Hill Bengali as Bengalis have a diversity of peoples with different accents.

They are minority in Tripura now constituting about a quarter of population. With the rise of ultra-nationalism during the rule of Communist Party, a section of Tripuris, led by a recently-converted Christian Mr. Bijoy Rankhel, organized a group of tribes for conversion, then killed Hindus and pushed for adoption of English script for Tripura languages, away from their indigenous Bengali script. Tribal languages use "Bengali" script as does neighbor areas of Assam, Bodo, Manipur, Chakma and a few others who have similar script, at times with minor change. On January 19, 1979, the Left government of Communist Party-Marxist made the tribal Kokbarak language as another "Official Language" of the state, not satisfying tribal extremists. Not being satisfied, on June 8, 1980 a group of tribes murdered in cold blood 255 of majority Hindu Bengalis in Mandwi village. It was so brutal that some of the babies and expectant mothers were killed with spear through their heart and belly. No one has been punished for that massacre. There is no memorial for those killed. What kind of democracy is that? Some local papers called the massacre as "worse than My Lai massacre" of Vietnam. Hardly any Indian, American, British, or Christian politician asked for trial of mass murderers. Is ignoring mass killing in India a Hindu disease? Is that why they are ignored in the world? Is that why Bangladesh genocide was never recognized by the U.N. whereas smaller cases are highlighted prominently? Bangla genocide was supported by Nixon Administration, and by all Muslim-majority nations. We have no problem highlighting pain of others. Please don't ignore some killing and cleansing. Being outraged, we wrote a protest to the Tripura Chief Minister, Dasarath Deb. Here is that letter of February 27, 1997:

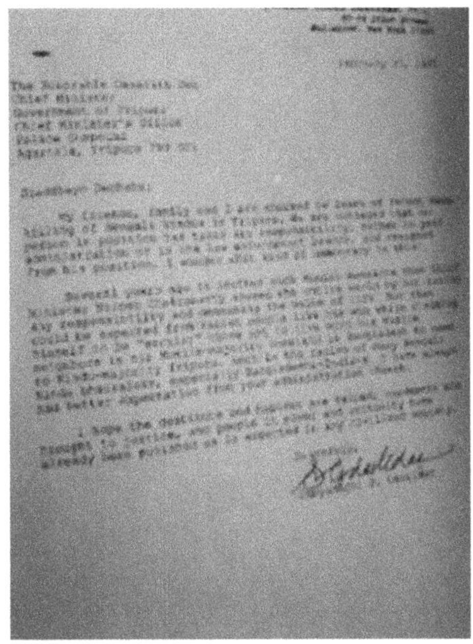

Entry to Tripura King's Palace

440

One Area of King's Palace facing a Lake

Tripureswari Kali (Black) Ma Temple, One of 51 Kali Pithas

(Grateful Sites) of Subcontinent

A Tribal Hindu Priestess at a Shrine

With Tripura Deputy Chief Minister Deb of Communist Party-Marxist

When Minority Lives, Homes, Ancestral Homesteads and Property Do Not Matter:

Bangladeshi papers on April 24, 2020 reminded us that 1,136 workers were killed when Rana Plaza collapsed, yet in 7 years no one has been held responsible for that death. Moreover, the owner of that eight-story structure built that building illegally on a poor Hindu-owned property, possibly by declaring it "Enemy Property" paying the owner nothing, nada, zero, when the owner still lived a few feet away in a shelter. The American Ambassador to Bangladesh pointed that out during a discussion on Rana Plaza, while rest of us ignored it. Why? That reminded us of Mrs. Mongala Saha, an indigenous minority, was sweeping fallen leaves early in the morning from the gated office of Local Guest House located at Chowrasta on Syedpur Road where Sachi was staying on Saturday, December 28, 2002. It was a nice new building. Seeing a stranger early in the morning, he introduced with folded hand, "Namaskar." She realized stranger was Sanatani. Finding a Hindu in her Muslim-majority land, she was eager to share her life story. "Look, I shouldn't be struggling like this at this late age in my life. We had quite a bit of land and many buildings of our extended family, including this particular land which belonged to my family for generations. All of our homes were destroyed in 1971 (during Bangladesh independence and Pakistani genocide) and our land was taken away from us. Now I have to collect leaves for fire to cook our food." Sachi followed her listening to her story as she worked with her broom. That dirt-poor aunt invited Sachi to her home for a cup of tea, that he couldn't do for his next appointment. Not far from that site our grandparents lived before 1947 partition. Later in the day, Sachi went to visit the old Pranab Ashram built by a Madaripur District monk, Swami Pranavananda, an anti-British Indian freedom fighter and founder of famous Bharat Sevashram Sangha order. He was imprisoned by British oppressors several times. Monk built a boys' hostel in 1910s for all poor students to promote education in rural areas, which was completely destroyed by the Army of Islamic Republic of Pakistan, and its Bengali Islamist allies, along with the ashram, monk's residence, Hindu temple, guest house, and more. Being that it was a Hindu institution, a Muslim family built an illegal two-story wooden building after 1971 genocide, without anyone's permission. Later, Probini Foundation of the U.S. built two student dormitories, and helped remove the illegal building from ashram property.

Back in Tripura state of India Sachi asked the workers at the Tripura tribal office why they want to change local Tribal-Bengali script to English, increasing distance within their society. They had no answer except to say that Christian Mizos and Nagas use English script. This is in a society where plains Hindu Bengali and hill Hindu tribes have intermarried for generations, breaking many taboos, and Tripura Kingdom was the first to adopt Bengali as its official language in the early Second Millennia, long before rest of Bengal adopted it. During Muslim rule in Bengal, ruling kings used Farsi as the official language, not Bengali. There are many Tripuris who became notable Bengali writer, educator and performer in Bengal culture. This is the same trap that British introduced in Bengal to divide Hindus and Muslims, but this time it was happening in free India under Communist rule in Tripura, and Congress rule in Federal Delhi. In India only violence gets result, generally at the cost of Hindu majority. In addition, Federal Indian Government under Congress Party, and Tripura under Communist-Marxist rule, amended Indian Constitution to give rights of two-thirds of the land area of the hilly state to one-quarter of the population so that the plains citizens – the Hindu Bengali majority – won't be able to live in two-thirds of that state, but hilly people will be allowed to live with Bengalis in entire state with two-thirds of the people, creating a new form of apartheid introduced by the British in India, South Africa and elsewhere. For a time, the terrorist group in Tripura was able to tear up many of the mixed marriages. Indian Constitution Amendment also provided for 25% of the population, the tribes, with 33% of the state legislature seats reserved for them in perpetuity. It will be like U.S. giving 75% of lands to tribal communities in Montana or Oklahoma, and 33% of state legislators. In India, and in democracy each group wants their share through election as Sachi found out during New York City School Board election mentioned earlier. Later, in 2017 trip to Tripura felt lot better. Still Sachi was asked to take protection while visiting Unakoti, a beautiful 7th Century, or earlier, rock cut Shiva and other temples, into stone mountains, barely 125 kilometers from her state capital, Agartala, taking over two hours in winding hilly picturesque road. It is certainly one of the most beautiful sites that we have visited anywhere in the world. We are not sure why Tripura and India hasn't been able to make it a tourist destination like Aztec Temple in Mexico City, Dubrovnik in Croatia, Xian in China, Inca shrines in Peru, Stonehenge in England, or Ajanta in India. It was a lifetime experience! Here is an interesting, and wonderful example of an old 7th through 9th Century cultural expression of indigenous, now called tribal, population in Unakoti, Tripura, located in northeast India. Because of its lack of publicity and accessibility hardly any Indian or foreigner knows about the loveliness. For more information, please see https://empireslastcasualty.blogspot.com/2017/02/unakoti-tripura-india-ten-million.html.

Stone-cut Mountain, Unakoti, Tripura

7th Through 9th Century Mountain Sculpture

7th Through 9th Century Mountain Sculpture

A Local (Tribal) Priest offering Puja

445

Picturesque Hilly Area

Picturesque Road Heading to the Site

Tripura is home to hundreds of thousands of East Pakistani/Bangladeshi Hindu refugees. Tripura became a plains Hindu-majority population after Hazrat Bal Hindu genocide of 1964 by Pakistan Army and its Bengali partners, when tens of thousands of oppressed-caste Hindu peasants were killed and millions cleansed for India. Sachi was a firsthand witness to some of those victims, when they were directly transported by train from East Pakistan border to Dandakaranya Refugee Rehabilitation area in central India, where his oldest brother Dada, Dr. Sankar Ghosh Dastidar, was a medical doctor whom he visited frequently. Rumors were spread in West Pakistan that Prophet Mohammed's hair kept in India's Hazrat Bal Mosque in Srinagar, Kashmir, was lost, thus Bengali Hindus had to be slaughtered, thousands of miles away, like animals during Id Celebration, or ISIS killings in 2010s. Did India or the world notice that? Of course, not. During that Tripura trip, on Tuesday, June 17, 2017 he was able to meet aunt Ila Mashi, Mrs. Ila Sengupta, a Hindu refugee from Barisal, Bangladesh whom he interviewed for our Partition Center Project, now saved on YouTube's ispad1947 channel. Within a month, on 2017 February, we lost her, heading to Mother's Lap, as locals said. Her family was happy to have her memory saved forever. In 2017 Sachi had an enviable privilege of staying in a real palace, first time in his life. It was the king's palace of Raja of Tripura, now Tripura Governor's Residence. He was invited by his former classmate Hon. Tathagata Roy, Governor of Tripura. Mr. Roy is a famous writer as well as a noted engineer. Palace was built in early 1900s. Earlier in 1998, Sachi crossed over from Bangladesh to Tripura through land border, with his New York friend Prasanta, and several Bangladeshis.

That was a time when Tripura was trying to break its landlocked position by developing links with Bangladesh. This was a new policy of helping each other's economy. During the rule of Pakistan, its policy was simultaneously hurting India, killing and cleansing of Hindu minority of Pakistan, and colonization of Bengali East Pakistan by minority Punjabi Muslims and their military of West Pakistan. We got a rousing reception at the border as we cleared our customs and immigration. Top officials of Tripura Tourism were present with rental cars. They had developed an exciting travel plans from visiting the capital Agartala to charming Udaipur with the famous old Kali Mandir – one of the 51 Kali Pithas or Centers where Ma Kali's body parts fell after Her death, to Neer Mahal Palace of Tripura king on a lakeside, to a lodge in

Unakoti, where we had the greatest gift of watching traditional *jatra* plays that continued till wee hours in the morning, which is unusual in rural area as people have to walk back in darkness, without street lights. We had to return back to our lodge in pitch darkness with search lights on hand, as others headed to their homes. This was really different. Getting to and from Tripura is complicated. It is only 200+ miles from West Bengal, India, as the crow flies, but crossing over Bangladesh. For most people is it a 3-day 1,000-mile or 1,600-kilometer journey around Bangladesh to Kolkata. Tripuris have to go east then north through Assam and Meghalaya, then west through north West Bengal, then south through West Bengal, instead of crossing 200+ miles via Bangladesh. It is best to catch a flight from Kolkata, if only one can afford and get a ticket.

It is also barely 40 miles from the Bay of Bengal connecting through southern Feni River via Bangladesh, or only 30 miles from Tripura's capital Agartala to Ashuganj River Port on the mighty Meghna River in Bangladesh. During Pakistani rule she made life miserable for East Pakistanis and Tripuris plus other Northeast Indians by not allowing access to rest of the world through the easily accessible Chittagong Port through road and railway links built during British colonial era. This would have economically benefitted Chittagong city and Bangladesh than West Pakistan, as the Port lost all the business from northeast India and Tripura, but economic benefit of the Bengalis was of no concern to Pakistani Islamists than pulling Bengalis, Hindus and Indians down. With the current (2020's) pro-development administration in Bangladesh, ousted in 2024, situation has changed for the better for both. There is a long way to go. Only in July 2020 goods flowed through Chittagong port on way to Tripura, and in November 2023 Bangladesh and India opened a rail connection with Tripura. But we are irrational people, often serving other's interest, not ours. We have to see what happens next after the overthrow of Mrs. Hasina Wazed's government on August 5, 2024. As Sachi stayed an extra day in Tripura, he couldn't get a flight out until after one week. Luckily his passport allowed him to reenter Bangladesh and leave the country by air. For holders of Indian passports, they needed to jump through many hoops. And Sachi's ability to rent a taxi from the border solved his problem. He hired a cab to take him to Dhaka Airport to catch a 30-minute flight to Kolkata. His first 90 kilometers drive west from Tripura border to Jatrabari Junction at the eastern edge of the Dhaka City took barely 60 minutes in that super-dense country with good roads. Then he got stuck in the notorious traffic jam of Dhaka City where next 9 kilometers took 90 minutes. He missed his flight but was fortunate to get the last flight out to Kolkata. What is worth mentioning that a 30-minute Dhaka-Kolkata flight with half the distance costs more-than-twice of Kolkata-Agartala Indian domestic flight that flies over Dhaka City.

As one travels, one realizes that India is more diverse under one flag than European Union from Ireland to Greece, and from Norway to Spain with 27 flags. Europe has barely two scripts, whereas India has dozen-and-a-half scripts. Europe has basically three forms of Christianity, whereas India's public holiday has all of those in Europe, plus a dozen more of faiths. Europe with centuries of warfare, has created linguistically homogeneous nations, with minor exceptions in Belgium and Switzerland. When there is diversity in nations, even in 21st Century, there are extreme strain, at times involved with bloodshed as in the Balkans, Spain, the U.K., Ukraine, Belgium, African and Asian nations. In wealthy nations of Europe, they have had space to expand in the New World and in new colonies, when they faced demographic pressure.

Partitioned Subcontinent and Expanding U.S. Continent: Traditional vs Pioneering Model:

1. India has to realize that their indigenous survival experiment is very unique, almost unparallel in history. There is no other nation, including Nepal sitting physically within India, that exists with their indigenous beliefs. Close to it is Israel, Greece, Ethiopia and Tibet in their uniqueness with their religious and traditional beliefs. Even Israel as a Jewish nation, receive support from many Christian-majority nations on the basis of her religious heritage. Thus, there cannot be any organization like Organization of Islamic Countries, European Union, African Union, Arab League, Organization of American States, or

international association of Anglican, Presbyterian, Catholic churches, and Christian, Buddhist, or atheist nations to mobilize with similar identity, if need be, although many European nations have become tolerant, secular, and less religious, even when a church is the official State Religion. Some have even become fatalist like Sanatani. In many gatherings putting a cross as a symbol, or decorating with cross has become more of a style than religion. Thus India, being one of a kind with long written history, must come up with policy based on self-defending nation, as she cannot come up with organizations like O.I.C. or O.A.S or E.U. For example, Pakistan, Malaysia, Gambia, Saudi, Kuwait, and many Muslim-majority nations' communal and discriminatory features are not looked down by the U.N., international bodies, and partisan media because of their number. Many nations have criticized India for creating a law for identifying their citizens that exist in all nations, including U.S. Some Muslim-majority nations and pro-religion groups have criticized India. It is good to do that. Yet, many of these nations treat many of their own citizens with non-Islam faiths impolitely.

Many nations do not give citizenship to their workers working for decades, but criticize West or India for not giving citizenship for illegal migrants who arrive at their nation. We have interviewed lots of people who came to India illegally, and now hold Indian passport through corrupt state police and bureaucracy, not the federal one. Don't all nations decide how one becomes their citizen? In a partition-affected country like India, it is even more serious. How many Muslim-majority nations, and Western democratic nations, have criticized Pakistan for constitutionally treating their indigenous, pre-Islam communities of Hindu, Jain, Buddhist, Christian, and Sikhs to be barred from many offices, thus treating them As fourth class citizens in one's own country? How many of us have shed tears for that? Should the persecutor and persecuted, oppressor and oppressed, slaves and slave-holders, Nazis and persecuted Jews and Gypsies, be treated equally? Which unbiased society does that? In 1980s, a close Muslim friend told us with disgust how in some Mideast nations' customs routinely destroy statues and pictures of deities right in front of believers, or how their holy books are thrown into trash. There are videos available on YouTube. What would happen if U.S., U.K., China, or Chile immigration did that with Islamic religious books in front of the believers? When Bangla-origin Rohingyas were cleansed by Myanmar for Bangladesh, we all objected. Fine. World and Bangladesh wanted them to go back. We support that. Rohingyas are decades old illegal Bangla migrants to Burma, now called Myanmar. British colonialism and local corruption have allowed that, but Bangladesh does not want them back. From a different point of view, does Bangladesh have no right to refuse them as they supported extremist Islamism, Pakistani genocide, and against her independence in 1971? At the same time, why World is not asking for Bangla Hindu refugees in India to be returned back? A new form of racism? Why the World Body is discriminating? Hindu lives not matter? Many secular Muslims support return of their minorities to their homeland. On the other hand, the corrupt Indian state administration has allowed many Royingyas to settle in West Bengal (2023) with West Bengal ID. As the federal government tried to return them back some communal and anti-India groups raised their voice in India, knowing fully well that how Muslim Rohingyas have murdered Rohingya Hindu minority in Myanmar. Videos are available on YouTube made by a human rights group.

Should we welcome our killers? Did U.K., U.S. or France welcome Nazi or ISIS or Taliban? Should Ireland welcome those who want to keep them as a colony? Or, should Cyprus welcome those who support partition of their island? One Mr. Rahman, a Muslim, told us how he was being harassed by Islamic activists when he protested Saudi Arabia's public beheading in 2010s of six foreigners in a festive atmosphere for spectators to watch. Same countries criticized India Government for coming up with a system of citizenship that they already have. They even criticized India for bringing Indian Kashmir state at par with rest of the Indian states. We haven't heard any criticism from the same nations and leaders when Pakistan broke apart Pakistani Kashmir into Azad Jammu & Kashmir (AJK), and Gilgit & Baltistan (GB). No one protested when Pakistani Kashmir was colonized by Punjabi Muslims, and killed and cleansed all non-Muslims. Some locals are protesting now. Please check YouTube of Mr. Bal Gupta, a Pakistani-Kashmiri-American Hindu whose 26 family members were murdered before he was able to flee to India. Local language was completely wiped out, with total cleansing of Hindus, Buddhists, Sikhs and Jains – the indigenous faiths. Just in May of 2020 Pakistan planned to hold elections in northern Pakistani Kashmir, now renamed Gilgit-Baltistan. Why Qatar, Turkey, Malaysia and OIC had no headache? Why didn't they ask for reparation and return of peoples like Bal Gupta? Army put them in a concentration camp in Pakistani Occupied Kashmir in 1947 (see YouTube's ispad1947 channel for Bal Gupta's story https://www.youtube.com/watch?v=ECVT7YMtTmo. On April 23, 2020, a noted Pakistani daily Dawn hinted repercussion on India because "80% workers are foreigners in Gulf Countries" for implementing India's citizen ID policy. It didn't explain why same policy in Gulf Countries is not objectionable that the workers cannot get citizenship there. India's daily Anandabazar Patrika also wrote about the threat on the same day. India was not taking any citizenship away, but making it normal like anyone else. Yet, Kuwait herself didn't give citizenship to Bedouins who lived there long before the King's family migrated there. Plight of Christians in Turkey is well known. Surprised? Did U.N. question that? Why Pakistan or Turkey not criticizing U.S. for not giving citizenship to 11 million illegal residents, while tens of millions of illegal migrants have received Indian citizenship? Similarly, on April 26, 2020 an esteem New York paper promoted anti-Hindu and anti-India article with tears on lockdown in Kashmir, but not a word on the most important news of the year when Bangladesh found and hanged killer Abdul Majid, hiding in India for 25 years. Majid murdered the Founding Father of the Nation, Sheikh Mujibur Rahman. The news was covered all over Subcontinent.

On May 3, 2020, a Kolkata paper *Kolkata24/7* wrote "Pakistan is complaining to IOC that India is promoting anti-Muslim hate." Almost all of these nations enforced mosque lockdown during Covid crisis, yet one pro-conversion Islamic group purposely disavowed the law to spread the virus in

India. So, victim must be blamed, not the culprits. Of course. The world accepts nation based on hateful constitution.

Bal Gupta, a Hindu Refugee of Pakistani Kashmir with 26 Family Members Killed

2. India also has to realize the limitation of non-violence. We believe non-violence is the best method, but American, French, Bolshevik, Chinese, Bangladeshi, and Indian independence were all bloody, violent, costing millions of lives. Gandhiji's genuine attempt failed as Britain, Muslim League Party and Islamic Leaders didn't cooperate with him in pacifism. Several millions of lives were lost, and tens of millions were ethnically cleansed. We don't call that a success of pacifist movement. This is complete failure. Martin Luther King, Jr. succeeded in America as he didn't threaten the foundation of the nation, but many African-Americans paid heavily. Mandela also succeeded, after loss of thousands of lives of Africans and non-whites, as the world was able to influence minority white Africans. We would argue, in both of these cases, Christ's sacrifice, healing power of love, and preaching of Christian churches helped ease the situation. This was not in the era of Crusade, or forced conversion. This was not the era of destruction of churches and shrines by conquerors, or World Wars, and wars between nations. Hardly anyone notices that in the holy book

Bhagavat Gita, Lord Krishna teaches Arjun how to fight against evil, even when that evil is your guru or your extended family. "Hindus" consider it sacred, but never follows it. There are many Hindus who try to figure out how they have given up on this lesson and have become fatalistically submissive, against self-defense, and for self-destruction. There is an old Bengali proverb saying, "*sakter bhakta naramer jom*," meaning "Followers of the rough (oppressor) but tough on peaceful (folks)." In the 15th Century Punjab region rose Sikh faith who militantly resisted Islamic oppression. Hindus consider Sikhs as part of their ethos like Buddhism, Jainism, or Vaishnavism. This was militant opposition when followers have to carry a sword like America's gun. Defending themselves from Mughal Emperor. The 5th Sikh Guru was beheaded in public. In Western region of India rose Shivaji in 1600s to resist Persian-Arab aggression. Rajput of Rajasthan resisted Mughal atrocities for centuries, and was never fully subjugated. These are exceptions. Then again, American style violence with gun, killing of humans or animals were avoided in traditional culture where every life matters. So, can a policy based on self-defense, and respect for all life be cultivated in modern world? Our gun culture evolved from our battle against indigenous Native Americans, and our fight against the British colonial power. This model cannot be applied if we believe in the rights of original inhabitants. Moreover, under President Jackson we created "laws" whereby we were able to clear indigenous population in the east through Trail of Tears driving them to new territory in the Midwest. We are still discussing this, not censoring it. This is America's greatness.

3. India must also completely wipe out caste racism, where is exists, as envisioned by many sages, and as it is forbidden in Indian Constitution. Many believe that new CASTE racism was created by 1,000 years of non-native rule of Islamic and Christian colonizers. As India urbanizes, and people head to schools, and migrate elsewhere, caste distinction goes away, as it has in cities and in many regions. Inter-groups, inter-religious and inter-linguistic marriages are happening regularly. This is going to solidify the nation, wiping out regional and linguistic differences, like in U.S and Europe. It is happening now, and

happened before, including in our family. There are many Hindu-Muslim or Muslim-non-Muslim, Hindu-Jain, Hindu-Christian, Buddhist-Hindu, Hindu-Sikh marriages in India. We have close friends in India and Bangladesh who have had mixed ethnic, linguistic and interfaith marriages. In America, as in Europe, interfaith marriages are common. Attending church has become less strident, like not going to temples. Non-religious civil marriages have become common in the West and East. When couples live by themselves away from extended family, identity becomes less of an issue. One has to look at Bollywood film industry of Mumbai, India of its high visibility with mixed marriages, divorce, multiple marriages, living together, and multiple partners are common creating a new narrative in India. But what is needed is not only it has to happen in India, but also in Pakistan, Bangladesh, Nepal, Afghanistan and in South Asia sharing the same culture and ethnicity. Tolerance must increase there too. Whatever the sectarian and neo-colonial press write, the bonding across cultures exists. Since the days of Middle Ages, such cross-cultural union have taken place. We know many such examples. One of the weaknesses of democracy is that free people are able to energize their sectarian base. So, in a large pool of candidates your identity gets highlighted, knowingly and unknowingly.

This happens in America, England, or France. That happened in Sachi's election in New York City. Thus, in a diverse pool of candidates an Arab may vote for an Arab, a Hispanic for a Hispanic, a Catholic for a Catholic, even in election in liberal place like the U.S. This is natural. If it strengthens racial, ethnic or religious identity, then it becomes a problem. In his election for New York City School Board in 1996 there were candidates who were White Catholic, White Protestant, Jewish, Korean, Chinese, Hispanic, and more. People assumed that different ethnic groups voted for their "own" groups. It promotes separate identity. This is a factor in democracy. Many believe that U.S. primary election does that too. What options democracy may have that lowers identity politics? India has been held up by her tolerant tradition and faith, not by language, culture or political party. "Far Right or Left" indigenism can strengthen pluralism, while "Extreme" religious and ethnic identity may strengthen separatey identity, but that may also strengthen majority identity, as it happened with President Trump's election. It is hard to predict the future. If the past 3,000-year history is any indicator, Indians will lose more land, face more massacre, face more ethnic cleansing, after losing Afghanistan, Pakistan, Bangladesh, Burma, Sri Lanka, Nepal, Tibet, and Indonesia identity wise. India's Congress Party was able to hold a diverse people together until Britain's promotion of racism of Muslim League Party in Colonial India starting with Muslim-Hindu Partition of Bengal Province in 1905 when no one wanted it, and treating freedom lovers with disdain to continue colonialism, and tearing non-sectarian Congress Party apart. Colonial Britain used the same divide-and-rule policy in Ireland, South Africa, Sudan, Cyprus, Fiji, Malaysia, Nigeria, Guyana, Sri Lanka, Palestine, Egypt, and in many more places. After Indian independence, the party that unified India, became a property of Nehru family. We don't know what would Jawaharlal Nehru think, if he is reincarnated! This is unfortunate. Even a foreign-born new citizen of "Nehru family," with only a few years on Indian soil, was regarded by the party as preferable Prime Minister than other long-term Congress activists. How would Americans react if a person like Mrs. Trump was on her way to become the President of America, just after few years of living in the U.S. Dynastic rule in democracy is bad, but very common. Should we treat white newcomer from Europe differently? Although several millennia ago, to integrate all races Indian sages created like Goddess Ma Durga with four kids and a husband all with different skin colors.

Did our secular imagery got confused during the rule by foreigners, Asian Islamic, and European Christian? It baffles us why no Indian Congress leader came forward to lead the party since Indira Gandhi was assassinated by her Sikh body guards. There were many capable Congress party activists. We have met a few of them. In the past seven decades India has moved towards a cultural harmony, that many Westerners said was impossible during partition. Some colonizers suggested that India will fall apart in a few years. We know many Pakistanis and Bangladeshis who are ardent supporters of India and Indian political system, in spite of false narratives of partisan press. Those folks also like their minority be given equal rights in their homeland. One often wonders why West, O.I.C. and the U.N. allowed Pakistani Islamist terrorists killing at least 174 people from 26 nations in Mumbai hotel of India not only go unpunished, but allow funds to flow to terrorists from outside unabated. Why have the same powers allowed killings across the Line of Control in Kashmir as reported in India and America on May 4, 2020 leaving 7 dead, and on January 1, 2023, and more? There are many more Muslims in India's Murshidabad district of West Bengal state, across from Bangladesh, than in all of Kashmir Valley. Why there are no daily terror in Murshidabad? This is certainly not a Muslim-Hindu issue, as hardly any Indian minority Muslim tries to flee India for the "Land of the Pure" called Pakistan. We can understand China's role, as Chairman Mao's Army marched to occupy India's Tibetan-speaking Ladakh region in 1964, as well as Tibet, once a part of India. China took advantage of Prime Minister Nehru's incompetence in newly independent India, and his inability of understanding China's motive. Nehru left three major problems for India's future leaders – Kashmir, Ladakh and Tibet – draining its economy.

4. In India, and in Pakistan and Bangladesh, it is important to teach students regional history; that we were not taught. History of Indian Independence Movement is a small part, often censored. Then there is regional distortion. Education is a state subject, which it should be. No wonder a top accountant in New York, a Kerala Christian, didn't know that Indian partition has displaced tens of millions of refugees, and millions lost their lives. On Tuesday, January 15, 2019 we were able to meet with the ruling anti-communist Trinamool (Grassroots) Party's Kolkata City Councilwoman elected from Eastern Kolkata. Generally, it is difficult to get an appointment. Days earlier we were asked by two of her workers to come to meet with her. The party had built an illegal structure next to one of the most polluted canals of the world flowing through the city. It is passing through a heavily built-up area. Decades ago, it was a swamp full of foxes and crocs. But now one can smell the canal from distance. As she arrived, there was a huge crowd of her well-wishers, and beneficiaries of Trinamool Party rule. All were standing outside. The small office was empty.

Once the men spotted Sachi, they pushed councilwoman and him into the office. Sachi asked her, among other issues, what is her *desh* or home? She replied, Faridpur, Bangladesh. Sachi told her that his brother-in-law is from Faridpur too living in the next block. When he told her that his sister and him just visited her homeland, and asked why her party or herself hasn't tried to protect the oppressed minority there, she replied that she never thought of that; her history was unknown to her. When Sachi asked, if she would like to help, she had no answer. When he asked why she is not cleaning up the canal, which is a health hazard, she answered, they tried, but gave up. Before they could continue further, a mob entered the room. During that visit, Sachi found how ruling party is deleting voters from the list, assuming they are opposition voters, as it was done during Communist-Marxist rule of West Bengal State. During our visit to Pakistan in 1989 a popular TV series based on Hindu epic Ramayana was being shown on Indian TV. On weekends it was run on midday. During a luncheon invitation of Sachi and family at a home in Lahore, several kids wanted to escape lunch to watch the series. The lady of the house objected watching Hindu epic, though she also recognized that as her heritage, but as a Muslim she couldn't watch that. Later during a walk in the neighborhood, little kids gave us a tour. Kids said that they watch the series regularly, and showed us how they have made bows and arrows carried by the main character Sri Ram. India and the Subcontinent won't be able to solve its socio-economic-political problems if only one part of the body is cured.

Tolerance has to be multisided. Recently, after the death of movie actor, Rishi Kapoor many papers reported that as a Hindu he ate beef, a prohibited flesh for Hindus. (See daily *Bhorer Kagoj*, May 1, 2020.) There was hardly any uproar. Communists to show their "secularism," at times forced beef on young Hindus. But when asked why don't they promote pork to Muslims. Their answer was, "We will simply be beheaded." Hypocrisy has limits. Criticism is good, and be encouraged; but not lies and sectarian racism. During the Coronavirus lockdown, one Indian channel started showing the popular Ramayana of 1980s. It immediately became a super hit with record viewership of 77 million (see daily

Star, May 2, 2020, and *Prothom Alo* of May 3, 2020, of Bangladesh). The previous record was that of an American movie with high teen viewership. Thus, a Hindu-named person, apparently a leftist, Prasant Bhushan, tweeted on May 1, 2020 "as crores (tens of millions) starve and walk hundreds of miles home due to forced lockdown, our heartless ministers celebrate consuming and feeding the opium of Ramayana and Mahabharata to the people." There is no record that Mr. Bhushan ever fed a poor or entertained one. Video was not shown by the government. And 1.3 billion quarantined people shouldn't be allowed any entertainment? Is this Left racism? It is continuation of false narratives, especially by people who are extremely selfish and hypocritical. Thus, increasingly young people in Bengal and eastern India, bastion of leftist movement, have turned against them. Recently some of the communist-turned-nationalist started bringing out document of historical oppression of majority Hindus by Muslims in Bengal when Muslims were a small minority, ruled by Farsi-speaking Muslim rulers. In 2019 they brought out a calendar with 12 major anti-Hindu atrocities in Bengal, each matching with a month.

2018 Calendar: Bengal Bleeds: Seven Decades of Jihad:

As people's, especially new generation's identity and human rights consciousness changes, new generations in the Subcontinent tries to overcome state and political censorship and have started to look back what their parents and grandparents avoided to speak, read and discuss. Here is an example through 2018 calendar of second and third generation refugees living in India looked back what their parents and grandparents have gone through, but censored themselves against speaking out.

Cover

January: 1964 East Pakistan Killing

February: 1950 Dhaka Killing

March: 1971 Operation Searchlight

April: Logang Massacre

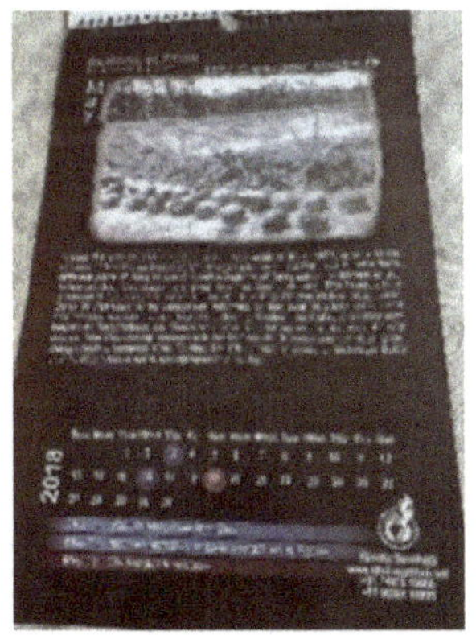

May: 1971 Chuknagar, Bangladesh
Hindu Genocide

June: 1971 Golaghat Massacre

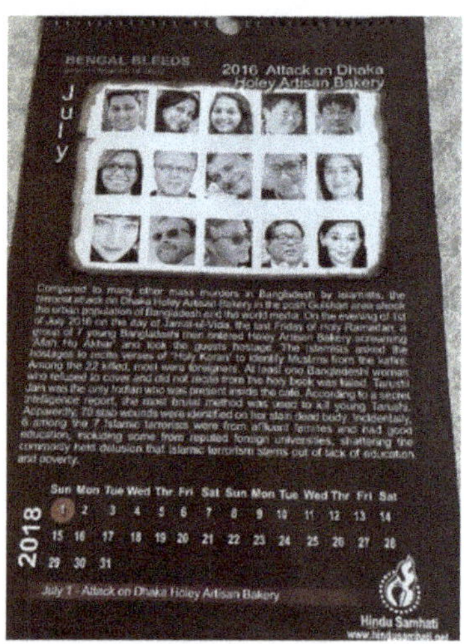

July: 2016 Attack on Dhaka Artisan Bakery

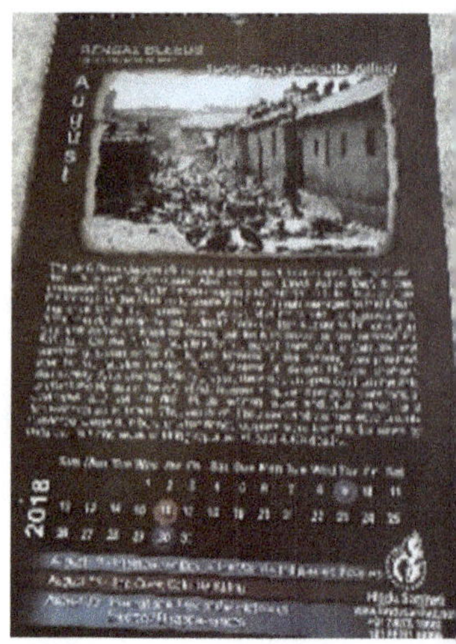

August: 1946: The Great Calcutta Killing by Muslim League Party during British Rule

September: 2012 Ramu Violence against Hindus

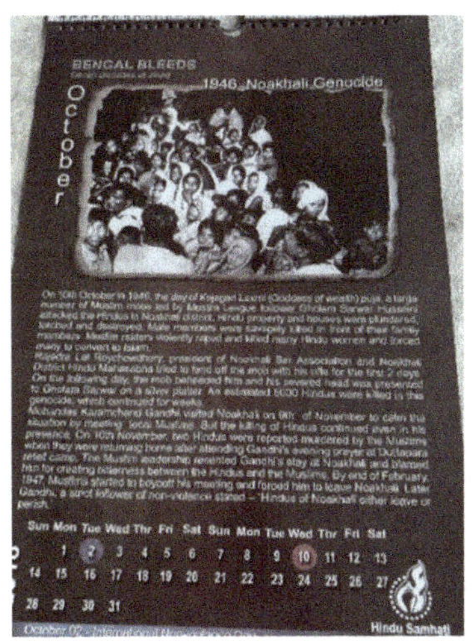

October: 1946 Noakhali Hindu Genocide, during British Rule

December: 1992 Hindu Bloodbath

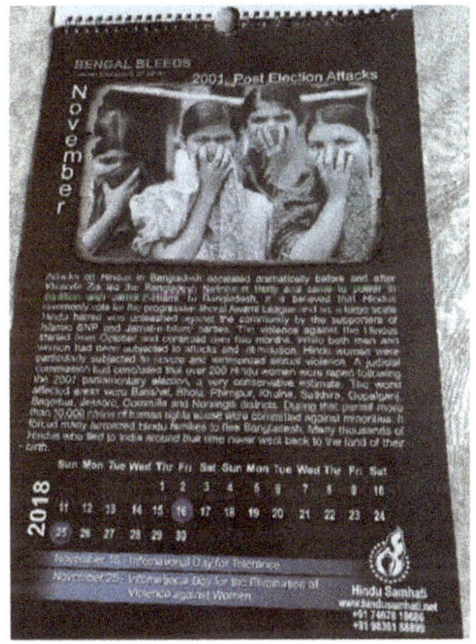

November: 2001 Post (Bangladesh) Election Attack

Then their 2020 calendar had representation of 12 major anti-Hindu pogroms/genocides. Unfortunately, no business, no media, or no political party agreed either to help or to promote the calendar. Does censoring history helps a nation? Would it have helped America by not teaching Civil War?

Here are 12 pages of 2020 remembrance calendar, yet not promoted by victims' ruling elite families' living in West Bengal and Tripura states of India.

Cover: Hindu Samhati (Remembrance) – The Fallen Monuments: The Saga of Destruction of Hindu and Buddhist Temples of Bengal by Arab-Iranian Invaders.

January: Dargah of Ata Shah, Atisha's Mahaviara, The Seat of Enlightenment Transformed into Madrasha (Islamic School)1, Gangarampur (Name of the Village), Dakshin Dinajpur (Name of the District), West Bengal (Name of the State), 1205 CE.

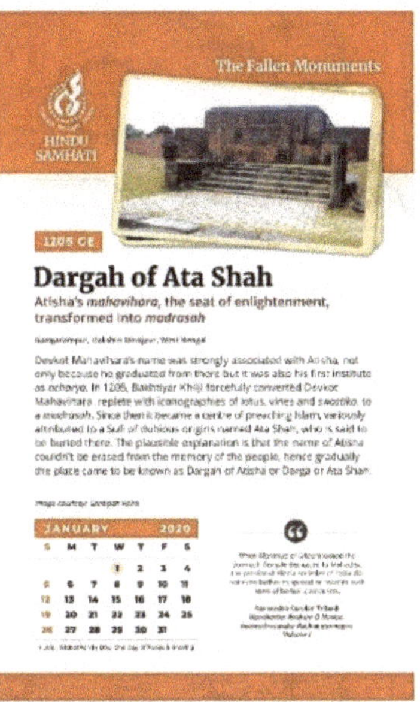

February: Pandua Minar, Sakti Peetha (Pilgrimage Center for Seeing Power) Desecrated and Converted into a Victory Tower and a Mosque, Pandua, Hooghly, West Bengal, 1295 CE.

March: Zafar Khan Gazi Masjid (Mosque), on destroyed Vishnu Wait of Kumbha Mela (Fair), Bengal's First Mosque, Tribeni, Hooghly, West Bengal, 1298 CE.

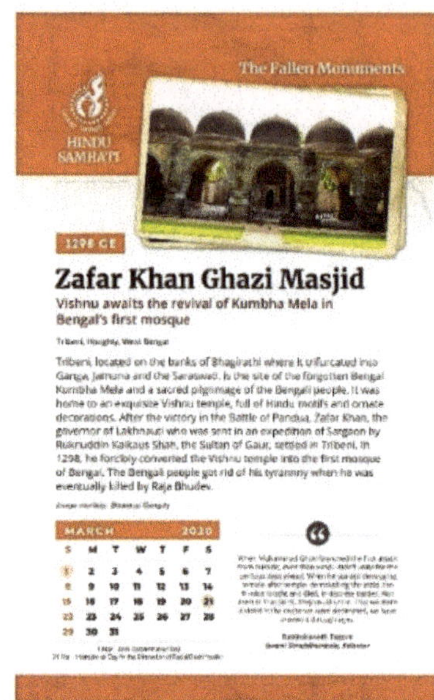

April: Adina Masjid (Mosque), House of Shiva Desecrated and Appropriated by the Khalifa, Pandua, Maldah District, West Bengal, 1368 CE.

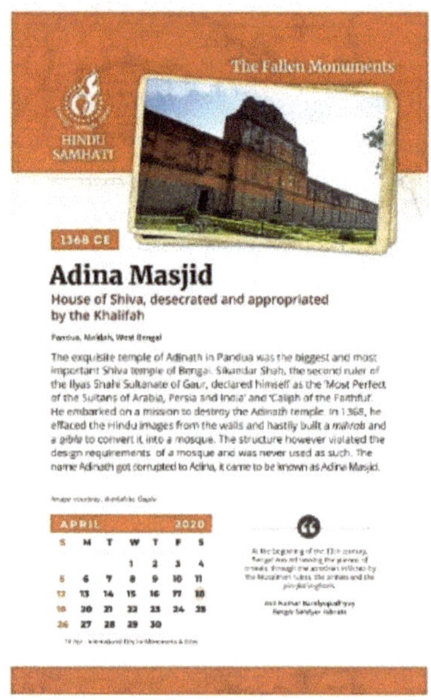

May: Eklakhi Mausoleum, Neo-Convert's Iconoclasm Wreaked Havoc on Hindu Temple, Pandua, Maldah, West Bengal, 1425 CE.

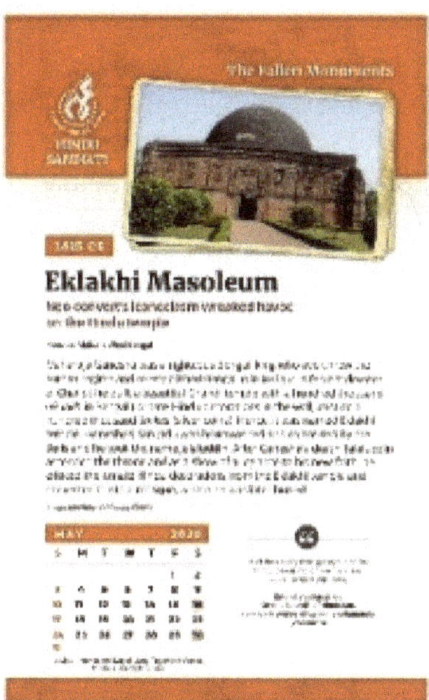

June: Chika Masjid, Temple Converted to Mosque and Used as a Prison, Gaur, Maldah, West Bengal, 1475 CE.

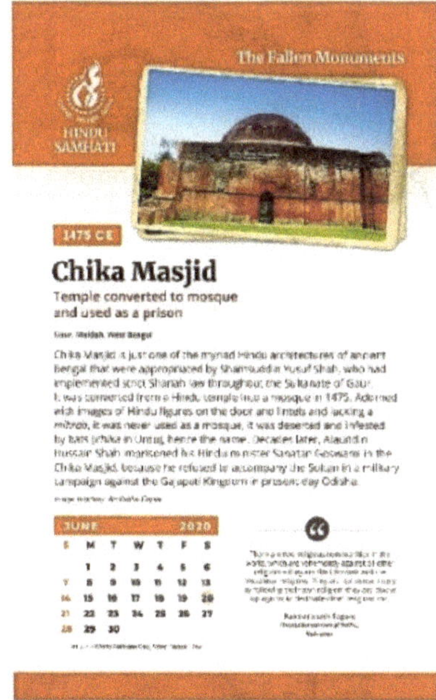

July: Majlis Saheber Masjid, From Wazir to Wali, A Tale of Butchery and Treachery, Kalna, Purba Bardhaman, West Bengal, 1490 CE.

The Fallen Monuments
HINDU SAMHATI
1490 CE
Majlis Saheber Masjid
From Wazir to Wali, a tale of butchery and treachery
Kalna, Purba Bardhaman, West Bengal
In the late 15th century, a Pathan commander named Ulugh Majlis Khan was the Wazir of the region comprising of present day Bardhaman, Kalna, Selimabad and Mangalkot, under the Gaur Sultanate. Khan's tyrannical administration was based in Kalna, where he decreed the construction of three mosques. The mosque at Denhankathtola was built in 1490 on a Hindu temple having an octagonal foundation, typically of Indic hexagonal columns and Hindu motifs of Sun, lotus, bell, deers etc. In his later life, Khan became a Wali and established his khanqah beside the mosque, which came to be known as Majlis Saheber Masjid and continued his mission to convert the Hindus by perfidy.
JULY   2026
S M T W T F S
            1 2 3 4
5 6 7 8 9 10 11
12 13 14 15 16 17 18
19 20 21 22 23 24 25
26 27 28 29 30 31

August: Hussain Shahi Masjid, Temple Destroyed by Khalifa's Right-Hand Man and Evidence Removed by Sufi Accomplice, Mangalkot, Purba Bardhaman, West Bengal, 1510 CE.

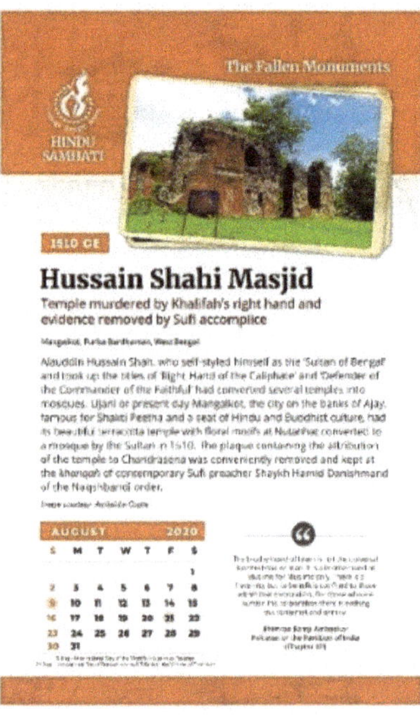
The Fallen Monuments
HINDU SAMHATI
1510 CE
Hussain Shahi Masjid
Temple murdered by Khalifah's right hand and evidence removed by Sufi accomplice
Mangalkot, Purba Bardhaman, West Bengal
Alauddin Hussain Shah, who self-styled himself as the 'Sultan of Bengal' and took up the titles of 'Right Hand of the Caliphate' and 'Defender of the Commander of the Faithful' had converted several temples into mosques. Ujani or present day Mangalkot, the city on the banks of Ajay, famous for Shakti Peetha and a seat of Hindu and Buddhist culture, had its beautiful terracotta temple with floral motifs at Nutanhat converted to a mosque by the Sultan in 1510. The plaque containing the attribution of the temple to Chandrasena was conveniently removed and kept at the khanqah of contemporary Sufi preacher Shaykh Hamid Danishmand of the Naqshbandi order.
AUGUST   2020
S M T W T F S
                  1
2 3 4 5 6 7 8
9 10 11 12 13 14 15
16 17 18 19 20 21 22
23 24 25 26 27 28 29
30 31

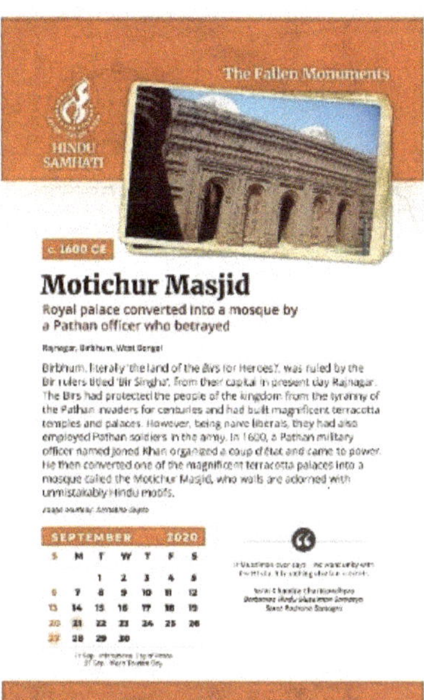

October: Kurumbera Garh Masjid, Fort Protected by Lord Shiva, Converted to a Mosque by a Zealot's Decree, Keshiari, Paschim Medinipur, West Bengal, 1691 CE.

November: Karta Masjid, Lone Survivor Listens to the Fallen Survivor, Who Cry in Silence, Murshidabad Town, Murshidabad, West Bengal, 1725 CE.

December: Suhrawardy Udyan (Park), Abode of the Mother's Shrine Demolished and Converted to a Park with a Graveyard, Ramna, Dhaka, Bangladesh, 1971.

One mixed experience of Dinajpur, North Bangladesh: Muslim Dargah of Atah Shah of January page of destruction of Hindu places reminded us of the ancient Kanta Ji Mandir of Sri Krishna. In 1990s we went to Dinajpur to help a school in the sweeper's colony run by Ramakrishna Mission. A real reward was the ancient Sri Krishna Temple. The shrine looked beautiful and could have been a tourist destination bringing thousands of jobs. Our other surprise was when the temple priest told us that the old deity of Sri Krishna and Sri Radha were stolen but hardly known to rest of the world. In the school area local thugs brought Muslim settlers to illegally occupy Hindu homes. We wondered what would have been the reaction in Egypt or Afghanistan if a symbol of the Prophet was destroyed by a group? Here are some pictures from Dinajpur.

KantaJi Mandir, Priests and a Cloth Covering the Missing Deity

Art Work on Wall

Slokas on the Wall

Standing with the Priest on Right

Taking a Ferry to Reach the Shrine

Gandhi School of the Oppressed run by Ramakrishna Mission of Dinajpur

5. One significant issue in public policy in India has been her attempt to copy Western model, especially British Colonial oppressor's model, and since late 1900s American model. There are many difficulties in blindly following Western model without adopting their work ethic, separation of teenage adult children from parents, independent living, family values, control of sexual desires, family orientation, marriage, relationship with younger and older persons, patriotism, mobility, and many more. There are good and bad on many of these issues depending on one's upbringing and value. In India, at several campuses when asked, no student replied that they had to work to support themselves. That is almost opposite in the U.S. In one campus in India students were planning to go on strike as there was talk of raising their tuition that remained the same for decades (about U.S. 50 cents since 2000), while some of the students were coming to campus on chauffer driven cars. In one campus bunch of rubbish was left in front of a building entrance. When asked why can't they volunteer to clean, a common response was, "It is somebody else's job." In many American campuses students volunteer to keep their campus neat, clean, and beautiful. In Indian culture students often develop personal relationship, calling their teachers/professors by a relationship, whereas generally we do not develop such relationship in the West, except for graduate students. Because of lack of gun violence in India, students develop politicization without gun, but they are more politically polarized than U.S., but gun violence and thuggery are common in America. In the U.S. a professor used to keep his watch on the classroom desk to maintain time.

On the very first semester a student stole his watch, and again decades later before his retirement someone stole another watch from a class. For another professor, some students stole his text book. Even in very poor India such tradition hasn't developed yet because of family values. With rapid urbanization and industrialization, TV, YouTube, TikTok and Facebook, values and identities are changing. Still, multiple marriage, value of work, single motherhood, premarital sex, divorce, work ethic to support oneself from early age, marriage age, and migration are influencing new identities in old culture. They are also adding new identities in the U.S.

6. Since 1947 independence there have been many aspects in India that have come closer. In 1947 lots of people in the South, East and Northeast were ignorant of Hindi, the major language of North India, and the Official Language of India, although 19 more languages are also treated as National Language. However, Bollywood movies, Boots of Indian Army who uses Hindi as its language of training and recruits from every corner of India, and poor Hindi speaking laborers found in every corner of India, have taught all Indians to talk in Hindi. India's tricolor was first hung by Netaji Subhas Chandra Bose of Indian National Army in Moirang in Manipur State bordering Burma (Myanmar) on April 14, 1944. This was the first liberated land in India where stands a museum. After visiting the museum, Sachi sat in the bus next to a local Manipuri boy, an Indian Army soldier, crying on Sachi's shoulder as he left home heading to Haryana in Western India, for a 3-day journey by bus and train. He spoke in Hindi from a border village in faraway Manipur. Then there is migration of people in other parts of India who use Hindi as the lingua franca. Actually, we were surprised to find Hindi as the common language in U.A.E, Oman, Maldives, and Singapore. Then within India, what people used to call "Bengali name" is no more "Bengali" but "All India" now. Bharatanatyam is not a dance of Tamil and Kannada, but is "All India" now, as Bhangra is no more Punjabi dance, or wedding dress is no more "Rajasthani," or pani-puri is no more "Gujarati," or pulao and biryani no more "Muslim," and "Dosa" is no more South Indian food, but "All India." "Sandesh" and "Rasogolla" is no more "Bengali sweet," plus "Naga" and "Kashmiri" shawls are "All India," just as vegetarianism or yoga are no more "Indian." We were surprised to know that "Smile of the Beyond" restaurant on Parsons Boulevard and 86th Avenue in Jamaica, Queens, New York City, next to Indian Subcontinent Partition Documentation Center, was the first vegetarian restaurant in New York established in 1971. American followers of meditation guru Sri Chinmoy opened it. By 2021, 50 years later, there are hundreds of veg restaurants in New York City, and most colleges and universities in the U.S. offer

vegetarian food. All these are bringing cultures closer. We believe India would be better served if All-India parties like Congress, Bhartiya Janata, or Communist, governed by bringing a diverse nation closer, not with 1,700 parties listed with Indian Election Board, some with extreme views of the nation and of the majority. It doesn't need to be a 2-party nation like the U.S., but not a 1,700–party state, some representing partisan or racist view, often anti-majority, of a small group in a nation of one-and-a-half billion people. In eastern India, even secular Communist Party has been a sectarian anti-majority in politics while its leaders chose not to live with majority Muslims in their homeland. To hide their hypocrisy, they have taken to majority bashing in eastern India, as mentioned earlier. In January of 2019 while visiting Kolkata, Government of India announced that from now on Kolkata Port, a real estate belonging to the federal Government of India, will be named after Dr. Shyama Prasad Mukherji, a former No. 2 of Shyama-Haq Bengal Ministry of 1941, a united Hindu-Muslim administration in Colonial Bengal under the Premiership of Fazlul Haq, a Muslim, and Dr. Mukherji, a Hindu, the youngest Vice Chancellor of Calcutta University during British Raj. All the Hindus and Muslims elected Premier Haq to be the Premier, and he chose Dr. Mukherji for a unifying position. On the eve of British partition of India, and partition of her Punjab and Bengal Provinces, Dr. Mukherji articulated the need for Hindu Bengalis to have a space for survival, not just for Muslims. There is a famous street in Kolkata named after him in his honor. To discredit Dr. Mukherji, a Bangladeshi-Indian Communist-Marxist Assemblyman representing an area settled by Pakistani-Bangladeshi-Hindu-refugees made vulgar and insulting anti-majority comments who gave him shelter in the new home. This is only possible in India. There were protests in Kolkata, and murmur in America. One of the Bengali-Americans wrote to him to which there was no answer. The letter reads like this:

January 31, 2020

The Hon. Dr. Sujan C, MLA West Bengal Assembly, Kolkata, India

Sub: Shyama Prasad Port: Writing on behalf of Bangladeshi-Indian-American friends and family, most of them of Hindu refugee-origin, as well as of many other Indian-Americans who were stunned, possibly a fake news of Anandabazar Patrika, about your statement on Dr. Shyama Prasad Mukherji and naming of Kolkata Port after him. There were discussions here in the Bengali-American community, and yesterday at the Punya Tithi Remembrance interfaith service on Mahatma's death anniversary.

I grew up in your area and learned a lot from leaders who because of their communalism chose not to live with the Muslim-majority neighbors in their (East) Pakistan/Bangladesh homeland, while calling one 'secular.' Thus during .... recent stay many W Bengalis called the 'left' as Communal Party of India. For us the 1st, 2nd and 3rd-generation refugees, if you change the name of West Bengal to Shyama Prasad, we may not have shown enough gratitude to his vision to find a shelter for us. In your constituency vast majority are Bangladeshi-Hindu refugee, including second and third generation. .... would appreciate if you could lead a drive for them to leave West Bengal to return back to their homeland of Bangladesh as many Palestinian, Israeli, Armenian, Irish, Cypriot, Balkans, African, African-Americans, Muslims are doing, as .... write. Moreover, you didn't mention in your sermon that Communists supported Colonial Masters in early 1940s, both communist legislatures in Bengal Province voted for Partition of Bengal, that Joyti Basu gave eloquent speeches in Colonial Bengal Assembly and in 1946 August in Maidan in support of Muslim League's partition plan, yet he chose not to live in his Muslim-majority homeland. We are also saddened that Assemblyman Somen Mitra doesn't know when or how Dr. Mukherji served with Premier Fazlul Haq. On behalf of all the Bengali native-born, refugees and their descendants, and millions of Bengali Hindus killed, we are urging a corrective measure for your churlish remark.

We are looking forward to hearing from you.

Later, someone called us and said that "Most likely because of the letter, the Bangladeshi-Indian-Refugee-communist legislator rose in the State Assembly and said, "Communist Party too voted for Muslim-Hindu Partition of Bengal in 1946." After that in 2021 election, one-time ruling with super-majority by leftist parties, lost all candidates in election.

Tolerance and Intolerance:

Democracy needs tolerance. How tolerant? India's tolerance has been self-destructive, not in year 2000s but from 1000s. Tolerance cannot be one sided. Mr. M.K. Gandhi's message of tolerance is the best model of governance, if that is possible. Gandhi knew more than anyone else as to its failure as he fasted in Calcutta on the day of India's independence and partition in 1947. He went to Bengal in 1946 in British-India to stop the Noakhali Hindu Genocide by the Bengal Province's ruling Muslim League Party. He traveled by foot for 46 days! A Gujarati-Bengali interpreter, a pre-monkshood traveled with him. (See Swami Purnatmananda, age 97 in 2021, interview at Partition Center's ISPaD1947 channel of YouTube.) India's birth was bloody, as was America's. U.S. was able to come to an understanding as it was able to demolish the entire colonial opposition. Moreover, there was no power internally who could resist the new nation. India's case was just the opposite. Its bloody birth was propagandized as examples of "Gandhian success," for a complete failure. Was it an example of unconditional submission? As mentioned earlier, every nation around India has cleansed indigenous population calling them "Hindu" their indigenous people of their land for India, with Jains, Sikhs, Buddhists and Christians – from Pakistan, Bangladesh, Sri Lanka, Burma, Afghanistan, Bhutan, Tibet (China), and even from Hindu-majority Nepal, and many Muslims and Christians from Burma and Sri Lanka. Unlike Arabs not accepting Palestine refugees after birth of Israel in

1948, and during 2023-2025 Hamas-Israel-Palestine war no Arab country accepted indigenous Palestinians to their nations. India took all kinds of refugees, most likely for not having a unified identity. Pakistan and China openly took Indian territory, using Indians' fatalistic mind. Sadly, most Indians represented by regional, linguistic or sectarian positions never came together to defend issues of "distant" state or ethnicity. India is a nation of nations. Each state or sub-state representing and governing that particular state/region sees itself as governing a "nation." We argue it has always lot more divisive than division in European Union. With the exit of Britain, E.U. model got stressed. Thus, when Tamil – Hindu, Christian and Muslims – were made non-citizen after Sri Lanka's independence and deported to India, only a section of Tamil Nadu state protested, not rest of India. Over half-a-million Tamils were deported to India from a small island of Sri Lanka, including parents of one of our neighbors in New York. Was there a cry from Hindus when tiny Bhutan expelled over 150,000 of her Nepali-speaking Hindus across the border to India and Nepal? Later, many of them were given asylum in the U.S. When Pakistan, including Pakistani Kashmir, cleansed about quarter of her population, who protested? Did any Telugu or Assamese complain? Why not? When China cleansed a large chunk of Tibet's Buddhist population for India, who protested? And when Pakistan Army and Bengali Islamists murdered 3 million people, mostly Hindus, who in India protested? Who in Muslim-majority nations protested? Which Western nation protested? Did China protest? What about Punjabis or Keralites in India? Why are Indians/Hindus so narrow minded? Fortunately, partition left India's Muslim population at home, unlike ethnic cleansing in Pakistan and Bangladesh. This is a good thing.

However, in the colonial Britain's apartheid-like Muslim Non-Muslim separate election, almost all the Muslims voted to be part of Pakistan, yet didn't go there after Partition. Has India been able to "Indianize" them instead of being pro-Partition? India didn't ban pro-partition Muslim League Party, yet Pakistan vanquished pro-united Congress Party from East and West Pakistan, as well as the pro-union Unionist Party of Pakistani Punjab. From time to time, Muslim

League's image of Islamic India has inspired many, even in Hindu refugee-burdened West Bengal. In the Bangladeshi-Pakistani-Hindu-Refugee-run First United Front Leftist Government of West Bengal included an Islamist pro-partition Muslim League member, but not any pro-union pro-Hindu party. Why? Even in Kerala in far south of India, Muslim parties have always been part of the government, Left or Right, but no pro-union Hindu party. Christian parties in Kerala have joined them too. Bengali communists have courageously defended rights of minorities in India, and the United States, but made no statements about rights of Uighurs, Mongols, Tibetans in China. Indian communists, most of whom are Pakistani-Bangladeshi-Indians, even opposed India stopping the Pakistani genocide in Bangladesh. We questioned an activist who was marching at Gariahat Road in 1971 summer with slogans equating genocide-maker Pakistani President Khan and genocide opponent Indira Gandhi as equal: "*Indira Mujib ek hai, Indira Yahya ek hai, and Mujib Yahya ek hai,*" meaning "Indira Gandhi, India's Prime Minister opposing the genocide, Mujibur Rahman winner of Pakistani election and imprisoned by minority West Pakistani military, later wanting independence of Bangladesh as the genocide began, and genocide maker Pakistani Dictator Yahya are the same." How could a genocide murderer and genocide protector be equal? Several thousand Indian soldiers gave their lives for Bangladesh's liberation. After the war ended Indian Army wanted a memorial in honor of those martyrs.

We thought there should be a separate memorial for Hindus as they were the target for extermination, much like separate Jewish memorials in Germany and elsewhere, and for Black-Americans in America. Many wanted a memorial in Bangladesh. Indian Army proposed a memorial to be built at their cost, next to East Bengal Football Club, that existed since the days of United Bengal in British India. Football Club's land belongs to Army. One would think all of India, West Bengal, and Bangladeshi-Indians would be overjoyed. It is like building a memorial in New York for 9/11 terror. But this is India, the land of extreme democracy. There was opposition from the Bangladeshi-Indian Chief Minister Jyoti Basu of the Communist Party-Marxist; opposition from the state opposition leader Ms. Mamata Banerjee, the future anti-communist Chief Minister. Ironically the head of Indian Army was a Bangladeshi-Hindu-Refugee, Gen. Sankar Roy Chowdhury. Political leaders refused to support a memorial at military's property of East Bengal club. Today's Bangladesh is locally referred as East Bengal. Thus, seeing this unimaginable dishonesty, a letter was sent on September 13, 1995 from New York appealing for a memorial for Indian martyrs as well as a memorial for Hindu genocide victims of Bangladesh War of 1971. The letter reads like this:

On behalf of our friends and family please accept …. heartfelt congratulations for planning to build a memorial for the (Indian) Army martyrs. This is long overdue. This means a lot for us. My deepest respect to the fallen heroes.

Wonder if you could build another memorial in Calcutta in honor of Bangladeshi Hindus, close to three million, who were murdered during our 1971 Independence War. A Martyrs' Monument dedicated to all the Bangladeshi murder victims stand in Savar near Dhaka. Such separate memorials of the victims of the Nazis are common in Europe. As Bangladesh becomes more anti-Hindu and anti-India, our secularists suggest that without such reminders of earlier atrocities it is becoming harder for them to fight institutionalized racism (communalism) in Bangladesh.

The letter was sent jointly to the Chief Minister of West Bengal Jyoti Basu of the Communist Party-Marxist, and Indian Army Chief Gen. Sankar Roy Chowdhury, with copies to West Bengal State Assembly Opposition Congress Leader Mamata Banerji, Hon. Pranab Mukherji, Minister of the Indian Congress Government from West Bengal in Delhi; several Kolkata newspapers, and U.S. Bengali associations.

Neither there was any action by the state and federal governments on a separate memorial, nor there was any acknowledgement of the letter. What is shocking is those leaders like Basu, Roy Chowdhury and Banerji were all Bangladeshi-Hindu-Indians, whereas Mukherji's wife was Bangladeshi, as were most others leaders, and media personalities, except one top Indian Army official who initiated the project who was non-local. Surprisingly the East Bengal (meaning Bangladesh) Football Club located on Indian Army property refused to share the property for building a memorial for Army victims of 1971 Pakistani Genocide and Bangladesh independence with Indian Army's help. Except for the non-local, all were directly attached to Bangladesh, but were opposing a memorial that those folks should have built. This would be like opposing WWII memorial in America by war victims in Europe! Unbelievable? Eventually, a memorial was built by the Indian Army in front of the entrance to Fort William Army Base, but not a memorial for 3 million victims. The fort on Hooghly River was the beginning of British Empire in Asia. This memorial is great! It is a bit away from the main travel areas of Kolkata, and lacks parking. In Bangladesh there are hundreds, perhaps thousands, of memorials in every corner of the land. Bangladeshi secularist Muslims are supporters of such memorials. A 1971 liberation memorial was built at Savar, about 30 miles west of Dhaka City. Unfortunately, after August 5, 2024 overthrow of Prime Minister Hasina of Bangladesh attack began on Bangladeshi 1971 memorial, and on Hindu minorities for no reason but racism. Why and by whom?

1971 Pakistani Genocide Memorial in Bangladesh

Britain entered India in 1600s through Bengal. Being the last colonizer, they established their military base at the lower point on Hooghly River, a tributary of Ganga. Thus, they were able to block access of other colonizers upstream – Portugal, France, Dutch, and Denmark, to reach their ports from the lowest or southernmost point of the south flowing river. Many Americans think even U.S. constitution is not perfect, thus comes amendments. 2020 U.S. election, and subsequent strain on our system is worth mentioning. Many think imperfections on U.S. citizenship as people born in other countries are not allowed to be the President. There are many presidents around the world from Guyana to New Zealand who were elected president born in another country. And in Presidential election weight of a citizen is lot higher in Wyoming, Alaska, and South Dakota that a citizen of California, Texas or New York. This it is imperfect. But, in the U.S. we can discuss, debate, and decide. We won't be able to do that in many nations.

Diversity of Ideas:

India's public policy must incorporate diversity of ideas as she is the only nation with diversity of religious practices within her initial religious faith. As a result, as mentioned earlier, it is the only large and diverse nation to survive after colonial divide-and-conquer rule of the British, and other European and Asian colonizers. Different kinds of racism that the British promoted through caste, language, and religion have been institutionalized in Indian politics. It won't be easy to eradicate mistreatment in a democracy, especially when your neighbors act differently including discriminatory practices, ethnic cleansing, and not treating citizens equally, but can't be discussed in world media. India has also to follow the ideals of non-violence as much as possible, but India's experience says it is bound to fail unless all parties, as well as her neighbors, and big powers also follow that. Thus, coalition in world politics based on similar values won't be possible, except for the European countries who have become pluralistic after the horrors of WW II, Enlightenment, and Reformation. In some ways, European Union (EU) countries are trying to follow Indian model, but with 27 flags. It has several strong military powers within EU, and some economic powerhouses. We hope Wuhan export of Covid-19 and Ukraine invasion do not upend politics of EU. So, for its survival India must develop self-defense. Since 1947 partition, India has lost parts of her territory first in 1947-1948 when Pakistan Army took large chunk of Kashmir by force as Prime Minister Nehru thought U.N. would act rationally, yet Pakistan didn't take all the Muslims she promised with creation of a homeland. Then again in 1962 China marched over India's Tibetan-speaking Ladakh Region, after colonizing Tibet. How many nations protested? In 1950 China marched her army to colonize Tibet, further weakening India, and Indian Civilization. Besides, one sided non-violence has no meaning. It has already proven to be bad. Gandhi was able to control of fratricidal majority in India. Thus, there was barely any cleansing of minorities from India. Western press rarely writes about natives being driven out from their ancestral land. Gandhi wasn't able to stop minority Hindu-Jain-Sikh-Buddhist-Christian cleansings from Pakistan, Afghanistan and Bangladesh. Tolerance and democracy should not be akin to self-destruction. Self-sacrifice is laudable for a cause. All armies are taught about that. In that respect Islam has done an excellent job. It is able to inspire hundreds of thousands of individuals to give up their lives to protect the religious belief. From ISIS to Al Qaeda, from Taliban to Jamat-I-Islam, and many more, all followers of Islamic faith are taught to make self-sacrifice for religion. They have produced human-bomb which pluralist nations call terrorist. So many young men gave up their lives for 9/11 terror. In the past 1,000 years no country could stop them. Many funded and applauded self-sacrifice. American-style self-defense with gun may challenge that. Citizens protect others, as we have witnessed from sacrifice of doctors, nurses, drivers, cleaners, cooks, garbage collectors, mailmen, deliverywomen, and more during Covid crisis. Gun violence emboldens antidemocratic forces and those with dictatorial mind. But it helps self-defense with a limit. There is a fine line for a nation to defend herself while teaching citizens self-respect, and gun violence.

World must fight against caste, gender, religious, linguistic discrimination, as she is doing now, but without guns, or with ammunition for self-defense, as taught by Sri Krishna. Nations must continue to teach self-defense.

There are many true believers worldwide who have spoken about deconstructing intolerance, and promote reformation in every belief. That includes many constitutions. This is not an Arab, Indian, or European issue, but it has gotten intertwined with India because of Muslim League Party demanded,

British acceded, and Muslims supported partition of India on the basis of Muslim and Non-Muslim division. Many authors from Egypt to India, Afghanistan to Algeria have written about reformation, but they all ended up in exile or dead. Even author Rushdie was attacked in New York. We need thinker's survival in their homeland, not in exile. Many think the war in Islam in Karbala when Prophet's grandsons were killed was the first attempt of reformation – which it was not, but the war ended in massacre even of the Holy Prophet's grandkids. Idea of any reformation ended there. Religion says Prophet is the last Prophet. So, any new idea within the framework is violently rejected. Thus, Ahmadian Movement arising from pluralistic India is declared Non-Muslim in Pakistan, Bangladesh and Indonesia. Calling one Baha'i in Iran from where the religion originated brings death penalty. Marrying a Christian, then becoming one brings death penalty in many nations. These traditions have to change. This is something beyond any one or any one nation. Many thinkers have written about it. And in world politics it is hard to discuss, when there is group behind one cause, howsoever unreasonable that is. Look at 2024 during Gaza war and destruction. Realizing that he was a minority ruling over a majority, Muslim Emperor Akbar promoted a Muslim-Hindu new religion called Din-I Ilahi. There were few takers from multi-theistic Hindus, but not from minority Muslims. We are afraid, America and the West has supported extremism when targeting others. Extremists from Ireland, Germany, Europe, Islamic nations, India, Iran, Israel, Africa, and the U.S. supported 9/11 terror. But 9/11 changed opinion in the U.S. and in many nations. We are thinking differently now. More to follow.

We need to promote interfaith and inter-linguistic and inter-group marriages. This is happening worldwide. In Muslim-majority nations when interfaith marriages take place, it should be left up to the newly married couple to follow any tradition without getting death penalty for blasphemy.

Unlike U.S., one more difficult task in India is teaching its own history which includes her regional sectarianism. During British era, one couldn't discuss oppression by colonizers. There was censorship on writing about oppression of majority population. Thus, we like open discussion of mass murder, destruction of shrines, ashrams, viharas, schools and libraries, transferring of wealth by colonial rulers, but not taking revenge in 21st Century. Secretive discussion of atrocities is undemocratic. Why should African Americans not be allowed to talk about oppression of Blacks? And, Jews by Nazis? Or, English oppression of Irish Catholics? Or, of Israelis by Hamas, or Palestinians by Israel? Atrocities should be condemned by secular press. In 1990s one of the very few Hindu communists not to leave his Muslim majority homeland was Mr. Sen. After his death in Barisal district of Bangladesh, communists in India, mostly his former Pakistani-Bangladeshi comrades who chose not to live with Muslims in Barisal District of Bangladesh, proposed to rename a Kolkata Street in Sen's name. Great! It was proposed by Barisal Seba Samiti or Barisal District Relief Organization of Kolkata, India. It began work in pre-independence era when educated natives of Barisal District living in capital Kolkata got engaged in building schools, colleges, bazars, ferry terminals, water supply, ponds, *ghat* steps to rivers and ponds, temples, and mosques in their native district. We were invited to their meetings because of our frequent trips to our Barisal homeland. Hearing this, Sachi suggested them to write to Barisal City Mayor to name one of the streets there instead of Kolkata. We are sure that the Barisal City Mayor, a Muslim, would have honored their request. Kolkata City renamed a street in Kolkata after Comrade Sen. Was it an honor or dishonor?

Indian Model?

For a country like India, its public policy has to be unique. Some are very difficult, others are not. Some harsh, others are not. India won't fit into single Asian, European, African, Islamic, Christian, Buddhist, Caribbean, Francophone or Hispanic model, for a one-of-a-kind nation. It has to come up with one-of-a-kind policy. It won't be easy because all her neighboring nations have engaged in ethnic cleansing and making legally indigenous pre-Buddhist, pre-Christian, pre-Islam people second class citizens. Because of Indian and Hindu narrow-minded linguistically-focused culture she ignored their pain since 1947. India is not an immigrant nation, yet she has taken Pakistanis, Bangladeshis, Sri Lankan, Burmese, Bhutanese, Tibetans, Nepalese, and Afghans cleansed from their nations. India's fatalism and tolerance have allowed small minority like Sikhs to demand a separate nation from India, but not in Pakistan where the religion was born and half the Sikhs lived there before 1947 partition. Like East Pakistani-Bangladeshi refugees in West Bengal, India, some Sikhs have focused on similar separatist mind and trying to partition India, but not in their Pakistan Motherland. Hindu Bengalis cleansed from East Pakistan and Bangladesh demand revolutionary rights in India, but not in their homeland. Small ethnic Christian converted communities like Mizo, Manipuri and Nagas tried separation from India, at the same time denying rights to their non-converted brothers and sisters. Oppressed Hindu groups from Sri Lanka, Bangladesh, Pakistan and Myanmar demand reserved seats in India's Parliament and State Legislatures, but not in their own homeland. This is India! This is fatalism!

India won't be able to solve her democratic polarization unless rest of the India's neighbors are equally democratic, pluralistic and tolerant. U.S. can't change other nations' constitution and civil culture, even when they are dependent on U.S. This is where world has failed, and exposed United Nations incompetence and sectarianism. This was exposed again during Gaza-Israel war. If South succeeded in dividing America, and continued slavery, should free Africans and Whites in the North keep quite if lynching continued there? Definitely not. Even the small Sikhs population have been highlighting their separate identity in India lot better than immense Hindu community. Bravo! Hindus consider Sikhs as a part of them, just as Jains, Buddhists, Brahmos and Vaishnavas.

Christians turned the violent death of Jesus Christ on a Cross to a pacifist movement. And the Day of Death turned into Good Friday, not a bad one. That was great which gave peace lovers to plead for a non-violent world. Wars were not eliminated in the past 2,000 years. In democracy small groups of people can influence a larger outcome, if they are able to organize themselves. In the U.S. it is easier with the Primary system when only 10% to 20% of the voters take part. Thus, if one can energize a small group to vote, then a small group is able to influence the state and national politics, and national policy. A bad example could be that of an avid Islamic Tablighi Jamati, who organized a huge meeting in Delhi, India at a mosque, in defiance of a national Covid ban. The huge gathering of thousands of devotees in April of 2020 included foreigners who traveled with false visas, and many crossed borders illegally. What would U.S. have done if such situation was found there? In many areas they created Covid crisis, including in Bangladesh. US Commission of International Religious Freedom (USCIRF), Malaysia, Kuwait, Iran, Saudi and many countries criticized India, instead of praising her. Moreover, one of the goals of Tablighis from its inception was to turn India into an Islamic nation. What would Americans do if they found out a group of folks were holding underground meeting to turn America into a communist nation? It reminds us of a meeting of Indian Muslims in Queens in 1991. It was great to see Indian religious groups and subgroups come together in the U.S. An Urdu-speaking Muslim from the Telugu-speaking southern Andhra State invited Sachi to join. There were songs and dances. But one speaker reminded attendees of the faulty Indian democracy, "Look, how Pakistan is better as there are no Hindu-Muslim or Muslim-Sikh riots." Some attendees appreciated the comparison, and clapped. During a break Sachi asked the speaker, "Are you suggesting that India should have cleansed all Muslims to avoid Muslim-Hindu, Muslim-Sikh riots, as Pakistan has cleansed all non-Muslims from the land?" He was surprised, as he never thought Pakistan as a land of non-Muslims. He didn't mind that Pakistan cleansed her indigenous population. This is not the deficiency of the speaker, but lack of transparency and lack of history lessons in Indian and Pakistani text books.

American Federation of Muslims from India, 1991

This is the result of bad Indian, Pakistani and Bangladeshi educational policies. Just as India's neighbors have failed in promoting secular, tolerant, inclusive policy, for no apparent reason, Indian politicians have promoted further intolerance, at times of smaller sub-ethnicities, or sub-groups, to get elected from a small corner of the nation. Thus, India has 117 political parties. In order to come to power, Indian Bengali Left propagandized Congress Party as promoter of Partition, but not the Muslim League Party. This was a false narrative. This narrative of some politicians was to hide their own anti-Muslim communalism as they were fleeing Islamic Pakistan, East and West, for India. The first Left Government in West Bengal included members of Muslim League Party that promoted Partition, but no Hindu nationalist, as mentioned earlier. In 1980s they murdered dozens of Hindu monks and nuns in Ballygunj area of Kolkata, possibly within 150 yards from where our parents lived. No one was arrested. No one was prosecuted even when pictures are available online. Then in 1990s they allowed Call for Prayers through mega speakers, even when the same politicians restricted use of loudspeakers for traditional Durga Puja, Kali

Puja, and other seasonal festivities. West Bengal High Court ruled use of loud speakers will be banned at night, and stopped use of drums and bells in many Hindu festivities that are conducted at night like Kali Puja, Shiv Ratri, and more. This tradition is continuing for millennia. Left government enforced that rule on majority Hindus, but when Muslims openly called for ignoring such rules, Leftists and later Trinamool party, refused to enforce the law, triggering polarization. Hindu festivities are yearly but Islamic call for prayers are five times daily. During 2020 Corona virus lockdown India was criticized for trying to arrest for holding illegal meetings by Islamic leaders when it was prohibited for all, but they did not criticize Bangladesh or Malaysia for doing the same restriction. India was not criticized by foreigners and U.N., to force Hindus to cancel festivities of Holi, Baisakh (mid-April) New Year, Akshai Tritiya, Buddha Jayanti, Rabindra Jayanti and more. Why? With Islamic Id celebration coming in April 2020, many Indian states and neighboring countries started loosening virus restriction. One hears complaints from individuals about double standard, but not on sectarian media. Are these censorships helpful? In West Bengal, India, many Islamic leaders have pleaded with the state government not to relax the virus lockdown but of no support from politicians (see daily *Kolkata 24/7*, May 10, 2020). Pakistan and Bangladesh didn't have any room for indigenous celebrations. Double Standard? Hypocrisy?

It is not the hypocrisy of international organizations and media, but Indian educational systems are equally responsible for fake and wrong information. Should Indians have only one world view? As mentioned earlier, Indian Freedom Struggle is rarely taught in Indian schools. Muslim League's two nations theory of racism is rarely mentioned in classroom. Leftist or rightist in India rarely mention Kerala's 1921 Moplah Malabar anti-Hindu pogrom when large number of Hindus were killed in Hindu-majority Kerala. British colonizers sent killers to Andaman Islands, not to British Isles. Indian Freedom Fighters were hanged and imprisoned in Andaman. We always wondered if that was a way of controlling Indian freedom fighters who were imprisoned in Andaman Islands, as Moplahs were allowed to settle there, but not the nationalists. Moplahs then started to give loud "Call for Prayers," subjugating Andaman's indigenous population. Discussion of Moplah killing of majority Malayalee Hindus in southern Kerala state of India is censored by the ruling Communist Party, and Islamists. Here are some pictures from the British Prison in the Andaman Islands in the Bay of Bengal.

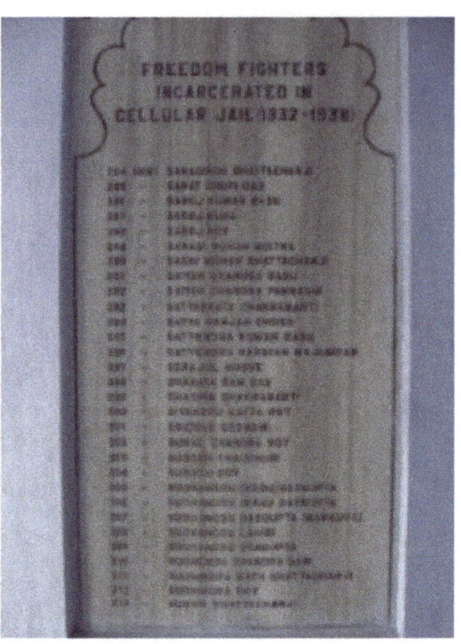

One of Hundreds of Tablets of Imprisoned Indian Freedom Fighter names.

Place for Hanging Indian Nationalist Freedom Fighters

Central Jail, Andaman

Names of pro-Independence Prisoners of British Oppression, possibly over 90% Bengali Hindus from East Bengal (Bangladesh) and West Benga

Mosque Established by Moplah Hindu Killers of Kerala, on Right

At a Beach Party

At Bay of Bengal

A Hindu Shrine in Andaman Islands

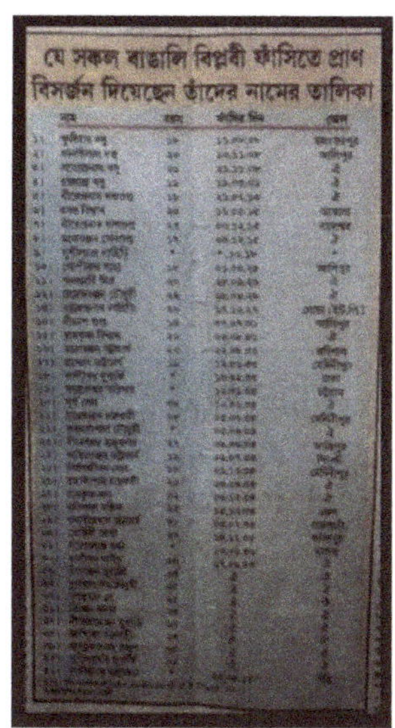

One Short List of Indian-Bengali Freedom Fighters Hanged by Britain

Bengali Hindus Killed in Assam in Post-Independence India

Family Values – West & East, U.S. & India, Work Culture & Family Culture:

Public policy of the two largest democracies are determined by several diverse, at times opposing values, history, culture, recent and ancient past, idea of family – nuclear vs extended, promotion of sexual culture vs control of one's urges, colonial rule, colonial oppression, gun culture vs suicidal pacifism, rule of law vs bribery and money, foreign involvement in socio-economic-political issues, love of nature and animal, science and technology, adoption to modernity, idea of wealth, social hierarchy, caste-and race-and-wealth-based racism, effects of indigenous culture, democracy, majority and minority politics, and so much more. With time, some contradictions have developed, others diminished. Some of these contradictions are not that different from contradictions between settler nations of North and South America of Europe-based cultures, and non-settler nations of Europe. Do we respect all life, including animals by becoming vegetarian or cultivate promotion of slaughter for food? Do we promote caste-like racism or color-based racism? Should we promote colonization by immigrants or promote indigenous traditions? Should we promote gun culture or nonviolence? How can we tolerate indigenous faiths while promoting alteration? Can we avoid superiority complex?

Then there are questions of values, including individual, family, and work ethic. Values change over time – individual, cultural, family, economic conditions, nature, weather, climate, and more. Western culture promoted "Conquering Mother Nature," whereas Indian/Hindu culture promoted to "Be a Part of Mother Nature." These are fundamental differences affecting people's DNA. Coming in contact with each other, it is changing cultures, and lot more. Technology is also associated with changing of values. For example, smoking was an element of status in the West blindly followed by the East. This is not true anymore as we found its ill effects. Hardly any movie in the 21st Century project smoking as a glamour. But through colonialism it entered the psyche of colonized Indians, Africans and Inca-Aztecs as white masters were smoking on all occasions. Ganja or weed smoking was a part of Indian culture for millennia through Lord Shiva's festivity, but looked down upon as a culture of uneducated and oppressed peoples by the colonizers and their Indian helpers, until it was approved in the West. Same with alcohol. Yet, cigarette smoking, imported from the West, entered mainstream in India, but with some reservation. Still many Indians hold cigarette smoking to be of higher class, although traditionally it was considered as something bad. In some Indian ethnic groups smoking in front of older persons is considered uncivil. So, smokers often hide the cigarette from older or respectable persons putting the hand with cigarette behind their back. Alcohol was considered even worse in India, although in 1990s it entered exponentially in mainstream. It is sad to think so many of our college classmates in India are dead due of lung cancer from smoking. Then there is pornography, and casual sex as seen on Western movies, TV and online shows, and now available via internet. In Indian culture sex discussion has always been considered very private, and pre-marital sex was never a part of the culture. This is also true for many cultures in the Mideast, Asia and Africa. On the other hand, Indian, Asian and African cultures allowed child marriages, others did not. Thus one-night stand, or casual sex was avoided from childhood, and in family culture of extended families, sex before marriage was unthinkable for most locals. Of course, Muslim kings had harems of women for enjoyment, that was considered "abnormal and unethical," but Muslim theologians didn't object. One Western theologian told us that in India one is urged to control sex urge from the childhood changing people's mindset, whereas in the West they do not, and adulthood meant casual sex. As most Hindu/Buddhist/Jain saints remain ascetic for life, control of one's sex urges has been a part of the culture forever. It is a part of the cultural DNA. Thus, electing a single man or a single woman as head of the nation or states is not considered unusual, unlike in the West. Being ascetic is considered a virtue. Thus, it is quite common in Indian culture for one to remain bachelor or bachelorette while serving the extended family. Joint culture of extended family provides a home for single persons. In India many politicians and famous persons remain ascetic. For example, in early 2010s several Indian State Chief Ministers were single woman or man: Delhi, Odisha, Tamil Nadu, Uttar Pradesh and West Bengal, with a combined population of about 500 million, and mostly headed by women, except Odisha. One of India's former Prime Minister, Atal Bihari Vajpayee, was single. It hardly crossed any Indian's mind that being single, or woman as leader is a problem. Such individuals were not elected in 250 years in the U.S. Indian Prime Minister in 2022, Mr. Modi, is a single person. On the other hand, as men and women have entered work force and moved away from home protected by extended family, seeing online easy pre-marital sex in the West, rape and abuse of women have increased exponentially in India, and in other developing nations. TV and online social media are playing a big role.

We believe, with the advance in technology and cell phone, attraction to pornography has also increased in India and Third World immensely. One Indian state legislator was seen watching pornography while on a session. Rape has also increased significantly. Repeatedly seeing sex acts could easily influence mind. It is like seeing ad. If there was no influence on our brain through ads why would businesses spend $25 million dollars for a 60-second ad? Then there is Hollywood movies which give a narrative of easy sex, many girlfriends, sleeping with strangers, living in mansions with dozens of cars is the norm in the West, especially in the U.S. These influence weaker minds. Nevertheless, in an open society balance of age-old teachings and influence of modern tools are coming into conflict. In traditional culture when marriage and virginity are considered two sides of the same coin, and where marriage is considered between two families, tribes or villages, not individuals, rape was considered a tool of family cruelty. During 1971 Pakistani genocide in Bangladesh rape was one more tool to destroy a population, as they abused 250,000 girls and mothers. (See Dr. Nilima Ibrahim, *Aami Birangana Bolchhi* [I am the brave woman speaking], Jagriti Prakashani, Dhaka; 1998.) Same abuse was used by Muslim League Party supporters in Noakhali in east Bengal in 1946 during British colonial rule by abusing tens of thousands of Hindu girls and mothers. Neither Britain nor Pakistan paid any price for the atrocities. (See Ashoka Gupta, *Noakhalir Durjoger Diney* [An Account of the Aftermath of Riot in Noakhali in 1946], Naya Udyog, Calcutta; 1999.) Prof. Ibrahim had to stop publishing stories of rape victims as entire villages in Bangladesh got identified with rape victim felling insecure. This is sad! This is shocking! This is bad! She stopped publishing more books on rape of Bengalis by Pakistani and Islamic soldiers. In one case when a girl became free and called her parents, they said to wait for returning home until they secure rest of the kids. Sad! Very shocking tradition! Prof. Ibrahim is Hindu married to a Muslim.

One must be aware of a problem to solve it. In many nations alcohol has gone underground, including Pakistan, Bangladesh and Afghanistan, and in Indian states where sale of alcohol is banned. Some give severe penalty to citizens for drinking, yet their military keeps alcohol open. During Covid pandemic Subcontinent governments came under criticism for not providing food to the poor. Understood. So, all state governments in India kept bazars open for people to buy food. For some reason most states where alcohol is legal allowed liquor stores to remain open. In many cities from Delhi in the north to Bangalore in the south to Kolkata in the east and Mumbai in the West there were long lines to buy liquor. Should states be providing free food to the poor to increase their appetite for alcohol? (See Indian papers of first week of May 2020.) This is another effect of modernism and Westernization. Thus, developing nations need to control gun violence, drugs, sex, technology, and alcoholism – all imports to her modern economy. Western societies are also adopting many Indian/Hindu values like yoga, meditation, vegetarianism, music, dance and to be a part of Mother Nature. Two radically different societies are coming closer by adopting other values.

Moreover, there is the issue of values, pluralism, tolerance, diversity in democracy. We often said that "India has too much democracy." This is because of traditional "Hindu" belief is a pluralistic tradition. It created space for women and men of all colors, for poor and wealthy, short and tall, fully clothed to unclothed, animals as pets and saviors, and more. Thus, in spite of bloody, merciless killing by colonizers for a thousand years, and cleaning of almost all indigenous minorities from Pakistan, Afghanistan and Bangladesh, there were efforts by Hindu majority to have their minority neighbors stay in their home. Pakistan became barely 1% minority from over 25% in 1941 census, and Bangladesh's indigenous Hindus came down from about a third to barely 7% in 2022. India's post-Partition Muslim minority who voted for separate homeland for Muslims rose from 14% to 17% in 2021 census, in spite of tens of millions of Hindu-Sikh-Jain-Buddhist-Christians coming to India. We often hear that "Indians and Hindus can't fight back." True. Within Hinduism Sikhs rose in the

Middle Ages in western India with armed resistance, and the eastern India rose extreme Vaishnav (Baishnab) pacifism. Many complain that Hindus do not follow what they say: "To every action, there is an equal and opposite reaction" dictum. During and after partition, did they react with their minorities like Pakistan did with their minorities? No. They are not able to respond to a popular Sanskrit proverb, "*Sathe Satthong samacharet*," or "Behave equally with evil forces." It is also possible that because of this infinite tolerance in tradition foreigners were able to colonize them, but it may also be true that because of such faith it is the only culture where traditional belief has survived as rest of the world converted. And she has been able to give full rights to her minorities who opposed her freedom. Very few nations are able to do so. She was able to create minority linguistic states, minority religious states, minority tribal states, and teaching in numerous languages.

In 1972 when Sachi's Jewish classmate took him to meet his family at Miami, Sachi was a bit surprised when he introduced him to his grandma, 86, and grandpa, 79. His mother said that the grandma got newly remarried. She hesitantly mentioned that "I am very happy as Ma doesn't only depend on me. Initially, I was surprised. But soon I realized what a good thing." It opened our eyes as in a non-extended family-oriented society, why such remarriage and new family is so important. We called Jay's mom Aunt Mashi or Mother's Sister in Indian tradition, that she liked very much. In 1987 she rushed to Long Island from Miami to meet Sachi's mom who was visiting them. Ma was widow then, just losing her husband of 67 years.

We noticed during our research that marriage for the older persons, or remarriage of a widow or widower is so rare in India that it becomes newsworthy taking space in page 4 of 6-page of daily papers. On February 22, 2022 *Dainik* (Daily) *Pratidin* wrote a story that a 54-year-old woman married a 60-year-old man. The day before, on February 21, 2022. the same *Daily Pratidin* wrote how a "young" 80-year-old woman married a "young" 80-year-old man. We are happy that papers are reporting this news than censoring them.

As society and economy are changing, it is important for Indian society to be more dynamic and adoptive, as Hinduism is in its core, like the U.S. For America it is a bit easier, as she has only to follow a tradition established only in the past 250 years, as opposed to India where many families or villages have traditions of 2,500 years! Simple symbolism becomes difficult barriers to cross. At times, what colored sari a bride is to wear becomes an issue, because the family has been doing that for centuries. Or, how many ladies should hold the welcoming flat basket *barandala* for the newlywed couple becomes an issue so that tradition is not broken. Whom to marry becomes an issue. Besides, the concept of money, earnings, work ethic needed for a dynamic industrial society is deep rooted as in the individual-oriented capitalist West. Moreover, to get elected, some parties promote parasitism or getting everything free. This has something to do with colonization of India for over a one thousand years. Elected politicians in the Subcontinent are not yet used to the term of "Balancing the Budget" or taxing citizens. For a long time, Pakistanis didn't have the idea of taxation. The idea of raising money to pay for public service was also absent in the Left ruled West Bengal and Tripura, both ruled initially by Congress Party, then by Communist Party-Marxist. A common phrase often one hears in Bengal is, "*Laagey taka debey Lakshman Sen*" meaning "When you need money, it will be provided by Lakshman Sen," a mythic donor with endless supply of money. This is also the result of a post-independence economic system where states had limited means for revenue collection. States are depended on the federal government for monetary help. Since year 2000, states got more taxing power, nevertheless, blaming "Central Government" for states' failure as an escape in politics, as in the U.S. This is often tinged with sectarianism.

The work ethic is also an issue in certain regions and certain sectors of India. In 2019, after receiving Nobel Prize in 2019, a young Dr. Avijit Banerjee recalled only after coming to America, he realized what is "hard work." Indians and Third World citizens are certainly capable of hard work, but it is not ingrained equally in all regions. Work ethic, entrepreneurship and adoptability varies in India from region to region. In America, culture of diverse immigrants has taken place through assimilation, love, constitution, and more. During the Left rule of India's West Bengal from 1970s through 2010s, a common phrase one heard in labor movement is, "*jacchi aaschhi poisa pacchi, kaj korley overtime pacchi,*" meaning "For coming and going, we are getting paid. When we work, we get overtime pay." There was hardly any discussion in Bengal for closing of 55,000 factories during Left rule See "55,000 factories closed in West Bengal," *Bartaman,* Aug 27, 2011; http://bartamanpatrika.com/content/rajya.htm. We are not sure how elite media would have reacted if those closures were under nationalist's rule.

Then there is "Family:"

Many of the Indian catastrophes, especially after Partition's mass killing was ignored by the world. Rehabilitation of tens of millions made homeless overnight by Islamic killing and cleansing of poor, middleclass, and educated families, were ignored by the elite press, and world media. The saving grace was the family structure that made people survive in a poor economy with no help. It is not that different from the plight of citizens of Sudan, Gaza, Ethiopia, and more. This is especially true of Bengali Hindu refugees in India. For West Pakistan refugees in India the ruling Congress Party passed an extremely racist Nehru-Liaquat Ali Treaty to deny help to Bengali Hindu refugees, favoring Punjabi, Sindhi, Pashtu, and Baloch Hindu-Sikh-Jain-Buddhist refugees in India from West Pakistan, now Pakistan, a much smaller number than Bengali Hindu refugees. Nehru was the Prime Minister of India and Liaquat Ali was that of Pakistan, both from northern India. Families have always been the backbone of India in collectively helping extended family members. Thus, one sibling of refugees often sacrificed to support the extended family, including aunts, uncles, grandparents, and cousins. An uncle may have taken in protecting many families. Definition of family is quite different from the West. In the West it is the nuclear family, mother, father, two kids, and the dog. In India it always includes grandparents, often uncles' and aunt's families, as often extended families live under one roof, with one kitchen, especially with paternal uncles. This is going down in urban areas, as space is a problem. We still remember in

Long Island elementary school IQ test our daughter Joyeeta included her residing grandma in the question as a part of the family. She got a zero for that answer. When we told her examiner that in our culture, the answer is correct. She was surprised to learn that. Generally, it is the grandma or the senior most woman who runs the family. One of my close Bangladeshi Muslim friends, who came to U.S. with a Lottery Visa, was able to sponsor 47 members of his extended family. By sponsoring them for immigrant visa, U.S. also acknowledged Indian culture's difference. In the West, boys and girls are encouraged to take charge as they leave home at age 18 heading to college. This is our narrative, although all families in the U.S. retain strong ties, though not living together. Moreover, in a mobile society people find jobs in every corner of the nation. Thus, in 1960s and 1970s when Indians were learning more about American culture, one constant fear was to grow old in America, and live separately in senior centers. Now, life has come to a full circle in urban, industrial India. Family size has shrunk just like in the West to one or two children for most urbanites. There are thousands of senior living centers, *bridhhabash*, and in *bridhhashram* or Ashram for the Elderly. One of our friends from New Jersey MonoDa, Older Brother Mono, lived in one such Indian facility in southern suburb of Kolkata, that we visited him in 2013. In reality, living separately at a facility has always been there in India, but not acknowledged culturally.

When the immediate family wasn't present, ashrams led by a swami (monk) or swamini (nun) provided shelter, including food, clothing and medical care. Then there is Varanasi (Banaras). For millennia old men and women headed to Varanasi for a holy death. Many Sanatani believe that if one dies there, near the famous shrine of Lord Shiva and where Lord Buddha gave his first sermon, one will have *moksha* or liberation not to be born again. Thus, India needs to revive her old habits of independent senior living in group setting, not discard it, for future change in family structure.

At the same time, an old traditional culture has to be flexible and adoptive. One American scholar at the 2003 American Academy of Religion conference in Atlanta reminded during a meeting of theologians that one of the reasons why

Hinduism survived after onslaughts of Christianity, Islam and atheism is because of its flexibility and being adoptive. Indians have been able to adopt with changing demographics, cross cultural mixing, and migration. It has already happened overseas. Our family friend Mr. Sudhindra Adhikary, is a Christian with a typical Bengali name, always wore dhoti outerwear. They are considered to be one of the first families to convert from pre-British Portuguese era of Christian conversion. Some Indian Christians keep a "Christian" middle name like Jayanta Christopher Ghosh; whereas in some areas families keep only "English" names as Christopher Ghosh.

Christians were always more tolerant than many others, maintaining local identity with local names and outfit. Islam always demanded complete Arabization of cultures. As Hindus transformed in the 20th Century, no Hindu devotee questioned when we saw African or European natives leading religious services in temples in New York, Botswana, South Africa, Ireland, or at Almaty, Kazakhstan, or in Kolkata and Delhi, India with Indian assistant priests, learning from Africans or Europeans about India's tradition. In India many temples are led by women, and from non-priest and non-Indian families. With more migration to and from India, the ethnic-caste definition is going to change for the better. We believe ISKCON, the pacifist movement spread from the U.S. has lot to do with this transformation, as well as actions of Sri Chinmoy in the U.S. of Chittagong, Bangladesh. In 1980s when a Hanuman Mandir (temple) was built in Hempstead, Long Island, one of its biggest supporters was an Indian Muslim. It was led by a Hindu female priestess.

A Temple in South Africa with Three African Priests

A Temple in Botswana with African Priest

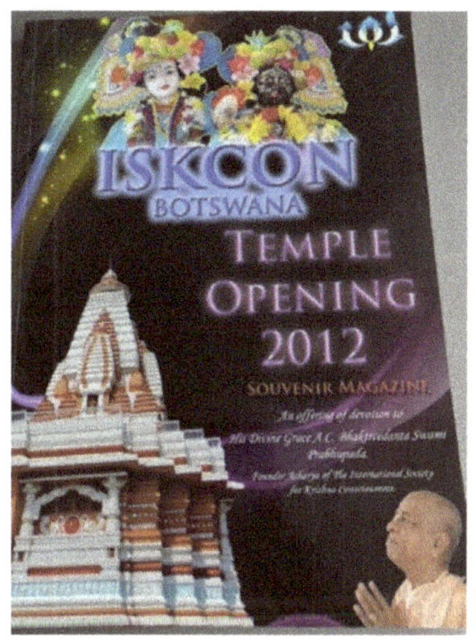

Botswanans Presented Their 2012 Temple Opening Book

With urbanization and college education mixed marriages are common. Non-traditional mixings are not shared by the elite press. Mother Sita, Lord Ram's wife, at millenniums old Ramayana, was adopted as she was found in a rice field, thus her name Sita. Lady Kunti was an unwed teenage mother, who let her son float down Ganga River to be picked up and raised by oppressed parents that no one finds dubious. Lord Krishna, one of the most revered of all avatars, was from oppressed cow herder group. To break some of the caste garbage that we have collected in our Indian society, one needs to highlight the positive. Since early 1800s Raja Ram Mohon, and Vidyasagar – meaning Ocean of Knowledge – pushed for many reformations from stopping of killing of widows among a small group of people, to widow remarriage – remarriage was despised in the culture – which soon became accepted as Vidyasagar had his son marry a widow.

Such reformations are possible in pluralistic religion. Ram Mohon started a new monotheistic religion, Brahmoism, deity-less prayer from Upanishad. He was influenced by Christian prayer service during his visit to England in early 1800s. In that era Hindu's were so defensive after a thousand year of foreign rule, that Ram Mohon traveled with cow in a ship to remain "pure." Ram Mohon started a social-religious reformation movement whose effect is still alive 200 years later. Those reformations have been accepted by the larger society. We wonder how many monotheistic nations would tolerate someone who says in public that "I am starting a new religion," or "We will reform our religion." Even today many Muslim-majority nations declare Ahmadis or Qadianis as non-Muslim, although they consider themselves as Muslim and follow Holy Koran. It was a nice experience when Shefali and Sachi were invited to the opening of Ahmedi Mosque in eastern Queens. Our Pakistani friend visiting us was excited to see that shrine during a visit to New York, as it is banned in Pakistan. Christians have done many reformations for centuries. Jews have reformed themselves many times. Begum Rokeya, a Muslim, attempted some reformation in Bengal, as did Ataturk of Turkey. Rokeya's experiment succeeded among very few, while Ataturk's has been toppled by Erdogan in 21st Century. In Bengal, India, Kazi Nazrul Islam, a Muslim, tried reformation through his mixed marriage, poetry, songs and literature so much so that many Muslim clerics declared him, kefir or non-believer. Sadly, an anti-thesis to Nazrul is an India-born Islamist-Military dictator practically stole Nazrul's dead body to bury him in Bangladesh, to make Nazrul a symbol of his Islamist intolerance. Nazrul was never a Bangladeshi, as he was born in what is India, and opposed Muslim League Party's racist-divisive policy that created Pakistan, and Bangladesh. Nazrul composed and sang many songs dedicated to deities, and offered puja at Hindu celebrations regularly. His married a Hindu, and gave his children Hindu or Bengali names starting another turn in identity of Bengali Muslims. As we mentioned, in 1970 and 1971 Sachi visited him at his home in Kolkata during his birthday celebrations when there was a kilometer-long line to touch his feet and pay respect, overwhelmingly by Hindus. He became completely disabled in the last years of his life. He was cared by a Hindu caretaker from Orissa.

Rule of Law, Not the Rule of Family Tradition:

To follow American system India has tried to have a neutral judiciary with appointments of people of all regions, religions, languages and genders. Unfortunately, the U.S. court system has become tainted with the idea of "Republican" and "Democratic" appointees who would behave with party ideology. This is bad. Very bad. Where is neutrality? If we already know the biased attitudes of justices, then where is justice? Abortion issue has exposed many of the justices to be influenced by theology, putting "American" ideology in difficulty. This was not supposed to happen. All nations must avoid biases of justices at all cost. Justices are human beings; thus, all of their feelings cannot be predicted all the time. India's traditional belief of wisdom through age, still influences some minds, but rarely followed. That old tradition was abandoned since Muslim and Christian rules at 1000 AD. It seems in 2024 America has come to follow India's belief in wisdom when the entire nation trusted their faith in two septuagenarians for the top two presidential candidates, not young folks in their forties or fifties, until it changed with Hon. Kamala Harris, a few months before 2024 election. Unlike America, in India's case Hindu genocide, ethnic cleansing of tens of millions from their homeland, and confiscation of ancestral properties of thousands of years by declaring them "Enemy Property" – thus officially declaring the indigenous pre-Islamic natives as Enemies of the State, but no fatalist is to challenge and remember that. This is anti-democratic inkling. Complete ethnic cleansing of indigenous minorities from Pakistan and Afghanistan, is not supposed to influence victim's mind. Why not? Why are we supporting Ukraine fight or Israeli fight? Why did we fight against Nazis? India survived only because of her extreme suicidal fatalism and tolerance of indigenous mind. With urbanization, migration of linguistic, religious and regional population, their victimization plays lesser role in life giving Indians in new post-colonial identity. Whether an all-India movement of pre-independence Congress Party will be able to bring the extremely diverse nation together in 21st Century is yet to be seen. After Congress Party's rule over half-a-century, now an all-India Bhartiya – meaning Indian – Janata Party (BJP) is trying to bring a very diverse nation together, yet it is naturally being challenged by sectarian forces, neo-colonialists, communal Left and Right, missionary forces of Islam, Christianity and China. We will not be surprised if tons of funding are coming from foreign countries with no interest of toleration and democracy in their own land. Will Mother India be able to reincarnate as a new Avatar? Jury is not clear yet.

In case of India, one more issue of tradition needs to be looked into. We grew up in a system in post-independence era of blind Westernization and negation of all things Indian, aka Hindu, aka Traditional, aka Nature Worship, aka Worship of all Life, much like what Pakistan, Bangladesh, and Afghanistan have done. Thus, lessons of *Khonar Bachan*, Words of Khona, was dropped from Indian life that guided her people for a thousand year. There were many practices that British and then neo-colonial Indian rulers rejected as taboos, without any science. Some of the traditions like yoga, *dhyan* (meditation), *sanyash* (priesthood), Ayurveda, treating any life as sacred which came with experience of many generations of trial and error, especially learning from Mother Nature were ignored. Thus, yoga and meditation were dropped from Indian life until it entered from America in late 20th Century. Why? Were these blind Westernization necessary? Why Indian freedom struggle is not taught in Indian books, but Bolshevik Revolution and WW II became more important? Keeping clean through hand washing, and leaving shoes before entering the main rooms, were considered bad "Hindu" practices. COVID-19 crisis has taught us that those traditions developed for good reasons where tropical diseases spread widely. This was one way of preventing that. In 2023 November, a new research result in the U.S. showed how germs enter our home through outdoor shoes. Makes sense. Modern India, Pakistan, and Bangladesh taught the old tradition of taking bath or shower before entering home when folks went to a cremation ground carrying a dead body on a cot on men's shoulder is bad ritual. Traditionally men, taking turns, depending on the distance to cremation area, carried the body on a stringed bamboo cot. Now, in COVID era it seems very logical when people carrying bodies with viruses are thoroughly cleaned before entering home. There are many viruses in tropical areas which ended life. It seems cremation is a better in tropical countries like India, burial is the only option in desert-like green free regions. In higher elevation, above tree line, Hindus and Buddhists bury, as there are no trees there. Many Hindus, Buddhists and Jains have a tradition of burying the dead in a Samadhi or Sacred Grave, especially for holy persons. With coming of Islam, burying the dead entered the culture as Muslims, and Christians bury their dead, as in treeless Arabia or Mideast the tradition developed. It is natural there. However, after each monsoon and flooding in the Subcontinent, newspapers routinely report that many "dead bodies have just floated away from graves." In dense countries like India or Bangladesh, soon it will be hard to find space for burial, especially in urban areas. Society must come up with new ideas. Christian Europe and America has already adopted new norms.

We were told it is a "taboo" when older persons asked us not to be near a newborn within the first six days from birth, when the mother and the baby used to be quarantined in a room. Usually there was a religious ceremony of *Shashti* or Sixth Day, opening the family relationship with the baby, thus securing the first survival barrier. On 21st Day of the baby's birth, there was another ceremony. Again, in old countries where most births took place at home, we think it was done to protect the baby and the mother from getting germs and viruses from strangers. And 6 days and 21 days must have been predictors of baby's survival, overcoming hurdle, when child mortality was high. Modernists taught us to ignore many "traditional taboos" of when to leave home, what and when to eat or not to eat, where to sit for chatting, and more. Some of those certainly make sense even today, but needs change with changing surroundings. Leaving blindly to follow something else is also a problem.

One of the good thing U.S. has been able to maintain is its two-party system. But, two party system and Primary Election have added a problem of minority rule. In many primaries, and low-level elections like School Boards and Village Council, and others at times the share of voter participation is in single digit. In my New York School Board election in 1996 the number of citizens who participated was small. This is normal. Representing the majority by a minority can result in racial, ethnic, and class tension. Minority rule contradicts the idea of democracy of majority rule. In almost 250 years we have been able to create a law-based culture, although we have many more steps to take. While in the largest democracy of India, minority rule has been institutionalized by Colonial Britain, especially with partition of India in 1947 based on a religious minority's demand. Then in independent India states were created where a former minority would be a majority, instead of keeping multilingual states. New states were created even for religious minorities. It will be like if U.S. creating Black-majority, Native American-majority, Irish, German, Hispanic, Catholic or Jewish majority states where White Christian-Americans are minority. Even in 2024 in many Indian states it takes decades to get a verdict for murder, property confiscation, non-payment of rent, sexual abuse, and on mundane issues. This is true in many parts of the subcontinent. On March 8, 2022 the daily *Prothom Alo* of Bangladesh reported that there are "One rape victim in every ten minutes," but hardly any repercussion. It reminded us of the tears of a homeowner in Ballygunj neighborhood of Kolkata. The homeowner returned back to Kolkata after retirement. He rented his home to a Pakistani-Hindu-Bengali-Refugee lawyer who refused give the property back to the owner. Renter didn't pay rent for years. Bribery of elected and party officials, and influence of refugee colonizers, allowed changing of the property to the occupier's name. This issue has created a serious housing and investment crisis in many states. Once visiting our parents almost 40 years ago in early 1980s, while talking to Ma at her roof garden, we realized the seriousness of forcible illegal confiscation and non-payment or rents, when Ma pointed out how many apartments are empty in just one block of two-story buildings. At least 30% of the apartments were vacant as owners found it is better to keep it empty than renting to someone, thus not getting any return of their investment. Sachi got energized to write an article on that issue, and Indian Planning Commission Journal, *Yojana*, published that in early days of his carrier. Surprisingly, in August 12, 2021, Kanika Debi, grandma of my granddaughter Lakshmi's 2nd grade friend in New York, said how she is planning to sell the unrented apartment in Kolkata, but not her properties in

Mumbai and Delhi, as Kolkata citizens are prone to confiscating illegally, started during Bangladeshi-refugee run party rule. Sachi wrote about that earlier in this chapter.

Indian Planning Commission Journal, Yojana

In South Asia, especially in Bengal, a myth developed that to be rich is bad. As a result, the Pakistani-Bangladeshi-Hindu-Refugee-run West Bengal politicians were able to confiscate indigenous Hindu land and buildings without much repercussion. In the U.S. money is able to buy local to national elections. No one hides that. In India Left or Right try to avoid that discussion. Although all agrees that to run for elected offices one needs money. We will not be surprised if foreign money from other nations, including non-elected regimes pour money for elections. In 2022 we learned how Russia and monarchies influenced 2020 U.S. election. In India many parties try to control the media, as in the U.S. One extreme case was in Kolkata of West Bengal State where the head of ruling anti-Communist Trinamool Party of Ms. Banerjee, the Chief Minister of West Bengal State, fired the editor of privately-owned largest daily Anandabazar Patrika on June 1, 2020. Since then, the paper has turned into an anti-India, anti-Hindu, anti-Bengal pro-colonization paper from pro-independence nationalist paper since the days of British era. It helped her to get reelected the following year. Everyone in the state talks about how she gives 10 million rupees of public money to the privately owned paper each month. We asked for further proof. There are discussions in social media. In 1995 daughter Joyeeta and Sachi met with her at her home in Kalighat, as we felt that she was a rising star of Congress Party. A few years later she quit the party and started her own political party: the Trinamool (Grassroots) Congress Party. The ruling Communist-Marxists beat her up many times, until she ousted them altogether from the Legislature. With the rule of Communists, then with Trinamool, the state has declined economically with no jobs and no wealth. The state is using its public funds for politics. In 2022 and 2023 several top politicians were found with tens of millions of cash at home, dozens of properties, cars, and bank accounts, but officially with a small salary. This is another form of corruption that has expanded in India, unlike U.S. where the funding comes from open private sources. Parasitism is problematic.

However, as all the Subcontinent nations, except India, have made them non-secular, single ethnic-religious nations, thus minorities are automatically Third-Class citizens and may not have any protection but ethnic cleansing. The problem is if the same minority is majority in an Indian state, what should their role be? Should they as majority in an Indian state protest and protect their brothers and sisters elsewhere? In America, if Blacks or Whites or Browns are attacked in one state should Blacks, Whites and Browns protest in another state? And in 2023-2024 Hamas-Israel protest in the U.S. has exposed the identity and value issues in a secular nation.

Identity and Nation Building:

Many visitors to India are often baffled as to how diverse the nation is culturally and ethnically from one corner to another, although they look alike. Even religious practices are different. Same deities are celebrated differently, at times with different look, belonging to the "same religion," although using the same Sanskrit verses. Unlike monotheistic religions the difference can be quite significant. Depending on sub-regional differences, Mother Durga may be worshipped with ten hands holding ten powers, at other places with eight hands, and some other region with only four hands, possibly because that region's plights were less severe than another region needing less protection, with more imagination. Thus, imagery and real-life experience create new ideas in pluralistic philosophy. Food, dress, social habits, idea about groups, class, states, languages, dialects, and ethnicity vary significantly, yet without hostility. Most of the time they welcome and tolerate each other. Colonialism for 1,000 years, treatment of the silent indigenous majority, and change of people's identity has had its implications. This is just opposite of America with English language and Christian guidance have created its identity. In case of America her identity has developed in 300 years, whereas in Subcontinent tradition has developed in 6,000 years. So, roots are very different. In the U.S. it is unthinkable for some states not to teach English in schools but receive same privileges as English-medium states. Visitors in India often ask what holds the nations together? Many books have been written on that. In our opinion some of the things that hold the nation together, not in any particular order, are: Bande (Vande) Mataram, Bollywood, Bihar, Boots, Babu, Bhakti, Bidya Debi (Vidya Devi), Buddha Deb (Dev), and more.

Vande Mataram is the National Song in Sanskrit that led Indian independence movement. The song praising the strength of woman defeating the demon was banned by the British colonizer. In this case woman was the Mother Nation. And saying the first two words, Bande (Vande) Mataram, Glory to the Mother, sent one to the British Colonial prison, including our grandma, grandpa, and two Mamu maternal uncles. Mother in this case is Mother Bharat (India) but that is not mentioned in the poem. This song depicts the nation being led by the Mother who is strong to make the nation free, yet motherly soft to Her children, meaning citizens. Projecting power of a woman, the Mother, contradicts the values of British Christians as well as Islam believers. This is one more reason that the song didn't become India's national anthem. It wasn't adopted as a national song to please Muslim League Party who didn't like Sanskrit, the mother language of all Indian languages. Atheist also opposed for no real reason, except for being anti-Congress, and anti-indigenous.

Accidentally, Rabindranath Tagore (Thakur) became the composer of two national anthems of India and Bangladesh, and music composer of Bande (Vande) Mataram written by Bankim Chandra Chattopadhyay in 1870.

Bollywood: is the Hindi movie industry located in Bombay, now called Mumbai, in a non-Hindi region of India, but pulling majority Hindi and non-Hindi regions of India together with their fantasy, music, recruitment and projection of real and imagined culture. Bollywood has introduced Indians of her ancient and distant cultures, and connected with distant lands from India and Indian cultures. We were surprised to see a Hindi movie being watched at a college dorm in Almaty, Kazakhstan, dubbed in Russian, as well at a TV channel in Peru dubbed in Spanish. But the songs were in Hindi without any subtitle. Bollywood has introduced India of many Western ideas, including pre-marital sex, casual sex, divorce, murder culture, LGBTQ, fantasy living, abandonment of families, and multiple partners pushing these norms in poor societies. This Bombay movie industry extends to Calcutta (Kolkata) to Madras (Chennai) to Bangalore (Bangaluru), and more.

Bihar: is one of the poorest states of India with hardworking peoples which contributed to India's cultural development before the days of Sri Buddha in 600 B.C. Many other divinities before Buddha also came from nearby areas. Now, because of its poverty Biharis find jobs of laborers, rickshaw pulling, street cleaning, shoe polish, construction, and more all over India, as well as top competitive bureaucratic jobs in India. Among many notable places of Bihar is Gaya and Nalanda. Gaya is a place where two rivers meet, and people go there to offer food and water to their ancestors. This could have been the reason why Buddha went there to meditate for his Nirvana. Nalanda is where a millennium-old university existed, until it was destroyed by a Muslim invader Bhaktiar Khilji in 1193 destroying 9 million books in that ancient time. He also destroyed Hindu and Buddhist shrines at Gaya until it was discovered by the British in late 1880s. So, book reading tradition must have existed for a long time. During my trip there with my older sister Didi to offer food and water called *pinda thaan* to our departed mother, we discovered through local guides called *pandas* who carried record book of ancestors who visited the site for the past 400+ years! Our *panda* guide told us that some Westerners and Easterners visit Gaya to offer food and water *pinda daan* to their ancestors. Biharis speak Hindi. All the elites needing their service learn to speak Hindi, the National Link Language, to hire them. Thus, one finds these workers in distant non-Hindi corners from Assam to Ahmadabad, Kashmir to Kanyakumari, and Kolkata to Kerala. Even though some Indian states are not teaching Hindi, including West Bengal and Tamil Nadu for their own sectarianism, but they depend on hard working Biharis to do their low-paying jobs. When their own citizens find jobs in other states, they use Hindi for communication. Sadly, in 2023, sectarian Tamils attacked poor Bihari workers in their Tamil Nadu state for ethnic cleansing, and in 2024 October state's Chief Minister condemned federal government for promoting the federal language.

Boots of Army: Those are not for oppression but bringing the nation together through diversity under one roof. Indian Army recruits from every village and every group of India, and their training is in Hindi. Thus, a diverse linguistic population learn one more language bringing them closer. We think most Indians speak or understand four or five languages. It becomes a natural part of life, lot like Europe where most people know more than one language. Once more reality was brought to us by an Army recruit from Manipur State, bordering Burma (Myanmar) in the east, as mentioned earlier. At the border exist the first city to be liberated from the Colonial Masters by the Indian National Army led by nationalist Subhas Chandra Bose. It is a national shrine. On Sachi's return journey to the state capital Imphal from the commemorative, bus took about two hours. There sat a Manipuri army recruit heading back to his 3-day journey to Pakistan border, telling in fluent Hindi how his life has changed, and how he will miss his family till his next vacation.

Babus (Mr.) are the bureaucrats of the centralized bureaucracy. Now there many Didis or Sisters as well. They are recruited through competitive national exam, and after that they go through unified training with one identity. They serve in every state and federal territory, irrespective of language, region, class, or religion. They have held the nation together, even when the ruling political elites are partisan or incompetent.

Bhakti means devotion. This is about faith. In case of Indians, especially Hindus, Jains, Sikhs and Buddhists it means devotion to the land without any militancy or partisan resistance.

Bidya or Vidya is the promotion of the idea of knowledge or learning. Goddess Saraswati represents knowledge and music. For millennia *pathashalas* or schools offered *vidya* by sages to common man and woman. This is a part of oral history as well. This has encouraged average citizens towards knowledge. And Lord Buddha, and Lord Jain's 600 BC-era onwards have promoted non-violence, pacifism, treating animals, plants, and Mother Nature with kindness. Animals and plants get protection in local beliefs as each deity has a *bahon* or pet, from lion to snake to mouse. Deities find shelter on flowers, trees, lakes and rivers, giving protection to that part of the nature. Buddha is the person who bridged Indian pre-history tales with real life. He is the last of the 12 incarnations or Avatars of God, only one with flesh-and-blood human in post-writing era. With Buddha, and Jain, of the same era they also highlighted the values of Sanatan or Traditional Belief as "Hindus" call themselves. Buddhist symbol of Ashok Chakra, 24-spoke wheel, connecting all directions of the world, is the symbol in India's tri-color flag. We don't know how many nations depict symbols of her minority religion or sub-sect in her flag of majority Christian, Muslim, Buddhist or Communist nations. Sacrifice for the family, for the nation, serving the society before oneself, Atma-Tyag or Self-Sacrifice, to the point one gives up everything. Thus symbolism in statues of Lord Jain is without any clothing. In folklore there are other kings who gave assets away, including the outfit he was wearing. This is to promote sacrifice, and sharing of wealth.

In 1960s in Calcutta of West Bengal State of India, our intelligentsia used to say, "We are building a nation without nationalism." Most didn't take part in Indian Independence Movement, although many nationalists turned communist after 1947 partition of India. Anyone going to temples or puja festival was projected as "communal" or racist, but not Muslims, Christians, Sikhs or Jains going to their mosques, churches or shrines, thus promoting a different kind of anti-majority racism rarely found in human history. To hold power and create division Britain encouraged anti-majority racism by promoting minority-sectarian policy of Muslim League Party in pre-1947 India. Contradiction was that the vast majority of the ruling Hindu-Sikh-Jain elites fled Islamic rule in their native Pakistan, East and West, for "Hindu" India. After Partition India gave them shelter. Congress Party which led Indian independence stressed on "nationalism," which brought India to freedom. India took many lessons from America, the first nation with a man-made constitution and democracy. The problem of new India was that all of its uniting nationalist symbols failed. The symbol that Gandhi represented was negated by the Left and the Right, as his policy of a century-old struggle to have a united India failed. Gandhi was able to save Indian minority Muslims who voted against him for Islamic Pakistan. Sadly, Gandhi wasn't able to save tens of millions of minority Hindus, Buddhists, Sikhs, Jains, and Christians in partitioned Pakistan, West and East. And then Gandhi was murdered by a Hindu fanatic leaving none of his symbols in action, except his memorial in Delhi. Neither his visit in 1946 to Noakhali in British eastern Bengal, now Bangladesh, where began a Hindu genocide under Muslim League Party rule of Bengal province; http://empireslastcasualty.blogspot.com /2022/01/gandhi-ashram-bangladesh-with-probini.html, nor his fasting in Calcutta saved any life. Gandhi fasted too on the day of Partition of India, and independence of Pakistan and India on August 14/15, 1947 but could not save non-Muslim minorities in Pakistan, including Bangladesh. Congress Party of India also banned "Hindu" groups after Gandhi's assassination, but didn't ban Islamist groups, although Islamist groups killed thousands of Indians, from Great Calcutta Killing starting on August 16 of 1946, to Noakhali genocide of October of 1946, and many more before and after the 1947 partition. Then the other symbol of independence nationalism, the flag, was also gone as the new flag was slightly different from the original flag of the Freedom Movement. Almost all Left parties denounced flying Indian flags in their political gatherings and mega

514

demonstrations with million in attendance. Flying only red flag with hammer-and-sickle was allowed. Rarely they flew Indian flag in their offices. (See, *Mukti: Free to be Born Again: Partitions of Indian Subcontinent, Islamism, Hinduism and Leftism, and Liberation of the Faithful,* Author House, U.S.A; 2015; and U.R. Link, U.S.A., 2021.) Only in 2021 before Kolkata Corporation Election Communist parties flew Indian flag in one or two rallies that became sensational news in local media. https://www.opindia.com/2021/08/westbengalcpimunfurl indiannatioal-flag-party-headquarters-first-time-75-yearssinceindepen-dence/ August 9, 2021. Mr. Gandhi was also denounced by the Left for being on the "Right." During Sachi's undergraduate studies in 1960s at our residential engineering college, one dorm had a stray dog who lived at the entrance of the dorm that some lefties named Gandhi. This is to insult him and his followers. This is when left was rising in Bengal. In all fairness to Indian political parties, flying Indian flag was banned by the British in colonial era, but continued in free India until an American-returnee went to the court to negate that law. This ban has entered Indian DNA as Indian flag is not displayed everywhere at every occasion as in America where the flag flies from gas stations to front yards to the White House. Sadly, Indians couldn't develop an independent mind. It was aided by extremists who opposed India's independence, supported by the pro-Colonial British Church groups in India who didn't support India's independence.

Gandhi Memorial at Birla House in Delhi where he was Murdered

Gandhi's Steps to the Meeting before His Assassination

A Gandhi Museum Wall

See https://empireslastcasualty.blogspot.com/2020/01/gandhi-memorial-at-birla-house-in-delhi.html

Gandhi Ashram, Noakhal, Bangladesh. Home Donated by Mr. Ghosh, Lawyer, after Gandhi Stayed There in 1946 for one night, during his Visit to Stop the Anti-Hindu Genocide under British Rule

Memorial of Several Acetic Gandhi Associates Were Murdered by the Army of Islamic Republic of Pakistan in 1971. Gandhi Went to Noakhali in 1946 to Stop Hindu Genocide and Mass Female Kidnapping and Abuse

See https://empireslastcasualty.blogspot.com/2008/12/educating-poor-and-orphaned-in.html.

Old Gandhi Statue at Noakhali, Bangladesh

Rebuilt Gandhi Statue at the Ashram, 2022, Honoring Sachi G. Dastidar for Help

At the New School in Gandhi Ashram, 2022

New Gandhi Memorial Institute Co-Ed School

Jayag Lake of Gandhi Ashram recovered from Illegal Confiscation by Sachi. An Illegal Mosque was Built on a Platform Top of the Lake to claim its Ownership

Sachi G Dastidar Honored at Gandhi Statue

The Great Calcutta Killing and Noakhali Genocide book

Rise of Anti-Communal Movement in India:

After a long time, in 2016 we saw a Left-style anti-communist mega march of Trinamool Party in Kolkata, blocking half the street instead of the entire street as was done by Left demonstrations. The party was of Ms. Mamata Banerjee of West Bengal which displayed Indian national flag as they marched through Kolkata streets heading to the central green space called Maidan, for a massive gathering. Flag was something new.

Trinamool Party Demonstration with Indian Flags,
Something new in Indian Bengal Politics

Citizens Trying to Touch Ms. Mamata Banerjee of Trinamool Party at Center

Trinamool came to power in West Bengal State of India in 2011 by ousting the Communist Party-Marxist-run Left Front Government. Left controlled over 80% to 90% of Assembly seats before being ousted. All nations have adopted some symbolism to bring their nations together, including people who sacrificed for their liberation. In sectarian India there is no remembrances of lives sacrificed for liberation from the British, for millions sacrificed during British and pre-British era, and in post-partition ethnic cleansing from Pakistan and Bangladesh, for tens of millions who found shelter in India. This is also a part of fatalism and subservient-ism. There is no discussion of oppression during Minority Islamic rule of India, including destruction of mandirs (temples), deities, killings, forced marriage, and forced conversion of the majority by a minority. It is a Hindu disease of having no memory, no way of commemorating the past and present, as their celebrations are with mythical deities. Ironically, many of our important deities are female, goddesses, from Mother Kali to Mother Durga representing strength when men couldn't defeat evil forces, to Mother Saraswati representing learning and education, Mother Lakshmi representing prosperity and wealth, Mother Manasa representing snake and wildlife protection, Mother Sitala, Mother Sita and many more. After independence none of these strengths could be used positively, as we were influenced by colonialism and rising anti-tradition ideology.

Since 2010s we have come to know of several Bengali groups, non-religious yet right conscious, some are 2nd or 3rd generation Pakistani-Bangladeshi-Hindu-Refugee-Indians, who want to commemorate some of the historic days and events of Bengali and Indian calendar – Noakhali Killing Day in October, Paschim-Banga Dibas (West Bengal Day) in June when in 1947 under British colonialism creation of West Bengal State was finalized, Partition Documentation Museum, Enemy Property Act of Pakistan which allowed Hindu minorities to be declared "Enemy of the State" and their property could be confiscated without notice and compensation, Ramna Kali Bari Temple Destruction Day when 900-year old Mother Kali's temple was destroyed by Pakistan Army with torturous killing of over 100 devotees, dirt-poor sheltered people, priests and priestesses; http://empireslastcasualty.blogspot.com /2021/12/rededicationoframna-kali-bari-mandir.html, Ananda Marg Day when 22 Hindu monks and nuns were murdered in broad daylight by communists and anti-Hindu thugs in the heart of Hindu-majority Kolkata; (https://empireslastcasualty.blogspot.com/2009/07/hindu-monks-and-nuns-killed-in-india-by.html), Nandi Gram Day where police and communist workers killed dozens of peasants to forcibly sell their land to a foreigner and many more; https://empireslastcasualty.blogspot.com/2008/12/nandi gram-bengal-india-communist.html. This is new in fatalistic culture.

Here's the killing site of Hindu monks and nuns in "Hindu" India without any arrest of killers in three decades, till 2024, although pictures exist in social media:

Hindu Monks and Nuns Murdered in Kasba (Bijan Setu)
Bridge at Ballygunj, Kolkata

Marching Groups Asking of Prosecution of Hindu Killers in Kolkata, India.

- *Picture: Courtesy of Social Media:*

Nandigram School: The Village where Scores of Peasants were Killed by Communists to sell their Property to a Foreigner

Nandigram School Kids

Martyr's Tablet at Nandigram, West Bengal, List of 17 Names of Men and Women Killed by Leftists

Finally, in 180-degree turn on December 2021 a conference and an exhibition was held in Kolkata on the 75th Anniversary of 1946 Noakhali Hindu genocide, and 50th Anniversary of 1971 Bangladesh Hindu genocide and Secular Bengali Muslim killings. It took 75 years to raise consciousness! We have had many forums in India on American, Russian, Chinese, and Cuban revolutions. Can a nation's progress be made ignoring one's own struggle, failure, and success? Does censorship help or hurt? Only recently, December of 2021, there was attempt by victim's descendants to learn about their families' experience through a "Bengali Hindu Genocide" discussion and exhibition.

Forum on Bengali Hindu Genocide, 11-12 December 2001, Kolkata

Can America, Europe, and Russia ignore sacrifices of WW I and WW II? Or, should China ignore Chairman Mao and its Revolution? India was taught to ignore its past greatness as well as subjugation. This is where identity of "Indians" plays a big role. Foreigners see "India" with one identity, but when a foreigner asks an Indian of identity, he or she sees oneself from one's distinct "regional" or "sub-regional" identity. We believe it is not that different from European Union as one political unit, and within it Polish and Portuguese, Italians and Irish see Europe differently. Just as in Europe someone may grow up not knowing German, in India one may grow up not knowing Hindi or Kannada, as they speak different language, and regional participation for India's Freedom Struggle varies widely. In the U.S. the nation has adopted many nationalistic symbols that bring the nation together and energize: The Flag, anthem, Thanksgiving, Fourth of July, Christmas, bugle at Memorial Day, gun, gun violence, slavery, anti-slavery, immigration, and others. In India every region of the nation did not take part aggressively for independence from colonial British-Christian oppression, or before British against foreign Islamic rulers many of whom treated indigenous population as kefirs to be treated as foreigners paying *jizya* tax to live in their own homeland. We are not supposed to say this. Religious conversion, whether by force or peacefully, changes convert's identity. Political conversion does that too. But, in our opinion, religious conversion is more serious and permanent in nature. Changing from Republication to Democratic party, or from Congress to Socialist or Dravida Munnetra Kazhagam party is lot simpler than changing from Islam to Christianity or from Hinduism to Judaism.

In one religious conversion there is death penalty sanctioned by religious doctrine. Thus, there is contradiction of history lessons. In India, some of the symbols that held the nation together has had to do with nature and nature-based festivities known as Sanatani festivities. Autumn Durga Puja of Mother Goddess is also known as Saradiyaa or Autumn Festival, and Holi as Spring Festival, and Rath Jatra or Chariot Festival as time for planting, taking home live twigs, and stocking ponds with fish as Monsoon Festival. Tiny number of groups celebrate Indian Independence Day in America, but almost all celebrate Diwali, Holi, Shiv Ratri, etc. After 75 years of independence, is it time again to rediscover her heritage as well.

Identity in America and the World:

Identity is a very big issue in any nation and for nation building, as was discussed earlier. At certain level all the population of the Subcontinent had "Indian" identity, but it changed with Persian-Turkish-Arab and British colonialism. From Afghanistan to Pakistan to Tibet, Burma and Sri Lanka evolved as new nations with partition and politics. Once independence came to Pakistan, soon Muslim identity changed. East Pakistan began struggle for independence from minority West Pakistanis culminating in Pakistan's Hindu Genocide, secularist extermination of 1971. In India ethnic identity created making states with ethnic-linguistic boundaries. In Pakistan, after Bangladesh independence began separate Muslim identities among Baloch, Sindh, Muhajir, Punjabi, Pathan, Kashmiris and many more. Some struggles are still continuing.

During Muslim rule in Bengal in the second millennium, the Bengali Hindus, then vast majority of the population continued teaching their kids Bengali. With conversation, learning Bengali was not so important to Muslims as they changed their identity. Thus, a learning gap developed with Hindu and Muslim communities which added to sectarianism. In 1700s and 1800s during British rule replacing Muslim kings in India, many top Muslim *pirs* or preachers in northern India and in Bengal proposed not to slaughter cows as they are respected by Hindus, to have a good relation with their Hindu neighbors, and cow slaughter is not done in Arabia. Their appeal was rejected by political leaders. Identity was changing. New converts started changing their name to Arabic or Persian names. Many traditions of Bengali lifestyles started to change. In late 1800s and early 1900s many Muslims intellectuals tried for Muslim Reformation Movement in Bengal, like the Hindu Reformation Movement of 1800s, but it didn't go far. Begum Rokeya Sakhawat Hossain, also known as Begum Rokeya, fought for women's liberation and fought against head and body covering for Muslim women. In 1980s an Indian-Bangladeshi-Muslim dictator grabbed the power in Bangladesh. To be popular, he pushed for head covering for girls when many Muslim-majority objected. When we visited a school in a rural area in southern Bangladesh, many girls complained against that. And one shouted out, "Kaka Uncle, but Hindus don't have to wear that." Some kids cheered. Then a wise one said, "But, then you can be identified in the street and can be abducted." Four decades later that identity has changed. Now many Bengalis in New York are sending their girls with head cover that their grandma opposed as a sign of oppression. And in 2022 a few minority Muslims were demanding head covering in the U.S. to identify as Muslim, but not with traditional Americans. They don't want to identify with struggling Iranian, Afghan or Pakistani girls who are opposed to head cover. Will they be able to give same rights to Christians, Jews, and Buddhists in their nations? In a democracy it is risky if majority identities are degraded. Compromises for any minority groups could influence the majority. It may bring political strain in democracy.

In some ways U.S. can become home to sectarian identity than a universal one. Back in the Subcontinent, in a high-density country, especially in urban areas people of diverse ethnic, linguistic, and religious groups, live next to each other, sharing their culture and habits, as there are not many hiding places. One has to walk to work and market. Thus, in neighborhood *baroari* public puja celebrations everyone participates, offers puja-prayers irrespective of one's ethnicity, thus introducing and exposing diverse traditions and cultures. In the U.S., in a car-dominated neighborhood, we rarely meet our neighbors for collective social relationship. Summer block parties are one way to bring us closer. Most blocks do not do that. In New York City Mexican regional groups may meet separately on the basis of one's separate identity. We will not be surprised if separate identity exists among immigrants from pluralistic countries like Indonesia, Nigeria, Pakistan, Switzerland, Egypt, South Africa, and more. In the U.S. our schools and colleges bring young people together. That is not true in many places, except schools and colleges with competitive entrance exam, as all colleges do not get students from every corner. It is changing. Soviet Union brought diverse population closer through Russification, and China through Sinification. India with her diverse indigenous population couldn't do what U.S., Russia, China, Brazil, or Mexico could do. In Sachi's class in Kazakhstan in 1999 he was told by his students that they belong to over a dozen "Nationality" among 20 students, but they all spoke Russian. They were Kazakh, Russian, Uzbek, Dungan, Kyrgyz, Korean, German, Ukrainian, Azari, Siberian, Jewish, Tajik, and more. From the Soviet era local ID cards showed those nationalities. During our tour of Kazakhstan, Uzbekistan and Kyrgyzstan, our driver with Kazakhstan ID but with Ukrainian name born-in-Siberia used to be questioned more than normal at border crossings. Our look confused our identity to many. We got invitation to the opening of an ashram of Sri Krishna at Almaty, Kazakhstan's capital, because of our look. The head of the ashram was a Caucasian American, who changed his own identity. The new institution Sachi taught, developed a research center, and published the first English language journal in Central Asia in 2000 edited by him, was earlier an institution to teach Communist Party bureaucracy in Russian. After the demise of Soviet Union, it changed to English-medium university of free-market management. What an identity change! It was great to see how welcoming Kazakhstan was. A former student of mine, now holding a top U.N. position, is still in touch with us, and stayed with us in New York while going for higher studies in the U.S.

Central Asian Journal, Kazakhstan, Editor Sachi G. Dastidar, 2001

Kazakh Culture statues, Almaty

Kazakh Culture statue, Almaty

In America, her identity was highlighted by its revolutionary leaders. One really good thing was that they didn't become anti-English as England tried to deny its independence. England's oppression in India and of indigenous peoples was very serious, but she was able to keep that under the rug. Many leaders like Gandhi, Nehru, or communist leader Jyoti Basu, were all educated in England, thus had a separate loyalty. They were the opposite nationalists like Sri Aurobindo and Michael Madhusudan, who studied in England but became very conscious of their Indian identity. From 1947 there were many opposition parties. It was not just the Muslim League Party who opposed unified India.

Most of its supporters stayed back in India, but were not provided leadership as how to become "pro-India." Even the Left movement's slogan, "Yea azadi jhuta hai," or "This is a false freedom" added to new anti-India force. Left members who marched in India but chose not to live with their neighbors in East or West Pakistan, but condemned India who gave shelter, but not the party who cleansed them.

As mentioned, Pakistan could claim its Indian and Hindu heritage, like India. But the term Hindu is a derogatory word for many there. This is true for Afghanistan as well. Since Islamization they have struggled to adopt either Arabic or Persian identity. There are millions of people who are comfortable with their pre-Islam identity. However, almost all of them are terrified of militants, and foreign funding from non-democratic states. Now some groups are pushing Bangladesh to become like Afghanistan. Since Islam is a very militant colonizing ideology allowed in killings of non-believers, including of pre-Islam indigenous peoples of Arabia, it is and will be hard to turn to pluralistic peace like Christianity or Jainism. In 1990s in our neighborhood in New York City we went to get gas for our car at 263rd Street. Seeing us, a friendly Pakistani gas station helper asked where we were from. We replied "Bengal." He asked, "Which Bengal?" We were extremely surprised as very few people in the world know that there are two Bengals. Sachi replied, "Both," and asked how do you know this. He said "I was a soldier there." We asked, "When?" He replied, "During Bangladesh war." We were shocked, and asked, "Did you go to kill people?" He nodded. I asked, "Did you go to kill Hindus?" He replied, "Oh to hotai hai," meaning "That (Hindu killing) always happens."

In open societies like the U.S., India or Europe it is possible to debate and discuss "Who's life matter?" In closed societies, this is difficult. We wonder how many Russians knew of the plight of Ukrainians since 2022 invasion. Or, how many Chinese know about Uighur's and Tibetan's plight in China? Or, in Hindu majority India, the plight of indigenous Hindu and Buddhist minority in India's Christian-majority Mizoram?

All nations try to come up with their own identity. Many nations have diverse population, and they often choose to identify themselves separately. Thus, Europe has an identity as European Union, and another as German, French, Andorran, Lichtenstein, Italian and Irish. Then within old countries like Italy, identities may vary from Milan to Rome to Sicily to Sardinia. It may vary in Ukraine from east to west. In Spain it may vary from Catalonia to Andalucía to Castella. For non-settler countries this is normal. As a result, sometimes in order to protect their identity, separatism with political struggle take hold. New settler colonial nations have certain advantage that they are able to create identity mostly determined by colonizers and elites. How much Cherokee or Seminole cultures are able to influence mainstream America, even within their territorial area? In a culture where one has to seek blessings from 14 generations of ancestors, it is hard to disconnect from the past, unless there is revolution.

Thus, after Indian partition, Islamic Pakistan was able easily force its majority Muslims not to learn its past tradition, and impose a North Indian Urdu language lot easily than India trying to teach common language Hindi. Pakistan faced linguistic opposition from the Bengali majority, although Pakistan did not face any problem by declaring herself an Islamic Republic where pre-Islam indigenous peoples would be constitutionally discriminated. In Pakistan of 2020 linguistic minorities of Baloch, Sindh, Punjab, Pathan and Kashmir have given up their own languages and scripts. Religious monotheism has played a very big role in changing psyche of diverse groups, whereas Hindu tolerance and pluralism have allowed even groups of a few thousand in a nation of billion people, demand and receive education in one's language. Pluralism is good for humanitarianism, but gets complicated for governance. Just imagine U.S. having 1,700 political parties in place of two, and each state offering education in separate languages! Just imagine New York City School Board offering instructions in 30 languages, as in City of Kolkata. In case of colonization, almost all the newly conquered older cultures gave up their languages and cultures. This is true for Arabization. A similar process also occurred with Christian-

European colonization of Africa, North and South America, the Caribbean, and Australia. One difference is that Europe, including England, has always had free thinkers who challenged European colonization and treatment of colonized peoples. Another advantage in colonizing North and South America, Africa and Australia, is that locals didn't have written scripts. Such challenge by enlightened Arabs used. Even in 2020, how many Islamic groups and governments in Muslim-majority nations came forward to condemn or criticize massacre of Yazidis in Syria and Iraq? In the Subcontinent we notice further change of Arabization as some give up their traditional outfit for Arabized one (see Ahmed, Mohiuddin, "Swadhikar thekey swadhinata" [From freedom of rights to independence] in *Prothom Alo*, March 26, 2020). Dhuti/Dhoti for men and sari for women is no more Bengali for some. Fortunately, there are debates in liberal circles in India, Bangladesh, and Pakistan about their common identity. West Bengalis are changing their identity towards America, while Bangladeshis are leaning on Arab and Yemeni outfit. If one comes to Jamaica area of Queens, New York City where the office of ISPaD: Indian Subcontinent Partition Documentation Project is located, one can easily find that identity change. A large number of Bangladeshi-American women have given up their traditional sari outerwear of women for Yemeni outfit with head cover while Hindus, Buddhists and Christians wear sari. Men gave up their outerwear after partition of Pakistan for Arabized outfit. Whereas, many women followers – white, black and Asian - of meditation guru Sri Chinmoy, whose ashram is nearby, wear sari, and men devotees wear white outfit, identifying with the ancient tradition, much like Mother Teresa and her followers adopting many Indian symbolisms in their Christianity.

Sachi met Sri Chinmoy in the "Heaven" at 32,000 feet in the sky while flying back from Chicago to New York City. Sri Chinmoy was returning after opening the 1992 Bicentenary of World Congress of Religions in Chicago, and Sachi was returning from a conference in Wisconsin, via Chicago. Since then, Sachi and Shuvo, with mom Shefali and sister Joyeeta have been honored by the meditation guru several times. Sachi was honored when in 2006 Sri Chinmoy asked Sachi for reading from his book, *Living Among the Believers: Stories from the Holy Land down the Ganges*. Meditation and yoga were new experience for Sachi and Shefali as those were absent during their school and college days in post-colonial India. Those were practically excluded in pre-independence India to fulfill the wishes of British-Christian colonial masters, and pro-partition supporters of Muslim League Party in their post-1947 independence Congress and Communist Party ruled West Bengal State of India. This was possibly true in other states, as education is a state matter in India. In 2022 Sachi fulfilled his desire to visit Sri Chinmoy home at Purba Sakpura, Chittagong District of Bangladesh, though he was not a member of his Meditation Center. Sri Chinmoy's surviving cousin welcomed Sachi with open arms like a true Bengali. See http://empireslastcasualty.blogspot.com/2022/10/visitingchittagog-home-of-meditation.html.

Sri Chinmoy Home in Chittagong, Bangladesh, 2022 with no one Living There

Sri Chinmoy Presenting the First Citation for Married Couples to Shefali and Sachi, 2007

Sri Chinmoy Ashram in Jamaica, New York City, 2021

In the West discussing and learning of their past and old traditions are not condemned. But there is pride among other converts for destroying relics of their ancestral past as the Bamiyan Buddha destruction in Afghanistan, Ramna Kali Temple destruction by Pakistan Army in Bangladesh, Somnath Temple destruction in Gujrat by Persian king, and thousands of such examples in India and Subcontinent. In many nations going to old shrines of their ancestors bring severe punishment. There are regular reports from many nations. No question that there is large number of tolerant citizens who take pride in their past. However, most are vilified. This has added a taboo in media and literary circle, but not followed by liberal media in the West. Censoring truth is not good. It is like hiding the death of Christ. In the subcontinent no discussion is allowed in most cases of atrocities and destruction.

Kutub Minar, Delhi: The First Victory Tower of Islamic Conquerors built with Destruction of 29 Hindu and Jain Temples, but Censored in India

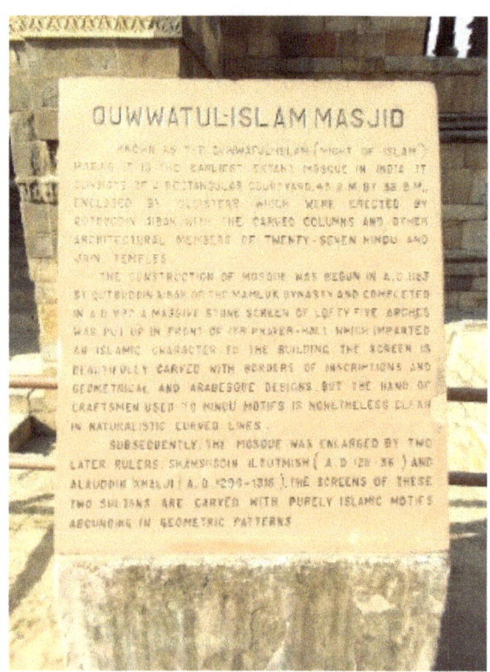

Kutub Minar Victory Tower Tablet from British Era Documenting Destruction of 29 Temples

Mosque Built at Varanasi on Top of Ancient Shiva Temple Hidden Behind Newly Built Towers

Krishna Temple at Mathura Built on the Walls of Mosque Built on Top of Ancient Krishna Temple. New Shrine was built Many Years after the Temple Was Destroyed.

The Mosque Sits on top of Thousands of Years old Krishna Temple, Mathura, Uttar Pradesh

Sachi Offering Durba – Grass Top and Flower in 1986 at the 900-Year-Old Ramna Kali Mamdir Temple Site of Black Mother Kali Destroyed by the Army of Islamic Republic of Pakistan with Brutally Killing of 100+ Devotees in 1971

Our identity changes routinely. One does not have to go far than studying Bengalis, as we carry Indian, Bangladeshi, American, Hindu, Muslim, Buddhist, atheist, colored and bald person's identity. Until 1947 when the Partition of Bengal and India happened, Bengalis were almost divided between Hindus and Muslims. Then we started to change our identity. (See Rafiuddin Ahmed, *The Bengali Muslims 1871-1906, A Quest for Identity*, Oxford University, New York, 1981, and Akbar S. Ahmed, *Jinnah, Pakistan and Islamic Identity: The Search of Saladin*, Routledge, London; 1997.) Separate identity with names didn't happen with Christian converts as they generally kept a "Christian" name as the middle name. This separate identity was used by the British colonial power to further divide Indi ans, and Indians gladly fell into that trap. Even in 2022 British Army's Nepali i.e., Gurkha soldiers asked for the same treatment as White soldiers (see *Statesman*, March 22, 2022).

Change is inevitable. In 1800s and 1900s with the rise of Indian nationalism, many Indians tried to learn from Reformation, English and European Enlightenment. They tried to adopt the best of both worlds. Thus, they pushed for identity from their language to culture to clothing. That included our British-educated father and British-honored mother. They taught us in Bengali medium in free India, not English. Within 50 years from independence India joined full speed for Westernization, not necessarily adopting their work ethic, individualistic values as opposed to family-based values of Afro-Asian cultures, promoting anti-racism values, and post-Industrial Revolution mindset of research. Still in India there is pull between "Indian" and "Western" cultures. There are discussions on promoting violence vs nonviolence, adopting nature-based living vs nature-dominating lifestyles, and more. Even in China, with a very long written history, proud culture and language, devaluation of their traditional religion for atheism, and for capitalism began under one party dictatorship. It also jumped full speed towards Europeanization. We were surprised that in many hotels, from Xian to Xinjiang, seeing our U.S. passport, the receptionists asked for our "English" names. They were surprised to hear that we didn't have one. This was quite reveling. And so many Chinese migrants in America give up their name and faith for American name and religion. A former Party official of China living in America asked, "Here in New York, I attend a Christian church. What church do you attend?"

Identity in Bengal, Pakistan, Bangladesh, India and the Subcontinent:

Issue of identity is always complex anywhere, but we found it is significantly different in old countries of Africa, Europe and Asia, versus new countries of North and South America, the Caribbean, and Australia. In the new countries immigrants knowingly arrive to give up many of their traditional identities, however, at times some of those identities are gradually adopted until it is localized in their new land via food, music, dance, restaurants, churches, and more. Thus, in an open America with English-Protestant identity when the Catholic Irish arrived in mid-1800s, they faced many issues from housing to employment, even in Boston. An open society allows discussion and debate of these. Since the Civil Rights Era as the nation opened up to Afro-Asian-Latino immigration, colored people from those continents have become a part of American identity. We have a feeling that if we were young, our passports would have been examined with extra care for its authenticity in many nations. Our looks give us an identity. One of really enjoyable moment came in Brazil-Argentina border – as mentioned earlier – when we were visiting one of the world's wonders, the Iguazu Falls, in a tourist bus full of Italian tourists. Every time the bus stopped some young kids would surround us to figure our identity. They were trying to figure out in what language we were talking. Finally, after three or four stops one of the parents came to us and asked in English, "Where are you from?" Our answer "New York" puzzled them. At the next stop the man came and told us, "We thought you are Indian." To which we nodded confusing them even more. In Rumania's Bucharest Airport our passport exam took lot longer than usual. We didn't fit their imagination. In the land border between Almaty, Kazakhstan and Bishkek, Kyrgyzstan, the harassment of Shefali was extreme, but as tourists one has to be prepared for that. Many Bangladeshis told us that at Kolkata airport, they have to pay bribe at the customs counter. We were surprised as we never had to pay a penny of bribe. Once as Sachi was traveling from Kolkata, India to Dhaka, Bangladesh, both Bengali-speaking regions, a 30-minute flight, he found immigration officers checking Bangladeshis harder than him. When he asked the officers, one of them showed newspaper articles showing 80% to 90% Bangladeshis travel with false passports. Once Bangladeshis came to meet us in Kolkata without any visa and passport. Visitors said that it was much easier and cheaper to do so than going through official paperwork. This is the other side of corrupt, poor and incompetent bureaucracy of Indian state of West Bengal, and the nation of Bangladesh. Like America, local police and bureaucracy are managed by states, not by the federal government in Delhi. Thus, in West Bengal all Bangladeshi Hindu refugees and Muslim settlers got their Indian passport by giving false documents, and through local bribery. Number is astronomical! Tens of millions of Hindu refugees got their passport, ID cards, through normal illegal process, as did illegal Muslim colonizers, through bribery. Very recently one murderer of Bangladesh's founding father Sheikh Mujibur Rahman and his family was found in Kolkata, India with Indian passport and local ID. The killer moved during Communist rule of West Bengal; (https://nenow.in/neighbour/bangladesh /another-mujib-killer-picked-up-in-kolkata.html.) Also, during Communist rule in 1990s journalists found that one of the communists elected to rural Gram Panchayat (village council) in eastern Nadia district of West Bengal state was

Bangladeshi. The elected person was an anti-Hindu activist of Muslim League Party there. In 1990s when we were visiting our teacher sister-in-law's family in Raina, Bardhaman District of West Bengal, knowing our research and writing, locals asked us to visit the Head of the Gram Panchayat Village Council who was from our ancestral district in Bangladesh. When Sachi asked the same old question, "How come an atheist like you fled your Muslim-majority homeland for Hindu India?" There was no answer. (https://empireslastcasualty. blogspot.com/2021/04/story-of-lovededication-and-tribute.html.) And very recently many Burmese (Myanmar) Rohingya refugees who fled to Bangladesh were found in West Bengal with Indian ID. This time paperwork was provided by the ruling sectarian anti-communist party. See (https:// www.sangbadpratidin.in/kolkata/uttarpradesh-ats-arrests-two-rohing- ya-youth-from-kolkata-who-helpmakingfakeidentitycards/ November 21, 2021; and http://www.anandabazar.com/state/%E0%A6% A8%E0% A6%AE%E0%A6%AD%E0%A7%9C%E0%A7%9F%E0%A6%9D% E0%A7%9C%E0%A6%96%E0%A6%A3%E0%A6%A1%E0%A6% A5%E0%A6%95%E0%A6%AA%E0%A6%B8%E0%A6%AA%E0% A6%B0%E0%A6%9F%E0%A6%93%E0%A6%95%E0%A6%B0%E 0%A7%9F%E0%A6%B0%E0%A6%9C%E0%A6%89%E0%A6%B2 1.105410;http://www.telegraphindia.com/1150114/jsp/frontpage/story _8332.jsp#.VLZXcmYo7IU January 14, 2015.) In May of 2024 a Bangladeshi Muslim parliamentarian was murdered in Kolkata, India with unbelievable butchery. At least six Bangladeshi Muslims were involved, plus one American-Bangladeshi. What it exposed that almost all of them, except the parliamentarian, entered India illegally through West Bengal border, and now hold Indian documents, including home ownership. This also explains how complex is governing India, as long as regional politicians are able to use corruption and racism against all-India politics. (See May 25, 2024, *Prothom Alo* https://www.prothomalo.com/opinion/column/brluyz8adw Why Bangla- desh MP is Killed in Kolkata?)

It is so rare to get a legal Indian passport with official place of birth in Bangladesh that when we submitted the application for a passport in 1986 for our mother the passport office located in Kolkata's downtown in Brabourne Road tried to return back the application asking for "Migration Certificate" because her place of birth was Barisal, East Bengal, India, now in Bangladesh. In 1905 Bangladesh was part of India, and hotbed of Indian independence movement. Sachi's Indian passport showing place of birth, plus Sachi's challenge in asking the counter officer of his "Migration Certificate" as he spoke with East Bengali accent convinced him to accept the application. Even in 2019 when Sachi interviewed many Bangladeshi Hindu refugees – including a taxi driver in his 30s, and a young man in twenties who was sent to Kolkata as a teenager when his father was attempted to be murdered second time in his Bangladesh hometown, had Indian passport and ID. A cocoanut vendor from Khulna, and a handyman from Chittagong living in West Bengal (see YouTube's ispad1947 channel for their interviews), all were honest by saying that they were carrying Indian identity documents, and all said that their life has changed from a homeowner to homeless, and from assured life to life of despair with hope! It may not be an exaggeration to say that possibly 99% of Hindu refugees in India got their paperwork by submitting false documents. They were joined later by Christians and Buddhists who were very small minorities, possibly less than 0.5%. This is where corruption helped the destitute. Can one imagine 99% of immigrants to U.S. or Canada or Australia get citizenship and voting rights through fake documents? And, many Muslim-majority also got Indian documents, including folks who confiscated Hindu homes and property, as mentioned earlier. Traveling through South Africa reminded us of India's West Bengal as so many of taxi drivers were from neighboring nations. They all said they just crossed the border. In poor fatalistic India legal and illegal migration of the persecuted and persecutor complicate conversation. In other regions of India citizens are completely unaware of this saga of ethnic cleansing and illegal citizenship. Many Muslims from the Bangladesh are settling in India using the same fake documents. Without illegal Muslim migration, their population couldn't rise faster than Hindus in West Bengal and India. However, in case of

Muslim majority illegal migrants from Pakistan-Bangladesh, many of the same individuals or their families forcibly confiscated Hindu properties through "Enemy Property Act" by declaring indigenous Hindus to be "Enemies of the State." Nowhere else in the world there are political parties who want to treat persecuted and persecuting equally.

This is also unparalleled in human history. During interviews with media personalities in the U.S. and in India we were baffled to get their reaction when they learned that Shefali's family and that of Sachi's, and possibly 80% of Indian-Bengali immigrants in America, are Pakistani-Bangladeshi-Hindu-Refuge-Indians, and that over 49 million Hindu minority are missing from Bangladesh Census from 1947 Indian Partition (1941 Census) through 2001 Census. (See *Bengal's Hindu Holocaust: Partition of India and Subsequent Change*, Publisher Garuda Prakashan, Delhi, India, 2021, and *Empire's Last Casualty: Indian Subcontinent's Vanishing Hindu and Other Minorities*, Firma KLM Publishers, Kolkata, 2008.) A highly educated Christian Indian Charted Accountant from Southern India said that in his state no one knows about ethnic cleansing of minorities. Sadly, on January 14, 2022 at a discussion with Bangladesh Minorities in America on Durga Puja Anti-Hindu pogrom starting on October 13, 2021, the Bangla Ambassador to the U.S., mentioned that the Hindu population in his homeland is going down since 1901 census, shockingly, he also said that only 25 Bangladeshis received Indian citizenship each year, thus Bangladesh couldn't be losing so many Hindu and non-Muslim minorities. This statement reaffirms the belief among religious minorities and secular Muslims that in Muslim-majority nations "Minority non-Muslim lives do not matter." He didn't tell us how they have evaporated 50 million+ Hindus from his homeland in barely five decades. He also gave false statistics of how many Hindus were killed during the 2021 Durga Puja Pogrom, and how many temples and deities were destroyed. (U.S. Senator Schumer informed Sachi in April 2023 that U.S. has approved millions of dollars to help 2021 pogrom victims.) Sadly, many Hindu minorities were arrested while trying to protect their families. Ambassador even tried to equate victims of pogrom and perpetrators of pogrom as equal. This is exactly what Pakistan Army and minority West Pakistan Administration said during 1971 genocide of Hindu minority and secular Muslims of East Pakistan. It reminded the group of an old Bengali proverb, "They think we are camphor." Camphor evaporates in thin air. Indian Government's new Citizenship Act of late 2010s was a big relief for persecuted minorities from Pakistan, Bangladesh and other neighboring countries. Founder of a relief organization in Kolkata had to flee his homeland when he was only 13, not seeing his parents for over 15 years. He is now involved with educating the poor in India.

Street Children Organization of Kolkata Gathered for Outdoor Lessons,
Founded in late 2000 by a Hindu Refugee

Street Children Group Meeting with Probini Foundation of New York in Kolkata, India

Identity has always been an issue in all nations and in nation building. However, one of the best places to study identity and nation building is India, and within India the partitioned provinces of Punjab in the west and Bengal in the east. Issues of identity may not be that different from partitioned India and Pakistan, Ireland and North Ireland, Cyprus and North Cyprus, Israel and Palestine, Sudan and South Sudan, Columbia and Panama, Serbia and Bosnia, Russia and Ukraine, Soviet Union with Estonia, Lithuania, Latvia, Mali and Nigeria, China's Tibet, Xinjiang and Inner Mongolia, and many more. In case of Punjab Province in the West Pakistan, cleansing of all non-Muslims after 1947 partition – Hindus, Sikhs, Buddhists, Jains, and many Christians – has settled the non-Muslim minority issue. In Pakistan in one stroke the Punjabi identity changed as schooling was done in North Indian new Urdu language written in Arabic script, not Punjabi, thus creating a new barrier between Pakistani Punjab and Indian Punjab. Still, at the grass roots level, there is tremendous warmth between groups that many are afraid of sharing in public. Our trips to Pakistan, Bangladesh and Sri Lanka exposed that. As our kids were horse riding in Pakistani Punjab and we were relaxing on the side, one man rushed like a bullet and said, "I am Bhatti, a Muslim, but we were like you, Hindu," then folded hands, bowed his head, and rushed back vanishing in one of the stores. In Pakistan, during one of our trips to Peshawar University, we were pleased to see that almost everyone wanted to take pictures with us in Indian outfit, and many scholars said, "This is our heritage" https://empireslastcasualty.blog spot.com/2008/12/first-war-of-indian-indepencence-1857.html. And in Lahore, the cultural and intellectual capital of Pakistan, we had similar experience. At another time at Lahore airport, a woman rushed to Shefali saying, "Didi, Older Sister, we are Hindu from Sind Province. You look like Hindu. I am taking my 90-year-old father to meet his brother whom we haven't seen since partition as he fled to India." We were able to assure them of needed assistance in Delhi too. We still wonder which of our identities brought closer to families!

There are risk takers in most nations. But, most of the individuals trying to learn and discuss about the past almost always end up as exile in Europe,

America, or India. Can social and intellectual change happen from outside? Doubtful. After lots of struggle Vasant (Basant) Panchami, the Fifth Day of Spring, has entered as a holiday in Pakistani Punjab for kite flying, although that day is associated with Seasonal Change of Mother Nature, and Celebration with Mother Saraswati, the Goddess of Learning, Music and Education. In Islamic nations celebration of their past tradition is very difficult. Still in 2010 several Muslim activists wanted to save an ancient pre-Islam Gor Khartee Hindu Shiva Temple in Peshawar, Pakistan. Sachi was asked by some activists to help them save their Hindu heritage.

He joined them and were able to save the *mandir* (temple) https://empireslastcasualty.blogspot.com/2013/05/gorkhatreegorkhuttreeshiv-amandir.html. Another contradiction in the Subcontinent is that such rebuilding may not be possible in Hindu-majority India as seeing such reconstruction may be called "communal" or "Hindu racism" or "Hindu fundamentalism" by neo-colonial Indians, pro-colonial foreigners, and groups seeking favor from anti-India foreign powers. As we mentioned earlier, if one is not taught history, people will not learn their past. If you are not taught about the War of Independence and 4th of July, how would we learn about that struggle? While visiting old downtown of Lakshmi Bag of Pakistan's intellectual capital, Lahore, shopkeepers welcomed us with open arms as "Indian" or "Hindu." Fine. We were surprised to see so many inscriptions in Sanskrit, the mother language of Indo-European languages. One host said, "These were owned by foreigner Indians." When we said, they were Punjabis, not foreigners. Shopkeepers were stunned and excited. One said, "How come I didn't know about that?" Then again, we rarely meet the folks on opposite side. One of the large dailies of Pakistan wanted us to write our experience. Sachi did that. At the same downtown as we went to a book store, we met the opposite, with the bookstore owner telling bluntly that he does not carry books written by Hindus. On the other hand, the populous Pakistani daily was eager to publish Sachi's three articles ending with the most populous Islamic holiday of Eid of 1990.

Here are some pictures of *The Pakistan Times* daily with Sachi's essays on Pakistan visit.

British Era National Museum of Pakistan in Lahore with "Indian" Symbols

India's National Symbol from Buddhist Era at the Museum

An Old Sanskrit Tablet

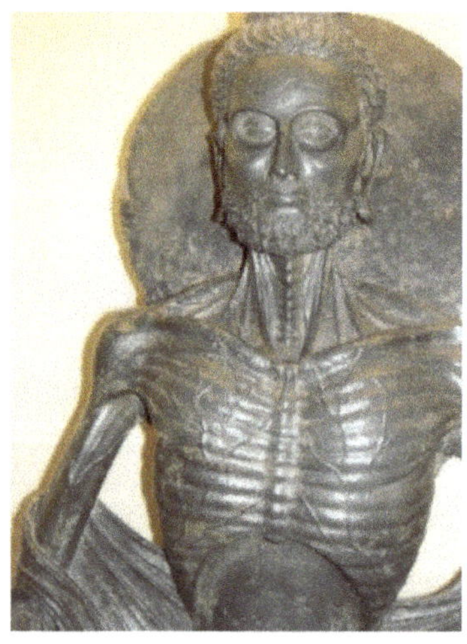

Fasting Buddha Statue at the Museum

Pakistan Tower in Lahore built After 1947 Partition

With Hostess Older Sister Didi, 3rd From Left, Prof. Nabila, right, at Lahore, Pakistan

A Neighborhood Park, Lahore, Pakistan

An Abandoned Sikh Temple, Lahore, maintained by Refugees Overseas as Sikhs were Cleansed for India at 1947 Partition

Nationhood and identity are complex, and one's perception varies based on teaching, preaching, brain washing, conviction, lessons from history, socialization, visits and more. Even within the Subcontinent, studies of Bengal before and after Partition opens our eyes lot more than Punjab partition with institutionalized division and complete ethnic cleansing. At the end of 1800s Hindu-Muslim population divide in Bengal Province was almost 50/50. Colonial Britain seeing this demography, and Bengal's leadership by her Hindus in India's Independence Movement, pushed for creation of a separate Muslim identity by partitioning Bengal Province into Muslim East Bengal and Hindu West Bengal, when nobody wanted that. Britain was able to polarize the population with separate apartheid-like voting system, when no Muslim or Hindu wanted that. Before and after 1947 Partition there was huge support for Pakistani Islamic identity, however, once attempts were made to wipe out East Bengali identity, East Pakistan turned around and ruling Muslim League Party got wiped out in early 1950s election. Then came the Language Movement for demanding Bengali to be a National Language of Pakistan. Several Bengali activists were killed on February 21, 1952, and changed Bengali Muslim identity from Islamic to a secular language-based identity. But Pakistan pushed for Islamization and Arabization, until the Bengalis won majority in Pakistan's first open election in 1970. Instead of handing over power to the majority Awami League Party,

(West) Pakistan Administration and Army engaged on anti-Hindu genocide and secular Muslim extermination killing over 3 million people – 90% to 95% Hindu – in just 9 months, and displacing over 10 million citizens outside, again 90% to 95% Hindu minority. This turn of identity narrative was changed again with the murder of Bangladesh Founding Father Rahman and his extended family in 1975, and then ruled by various intolerant dictators. And again after 2024 overthrow of Awami League administration, new identity problem has emerged.

Each time extremists came to power in Bangladesh, they started their act of ethnic cleansing. Sachi was a firsthand witness to 1991, 1992 and 2001 pogroms when he visited many destroyed and desecrated homes and villages. Even during the pro-secular rule beginning in 2008, identity issues remained. To create separate identity new words are added in language, and a pro-Islamist government in Bangladesh changed the Bengali calendar, so that it doesn't match with her neighboring Indian Bengal, and the broader Indian calendar. In this identity issue has entered Islamic *madrassa* schools. In one madrassa an 8th grade Bengali book didn't include any literature from a "Hindu-named" person, whose writings from 1700s onwards possibly contribute 80% to 90% of Bengali literature. When asked, the headmaster said that he has no idea as to why it doesn't contain any writings of minorities as the books are provided by the Government. To change Bengali identity further, a political-religious force is working to confiscate ancestral home-land-property-pond-business by calling them "Enemy (now Vested) Property." Pakistan created that racist law for confiscation of indigenous minority assets without any compensation and notice.

Identity change is also happening in India's states, but at a different mode. In India different linguistic-ethnic groups live and work together in all corners of India. Thus, as in Europe, most Indians speak many languages, live and eat together, and even intermarry. In Bangladesh it is changing as well. Recently, one of the prominent Bangladeshi intellectual Shamsuzzaman wrote that "During our Islamic Eid holiday we wore beautiful *dhuti* and *punjabi* shirt," which will be unthinkable now ("Eid of Bengali Muslims," Shamsuzzaman Khan, *ISPaD:*

The Partition Center Journal 2020, 13-15; and in Bengali, *Prothom Alo*, May 22, 2020.) Wearing *dhuti* by Muslims still continues in West Bengal, though people assume money is flowing to them from intolerant societies to bring Arabized identity. In January of 1982 our family was present at the annual Saraswati Puja of the Mother Goddess of Education and Music in Kolkata. Everybody kept their books at the Feet of the Deity for blessing, including books of babies. Before the service started, we noticed a group of five men on our rooftop garden waiting for the puja service to start. They were workers of father's construction agency. All were wearing formal *dhuti* and *punjabi* outerwear. In India, for these types of celebrations people often invite themselves. We invited them to our living room where the puja service was taking place.

Dad didn't know they were there, but was very happy to see them. They offered *anjali* flowers to Ma Saraswati like everyone else, and then waited for Prasad or Blessed Food offered to Ma Saraswati. Hearing we've just returned from Bangladesh, the first thing they asked at the rooftop garden, "Do Bangladeshis speak Bengali like us?" After some queries they asked, "Do they offer *anjali* to Ma Saraswati like us Muslims?" This is the first time we learned that they followed Islam. I couldn't answer their question. In mid-1960s in our undergraduate engineering college election of Chair of Saraswati Puja Committee was won by KarimDa, Older Brother Karim, a Muslim, without any religious tension. Most Hindu festivities are cultural festivals like America's Thanksgiving or 4th of July festivities but containing region-based cultural activities. And in 2010 we were heading to Bangladesh border crossing at Bangaon 70 miles east of our home in Kolkata. Sachi took a commuter train. A family sat next to him. They were going to finalize a marriage deal. At times the man chatted with Sachi. He was wearing *dhuti* (dhoti) and the women were wearing sari. They were wearing "loha" iron bangles of married women, but not "*sankha*" conch shell wedding bangles, a typical of Bengali culture, also followed by Buddhists and Christians, tribes and non-tribes. They were a Muslim family. One thing stood up in our mind as the father was continually cursing his early-teen boy for wearing pants and not *dhuti*. The father didn't like his son following Western identity.

Hindu-Majority Partitioned West Bengal:

Hindu-majority partitioned West Bengal state came into existence as Colonial Britain planned to divide the nation of the basis of Muslim-Non-Muslim partition. Muslim League Party which governed Bengal Province wanted the entire region, including non-Muslim Assam and Northeast India to be included in Islamic Pakistan. Resistance for the entire province to go to Pakistan came from all over India, but was led by one of the true patriots of India's independence war, Dr. Shyama Prasad Mukherjee. Dr. Mukherji was the youngest doctorates of Calcutta University, then India's leading university, became the youngest Chancellor of the University, a leader of Hindu Mahasabha (Assembly), and in 1930s was chosen by Mr. Fazlul Haque, a Muslim, and the leader of the ruling Praja Krishak (Workers and Peasants) Party of Bengal, to be his deputy, pushing the idea of Muslims and Hindus living together, against British plan. Britain encouraged communal division, and to ignore Independence Movement. To punish Bengal Colonial masters moved the capital of British India from Calcutta to Delhi. Before Partition, Muslim members voted to keep Hindu-majority western Bengal to be part of Islamic Republic of Pakistan, while all Hindu legislative members of Congress Party and two communists – Mr. Jyoti Basu (of Dhaka eastern Bengal) and Ratan Lal Brahman, a Nepali-speaking from northern Bengal, voted for partition, making West Bengal joining India. Idea of this division and a recognition of Hindu majority areas of the province came from Dr. Mukherji establishing existence of Hindus in British India. Irony of ironies of a Hindu leader claiming to represent oppressed Hindu Bengalis of eastern Bengal, Mr. Jogen Mondol, through his Scheduled Caste Party supported Muslim-Hindu partition of Bengal joining racism of Muslim League Party. He became the first Law Minister of Pakistan, but then fled Pakistan for India, as mentioned earlier. Hindu sages, rising from the oppressed, Hari Chand and Guru Chand, of current Bangladesh, were the biggest protectors of Hindus. Seeing merciless massacre of oppressed and poor

Hindus, Mr. Mondol fled to India which he earlier criticized as imperfect, but submitted his 20-page resignation letter documenting tens of thousands of Hindu murders in East Pakistan, now Bangladesh. Mondol fled to India, and soon ran for Indian Parliament (see Appendix A of *Bengal's Hindu Holocaust: Partition of India and Subsequent Change*, Publisher Garuda Prakashan, Delhi, India, 2021). Would U.S., Canada, Britain or France allow someone to run for office who not only gave up his citizenship, but also acted for nation's destruction within days of return? This is fatalistic suicidal India.

While visiting former Soviet Republics in Central Asia as well as Baltic nations reminded us again the question of identity. In Estonia's Tallinn it seemed everyone spoke Russian, while the writing in public was in Estonian. Same was true in many Central Asian and Baltic nations. Trying to come up with a new identity while bypassing some others can create new problems in new nations. Uzbek and Kazakh are changing their scripts which may add new issues that did not exist before. As long as free expression is censored, these new identities may not pose serious problem, but in open societies they may add to political problem. Uzbekistan's Fergana Valley was a wonderful place to visit. It is where the first Mughal King Babar came from and colonized India, bringing a strong Persian-Islamic culture to India. Babar loved fruits from Fergana. During our visit to find Babar's birthplace we ended up in bazars of Fergana, Marghilon, Andijan, and Namangan. In every market Shefali was mobbed as "Hindustani" offering her flowers, food and drink. Locals were impressed with her "Indian" identity. And at the new Amir Timur Museum in Uzbekistan's capital Tashkent, the lady at the ticket counter seeing us "Indians" started speaking in Hindi that she learned watching Hindi films, and asked if we are carrying Indian coins. An Uzbek professor asked us not to visit the "Killer Timur Museum" as Timur beheaded tens of thousands of Indians because he couldn't forcibly convert them to Islam, although Timur himself barely converted himself. The professor gave us an English newspaper containing that story. Tajik, Uzbek and Kazakh are struggling for new identities, altered from Soviet era.

The polytheistic identity is unable to protect peoples whom others persecute with partial identity. During British Raj it ruled not only today's India, Pakistan and Bangladesh, but also neighboring Burma (Myanmar), Sri Lanka (Ceylon), Malaysia, and Maldives. It also had arrangements with monarchies of Nepal, Bhutan, Afghanistan, and Buddhist Tibet, which they considered "Indian". As each country gained independence, they cleansed their indigenous minorities with non-majority identity. Which part of India fought back? None. No Hindu-majority area, or Muslim-majority nation complained during 1971 Islamic Republic of Pakistan's genocide. Sri Lanka committed genocide to preserve their Buddhist-Sinhala identity, not that different from separate identity of Pakistan. Some world powers put restriction on Sri Lankan leaders, but soon they came to power with Buddhist ultranationalism. Those leaders defied restriction and visited India's holy city of Varanasi. After Taliban came to power in Afghanistan in 2021, the number of Hindus, Sikhs, Christians, and Buddhists may have come down to single digit. All fled to India, not neighboring Pakistan. Dalai Lama's protest with notable world figures hasn't changed China's colonizing and cleansing policies. They have made Tibetans minority in their own land. Communist propaganda in India of ideal ways of protecting tribal minorities in China encouraged us to visit those wonderful tribal lands with non-existent tribal-ethnic identity. In Kashgar, Uighur many Pakistani-Kashmiri traders welcomed us as their own, and directed us to a nice Pakistani restaurants for Indian food. Identity was knowledge of Hindi, and Shefali's presence. There were no woman travelers with them, so Shefali's presence was welcome. On our trip, we crossed over to Pakistani Kashmir at 14,000 feet Khunjerab Pass. We had to abandon our Chinese bus, and climb a mountain at that height to catch a waiting Pakistani bus on the other side of the mountain. All the Pakistani men traveling with us helped us with our luggage and made sure that the bus didn't leave without us. We were the last to come to the bus. As soon as we arrived at the bus all of them cheered. The bus left immediately, after a check by the border guard. At the first stop at Sost we became special guests to the entire village welcoming to their home. At the only restaurant open they were watching a Hindi Channel of Indian TV. So much for developing a separate identity. Next day we took a car to Hunza, where we joined the king's hotel which had a beautiful view of Nanga Parbat, a Himalayan Mountain. Then we took a bus to Gilgit. When the bus stopped at Gilgit, a lady sitting next to Shefali at the bus pulled her hand to take us to her home, asking us to cancel the hotel we reserved. Next day, 14th of August, the Independence Day of Pakistan, we had the weirdest experience anywhere in the world: among thousands of locals enjoying the holiday, playing cricket on the street, buying groceries, and walking for leisure, there was not a single woman. Even the hotel workers asked us to wait until the crowd thins out. See http://empireslastcasualty.blogspot.com /-2007/11/xinxiang-kashmir-karakoram-highway.html. Later local shop keepers welcomed us as their uncle and aunt, as Indian not Americans, as part of their own identity. Yet, many secular Muslims told us that for many Muslims their identity changes after attending Friday prayer at mosque, then listening to *khutba* Islamic lectures with virulent, racist, anti-Hindu, anti-Christian, anti-Jewish, anti-secular, anti-non-Muslim, pro-violence speeches. Because of racist, pro-violence history of some nations, few have banned *khutba*, but not India. And, if India bans it, then even those nations who have banned it would complain as "racist policy." Organized religions in churches, synagogues, viharas, and gurudwaras have sermons by their preachers to counter organized hate, and response to hate, if any, but not Hindus for whom puja service is flower offering rituals. There are no sermons.

American and Indian Public Policy:

Public policy of the U.S. and India have evolved in two different ways, both influenced by British colonization. U.S. won a militant struggle, and brought back "people's power." In a recent trip to New York in September of 2021, Bangladesh Foreign Minister Dr. Momen, a former Bostonian, reminded attendees at a forum in Jackson Heights, Queens, that British wanted to give up America in 1776 as it was costing Britain money, whereas their Indian colony was bringing in tens of billions of dollars each year. In 2021 we noticed efforts to restrict voting rights in the U.S., bit it was not widening. This imperfection extended to Presidential election, and also to Supreme Court. Even four years after Presidential Election there are people who still believe that presidential "election was stolen." Our Supreme Court is in a very unfortunate stage, when Supreme Court judges vote on party lines diminishing their neutrality. It implies that our judges vote on the basis of party, and not based on merit. If judges of distant nations, Indonesia to Ireland, New Zealand to Nigeria, say our judges are partisan, would it affect world judiciary?

How we treat other genders, especially women, is influenced by upbringing and culture. Even in 2022 overwhelming majority of marriages in South Asia are introduced marriages, where family members or friends introduce partners, thus pre-marital sex is rare in most towns and villages. This is true for a large number of nations of Asia and Africa. Some of the pre-marital sex questions asked at the popular "Family Feud" TV show would be irrelevant in Asia and Africa. In some Asian and African countries polygamy is legal, as is child marriage, and easy divorce. Some other places it is the opposite.

Abduction of women and girls began in British era when tens of thousands of mothers and girls were abducted during Noakhali Danga of Hindu genocide of October of 1946. Mr. Gandhi went to Noakhali to rescue the victims and stop the killing. His effort failed. Western press writes about parochialism in India, but they avoid discussing notable mixed-marriages of Mrs. Aruna Asif Ali, Mr. Nazrul Islam, Mrs. Sucheta Kripalani, Mrs. Indira Gandhi, Mr. Jatindra Mohon Sengupta, Mr. Rajiv Gandhi, Mr. Indrajit Gupta, Mr. Irfan Khan, Mr. Sharukh Khan, Mrs. Sutapa Sikdar, and many more notable persons. One American theologian reminded us that while West promotes female body but Indian and Hindu scriptures promote abstinence. Promotion of female body is everywhere in the West. One has to watch outfits at Summer Olympics to understand sex promotion. In spite of economic backwardness all the nations in the region elected woman to head their nation – Sri Lanka, India, Pakistan, Bangladesh, Burma, and Indonesia, without any social upheaval, as many deities in Hindu mythology promote women's strength. We understand that one of the drawbacks of Mrs. Clinton's run for President in the U.S. was her gender.

Public Policy for Ordinary Citizens Vs State Power:

After 250 years of making laws, the United States has become a nation run by lawyers. From school boards at the lowest grass-roots level to nation's presidency all are dominated by lawyers. Law making is made easier by lawyers. That is certainly not true in the largest democracy of India, where some lawyers sit under banyan trees to meet their clients, not in air-conditioned offices. American Law practice works from the smallest state to the largest state to small suburbs. Migration of population without any special identity has made this protocol easy. Like Europe in India each state and sub-state maintain their separate identity, separate laws, and subculture. Although strangers are welcomed in another state, but assimilation takes lot longer than an immigrant nation. An Estonian of European Union may be welcomed in Spain, but becoming Spanish takes lots of time. May be centuries. A French is certainly welcomed in Poland, but does not automatically become Polish because they are in European Union. But it doesn't take lots of time for a New Yorker to become Floridian, or a Carolinian to become a Californian. We mentioned earlier that how after 700 years and 500 years of living in Rajasthan some families were still known as Bengali, as they were expected to maintain that identity. At their temples both the families wore traditional Bengali outfit, and spoke in their ancestral language with Rajasthani accent. Whether it is good or bad, people have to determine.

In India assimilation varies state wise. In smaller border states like Tribal-majority Nagaland, Christian-majority Mizoram, or Muslim-majority Kashmir there have been attacks on non-converted indigenous population. Why no discussion on people who vanished? Moreover, Indian Kashmir has a small population of five million of India's 1,300 million population. We wonder is the current terrorism in Indian Kashmir has anything to do with bordering of Islamic Republic of Pakistan? Many people on all sides of the partitioned border have asked, would it have been better for India to have a complete population exchange, as it has happened one-sided in Pakistan, and Pakistani Kashmir? This is a very, very bad question. Mr. Bal Gupta, was cleansed from his Pakistani

Kashmir home with a loss of 26 members of his family who were brutally butchered. (See YouTube's ISPaD1947 channel for his interview.) How many T.V. channels interviewed him?

Forgotten Atrocities: Memoirs of a Survivor of the 1947 Partition of India by Bal Gupta

Violence vs Non-Violence in Democracy:

This is certainly a contradiction. Though we preach non-violence of Upanishad, Vedas and words of Buddha, Jain, Jesus, Sri Chaitanya, and Gandhi, but in real politics violence wins. There is a famous saying, as the foreign colonizers came to Bengal, and started to oppress and kill the indigenous people and attacked peaceful march of Sri Chaitanya who said to the foreign oppressors, "*Merechis kolshir kana, taboley kee prem debona?*" meaning "Just because you've hit me with broken pitcher, am I not going to give you love?" For the U.S., violence is ingrained in our DNA as the nation was created by a violent overthrow of the British rule. We encouraged gun violence with Constitutional Amendment. In India, Gandhi failed to convince Islamists for a peaceful cohabitation. Result was killing of millions of people, mostly Hindus with some Sikhs, Jains, Buddhists, and some Muslims in Punjab, and making tens of millions homeless, like our extended families, and almost 80% Bengali-Indian-Americans are Pakistani-Bangladeshi-Hindu-Refugee-Indian-Americans. Gandhi was murdered by a Hindu fanatic as he couldn't protect Hindus while he protected Muslims. Unfortunately, there is still anger against Gandhi in Left and Right because of his failure.

We want peaceful solution. But, do we notice peaceful demonstrations? U.S. openness is lot higher than many other nations. Black Lives Matter protest shows that we pay attention when there is protest. This is human nature. On December 20, 2022 Pakistan's Foreign Minister Bilawal Bhutto Zardari at an interview with BBC TV called Indian Prime Minister Modi as "Killer of Gujarati Muslims," but didn't say a word when minority Muslims burned to death coaches full of Hindu mothers and kids at a train station which started a retaliatory action by some protesters. He didn't expect "Hindus" believe in "To every action, there is an equal and opposite reaction," as no Hindu ever reacted even after killing of 3 million in 1971 in just 9 months by his grandfather's army of Islamic Republic of Pakistan. Neither Pakistan, nor any state punished any of those mass murderers. Why Bilawal has no sorrow for 3 million killed by his army? Why doesn't he drop a tear for 59 mothers and babies burned to death by pro-Pakistani folks? Did he support protest by pro-Palestine activists and pro-Israel activists in the U.S. during Gaza-Israel-Palestine war of 2023-2025? We thank protesters. On the other hand, Indians know how to be silently slaughtered. This suicidal fatalism is beyond description. There is a saying that as living being a cow fights back when her calf is taken away, pigeons fights back when their baby is touched in their nest, a mother snake attacks when someone approaches her den; do indigenous mothers, fathers, uncles and aunts fight back? Why not? Have they lost instincts of living creatures? Why? How? In eastern India why ruling Right-Left-and-Center do not fight to protect their families? Thus, no one knows of their plight. Millions of minorities have been killed, cleansed and raped by believers in our homeland. How many of us know that? Why blame others? How can they change their suicidal fatalism, and self-destroying tolerance? It seems, world only responds to violence, not to non-violence. It is well known that Gandhi's idea of non-violence is great which completely failed to keep the nation united as neither colonial Britain nor separatist Muslim Langue Party believed in that. Britain ruled the world with her army with direct association of monotheistic-religious oppression of indigenous traditions. From its inception Islam has been a militant movement engaged in militant damage of indigenous traditions. Preaching is fine, but reality is different. Did free thinkers win in Tiananmen massacre? World still remembers that only because some free-thinking Chinese pay homage on June 4 of each year. If they were like Indians, no one would remember that date. How many of Indians remember on what day Bengal was first partitioned by the British to start their racist Divide-and-Rule and Divide-and-Conquer policy? Or, any British, Indian, Bengali, Muslim or Hindu remember when did Noakhali massacre began under Muslim League Party during British colonial rule? Or, remembers the day when 20 Hindu monks and nuns were murdered in broad daylight in the heart of "intelligent" Hindu-majority Kolkata, also known as 'Liberal,' 'Left,' and 'Intellectual Capital of India'? And who remembers how and why India was partitioned? Because of America's textbooks we still learn about our 4th of July, and how we avoided partition after American Civil War. Luckily, we aren't ruled by foreign power, then and now. Still in parts of the nation, even in 2020s, denial of rights to minorities, and women are seen with nostalgia.

That idea has taken root in many states attempting to deny voting rights to some. This is happening in barely 150 years from Civil War in the world's strongest and longest democracy! But we are able to discuss and debate, assuring our bright future.

We hope peace wins over violence, and no one is made homeless!

Conclusion

We are fortunate to receive blessings and warmth for over five decades of journey in two of the largest tolerant democracies of the U.S. and India, as well as to over 125 nations, islands and territories of colonized, decolonized and uncolonized lands in all seven continents. Recently, after completion of this memoir-based book project – first part published was with Mr. Shuvo Ghosh Dastidar – it was very uplifting to receive a response letter written on November 4, 2024 from our President Biden after my protest against another pogrom in my Bangladesh homeland starting on August 5, 2024. It started with nation's elected Prime Minister Hasina's overthrow, but for no reason her pre-Islam indigenous Hindu minorities immediately became target for oppression, sex abuse, killing and cleansing by religious terrorists. Possibly for the first time since Noakhali genocide in 1946 during British colonial era – when Britain didn't punish any of the mass killers and kidnappers – and Partition of India in 1947, there was worldwide protest including protest in the U.S. by presidential candidate and former President Trump, but there was no immediate protest from the Hindu-Bengali rulers of Indian states of West Bengal and Tripura run by East Pakistani-Bangladeshi-Hindu-Refugee-Indians. Shocking? Unbelievable? The number of indigenous pre-Islam minorities is easily 50 to 60 million refugees with their descendants living in West Bengal State, and in rest of India. This is India's and Hindu's suicidal-fatalism! In addition, former U.S. Congresswoman Ms. Tulsi Gabbard sent written protest, as well as Indian Congress Parliamentarian from the southern state of Kerala, Mr. Sashi Tharoor, a former U.N. official. Indian Vice President and former West Bengal State's Governor Mr. Jagdeep Dhankhar, and an Indian Parliamentarian from West Bengal State, Mr. Jagannath Sarkar, also protested. All oppressed peoples really appreciated that. Sarkar being the only noted Bengali-Indian to protest their ethnic cleansing. Even Hindu religious monks in partitioned Hindu-majority West Bengal, India had to get permission from the State High Court for their march to save Hindu lives. Is it a form of censorship or support for self-destruction? This was extremely important and exceptional event in India against world's oppression of indigenous peoples. There were worldwide protests of the new 2024 pogrom, but not by the refugee power-holders in India. This is suicidally-fatalistic India! Secular Bangladeshi Muslims were marginalized as well. As usual, no Muslim-majority nation opposed or criticized this oppression, but criticized Palestine war of Israel. One U.S. Senator also wrote back to us on the current (2024) Bangladesh issue. Yet, the devastation is still continuing since August 5, 2024 since the ouster of Prime Minister Mrs. Hasina Wazed.

Envelope of President Biden's Letter to Sachi G. Dastidar, November 4, 2024

Teaching of Human Rights, and Politics of India and South Asia for decades, and traveling in partitioned Subcontinent nations of India, Pakistan and Bangladesh, including our ancestral home, exposed us to the warmth and contradictions of tolerant, intolerant, religious, racist and atheist parties and nations, which was quite revealing. We are sure our experience may not be the same as others, as it depends on one's expectations, values, families and beliefs. In addition, being a refugee and as well as an immigrant, and traveling with family, added to our experience and learning. We were welcomed to so many strangers' homes in Asia, Australia, America and Europe, including by majority Muslims in Bangladesh and Pakistan, as well as by non-Muslim minorities there. Our learning hasn't ended, and we hope to continue to learn from others.

May Mother Nature bless us all!

SHORT BIO OF
SACHI G. DASTIDAR

Sachi G. Dastidar is a Distinguished Service Professor Emeritus of the State University of New York, Old Westbury. He has also taught in Kazakhstan, Ireland, India, Florida State and Alabama A&M University. He was elected to a NYC School Board. He has authored over 25 books and Journals, and has written over 150 articles. He was born in India to Hindu refugee parents who fled their home of 500 years after a pogrom. Since finding their ancestral home he established Probini Foundation which educates poor and orphaned children in 33 schools in Bangladesh and India; and later established Indian Subcontinent Partition Documentation Project. One of his first articles in weekly Desh on Partition of India, Ai Bangla Oi Bangla (This Bengal that Bengal, 1989) was written about in almost all the papers and journals in Indian Bengal and in Bangladesh, with the largest-circulation Indian newspaper reviewing it twice. His Empire's Last Casualty: Indian Subcontinent's Vanishing Hindu and Other Minorities, Firma KLM Publishers, India, was quoted in US Congress.

His has received two Senior Fulbright Awards, honors from residents of Mahilara, Madaripur and Uzirpur villages (Bangladesh), India's Assam Buddhist Vihar and West Bengal's Durgapur, from Kazakhstan Institute. In Uzirpur, Bangladesh a new "Dastidar Sanskrit College Building" was dedicated in his honor, and a Marble bust was unveiled in Malikanda, Bangladesh.